FROM

the girl next door

WINTER'S

book two

ASHES

AMY LEIGH SIMPSON

From Winter's Ashes
By Amy Leigh Simpson

Copyright 2016 Amy Leigh Simpson

Cover Design, Jeremy Stehlick
Editor, Andrea Ferak

ISBN-13:978-1985098480
ISBN-10:1985098482

For more information on this book and the author visit: www.amyleighsimpson.com

What others are saying about
The Girl Next Door Series

"With smart dialogue, plenty of romantic tension, and well-crafted sentences that pull you right into the scene, Simpson is brilliant with a pen."

-Amy Matayo
Author of *The Wedding Game* and *Sway*

"Amy Leigh Simpson is a brilliant wordsmith. Wow. This author knows how to write fresh and feverish! This book has edge and wit and lots and lots of lyrical goodness that made my little writer's heart pitter patter to a happy beat."

-Nicole Deese
Carol award-winning Author of *The Promise of Rayne*

"One word persistently leaps to my mind as I read and reflect on this delightful story... HOT! ... There is nothing dull, cool, or mediocre about this story! It is a blazing FIRE of brilliance!!!

-Faithfully Bookish Blog

"I highly recommend this series from Amy Leigh Simpson. I'm grateful to have discovered her series and lovely writing and look forward to discovering more of her stories. From Winter's Ashes is a timeless romantic, suspense love story encompassing forever friendships, complex relationships, deep manipulations, engaging mystery, and sweet charm."

-TeriLyn
Amazon Reviewer

"Yet again, Amy Leigh Simpson weaves an incredible tale ripe with thrilling suspense, witty dialogue, and dazzling romance."

-Pepper Basham
Author of *A Twist of Faith* and *Charming the Troublemaker*

"Sparks sizzle in Simpson's sophomore novel. Ripe with tension, danger, and the pain of the past, you'll be ripping through pages to see what happens next. Grab your oven mitts before you pick this one up, you're going to need them."

-Jill Lynn
Author of *Her Texas Family*

"If you're looking for a sit on the edge of your seat, don't turn out the lights and don't go to sleep until the last page is turned read this summer, From Winter's Ashes is it! Wonderful characters with real hurts to overcome, romantic tension, intrigue, yikes moments and everything in between, Simpson has created another delicious novel that will sweep you away and hold you captive until the very end. Don't miss this one!"

-Catherine West
Author of *The Things We Knew* and *The Memory of You*

"Simpson's books are fast-paced romantic suspense that keep the reader reeled in from beginning to end. The author has a lyrical voice that is fresh and quirky."

-Julia R.
Professional Reviewer

"This is one hot book--and not just because the hero is a firefighter! Sizzle crackles off the pages as the two well-drawn main characters try to elude a pursuer with murderous intent. Turn up the AC and enjoy!"

-Irene Hannon
Multi-award winning author of
Dangerous Illusions and *Tangled Webs*

For my big brother, who bears little resemblance to Finn, but has a heart full of fire, and is every bit a hero.

December 5
Kirkwood, Missouri
9:47 p.m.

Prologue

For our battle is not against flesh
and blood ... Ephesians 6:12

*G*od is just.

The echo of long diminished voices twined with the dark thoughts crowding his skull. *"Right."* The rancor in his voice a sharp intrusion in the fragile silence.

Years of faithful church attendance taught him plenty about God's wrath, even God's promises. Where was *God* now? More importantly, where had he been *then*?

Justice? What a joke.

If God was just, then he wouldn't force a man to take matters into his own hands.

Pulse steady, breath even, he clung to the shadows of the bungalow, awaiting her return and the final installment of his revenge.

As he pictured her curled up in the sheets, his memories slipped loose from their moorings, fragmented pictures snapping like electrical surges in an unstable power grid. Tears clouded, and the suffocating press of twilight had him completely blinded to the present. But his anger, his all-consuming anger was sharp and sure despite the misfires in his mind. It was that righteous anger that smothered his conscience and every lingering ounce of apprehension about his mission.

The fact that he was alive to fulfill this duty was the only consolation. The beat of his empty heart, each sour, life-giving breath just bitter reminders of the injustice of his now shattered existence.

A beam of light sliced through the darkness as a car pulled

in to the neighbor's drive.

Anticipation kicked in, pounding hot and furious through his veins despite the chill of the December air. Oh yes, he'd have his justice. Tonight. Long before the sun rose on the ashes of tomorrow.

A soft giggle drifted over the crisp breeze, the crescendo of voices signaling their approach. He siphoned his breath.

"Thanks for walking me home."

"Are you sure you don't want to come over for a drink before we call it a night?" The husky voice was laced with an invitation for something more.

Shuffling feet brushed the splintered porch steps, and the sound of dangling keys chimed in the night.

"No. Sorry. I have an early morning, but thank you for dinner, Max."

"Sure. Hey listen, I'm going to a medical conference for two weeks, leaving tomorrow, but when I get back I'd love to take you out again. That is, if it's not too weird dating your neighbor."

"Well, I suppose I might consider another date. First one wasn't *totally* unbearable." The smile in her voice was unmistakable.

"I'll be sure to up my game for next time."

"Good night, neighbor." The groaning of strained hinges mingled with the silence as she entered her doom.

"Good night, Joselyn. Sweet dreams."

Not likely.

Chapter 1

Finn Carson

"**I**'m all in." Finn Carson slid the stacks of poker chips to the center of the table, his tone, if not the impressive wager, challenging anyone to cross him. The pocket aces in his possession were basically a sure thing, considering Ryker and Jones couldn't bluff to save their lives, and Wally, well, he could lift a ton, but he sure couldn't spell it.

"Dang it, Finn! Why do you always have to push it to the limit?" Jones threw down his cards. The low hanging light etched out all the angles of his adolescent scowl before he shoved away from the table to sulk in the shadow. As usual. "I hate poker."

"No you don't, Jones, you just hate losing." Finn kept still to avoid any tells but let his arrogant grin taunt the man-child.

"Only to you. You always win."

If only that were true.

Finn forced his thoughts back to the game. Poker provided a nice distraction. Of course, winning didn't hurt matters either. Organizing these tournaments on quiet nights at the firehouse had become about more than a little friendly competition and a way to pass the time. It was about needing a win. And lately, it was the only way to get one.

The stillness in the station was unnerving. Deepening shadows from the edges of the dark room had become nagging ministrations, tempting them all to give in to the call of night.

"All right, any takers?" As the men considered, Finn held

on to his neutral expression. Maybe he shouldn't have gone all in. In only moments, the game would be over and the guys would be ready to hit the hay. And despite his exhaustion, the last thing Finn wanted to do was go to sleep.

Normally white noise soothed him, but the hum of the emergency exit light at his back might as well have been the cheese grater they'd used at dinner for the way it seemed to scrape away at his eardrums. And ironically, a remnant of the charred vapors from Wally's dinner preparation of blackened spaghetti sauce still clung to the air hours later. The bitterness of the stench filtered through to his mouth, torturing his taste buds for a second time tonight.

Ryker folded, and all eyes zoned in on a bewildered Wally.

Finn swallowed, letting his thumb skim over the smooth surface of his spade to calm the surge of restlessness.

"I, uh … I guess I'll … call?"

Finn slapped down his cards. "Tough break, pal."

"Aww, you win. I only got these five and seven of hearts." Wally shook his big head in defeat.

Finn blinked twice. "Are you kidding me? You have a flush."

"I do?" Wally's expression morphed into something akin to enlightenment. "Does this mean I won't be on bathroom duty for once?"

Finn rolled his eyes to make light of his agitation. It was just a game and there was no money on the line, but he still hated to lose. And very seldom did.

The ribbing and heckling commenced as Jones scrawled "J.P. Wallace" on the wall, knocking Finn's long-standing winning streak off the record board.

"Anyone up for another round?" Finn asked, feigning indifference. The resignation on their faces spoke before any of them needed to. "Fine. Wouldn't want to deprive you ladies of your beauty sleep." The deliberate taunt was met with good-natured insults as they cleaned up and filed out.

Finn granted Wally a congratulatory slap on the back.

"Good game, buddy." He was a simple lug, but maybe he needed a win more than Finn did. The thought unbound a twinge of tightness gripping his lungs as the men climbed the stairs and divided into their rooms. But not long after the lights were out, Ryker's heavy breathing filtered into the silence while Finn continued to stare into the dark, searching for rest in the blanket of black and pleading with God for a break from the nightmares. There was nothing to see, yet he could feel the haunt in the room like a monster in the closet, the tremble in his bones warning of the terrors that awaited the vulnerable moment when sleep dragged him under and left him utterly defenseless against the invisible enemy.

Restless, he rolled over and bunched the pillow under his head. He hadn't told Cap, but the lack of sleep was starting to affect his performance. Doubt and fear wormed through the cracks in his armor, taunting him for his weakness. So far, only Ryker knew about his insomnia and night terrors. And Finn wanted to keep it that way. He didn't need the guys badgering or second-guessing him. He was doing enough of that on his own.

And yet, as guilt baited his conscience, and the slow, painful torture of each passing night robbed him of another piece of the man he used to be, he squeezed his eyes shut and pleaded again, exactly like the night before.

God, please don't let anyone else lose their life because of me.

The blaring alarm jolted Finn upright. Ripped from the nightmare, a scream caged in his throat and labored breaths heaved from his chest. In the time it took to kick off the sweat-soaked sheets he'd regained his bearings enough to get his pansy-ass out of his room and down the pole to the engine bay. In seconds he crammed his feet into his boots, tugged on his turnout gear, and vaulted up to his spot on the truck.

He secured his helmet, shrugged his shoulders, like he'd done a hundred times. But the moment he stopped moving it all slowed, funneling a sinking dread into a ball of lead in his stomach. What had once felt like a suit of armor now felt like eighty pounds of excess baggage.

Less than two minutes after the alarm had sounded the fire truck left the safety of the Kirkwood Fire Station and wove through the sleepy streets of the quaint West St. Louis County suburb—one of few that had yet to be hit by the Five-Alarm Arsonist.

The truck ground to a stop, and Finn froze. "*Oh, God.*" A plea. A prayer. Because the magnitude of the blaze ravaging the small Craftsman-style home warned that the serial arsonist may have struck again. A canopy of tangled branches from the aging sweet gum and white ash trees caught the whipping lashes of fire, slashing vibrant flames through the dark, silky canvas of night.

After seven years as a firefighter, watching someone's home burn to the ground still twisted his gut. A home was a storehouse of memories, a refuge from the harsh realities of life, a foundation for a family. And since he didn't have any of those things, Finn was, in a sense, homeless.

"Yo, Iron Man! Look alive, it's a hot one!" Ryker's yell brought him back. Finn swung down from the truck, his boots hitting the icy pavement with a hollow thud to match the ache in his chest. It was no time to dwell on it, but the reminder of all his failures blazed like the house in front of him. A lost cause.

"External attack, boys! Something nasty is feeding the beast. That's no ordinary blaze." Captain Reynolds further confirmed Finn's suspicions and barked out orders. Finn forced his legs to hustle to his position on hose duty like a first year probie. *The sidelines.* His chest sank. Each job was important. Critical. But to Finn, stretching the line wasn't the same as riding the *irons*: forcing entry with a Halligan bar or an axe, ventilating the fire floor, and searching for victims. Yeah, once upon a time, he'd felt like he was living up to his nickname. Invincible. Like the fire couldn't touch him.

Those days were gone.

A frozen blast of wind fingered through his gear and grabbed ahold of him. The elemental combination of fire and ice shouldn't have given him pause considering his occupation and the time of year, but they hit like shock paddles to the heart. He couldn't explain the odd jolt nor why there was some ghostly intuitive unease prickling his senses. Other than the obvious, something was very wrong.

The only sound carrying on the bitter wind was the wicked laughter of the fire. And yet Finn could *feel* someone crying out. Calling to him.

With no regard to the past or the possible suicide mission ahead of him, his legs burst into motion, lured in by the call of the fire and the mysterious premonition.

No! Finn fought against the drowning urge, pleaded for his training and common sense to prevail, but the force was relentless. Powerfully persuasive. The determined pursuit of his body willed by a force stronger than his paralyzing fear.

His heart stuttered in his chest, his skin tasting the flames even from a distance. But he couldn't turn back, even as every fiber of his being begged him to retreat. The heat swelled, slapping his face as he secured his respirator.

"Carson?" Cap's voice cut in from the radio at his collar. "We're using an exterior attack. Get away from that house! That's an order—"

Insanity prevailed. Finn clicked off the radio and took his first intentional step toward the prison of fire.

Please ... guide my steps.

Chapter 2

Joselyn Whyte

Time's up. I am officially an old maid.

An intense, sweltering heat forced Joselyn to toss off her numerous covers. Not a normal occurrence, especially not in the dead of winter. Holy heat wave! At twenty-seven, wasn't she still too young for a hot flash? Were her eggs expiring already? A depressing thought but the only one that seemed to make sense in her drowsy state. Something pricked in her throat, ripping a hacking protest from her lungs. Her head pounding, her skin fevered, she managed to sit up—step one in peeling her tired body out of bed to check on the erratic furnace. The thing was likely half as old as the one-hundred-year-old house. It was a marvel it could still cough out any heat at all, let alone keep it at the balmy seventy-eight degrees she preferred.

Times like these she wished she had a man in her life. But loneliness, it seemed, was her affliction. *Boy, there's another cheerful thought.* And what was that smell?

The salty perspiration beading on her top lip released its hold and invaded her parched mouth. Joselyn swiped the moisture with the back of her hand and then propped her arm on the always empty side of the bed. But instead of being met with the chill of vacant linens, heat pressed against her palm.

Man, it's hot! She'd thought to utter the sentiment aloud, but the words hadn't formed, another cough raked up her throat instead. Then again, it was so hot the scorching air barely touched her lungs before little bursts of fire zinged in her chest. That observation alone should have cut through the disorienting haze, instead she yawned, pulled down the sleep mask, scrubbed her hand over her face, and pressed her fist against the heartburn. Was she getting sick? She felt like she'd been trampled by a horse and dragged through a blistering desert.

Light teased her vision, but her eyelids remained unnaturally heavy. The mask was gone, so why were her eyelashes stuck together? And why did her brain feel so … fuzzy? She hadn't even drank on her date. Had she?

She rubbed her eyes. Rubbed harder until the pounding in her skull intensified instead of lessened. Something was definitely wrong.

When she managed to coax her eyes open a scream tore loose but instantly dissolved like kindling in a bonfire. Her lungs ached, each burning breath seemingly laced with razor sharp fiber glass, and her vision hazed with a blinding ultraviolent hue to match her surroundings. *"Fff-Fire. Fire!"* She coughed up the words though she couldn't hear them.

Somehow she stood on wobbly legs and plucked out her earplugs. The mask and plugs had lulled her into a coma while her home burned around her. She cursed the noises from the creaky, old house for driving her to use them.

Oh, not good. Flames devoured the walls and danced across the floor to where she stood. The roar of the fire invaded the small shred of concentration she possessed, siphoning away her options faster than the breathable air. Ripping the comforter from the bed, she inched toward the only window in the room.

Desperation shoved back the drugging fatigue. But the fire only seemed to laugh at the futile attempts of her numb, shaking fingers fighting a losing battle against the ancient window latch. The drop from the second story wouldn't be fun, but escaping through the window was the only option. Aside from burning alive.

Think. Think!

Joselyn scanned the blazing room, scrounging for something to smash the glass. The nightstand was caged by fire on the other side of the bed. Nothing but pillows were within reach.

The corners of her vision curled in like lit paper. Prickles of sensation grew to a quick boil beneath her where she felt her feet sizzle against the smoking planks of the wood floor. Stepping onto the edges of the comforter, she wrapped her arm in the rest and, with more power than she thought she could muster, thrust her elbow through the window.

Yanking free, the glass tore away the fabric and through to her skin. Before she'd gulped even one breath of fresh air, hungry white fire shot toward the new source of oxygen, engulfing her escape.

She stumbled away, the writhing mass of heat bending her equilibrium and pitching the room like a ship being tossed on waves of flames. Wheezing from the chokehold of the smoke, Joselyn pressed the sleep mask over her mouth and collapsed to the floor.

Fiery blades licked at her flesh, each wicked lash leaving the bite of a burn. She pulled her knees in tighter, huddling in a tiny ring of fire, awaiting death. She tried to scream, but the air, charred and lifeless, evaporated before it hit her throat.

Please. Take me now. She didn't know who she was pleading to, but she closed her burning eyes and envisioned the words as a prayer. If anyone was listening.

Inexplicably, sorrow and resignation gave way to a renewed determination. With strength she knew she didn't have left, she managed to stand back up and encase herself in the comforter from head to toe. Struggling to hold onto consciousness, she ran blindly through the wall of fire toward the door until she smacked into something hard. Her legs gave out. Arms surrounded her. Weightlessness and relief invaded her body, drenching down to the bleakness in her soul. And without a final thought, poetic or otherwise, she surrendered to the end.

Beep ...

The scream of squealing tires on slick pavement ...
Beep ...
Phantom drifts of burnt rubber and gasoline ...
Beep ... Beep ...
"No." She whimpered. *The sharp, relentless pelt of hail ... the cutting cold ... the sting on her exposed skin ...*
Beep ... Beep ... Beep ...
"Run, Joselyn. Do you understand me? Stop crying and run!" The voice a mere wisp of pale smoke in the darkness.
Beep ... Beep ... Beep ... Beep ...
"No!"
"She's tachycardic."
Is someone there?
"Get me—"
"Wait! It's slowing down," another voice interrupted. "It looks like she's having a nightmare. Miss Whyte. Miss Whyte, wake up."
The voices jumbled. A cold touch. A quick flash of white in each eye. Her stomach crimped.
"Joselyn, can you hear me?" The voice pleaded.
"Please s-save h-her." Joselyn's breath caught on a hiccup. Stiff cotton brushed her cheeks, and antiseptic-scented air pooled in her nostrils. She blinked her eyes open, and the strange beeping noise slowed. "Wha—" She wheezed, the razor sharp air cutting off the word. "Where is ... where am ...?" Violent coughing shredded the rest.
A blur of blue scrubs and bright lights came into focus before her brain could construct a full question. "Shh. Good morning, Joselyn." The nurse soothed as if speaking to a traumatized child. "It's all right. You're in the hospital, you're fine. There was a—"
"A fire ... I remember." Splintered pieces of memory cut through her mind. The heat. The pain. The hopelessness. She squeezed her eyes tight—felt tears burn behind her eyelids as she relived the tortured moments before her death.
Only ... she wasn't dead.
She braved a glance down to inspect the damage. All she

saw was a long white bandage on her right forearm. *That can't be right.*

The nurse touched her shoulder. "Joselyn, dear, you are a living, breathing miracle. When the firefighters got to your home it was engulfed in flames. The young man that found you said your clothes were nearly burned off and every square inch of your house was consumed. Somehow, by the grace of God, there's not a burn to be found on ya. All you got is a bit of smoke inhalation and sixteen stitches in your arm. You'll be right as rain in no time."

"What?" She croaked. *Impossible.* She'd felt the fire, remembered the wicked touch of the flames as she'd prepared to die.

Kicking off the covers, she bent a leg and pulled her foot into her hand. Nothing but pale unbroken skin. As if all evidence of the fire had been washed away. Her vision blurred, her nose prickled like a pin cushion, and the haze of tears and disbelief made the room swim around her.

A pager sounded, and one of the nurses excused herself.

"You musta had some angels watching out for you, girlie. Well, that, plus that large hunk of hero who rode in like a white knight and rescued you." The silver-haired nurse with deep laugh lines bracketing her wistful smile sighed dramatically, patting her chest.

White knight? Joselyn's mind raced back to the last semi-lucid moment she could remember. Powerful arms surrounded her as she collapsed into his embrace. And then, in the split second before she'd surrendered to the darkness, she'd felt relief so deep that it lingered now—stronger than the fear from the fire, more powerful than any emotion she'd ever carried.

"… still in the waiting room."

She shook her head, blinking away the encroaching tears. "Huh?" Perhaps the potent combination of smoke and fear had brought on a hallucination. "I'm sorry, is my father here?"

"That's right, someone said you're Declan Whyte's

daughter."

Joselyn could only nod her confirmation as the nurse continued. "I'm sorry, dear. That cutie-patootie firefighter got ahold of him, but unfortunately your father is out of town on business. Said he'd be back the day after tomorrow, I think."

Joselyn hardened her jaw; ground her molars with enough force to shave away enamel. But that only intensified the pain spearing through each temple, so she tried to massage the ache except the heart-rate-finger-clip-thingy jabbed awkwardly against the tender spot on one side. Giving up, she let her head fall back against the hospital bed and closed her eyes to try to hide the hurt, both physical and emotional. "Uhh, you said the firefighter called my dad?" The words scraped like sandpaper.

"Yeah, he seemed to know how to get through to him. You were out cold when you were admitted. We didn't have the emergency contact information, and your father is one difficult man to get in touch with."

"You have no idea," Joselyn mumbled.

"Well, the doctor will be by in a little while to go over a few things. Your call button is here on the bed. Do you need anything before I go?"

It all felt like a bad dream. One she couldn't fully remember. The slivers of surviving memory only served to revisit her pain and panic yet leave her with more unanswered questions. Was there anything left of her house? Where would she go? How could her dad not be here? Did anyone else know she was here? Did anyone care? How had the fire start—

"Sugar, you okay?"

Joselyn glanced at her name badge. Shelby. She looked like a Shelby. Sort of sweet and southern, with soft, caring eyes. Digging deep, she recited the familiar words. "I'm fine. Thank you, Shelby."

With a reassuring pat of her hand, Shelby turned to make her way out. She paused by the door, and Joselyn released the breath she'd been holding. *I lied. I'm not fine. Please, don't leave me all alone.*

"By the way, your hero is still here. Been waitin' to see you."

So *not* what Joselyn had expected her to say. And as if her body knew something she didn't, Joselyn's heart set off at a gallop. A series of escalating beeps exposed the silly flutter zipping through her veins. Shelby cast a knowing smirk at the screen.

Stupid heart-rate monitor!

"Oh, my. This is better than my programs. Shall I send him in?" She raised a puckish eyebrow.

"Umm, y-yeah. I guess that'd be okay." Joselyn cringed. If she couldn't play it cool with the nurse, how big of a mess was she going to be for the supposedly hot firefighter guy? *Hmm ... hot firefighter. Such dramatic irony.*

Shelby set off in her plotting, and Joselyn tried to calm her fraying nerves. Didn't the nurse say that when her rescuer got to her all her clothes had burned off?

Great! So he's already seen me naked! And not like standing or attractively posed—not that it would have occurred that way anyhow; exhibitionist ventures, so not her thing—but slumped and unconscious in his arms. *Oy vey!*

And any moment now her "Whyte knight," as he would probably be dubbed, would waltz in to discover her all crusty and scraggly in nothing but a limp, mint green hospital gown.

There was no explaining the sudden bout of self-consciousness. She didn't even know the guy. Yes, she was lonely, but she wasn't desperate. So it didn't matter what she looked like, she assured herself. It didn't even matter what *he* looked like. He was her hero. She owed him her deepest gratitude. And even though Shelby's high praise of his appearance chimed back through Joselyn's ears, what intrigued her were the feelings her rescuer had stirred when he'd held her. Had he felt it too? Was that why he'd stayed? More likely he'd recognized her and was looking for a reward.

Calm down, Joss. You survived a fire. You can do this.

A gentle knock put an end to her internal pep talk. Aiming to soothe the raspy sound of her newly acquired smoker's lung, she cleared her throat. "Come in." Sadly, a guttural cough spewed forth, turning her voice box into something akin to a trash compactor. Lovely.

The doorway was set back and wasn't well lit, but she saw wide shoulders tapering to a strong, trim waist, and a value pack of thick muscles all wrapped around well over six feet of hard man.

"Hey, Joss." The nickname floating on the waves of that deeply resonant voice felt like a warm, callused hand grazing her skin. The room might be a little chilly, but it was the familiar caress of that rumbly baritone that gave her goose bumps.

Joselyn yanked the heart-rate monitor from her finger to silence the wild, runaway beeping and prayed she was wrong as she waited for him to step out of the shadow.

Finn Carson

"Uhh ... are you all right?" Based on her rigid posture and frozen slack-jawed expression, he wasn't who she'd been expecting. He stepped closer to the bed and bent over to make sure she was still breathing.

Okay, Finn. Be nice. She's just been through a trauma.

She gave an exaggerated blink. "*You're* the one who saw me nak—I mean, rescued me?"

He straightened, shoved his hands into his pockets and shrugged. "Guilty."

A lock of silky black hair slipped from behind her ear, swaying for a moment like a pendulum measuring the awkward pause. Even more gratifying than catching Joselyn Whyte off her guard—and her high horse—was the remarkable shade of red filling her creamy cheeks.

Well, whaddya know, she might not be a cold-blooded reptile after all.

Traumatized woman. He forced himself back on point. "Yeah. I was working last night, and I ... found you." Finn's fingers skimmed the fine fluted edge of a spare poker chip in the pocket of the clothes Ryker had brought up. He'd lost last night's game, but in light of the miraculous rescue, he supposed it might be his lucky chip.

Her eyes remained wide and unblinking. "*You* were the one I ran into, the one who held me?"

Held her? More like carried her down a flight of crumbling stairs. Was it really so hard to believe that *he* could be her hero?

"Uh, yeah, Joss. It was me. Look, are you feeling okay? Because I can call a nurse back in here. You seem a little confused."

And maybe it wasn't the first time. When she'd woken in the ambulance, she'd reached out for him, grasping not only his hand but holding his eyes in hers with a vulnerability that dismantled the wall of animosity they'd built between each other over the years. Without uttering a word she'd communicated that she needed him. So he stayed. Her eyes had been a little bit glazed and wild, but he'd been sure she'd recognized him. And why wouldn't she? They saw each other often enough—unavoidable seeing as how this snobby little nightmare was best friends with his sister, Sadie.

But now, seeing the shock steal back the warm blush from her fair skin, returning it to that cold and flawless finely dusted snow, he knew she'd been delirious. And if nothing else, her unquestionable awareness of their mutual disdain told Finn that while she may have lapsed for a moment in the ambulance, her memory hadn't suffered any long-term effects.

Pity. She looked a lot prettier without the scowl.

"I'm fine." She sniffed. "So do you know if there's anything left of my house?" From all the passion in her tone, you'd think she was talking about losing a penny on the street.

"I haven't been back to the scene since last night. But I heard everything burned up. I'm really sorry."

The slender line of her jaw tensed, and something in her eyes dimmed. "The nurse said you got in touch with my father." Her tone fell flat, indifferent.

Did this girl not possess an ounce of feeling?

"Yeah. He said he would be home in a couple of days. Told me to have you call when you were awake."

"Is that why you're here? He bribed you to stay?"

"Pfff, no." Finn replied a little too quickly, soothing the twinge of his conscience. He'd refused Declan Whyte's unscrupulous offer, but the whole conversation had made his skin crawl. "Not everyone can be bought. I just wanted to make sure you were okay."

Back in high school Finn aptly nicknamed Joselyn "Snow Whyte" because while most girls he knew were emotional schizophrenics, Joss always wore a cold and stony armor—impenetrable by any mere mortal born without a silver spoon and stones of steel.

After speaking with Declan Whyte he could see the apple clearly hadn't fallen far from the elitist tree.

"Where's Sadie?" Joselyn asked.

"I haven't called her yet. I wanted to know what was going on before I put everyone in a frenzy." That was only part of the reason he hadn't contacted his sister, but Joss would learn about the rest soon enough.

"I, uh, I guess I should thank you."

"I guess you should." *Oops.*

Her violently beautiful eyes narrowed, another scowl twisted the softness from her pale pink lips. "Why, thank you, Finn. You're my hero."

They always seemed to bring out the worst in each other. It was an ongoing war, and as they say, old habits die hard. He released a slow, smug grin, maintaining his role. "Glad you're finally seeing things clearly."

"It's amazing there's enough space for your ego in this room. Be careful with that big head as you leave; it might not fit through the door." Her raised eyebrows issued a silent challenge.

He took the bait. "Did they say PMS was a side effect of your condition, or is it just my unmatched hotness that awakens your estrogen from its deep freeze?" *Oh, boy. Too far.*

Their eyes locked, and venom sizzled between them. But draped in a hospital gown, smudges of burned embers staining Joss's porcelain skin, tubes attached to her arms, his steam dissipated. And wonder of wonders, her she-devil ferocity seemed to melt away too, leaving him strangely suspended in the exotic violet-blue of her eyes. The hue so complex and mesmerizing he felt ensnared in the riddle of the silvery blue striations, thinking he'd simply imagined the mirage of lilac that sparked brightest when those eyes were firing at him. Finn tried to swallow, but the starchy hospital air lodged in his larynx like dry toast.

A knock at the door announced the arrival of the nurse a mere second before she bustled through with a vase overflowing with white blooms. "Joselyn, is everything all right?"

Joselyn's eyes flitted away in a daze. "Huh?"

"Oh, psshh. You must have leaned on your call button by mistake. Oops, and the clip fell off your finger. But these flowers came for you, so I guess it wasn't a wasted trip."

As she placed the extravagant arrangement on the table, Finn snapped out of his stupor and backed away from the bed, tugging at the muscles in his neck strained from either the rescue or from sleeping propped up in the waiting room. Perhaps both.

"Don't let me interrupt you two." She shot an indiscrete wink at Joselyn before the door clicked softly behind her.

Several excruciating beats of silence passed while he perused the speckled pattern of the floor; the nurse's suggestive comment lingering like a stink no one would claim.

"Hey, Finn?" Joselyn's tone was achingly fragile. Surprising. And though he didn't often care for what spewed from her smart mouth, the husky quality of her voice pulled his strings with a distinctive and regrettably appealing tug.

He willed himself to look at her, and something in the tired depths of her eyes unraveled his resistance. He'd always been a sucker for the weak and wounded.

Seconds lapsed, her mouth opened and closed, pursed to one side before she bit the edge of her bottom lip. "As much as I love fighting with you, do you think maybe we could put our swords away for one day?"

It was as much emotion as he'd ever seen from the ice princess, and she still wasn't giving him much. "I suppose."

She unburdened a sigh and leaned her head back. The stress that was palpable only moments before started wicking away from her tensely folded body until she looked almost soft and pliant, but not quite.

Taking the moment to observe her, a coiling sensation churned in the pit of his stomach. In uncharted waters, the air, untainted from their usual sarcastic bickering, seemed much too intimate, exposing. Before he could stop them, the teasing words rolled off his tongue. "Did you say that you *love* fighting with me?" The question itself was benign, but combined with the tone and the suggestive wag of his eyebrows he was begging for a lashing.

To her credit she didn't retaliate, merely lifted her delicate arms in frustration and closed her eyes.

Finn was tempted to apologize, but those words were less inclined to cooperate. He hadn't even heard the knock on the door, but there was a man in a white coat approaching the bed, introducing himself as Dr. Jose Nunez.

A thick accent coated his words. "I'd like to go over a few things on your blood work that came back. But before I get into that, are you currently taking any prescription medications?"

Joselyn shook her head. "No. I take a multivitamin every day, that's it."

"Are you sure you don't remember taking anything yesterday? Perhaps a sleep aid?"

"No. I don't sleep well, but I've had bad reactions to those kinds of drugs in the past. Though that was years ago. To be honest, I'd rather deal with the insomnia."

It felt like eavesdropping. He considered stepping out, but something planted his feet in place, some unspoken suspicion. And since Joselyn would no doubt rather peel wallpaper with her perfectly manicured fingers than have a conversation with him, he resolved to stay and find out firsthand.

"Miss Whyte, we found a large amount of a barbiturate known as secobarbital, or more commonly, Seconal, in your system. This type of drug is used to induce sleep, reduce anxiety, control seizures. And—"

"*What*? Someone drugged me?" A white wall of panic washed over her face again. Her trembling fingers knotting together in a self-soothing gesture that didn't appear to be working.

Finn hadn't remembered crossing the room, but found himself at her bedside. His protective instincts momentarily trumping his stubborn pride.

"So it would seem. And from the high concentration we found in your blood, it's a miracle you were able to wake up at all. It was about enough to knock out a rhino."

"Great, another *miracle*." Joselyn dropped her head into her hands and seemed to check out.

The doc arched a dark brow at Finn in question.

"So what you're saying is … someone was trying to kill her?" Finn's inquiry drew her face out of her hands and into a mangled expression of terror he'd do anything to erase.

Dr. Nunez sighed. "I don't know. But it would seem this whole thing was no accident. We'll alert the authorities so they can look for foul play. I'm sure someone will be in touch. On the bright side, you're free to go this afternoon."

Well thank you, Captain Bedside Manner. Finn grappled with the short leash of his temper. The treat 'em and street 'em philosophy wasn't very tactful given the bomb he'd dropped.

But the man barreled on. "I want another oxygen treatment and we will check your carbon monoxide levels once more, but your chest x-ray looks good, as does the rest of your blood work. You should schedule a follow-up appointment, but the stitches in your arm will dissolve and you'll be heading home, good as new."

Finn might have growled. Was this guy for real? What was she supposed to do with that information? And where was she supposed to go now that her house had burned down and she was told someone might want her dead?

Joselyn couldn't seem to speak. Or move.

The girl Finn knew was a force of nature. Strong. Stubborn. Impossible. But this Joselyn ... she seemed frail. Helpless.

The chaotic misfiring of all of Finn's instincts had him feeling helpless too. He doubted someone as prickly as Joselyn would welcome a shoulder to lean on, but how else could he comfort her without physically touching her? Maybe information would be better.

"Okay. I'm gonna call the chief and see if they found anything. Signs of tampering, accelerants ..." Finn placed a hesitant hand on her bony little shoulder, lowering his voice. "Will you be okay for a few minutes?"

She bobbed her head, granting his leave, so he pulled his phone out of his pocket and stepped out into the hall.

After receiving the rundown of the scene from the chief, it was time to call Sadie. She was going to be livid that he hadn't called right away, but he had his reasons. His finger hovered over the send button. She deserved a little happiness. This would certainly put a damper on things.

Sorry, Sadie. Please forgive me for ruining this for you.

Chapter 4

Joselyn Whyte

It was the first trickle she feared the most, yet it slipped through regardless. A single tear like a wet blot seeping through fibers of satin. One drop. Two. Dripping down with emotions she kept on ice, the very ones that were now fleeing from their frozen cage, spreading like infection, and filling her lungs until Joselyn was in the throes of a near panic attack, gasping for breath, dry drowning in her hospital bed. Despite the sudden weight sitting on her chest, the emptiness of the cold, empty room echoed back to her hollow heart, a reminder of the stain on her life and the cruel truth of her existence.

Joselyn Whyte was a marked woman. Tragedy her very own heat-seeking missile—well, maybe *heat* wasn't the right word since she could never stave off a chill. Regardless, it was clear that the devil had her number.

You're all alone.

The voice in her head taunted, or maybe it wasn't in her head. More of a wicked whisper in her ear. The premonition shivered down her spine as the room suddenly felt occupied by something dark and terrifying.

Concentrating on drawing deep, even breaths, she shook away the unease and pulled on the thin woven blanket, fisting the flimsy warmth in her fingers.

How could her father not be here? Declan Whyte was an important man. She was accustomed to his absence, but somehow she'd deluded herself into thinking that the Whyte Empire would relent for one day, given the gravity of the circumstances. But, no.

Her father's unfathomable success, a sneeze shy of Donald Trump's, was never enough to quench his determination to take over the world. And now, with his precious Senate campaign ... well, there was no questioning the man's priorities.

Warring against her disappointment—not to mention her better judgment that warranted the silent treatment—she lifted the phone from the bedside table and set the drudgery in motion.

The ringing droned on and on, and righteous anger fired up in her gut. "*Jerk.*" She slammed the receiver back into its cradle, seething at his brush-off. Eyeing the grandiose bouquet of lilies set her anger on the brink of rage. As if flowers could make up for his absence? The sweet, lilting fragrance made her want to punt the sorry consolation down the hallway. Untucking her feet from the covers, she forced her achy limbs across the room. *This oughtta be good.*

Sorry for your loss.

Nice. *Real* nice. Not just the canned phrase and the unsigned card, but white lilies. *Funeral flowers.* At least, they were what her father always sent for such an occasion—mostly to his employees or their grieving families. Family. She grimaced. When had that become such an acrid word? The Whytes didn't have any family to speak of. Two people obviously didn't constitute a family. Or rather Declan Whyte was too busy to attend to anything so trivial. Too busy to visit his only daughter in the hospital. He probably wouldn't have bothered to come back to identify her charred remains.

He would've just sent white lilies.

The door flung open, and her anger left her. Sadie took the room in two strides and threw herself into Joselyn's barren arms.

"I came as soon as Finn called me."

Joselyn looked over Sadie's shoulder and spotted her brother in the shadowed doorway. His jaw flexed and caught a sheen of light, highlighting the angles of his face and sculpting chiseled features out of stone.

"Joss, is everything okay?"

"Yeah, I'm fine." *Keep reciting the words. Maybe even you will believe them.*

"I called Archer. He and Sal are gonna stop in, if you're up for it."

With only the mention of the man's name, Joselyn's heart buoyed at her friend's undisguisable happiness. Sadie and her FBI boyfriend, Archer Hayes, had only been dating a few months, but it was the kind of romance right out of a storybook—if there was one where two people fell in love while trying to catch a killer. Still. It was so sweet it'd be sickening if it were anyone but Sadie. She'd been through so much and deserved the very best.

Joselyn would settle for mediocre at this point if it could cure her loneliness. Sad, but true. Which was why she'd agreed to another date with her neighbor.

When she looked up from her introspective moment, Sadie and Finn looked away quickly, then exchanged worried glances in some sort of mind-melding, nonverbal sibling speak she resented and envied in equal measure.

"Sorry. I was just … thinking." *Of what? Think of something or they are going to have you admitted to the psych ward.* "I'm supposed to be released today, but it's obvious I can't go home. And the press will swarm a hotel within an hour."

"You're staying with me." Sadie squeezed Joselyn's hand.

"No." Joselyn shook her head adamantly. "No way. I don't know how much 'Captain Ego' told you, but this fire was no accident. Someone was trying to kill me. I won't drag you into this."

Sadie smirked. "*Ego* did tell me. But—"

"Hey!" Finn protested the continued use of the idiotic moniker.

"Sorry. Truth." She patted her brother's arm in consolation. "But I'm not taking no for an answer, Joss. Besides, Archer and his partner, Sal, will take turns keeping an eye on us."

"But—"

"You can save the excuses; it's already in the works. Archer has an in with the Kirkwood PD. They agreed to let them in on the investigation, so Archer and Sal will ask you some questions and we are all gonna strategize." Sadie's turquoise eyes, perfect replicas of Finn's, flashed with mischief. "I've cracked a case in my day, remember?"

Joselyn smiled, relishing the small wonder of happiness amid the wreckage of the past twelve hours. "How could I forget your nauseating happily ever after? It's only been, what, three months? The story's hit the bestseller list in my ears alone, you broken record." Joselyn let her words taunt playfully, "Love conquers all. We know."

Sadie snorted indelicately and adorably. "You just wait. Someday you'll find the right guy, and you'll be as ridiculous as me."

"Oh heaven help us all, the world will be ending." Joselyn giggled back until her gaze collided with Finn's. His indecipherable expression stole her amusement. She curled her fingers into the threadbare gown where the excess fabric hung at her thighs.

"Sooo, how was your date with the *doctor*? Sparks fly?" Sadie clamped a hand over her own mouth. "Oops, sorry. Too soon for fire humor?"

Releasing the wrinkles she'd created with her fists, Joselyn shook her head, chirping out another giggle. The girl knew exactly how to cheer her up.

Sadie scrunched her nose. "Some other time, perhaps."

"Full report when I've de-singed." Joselyn grinned and wormed back into the hospital bed, covering up her not-so-fashionable attire moments before Archer and Sal made their entrance.

"Hey, Joss. How're you holding up?" Tall, dark, and so very handsome, Archer approached her bedside with his sidekick. The lilies were overrun by the smell of men—a clean, spicy, masculine air that was an easy preference over funeral flowers.

"Oh, I'm peachy. Sal, nice to see you again."

"You, too. Sorry about your house. Extra crispy, hold the tasty, huh? That really sucks." At Archer's not so subtle nudge Sal glared back at him. "What?"

Archer huffed his exasperation at his guileless partner.

"You two could have your own sitcom." Joselyn couldn't help but smile, feeling remarkably at ease, given the circumstances.

Sal brightened. "You know, that's not a bad ide—"

"*Don't* feed him any ideas. So, give me the rundown?"

Finn cleared his throat. "I called Chief Barrett. The investigation is underway, but they haven't found much. The bomb and arson unit's working on accelerants and origin. They'll know more in a couple of days, but the timing is consistent with the Five-Alarm Arsonist."

"Have they made any progress with that investigation?" Archer snaked his arm around his girl and glued her to his side. Noticing the way his thumb traced the curve of Sadie's waist made Joselyn painfully aware of how pitifully deprived she was of human contact.

"No leads for six months now. He's claimed six buildings and two victims. Each new location a little more brazen. Word is the firebug started with kerosene and has since progressed to homemade pipe bombs at the last target. It all appears random—except for the fact that he strikes on the fifth of each month. This is no exception." Finn shoved his hands into his pockets and rocked back on his heels.

"Well—"

What was sure to be Archer's plan of action was interrupted by the blare of the bedside phone. Joselyn startled. Reaching over to silence the shrill ringing, she answered the phone and held up a finger to the group.

"Hello?"

"Hello, Joselyn. It's your father. You all right?" His voice was all business, as usual.

"Well, I'm alive. Can't say the same for my house."

"It's high time we get you a more respectable residence anyhow. Never understood why you'd choose to live in that hovel."

Her eyes rolled in reflex, her shields rising against the sting of his thoughtless words. "Oh yes, what a *relief* to be rid of my home and all of my possessions. And as an added bonus we now know someone torched the place on purpose. Quite the load off my mind, let me tell you."

Silence reigned for a long moment. "That can't be right. Are you certain?"

"Your concern is touching. Sadie is here with Agent Hayes and Agent Sal … ivas?" She lingered over the pronunciation of his last name, and Sal confirmed with a wink. "… of the FBI. And Finn Carson is here, too. I believe you spoke with him already." She let her eyes flash on Finn. Burly arms were crossed, expression guarded, yet his steely eyes seemed to penetrate the wall between them. The one very clearly marked *Keep Out!*

"Put me on speaker."

"What?"

"Joselyn, do as you're told. Put me on speakerphone."

"Dad, it's a hospital phone. I'm pretty sure there's no speaker. And my phone bur—"

"Tell that Finn fellow to answer his phone." Click.

No sooner had Joselyn eased the phone from her ear when a jolt of AC/DC's "Back in Black" blasted from her rescuer's pocket.

"Hello?"

Joselyn still hadn't found her voice, when Finn continued with "Yes, sir."

"Can everyone hear me?" her father called out, his tone as firm as his staunch Scottish accent.

A chorus of affirmations rang out.

"Now I am assuming the FBI is not officially involved in this, correct?"

The rigid taskmaster strikes again.

Archer chimed in. "We will be working in tandem with

the police and state fire team. Our main concern is to keep eyes on your daughter, make sure she stays safe until we find this guy."

Declan's condescension reached through the airwaves like an infuriating pat on the head. "Well, that's a swell sentiment, young man, but I think I'd like to hire some additional protection as w—"

Oh, no! "Dad, if you sick Gill and Royce on me, I promise I will never speak to you again." That drew a few curious glances. "Your Scottish goons are about as subtle as socks with sandals. And, if you must know, Gill's lazy eye has a distinctive leering quality that makes me itch."

"What would you have me do, Joselyn? The company Christmas gala is in two weeks. It's early yet, but I need you there to rally support for the campaign. It's obvious you can't go alone, and that doctor you went out with could be overpowered by an angry Girl Scout."

"Are you kidding me?" Her face burned, more from fury than embarrassment. "Our first date was last night! Have you had them tailing me, again?"

The last time Declan had her followed, she happened to be going to her annual ob-gyn appointment. Gill, rocket scientist that he was, started spouting ideas to her father about an unplanned pregnancy. What the oaf didn't know when he barged in on her breast exam, was that she'd gone on a Ben & Jerry's bender for two weeks, drowning her sorrows from a slew of horrendous blind dates in Chunky Monkey and Half Baked. The "baby bump" Gill imagined was three extra pounds of heavenly, albeit reckless, indulgence.

She didn't need an answer and didn't give her father a chance to give one. "You know what, this conversation is over." She fired an expectant glare at Finn to hang up. He shifted his weight, looking conflicted.

"Fine." Her father snapped. "But you'll need an escort— preferably someone who can pose as a boyfriend to avoid suspicion for the campaign. I'd really like to keep this under the radar. We don't need a scandal throwing away all the good press I've been getting. And it sure wouldn't hurt to *soften* your image a bit."

Joselyn bit back an angry retort and a few tenacious tears fighting for release. Could there be a more selfish human being on the planet? The tender places ached from the continued blows of his words. Not soft? She was bruised all over. Not that he cared to see. And what scandal? Wasn't she the victim in all this?

Hurt after hurt swelled up in waves, threating to drown her in the drone of names of possible suitors that would play the part to perfection. Every mortifying word airing in front of the studio audience at her bedside while her aching head screamed at the indignance of his meddling. She wanted to close her eyes, click her heels, and be anywhere but here. But once Declan Whyte set his mind to something, not a soul with breath could escape the path of his personal tornado. She looked to Sadie and was met with a forced smile and a helpless shrug.

"I could do it." Sal stepped forward, resting his hand near the head of the hospital bed. "It sure wouldn't be hard to pretend to like you for a few weeks." He winked and flashed her a sweet, goofy grin.

Her cheeks warmed. A hint of relief melted slowly through her tense muscles like a drizzle of honey in hot tea. Sal was definitely attractive. About six feet tall, ultra-lean, if not a little wiry—or maybe he simply appeared compact compared to Archer and Finn. Sal, whose first name was actually Dorian, had Hispanic roots ensuring him an enviable year-round tan, offsetting perfect white teeth and yummy dark chocolate eyes. From their few short encounters Joselyn knew him to be hilarious and easygoing. Maybe this wouldn't be too bad. Anyone would be better than one of her dad's minions.

"No. *I'll* do it."

Her eyes snapped to the newest volunteer. *Uh, oh.* Something fired low in her belly, probably her ovaries bursting into flames.

Finn. He was a different sort of handsome—and he knew it. Too aware of his all-American good looks, he'd used his cover-model crop of tousled, sandy blonde hair, gemstone-colored eyes, and athletic physique against the opposite sex for as long as she'd known him.

But looks were deceiving. Under no circumstances would she fall prey to those sparkling eyes. Not again. She held his gaze hard, strengthening her resolve to stay immune to their mysterious allure.

But then why did it feel like she was surrounded by quicksand?

"Who's going to do it?" Her dad's puzzlement broke the stunned silence.

"Finn." Sal answered, his eyes darting between Joselyn and the jerk.

"All right. Probably better it's not a cop. Those vultures in the press will be all over that, and it might make it more difficult for you lads to quickly flush out the threat. Besides, Mr. Carson has what appears to be a Guns 'N Hoses boxing title and a concealed carry license to his name. He should be able to handle this fool's errand until we put this nonsense behind us. It's settled then. Finn, we'll be in touch."

The line went dead, and Joselyn was certain her ears had played a cruel trick on her. Sweeping her gaze across the silent room and taking in the numb faces, she settled again on a horrified and equally bewildered-looking Finn. *Oh, crap.*

Joselyn withdrew her thoughts about Gill and Royce. There was a worse choice.

And she was looking at him.

Chapter 5

Finn Carson

What. Just. Happened? Had he blacked out? Was that really his voice that volunteered to pose as Joselyn's boyfriend for the next few weeks? *Take it back. Act like you were joking!* But before he could relinquish his asinine offer, Joselyn's father had gone and a collage of suspicious and confounded faces had zeroed in on him.

Now what?

He didn't even have time to sputter about when and why the mighty Declan had run a background check on him because Joselyn's velvety calm voice somehow pinched his ear.

"Finn? I'd like a word with you in the hall."

Wait, no. *Oww.* Not her voice. Her *fingers* pinched his ear. Helpless, his body bent, cartilage twisting, she hurled him—with uncanny force—out the door.

"Oww!"

"What on earth were you thinking?" Her eyes narrowed, claws resting on her hips.

He touched the flap of flesh to make sure it was still attached to his head. "I'm sorry, did you say something? I seem to be having problems with my *ear!*"

"Explain yourself?" She exaggerated each syllable.

Wish I could. "Uhh …"

"You have no idea what you just did. Do you know who you're messing with?"

He fought back a smug grin, and failed. "Sorry, sweetheart. You don't scare me. Can't be more than a buck twenty soaking wet." Although the force behind that ear trauma suggested otherwise.

"Not me, you idiot! My dad!"

"You wanna yell a little louder? I'm not sure the deaf lady in 5201 quite got that."

Curious glances from the nurse's station were now fixated on their display of what was soon to be front-page-gossip-rag material.

Joselyn grabbed his shirt and tugged him farther down the hallway. The harsh florescence ignited the white hot fury in her eyes. Her voice pitched lower, but her intensity held firm. "You don't understand. You penned a deal with Satan. Declan Whyte stops at nothing to get what he wants. And right now what he wants—aside from his billion-dollar empire—is a seat in the Senate. As if our lives weren't enough of a circus of speculation, *now* you can add another telescopic lens.

"He's going to have a whole story about our relationship to the press before they get a chance to interpret it for themselves. Then, you and I are going to be spied on to confirm the slew of lies he fed to them. Which means that we will actually have to spend time together and act like a couple, or my dad will have both of our heads."

If steam could shoot from a person's ears, Finn would be witnessing the phenomenon at this very moment. She did still smell faintly like a bonfire. Who knew the ice princess could get so steamed? Finn wrestled down a chuckle of sudden amusement when he pictured Joselyn's face a sickly shade of green as she chanted, "I'm melting." And since she hadn't slapped him, he figured he'd done an adequate job pretending to follow her rant instead of picturing her as the Wicked Witch.

"Dysfunction, arson, murderers, that stuff won't fly, and he's got enough muscle to make sure it stays hidden, for now. Nothing sells like a squeaky clean, happy family free of …"

His mind raced a 10K around her rambling thoughts as the

situation weighed in. Okay. This was bad. It was obvious she needed a protector of sorts at her side, but was he really up for the job?

The chief had ordered Finn on a mandatory two-week sabbatical to clear his head and recuperate. He hadn't taken any time off in the last two years, and even after the Monroe incident four months ago, he'd worked himself into the ground, refusing time away from the station. Punishing himself.

"Finn, are you even listening?" She rammed her fingers through her silky tresses and heaved her exasperation. "Look, you don't like me."

"Nope." He fought with every word scrambling in his head, yet this one rose to the surface with certainty.

"Perfect! I don't like you either, so on this we agree. What I don't understand—"

"Can you shut your trap for one second so I can say something?" His voice snapped more than he'd intended, and he saw her flinch.

Her teeth scraped across the corner of her pouty bottom lip. Then she crossed her arms and waited.

He glanced around, and shaved the harsh edge off his tone. "Listen ... I guess we're going to have to grin and bear it. But I certainly don't have to justify my reasons to you." He lowered his gaze to where the soft flesh of her lip surrendered from her bite, inexplicably frozen there. A blush of the palest pink stole back into the tortured petal of skin, and he could almost hear the pulsation that fluttered at her throat. She swallowed hard. Finn followed suit, forcing a swig of oxygen through his suddenly parched airway.

"*Dr. Vreeland to OR 3... Dr. Vreeland to OR 3.*" The page over the intercom jolted him from the trance. The hospital halls came alive, beeps and murmurs emerged once again from the background.

"There's a killer on the loose, and like it or not, your life is in my strong and capable hands."

She rolled her eyes.

"Now, let's kiss and make up and get this show on the road." He threw in a wink, just to tick her off.

"Ha! Right!" In a huff she turned and took on a fitful strut back toward her room.

Man, she riled easily. *This is gonna be more fun than I thought.*

"*Firefighter Finn*, is that you?" The squeal came from a curvy blonde strutting down the hall.

Finn saw Joselyn stop dead in her tracks. Her head craned around like that crazy girl from *The Exorcist*.

"*You* never called me, mister." Blondie's overly glossed lips formed a petulant pout as she approached.

He made sure to catch the priceless dumbfounded look on Joselyn's face before he turned and tossed his memory for the name of the vaguely recognizable "badge bunny" he'd helped pry from her car after a wreck. "Oh, I ... uh."

Movement from Joselyn's corner of the ring drew his eyes to her instead. Her gaze looked effortlessly sultry compared to the saccharine seductive looks batting from blondie's heavily-lined eyes.

A devious smirk played across her lips. "Oh, *Peanut*, there you are." Joselyn's words escaped on a syrupy grin.

Reality buckled at its hinges as Joss closed the space between them, slipped her arms around his waist, pressing the front of her body flush against his side. A fire swirled in his belly right before his stomach plummeted to his feet. His befuddled senses left the rest of him frozen on the spot.

"Who's your friend?" Joselyn spoke close, her warm breath tickling his cheek.

He looked down into her wide, innocent eyes. *Oh, she's good.*

So good he was once again completely disarmed. And disturbed. He would have thought the uptight princess would be all stiff and twiggy with this little charade, but he was loathe to notice she was both very firm and *very* supple in the most unnerving way.

"Peanut?" The question from bystander Barbie whose

previous advances he'd politely dodged and whose name eluded him.

"Oh, yeah." Joselyn shrugged. "Our little nickname."

She did *not* just wink!

Finn felt his jaw drop open, a mystified laugh escaped from his stricken lungs. "Wha—"

Before he could even attempt to defend his manhood an enlightened O formed on the blonde's sticky lips and she released a snort. "Gotcha. I'm Nikki, by the way."

Joselyn released one hand to greet Nikki, then promptly reset her trap. "It's always nice to meet one of Finny's old friends."

Joselyn smiled up at him with artfully acted pride in her eyes while he struggled to loosen his shackled tongue. Small talk ensued for a mindlessly fast blur of what couldn't have been more than a minute until Nikki disappeared down the hall.

Joselyn held her station, and Finn realized his arm was now wrapped around her tight little waist, his large hand spanning down over the curve of her hip sheathed only in the wispy thin hospital gown.

She lifted to her toes and leaned in an inch from his ear. "You are so going to regret this."

Finn's pulse spiked, his senses acutely honed in to her breath warming his previously traumatized cartilage and her fingers skimming across his low back in withdrawal. "I already do." He matched her glare as she pulled her hips away, pivoted, and sauntered, a bit too smugly he thought, back toward her room.

"Oh, Joselyn, dear."

She turned, triumph in her tight-lipped smirk.

"I know you are very proud of your *assets,* but doll, this is a public place, and you know I don't like to share. Perhaps you should cover up, save that for daddy for later." He bounced his eyebrows for effect.

Sheer mortification splashed across her face before she jerked at her gaping hospital gown and ducked into her room.

Ladies and Gentlemen: Round one, goes to Finn Carson.

"It's okay. I'm gonna get you out of here. Hold on tight." Finn's lungs screamed to be heard over the hiss and roar of the fire. Flames slithered toward the full-sized bed tangled with blankets, cornering him to the back wall, further from the door.

Clutching the frail, trembling body in his arms, he felt her frantic, muted sobs vibrate against his chest. The options were dwindling. His mind raced against a ticking time bomb for an escape.

"Please, show me a way out." The words were eaten up by the flames, and Finn wasn't sure they'd actually escaped his pleading soul.

The room seemed to spin around him. Throbbing pain ricocheted from various wounds in breath-stealing pulses to his brain and back for maximum effect. But none could touch the blistering agony of the still sizzling skin on his neck wailing in his ears louder than the raging inferno.

Something crunched under his feet. Looking down, he strained to make out a scattering of LEGO's on the floor near what used to be a Barbie Dreamhouse. Kicking the toys aside he tested his weight against the loose floor board. If he could keep the flames at bay for two more minutes it just might work.

Had to. Or this fiery grave would claim them both.

AC/DC called to him beyond the deep daze of sleep. Cracking open one eye, the nightmare fell away and he squinted against the harsh glare of sunlight. While he struggled to soothe his labored breaths and acclimate to the present, he let the phone call roll over to voicemail.

God, will these nightmares ever end?

A soft whine registered near his ear. Angling his head, he found himself nose to nose with his new roommate Dodger. His scruffy rescue mutt's front paws were propped atop the mattress, his tail battering the nightstand in metronomic time as he rolled out his sloppy tongue in greeting. Finn wiped away the remnants of the kiss before giving his little Benji-lookalike's ears a hearty scratch.

Rolling out of the torture chamber, Finn trudged down the narrow flight of stairs from the open loft bedroom to his kitchen and evaluated the meager contents of his fridge, the gust of cool air belatedly reminding him of his state of undress. He shrugged, took several long swigs from a carton of orange juice, and scratched his chest. Bachelorhood certainly did have its perks.

Licking sounds emanated from Dodger's jowls.

"Sorry, pal. This jug's mine." He burped and replaced the carton. "Let's get you some breakfast, huh, boy?"

If at all possible, his feathery tail flitted faster, causing his whole body to wag in opposition.

Wandering to the cabinet, he replenished Dodger's stockpile and was pleased to find half a box of Cinnamon Toast Crunch for himself. Knowing there wasn't any milk he took the box to the couch and snacked on the dry, borderline stale, cereal while *Sports Center* informed him of the news.

His phone called out the classic rock anthem, echoing down the two-story ceiling from his bedroom. Not remembering anything pressing for the day, he slouched further into the couch. Months of restless nights made Finn's body beg for complacency, yet his tireless mind spun toward distraction. This forced leave of absence might be the death of him. The empty days ahead a mocking reminder of his fears and failures.

Fortunately, it was Saturday, his favorite day of the week. The day he got to spend with Kendi, the only girl who'd ever truly owned his heart. Hopefully she wouldn't be exposed to any of the media storm that would be following him for the next few weeks.

After getting ready, grabbing his phone, and procuring Dodger to his leash, Finn headed out to the parking garage to his truck. The growl of the diesel engine reverberated from the concrete walls. Dodger paced the bench seat, ready to ride.

The redundant ringtone beat out just above the old Ford F-250's rumble, reminding Finn that he'd ignored his calls all morning. He regarded the screen: *Private Caller,* and answered it anyway.

"Hello?"

"Please hold for Declan Whyte."

And so it begins.

Chapter 6

How in the hell had she survived that fire? It'd been perfect. Every last detail measured with inscrutable accuracy. He would know. He'd planned it for a year. It was impossible. *Impossible.*

The odds calculated in his mind, numbers scratching out like chalk against the deepening black. All the variables had been considered. It wasn't possible he could have missed something. The unnatural heat of his handcrafted "Whyte" flame should have cremated her in minutes. And he'd been merciful enough to ensure she'd sleep through the incineration, imprisoning her in her own body. His rage blazed even hotter with the injustice of his failure; the poisonous hatred feeding the madness he was beginning to own, even appreciate.

The ghostly screams echoed in his skull, bounding around until he tasted blood from his cheek. He swiped the sting with his tongue; the tang soaked into his taste buds, awakening the empty ache in his stomach.

He pulled the car away from the curb near the blonde girl's condo, knowing he'd need food before he came back tonight.

All his careful planning had been decimated by an idiot, rogue firefighter with a death wish. Perhaps any plans he made were bound to fail. Plans were supposed to be reliable. But life proved to be anything but.

Maybe just once he'd try his hand at impulsiveness. See how that worked out.

Yes, a sense of rightness flowed through his veins. He'd

try again.
The sooner the better.

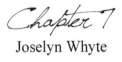

Joselyn Whyte

"**S**eriously, I'll be fine. I do not need a babysitter."

Sadie grabbed for her phone as Joselyn raked it out of reach. "I'm not leaving, it's too soon. I'm calling to cancel."

"You already said Sal would drive by later and check on me." Joselyn held the phone above her head. Her five foot nine inches gave her a distinct advantage over Sadie's five three. "Weren't you just complaining about *lover boy* working so much that you've barely seen each other in weeks?"

Sadie opened her mouth, but Joselyn blocked her protest. "—That's like a fourth of your entire relationship."

Sadie stuck out her tongue and started poking at Joselyn's underarms. "I still don't like it. Just let me call Finn—"

"NOOO!" Joselyn giggled and swatted her best friend's prodding fingers. "Stop that! Look, the doors will be locked. Plus, when Archer escorted us home from the hospital yesterday I could tell he had his eyes peeled for a tail. No one could possibly know I'm here. I'm fine. I promise."

Joselyn was no stranger to Sadie's condo so it was easy to feel instantly at home. The warm neutral colors, the tired wood floors, and all the soft, cozy upholstery made the space feel like a Pottery Barn-inspired retreat.

Sadie shook her head, crinkly blonde waves had sprung from her ponytail and were loose and wild against her pretty heart-shaped face. "Don't make me pull out my tae kwon do moves on you, Joss. I'll do it." She narrowed her eyes, lips twitching against the tugging grin.

Joselyn huffed and eventually extended the contraband. "Suit yourself. But if I had a gorgeous man asking me to go to … Where is he taking you again?"

Sadie relaxed from her ninja pose and accepted the phone. She hugged it to her chest with an overly embellished dreamy sigh and fell back onto the cream slip-cover style couch. "The only clue Archer gave me is that I need to dress up. I wonder if the FBI has some kind of banquet or something."

Collapsing down on the couch beside her, Joselyn tapped her lips. "Hmm. Only one way to find out."

"But I won't be able to enjoy myself if you're alone."

"Please. I could use a little rest from this whole ordeal."

"Can I at least call and check in on you every hour?"

"So much for getting some shut eye."

"Joss, that's my best offer. It's that or I call Finn, or Fish and Clausse to babysit."

"It's Gill and Royce." Joselyn let her giggle slip out.

"Perfect! Gill and Royce it is."

"Hold the phone, short stuff. I will confiscate that thing again and give it a swirly before you so much as dial the area code."

Sadie snorted. "Okay, okay. But I will be checking in every hour, so you best keep your phone close by or I'll have a SWAT team swarming this joint in a matter of minutes, capiche?"

Joselyn knew Sadie was likely joking with that threat and was tempted to feign outrage to keep the banter rolling, but the dead-serious concern in her friend's eyes froze her retort. How long had it been since someone had looked at her like that? Like they actually cared. Afraid the tremor settling in her throat would give her away she answered by crossing her heart with her index finger.

"Good enough. Will you help me get ready? I don't have the slightest idea what to wear."

"Hmm. Well, I know of this fabulous little boutique that's sure to have what you're looking for. And lucky for you, I so happen to know the owner."

Sadie grinned. "How fortuitous. But I'm sure I have something passable here."

"Oh no, my dear. Passable simply will not do. In the words of Coco Chanel, *'Dress shabbily and they remember the dress; dress impeccably and they remember the woman.'* Let's go make you even more unforgettable."

After scavenging Charisma—Joselyn's boutique clothing store in Downtown Kirkwood—for a stunning vintage sea-green lace sheath dress for Sadie's date and some everyday fare to tide Joselyn over for a few days, they returned to the condo all shopped out.

Joss helped Sadie primp to perfection and then submitted to a long, searing shower. With no place to go, and every intention of giving Sadie and Archer plenty of time to greet each other privately, Joselyn dawdled under the steamy spray, scrubbing herself pink with a whipped sugar body polish and treating her slightly charred hair to the dated hot oil treatment she'd found tucked in Sadie's hall closet.

Passing what had to be at least a half an hour of sauna-worthy bliss, she threw on a slim cotton robe and twisted her long, raven-colored locks into a towel. The cool air from the hallway chilled the smog of moisture coating her skin as she crossed to her bedroom.

But something stopped her short. She leaned against the door frame, listening again.

And then she heard it. Were those ... gun shots?

There was some sort of commotion and then *bang, bang!* Louder this time. And so close a tremor pulsed through the walls.

A scream trapped in her throat, and Joselyn lunged forward into her room, stumbling over her noncompliant size eights in an uncoordinated panic. She closed the door quietly in spite of the racket and twisted the flimsy lock. Stepping back shakily, she flattened herself against the wall. Think!

Think!

She needed to call for help, but her phone had been a casualty of the fire and the landline was in the kitchen. Joselyn bit down on her lip, straining to hear. Voices barked garbled messages she couldn't begin to untangle in her frazzled state.

Why were they yelling? How had they gotten inside? And what the heck were they shooting at?

Oh no! What if they'd shown up before Sadie and Archer left?

She touched a cold, quivering hand to her lips. Her fear was asphyxiating, every terrorizing scenario she could think of pummeled her from every side until she'd been bruised and beaten with the only sensible conclusion.

Whoever burned down her house had come back to finish the job.

Her weight sagged into the wall and the towel unfurled from her head, her wet hair now blotting through the lightweight fabric at her shoulders. The wall rattled with another barrage of gunfire. She shivered. For the second time in as many days the cold truth gripped her. *This is it. I'm gonna die.* Squeezing her eyes shut, she tried to breathe, tried to think past the consuming despair and helplessness.

Sadie! If they had Sadie, Joselyn couldn't cower in her room. She had to act.

Fortified in her decision, she felt a strange sense of strength and resolve fold around her body like a shield. A sense of déjà vu tingled down her spine, though she couldn't say why. She stepped back out into the hall, belatedly realizing she was about to confront armed intruders without a single defense.

Halting in the shadowed hallway, Joselyn recalled seeing an old baseball bat propped inside the closet. Her fingers closed around the door handle, deftly cracking it enough to snake in her arm.

Yahtzee.

She gripped the wooden handle, wincing at the pull of her

stitches, and raised the weapon to her shoulder. It was no match for a gun but somehow her confidence was overwhelming her common sense. *Sadie. You're doing this for Sadie.*

The voices hushed in conversation as she tiptoed closer. She could almost make out what they were saying. John. She definitely heard the name John.

Almost there.

A few more steps brought her to the shadowed opening of the living room. She'd decided to take her first peek when a figure rounded the corner and slammed into her.

"Ahhh!" The sound of her scream punched through her illusion of confidence. The terror made her frantic, and she sent the seemingly weightless bat into attack mode.

"Hey! Oww!" Strong fingers immobilized her wailing arm and the rest became a blur of struggling limbs and smothered grunts. In a scant moment of clarity she consciously brought her knee up hard and fast.

The hand on her arm dropped away, and the man fell back into the light. Before Joselyn could initiate her escape she caught sight of her assailant. One she would recognize anywhere.

"Finn?" Releasing the bat, she sank to the floor beside him. "Are you okay?"

He'd gone fetal, hands cupping his groin, face scrunched in silent agony. With great hesitance she settled her hand on his side. He hissed out a breath and shrank back from her touch. "Umm, is there anything I can do?"

"Haven't you done enough?" he growled.

Her spine whipped straight. "Oh, I'm *sorry*. I wasn't aware you'd be prowling around the living room uninvited. What do you think you're doing here anyway?"

Wincing, he propped himself up to a seated position. "Geez, girl, you sure do know how to show a guy a good time."

It was obvious he was in pain. But after the start he'd given her she couldn't muster a whole lot of remorse. It was his own fault, after all.

At this point she wasn't even upset with him, only grateful she was still alive to laugh about the misunderstanding. Though she suspected Finn wouldn't appreciate her laughter at the moment. So instead she bit back a grin and offered him her hand.

Though he was glaring up at her, she thought she saw a glimpse of a smile hiding somewhere in those much too pretty eyes. His hand was warm and rough-skinned, a compelling contrast to her always chilled yet pampered fingers now completely swallowed up in his grip. When he was to his feet, she assumed he'd let go. But he held on, and some kind of magnetic trance planted her in place. A hot rush flowed through her, heating feverishly in her cheeks.

Joselyn wasn't sure how long they stayed like that. Time slowed and her brain turned to haggis. Finn's body was so close she could feel the heat of him. And as always she was so very cold, and so very lonely, for a split second she considered closing the gap between them and filching a free embrace. Her fingers fidgeted in her moment of indecision, except the movement resembled more of a caress than a spasm and that flame in his eyes bumped up to scorching.

His grip tightened, she shifted her weight forward, and—

Sadie's landline rang.

Spell broken, Joselyn jerked her hand free of the ridiculously long handshake, turned tail, and sprinted to the kitchen. She bobbled the cordless phone twice before managing to finagle it to her ear.

"He-Hello?" She cringed at her breathless tone.

"Hey, Joss." Sadie chirped. "I know I haven't been gone an hour yet, but I wanted to check in. Finn showed up as we were leaving, and you were still in the shower. I assume you know that by now." The tint of remorse in Sadie's voice was overshadowed by her obvious excitement for her date.

"Yeah. Great, thanks for the heads up."

"I know. I'm sorry. I promise I didn't call him to play babysitter. Archer did."

"Uh-huh."

"I won't harass you with phone calls now that Finn's there. But make sure he doesn't crank up the new surround sound Archer installed too loud. It's pretty intense, and since I finally have new neighbors I'd rather not rattle those flimsy walls and scare them off the first week."

"Pretty intense, is right." Joselyn mumbled.

"Oooo. Okay. I think we're here. Play nice, now. Love you!"

"You too. Have fun." Joselyn disconnected the call and tried to shake off the nervous energy still making a mockery of her cool and confident façade. A handshake! If she could gather enough oxygen, she'd probably laugh. After a few deep breaths she returned to the scene of the crime.

"Interesting choice of weapon, Joss. Did you really think you could brain me to death with this thing?" An amused Finn was in possession of his ever cocky grin and ... an umbrella?

"For real? I thought I grabbed a baseball bat."

He glanced up. "Oh Jesus, you are a merciful Lord. But you, little missy, need to explain why you tried to beat me with a baseball bat." Something shifted in his stare. Amusement drained away leaving nothing to read but a suddenly averted gaze and pronounced chug of his Adam's apple.

"I heard gun shots. And then I heard some yelling and talking. I thought—" More gunfire drew her attention to the TV. She dropped her chin to her chest and exhaled a humorless laugh. *Die Hard.* That explains it."

"That's all you have to say?"

"Well," she shrugged in defense, "I must be a bit on edge, what, with the attempted murder and all."

"You could have destroyed future generations of little Carsons. I think I'm gonna have to hear an actual apology." He crossed his well-muscled arms over his chest, making her take note of the man that had taken shape from the boy she'd known in high school. Remembering that one and only time those arms had held her. And then ruined her.

Thank goodness Sadie called when she did.

"Not a chance. *You* were not supposed to be here. I was simply defending myself against an intruder. So, if you wish to procreate in the future you should be sure to give a girl a heads up. A simple holler down the hall would have saved little *peanut* the trauma." She lifted her chin and held his stubborn gaze.

"Tell me something. Is it your curiosity that's driving this slander?" He raised a devilish eyebrow.

Heat strangled her neck. "No!"

"You're trying to invent a flaw because you can't find one?" He took a step closer.

She felt her ears warm beneath the cool drape of her hair. "Pfff! As if—"

Good. Because as much as I'd like to set the record straight, I am not putting out on the first date." He smirked, laugh lines forming at the corners of his eyes.

It all felt a lot like flirting. But it couldn't be. Not with their track record.

"But for Pete's sake, could you put some clothes on? I may not be able to stand your particular breed of snooty princess, but a man can only take so much of you parading that hot little body around. It's starting to mess with my head." He averted his eyes again, and Joselyn felt the blood drain from her face.

And then she looked down. *Oh bloody hell.* The ultra-lightweight jersey knit of the short robe was plastered like cellophane to her damp skin. There was no mooning this time, but the scuffle had loosened the tie at her waist making each lapel of white fabric meet to create a plunging neckline worthy of a Hollywood starlet. Joselyn stared at the rather graphic display of her modest curves, mouth gaping and mortified for a beat too long before self-preservation kicked in gear and had her running for her room.

"How does that keep happening? And with *him*, of all people!" She fell back onto the bed, not sure she could ever show her face to him again.

"I can hear you, you know?"

As his voice bounded down the hall, she winced, pressed a pillow over her head, and considered hiding under the covers for the remainder of the evening. It only took a second to decide that that tactic would only fuel his antagonism, so she threw on a pair of black yoga pants and a time-softened white and green baseball tee, courtesy of Sadie. After tossing her straight damp hair with her fingers, Joselyn closed her eyes, absorbing every ounce of composure she could muster, before making her way back out to Finn.

The nerves she'd fought to wrangle came flooding back through her stomach the moment his eyes touched her. She was completely covered from neck to toe, but his gaze seemed to strip away every ounce of confidence, leaving her feeling naked all over again. "Umm, so, you never did mention why you came over."

"Well … Archer has had this thing planned for a while, and I wanted to make sure it still went off without a hitch. I figured Sadie would pull out because of what happened. That's why I held off telling her about you being in the hospital."

"I see. Well, she tried to stay. I wouldn't let her." She found herself incessantly tugging at the bottom of the shirt.

Finn smirked knowingly like the arrogant jerk he was. "Maybe we should sit. Gonna be a long night if we don't."

"Gonna be a long night either way," she mumbled.

He coughed up a laugh as he settled next to her on the couch.

Joselyn leaned back into the soft canvas cushions, gathering her knees to her chest to put a barrier between them. "Give a girl some space, would you? And maybe tone it down a bit on the aftershave, Romeo. Stuff's kind of nauseating." In reality, his warmth and nearness were both more potent than the fresh spicy scent currently hot-wiring her salivary glands. And it was only nauseating because she wanted to purge herself of her body's absurd responses to a man who was, for all intents and purposes, her nemesis.

Said nemesis smiled, revealing heartbreaking dimples in each cheek. She'd forgotten about those. *Why does it feel like he's in my head?*

"You're gonna fall so hard." It seemed he found his own vanity amusing.

"Oh, for—now I really am gonna be sick."

"Ha! Settle down, Snow Whyte, I was only teasing. But—"

"Don't call me that!" She snapped.

He held up his hands in surrender. "I was going to say we need to work on looking more comfortable together. As it is now, even our body language says we're both contemplating strangling each other. Pasting a phony smile over it won't fool anybody. Least of all, the media. Who, we all know, have an unhealthy fascination with you, for some unknown reason."

They weren't touching, but the inch between his muscular thigh and her frozen toes wasn't enough to slow her pulse. But as his words sunk in, it all clicked back into place.

"Ahh, he got to you. Didn't he?"

"What do you mean?" Finn stretched his arm on the back on the couch behind her head, sweeping her hair off where his hand came to rest on the cushion.

Brain cells scattered then quickly reassembled. "Declan Whyte's noble plan of action. He reeled you in. You're a goner. I can see it in your eyes."

Eyes that strayed in denial. "No. I simply listened to what he had to say. He seems concerned about you, and he has the experience to know how to handle this. To keep you safe."

"You realize you sounded exactly like him right then. Did he coach you? Give you cue cards? Talk about falling. Wow." She let her dismay leak out in a slow, patronizing shake of her head. "I was gonna give you more credit than that. But oh how the mighty have fallen."

"Whatever. The way I see it, I'm doing you a favor." He let that settle for a moment, then his eyes narrowed. "You're going to have to stop it with those sour faces. From this point on I'm your dreamboat. The wind beneath your wings. And don't forget, your 'knight in shining turnouts.' For our first exercise in civility, you may spend the remainder of the evening gazing at me adoringly, for practice. Don't worry, it'll come naturally soon enough." He winked.

Joselyn indelicately snorted her disgust. That strangling idea sounded better by the minute.

"It's either that or we snuggle and watch the rest of the *Die Hard* marathon?" He leaned in closer and wagged his eyebrows.

"And what's behind door number three?" She fired back. "The other options seem like cruel and unusual punishment for a traumatized woman."

"Hmm … option three, we make out on the couch until Sadie and Archer get home."

Joselyn felt her jaw dislodge. "You wouldn't dare."

Finn licked his lips, leaning in until their noses almost touched. "Try me."

Nuh-uh. Nope. Not happening. And as exhausted as she was, she knew she had to remain fully alert. No letting her guard down. She yawned. No way. Not for a single second.

"Mommy, daddy? Please wake up. Pretty please. I'm scared." She pleaded again. Her voice a broken little wisp of desperation.

After the violent shriek of the tires and deafening roar of twisting steel all had fallen silent. Her screams had faded to intermittent hiccups and sniffles. The eerie hush of the falling rain like a blanket of white noise smothering the wreckage. Minutes or hours might have passed as her small body, suspended inches from the crushed roof of the car, wriggled against the cutting pressure of the seat belt.

Then a groaning sound. A snippet of hope that her

parents had survived. She whimpered, fresh tears dripping in the already frozen tear tracks down her forehead. Never had a sweeter sound graced Joselyn's ears than when her father's gruff accent assured her she wasn't alone.

"Charisma? ... Joselyn?"

"Daddy. Oh, Daddy, I'm here. I'm—I'm scared." She shivered hard, trembling uncontrollably from the cold that had long ago soaked through her winter coat.

Her father didn't assure her everything would be all right. Somehow she knew nothing would ever be all right again.

Within moments he'd snaked his body through the hole of the driver's side window and crawled to the opening behind him. His trembling hands released the seatbelt and braced her dangling body's impact with the roof of the mangled car. Small shards of crumbled glass ground into her scalp as he wrestled her through the jagged window opening.

And then he held her tight, treasuring her survival for a fleeting moment as the rain turned to pelting hail, crashing down to earth, striking without mercy. Pungent vapors invaded the security she felt in his arms, singed her nostrils with each whimpering breath.

He pulled her back to look at her. His eyes sharp and assessing even as tears escaped his blue eyes to mix with the smears of blood on his handsome face. She realized she'd never seen him cry. And wished she never would again.

But with one blink the tears turned to panic as he looked toward the dangling electrical wires by the front of their upturned family sedan. A spark spit from the end.

Ripping her to her feet, he shoved her away. "Run, Joselyn! Do you understand me? Stop crying and run!"

Like everything else, her blood turned to ice. Inconsolable sobs racked her skinny body. She reached for him, desperate for comfort, for assurance from the fear that was so paralyzing. After those long lonely moments in the car, the thought of running off alone was more terrifying than anything else she could imagine. Her father screamed and shoved her again before he limped around to the passenger side that had received the brunt of the destruction.

After a beat of hesitation she followed him, keeping a safe distance. Her father's footprints marred a deep red goo spreading on the icy ground.

She watched in a trance. His strong arms warred against the weight of the car; sobs and cursing marked the strange silence of the storm. He looked up again when a strong gust sent the wires flailing on the wind. "Joselyn, run!"

The anguish and terror in her father's voice jolted her into action. She ran.

Hissss ...

But the sound made her stop and turn around.

"BOOM!" A flash of heat and light erupted. Invisible arms gripped her and threw her to the ground, her back landing in perplexing pillowy softness against the frozen road. A burst of fire exploded above, propelling a river of flames an inch from her face.

As if seeing it from underneath protective glass, she felt nothing. Nothing but the resounding certainty that she'd just lost everything she loved.

Chapter 8

Finn Carson

Y*ou asked for it.*

Finn was trapped. Over the course of the evening he'd taunted Joselyn, gambling with her obvious disdain for him, knowing it was a sure thing. He never imagined she'd fold.

But he'd miscalculated. And now he was trapped. Literally ensnared in Joselyn's web when she'd fallen asleep, nestled under his arm.

Okay. So, it didn't start out that way.

It started when she'd relented and picked option number two. The snuggling, *Die Hard* option. Only, it wasn't much like snuggling. More, Joselyn jabbing her elbow into his side as she leaned into him about an inch. Maybe that was what the ice princess deemed snuggling, and it was fine by him because he'd only been slightly serious about the options he'd presented. After all, if they had a prayer of pulling this thing off they needed to work on their believability. But now …

He looked down at Joselyn. His arm was draped around the back of the couch. Her bony shoulder and elbow had been the only points of contact during *Die Hard 2*. But then she went and fell asleep, and in doing so, she folded into him. Her head finding its way to the front of his shoulder, eyes fluttering gently with each steady breath.

It seemed harmless enough until she resettled and nuzzled closer. Her slender hand drew up and came to rest on his chest. One long, slender leg hooked around his thighs, making every inch of him from neck to knee her body pillow.

Something sparked along his nerve path. A sort of tingling awareness radiated from the cool touch of her spread palm. And it wasn't the first time he'd felt it.

When she'd helped him off the ground he couldn't seem to let go of her hand. It was as if a thousand volts zapped it in place.

And let's not forget her seductive performance at the hospital and the brain-scrambling effect it had on him.

No, let's.

He'd written it off as a fluke. Now, he was less sure.

When he attempted to wriggle loose she clamped on tighter. So he tried to find something else to watch. Tried to think of anything but the feel of her magnificent body wrapped around his. But every time he touched her, liquid fire squirmed beneath his skin. It was … disturbing. Wrong. And it didn't make any sense.

He hated Joselyn. Feeling something for her would only further break what was already broken. The past couldn't be undone, which meant they didn't stand a chance.

Besides, Sadie was the real reason he'd volunteered for this ridiculous charade. Tonight was an important step. It took real courage to believe in second chances, and Finn would do anything, including snuggling up with the enemy, if it meant protecting his sister from any more heartache.

And, yeah, maybe he had something to prove to himself too. Maybe that's why he'd volunteered. If he could keep this little nightmare safe, perhaps he'd quiet his too. But he had to stay focused, alert, tuned into every threat, every inconsequential detail. He wouldn't fail at this. It was time to reclaim himself.

But even with that thought in his head, his eyes grew heavy, his head dipped, and something sweet filled his lungs. What was that? She smelled like … Christmas. For some hideous reason it drew him and he was the helpless passenger of a drive-by sniffing. Bending his neck, his mouth made contact with the silky softness of her lustrous hair. Mmm. He hummed under his breath. The aromatic blend of sugar and peppermint seduced his higher functioning until he was incapable of doing any more thinking.

And ironically, the last rational thought he recalled traipsing through his mind was that thinking was overrated.

Something thrashed against his chest, startling him from a rare, peaceful sleep. His eyes jolted open to find … Joselyn. On top of him. Her face pressed against his neck, fingers twisting the sides of his shirt, hips unnervingly aligned, and her whole body convulsing with hysterical tremors.

Taking more stock of the situation he noticed that their legs were tangled together and both of his arms were fastened around her, holding her tight.

Why were they on the couch together? And what was wrong with her? He removed his traitorous arms from the object of his disdain, and a horrified scream rent from her throat. Without a thought, he surrounded her again, and she fell silent, pacified by his embrace but still whimpering against his damp neck.

"Joss, wake up." He shook her gently. "Joss." He shook a little harder.

A deep gasp filled her lungs. For excruciatingly long moments she clung to him, burrowing deeper, seeking refuge. A desperation in her touch as if she was holding on for her life. He felt the moment awareness took hold. A half a second later she'd shoved off of him and scrambled to the other side of the couch. But then he saw her. Really saw her.

Tears bled down her face, refilled and magnified the terrified look in her eyes—a look that would haunt him as long as he lived.

"Joss, it's okay." But it wasn't okay. He felt the same terror he'd seen on her face every time he woke from his nightmares. Yes, life moved on. But the past was an abuser with an insatiable appetite for pain.

He touched her arm in comfort, but she jerked away and buried her face in her hands. Her muted sobs evidenced in the quivering of her shoulders.

And then, as if he'd imagined the whole thing, Snow Whyte returned. Her spine straightened. Elegant fingers delicately dusted away the tears from splotchy skin and her stricken expression wiped clean into a placid mask. "Sorry about that." She sniffed.

"Uhh … Are you all right?"

Joselyn nodded, the lines of her face now smooth and serene. "I'm fine." But despite her mannequin act her lip trembled. She bit down on it to squelch her tell.

It wasn't at all funny, but Finn fought the urge to smile. Her façade was slipping. He'd caught a glimpse of vulnerability behind the screen of indifference.

Maybe Joselyn Whyte had a heart after all.

Ahh. It was amazing what a decent night's rest could do for his disposition. Finn rolled out of bed with a spring in his step, had a good morning wrestle with his pup, and then scrambled some eggs for breakfast, replaying the events of the night before in his mind.

Joselyn had retired to her room long before Sadie and Archer returned from their date. Since Finn was restless he utilized the downtime to prepare a lesson for the youth group kids he mentored—and to keep his mind off of other things.

Though emotionally the evening had run the gamut, he felt oddly rested. He'd only woken from his nightmares twice—a refreshing change of pace from the usual bihourly shock therapy. He couldn't recall what he'd dreamt about after he'd collapsed into his bed at midnight, but he woke up feeling better than he had in months.

After taking the pup out to do his business, Finn showered and dressed in a plaid button up shirt in shades of blue and gray, dark blue jeans, and gray Converse, taking a few more moments to peruse his lesson plan. The scriptures noted were hard-hitting, and he swallowed back a derisive laugh at the irony of the truths he'd planned to teach today.

Though he'd been raised by stern but warm parents, for many years he'd struggled with feelings of inadequacy. The middle child, Finn took second string to his talented, athletic, and good-looking older brother, Jay, in every arena. Their younger sister, Sadie, may not have become the frilly debutant his mother had tried to fashion, but she'd been insanely bright and driven and rule-abiding. So Finn, not having any particular niche or talent, had honed and perfected his bluff early on, wielding confidence like a shield to cover nearly desperate longings to earn acceptance. To be more than merely adequate and overlooked. And to maybe, for once in his life, be chosen first.

So yeah, maybe he was still there trying to prove himself, but he wanted to protect these kids against the burden of expectations. The constant shame of trying to earn grace and favor that were instead freely given yet still so difficult to grasp. Helping them find acceptance nibbled away at the load of guilt he now carried—tremendous, suffocating guilt that wasn't meant for his shoulders, but both weighed him down and circled overhead like a vulture, ready to devour the crumbling remnants of his faith.

Obviously the lesson was as much for him as it was for the kids. Hopefully they'd do a better job applying it to their lives. Because the Monroe fire had burned more than an old house and the skin on his neck, it turned the last of his hope to ash. So he'd put his shields up and smile like he hadn't a care in the world. A lesson he learned from Snow Whyte herself way back when. Fake it till you make it.

Oh yeah, he thought without a hint of mirth, he was one helluva role model.

After Finn and the teens wrapped up their small group meeting in the gymnasium, they shot some hoops and then Finn headed up to the sanctuary for the late church service.

The powerful swell of music was a tangible presence. He tried to cling to the promises painted so eloquently with lyrics, tried to absorb the words to fill up the barren and weak places still festering from old wounds, but the harder he tried to grab onto the truth he knew so well the more it seemed to slip through his fingers.

He scanned the crowded room until he found Archer towering over, well, everyone, and went to claim the seat next to Sadie.

"Where's Joss?" Finn whispered when the room quieted. He was pretty sure Joselyn had never set foot in a church before, but he had assumed, for safety reasons, she'd be in attendance with them today.

"She had some stuff she needed to do this morning. I know she's supposed to be with an escort, but she left before Archer picked me up. I did all but barricade the door."

His heart beat a little faster. "You know where she went?"

Sadie nodded. "I did tell her that for the remainder of her stay she will be joining us for church. It is the safest place for her to be since we're all going to be here anyways. She wasn't too happy but promised she'd start coming next week."

"So, where is she?" Finn crossed his ankle over his knee, his erratic foot giving away his sudden unease.

"Finn, she's fine. And she's entitled to have her secrets. If you wanna know, ask her. Maybe it will help sort out whatever this beef is between you two."

"But—"

"Shh. The sermon is starting, and Francine Walters is giving you the stink eye." Sadie squinted at him, then clenched the shoe that jittered near her leg, stopping the motion. "Would you relax? It's not likely she'll have a protective detail twenty-four seven. She's safe where she's at. Have a little faith, okay?"

Finn tugged his foot free, crossed his ankles, and slouched back into the seat, giving his best imitation of relaxation.

This was already harder than he'd thought. And with Joselyn Whyte, that was the one thing he could always count on.

Streaky beams of winter white sunshine escaped through the clouds, and the silky breeze exhaled the last breath of autumn's warmth for the year. The rare elemental beauty of the day stripped away the anxious feeling in his chest until all that remained was Finn, his bike, and the open road. He didn't normally take the motorcycle out during the colder months, but since the temperature was mild-ish, it would likely be his last chance to ride until spring.

The wind took on a bite as he zipped around the back roads while making tracks toward Sadie's place. She'd prepared some sort of baked-ziti thing and invited the whole family over for lunch. Joselyn too. She'd also mentioned Joss would be meeting with the investigators and the insurance adjusters tomorrow. He knew the St. Louis Regional Bomb and Arson Unit had already conducted their investigation with the fire dogs, but if they needed to speak directly with Joselyn at the scene something wasn't adding up. That information, coupled with the way she'd gone rogue today, set his nerves back on high alert.

They knew nothing about the crime—and the same about whoever tried to kill her. If someone truly had. Granted, it'd only been two days, but when time passed uneventfully, bit by bit they'd start to let their guards down, leaving the killer to his own devices to strike again.

Finn couldn't fail at this.

Not again.

The ride to Sadie's was too short. He still felt all pent up and off-kilter, but another twenty-minute ride wouldn't be nearly long enough to get his crap sorted. And while he wasn't willing to face Sadie's wrath by bailing on lunch, when he'd pulled up and saw Joselyn's fancy white Range Rover, he was sorely tempted to gun it right back out of the lot.

His crew must have done a darn good job containing the blaze if her detached garage survived the fire. He didn't know how she'd retrieved her pretentious rig, but spoiled, rich kids had ways of getting what they wanted. Or buying their way out of trouble. His best friend, Cody, was the same way.

The thought of Cody and Joselyn in the short jumble of his mind brought back memories he'd rather forget. Bitterness soured his stomach, and his contempt for Joselyn revved anew in sync with the final rev of his Honda Nighthawk's engine.

Well, his confidence might be slipping where Joselyn was concerned, but his anger would work just fine.

Chapter 2

Joselyn Whyte

"**E**xcuse me. Where do you think you're going?" A portly woman with a snarling expression rushed out from behind the nurses' desk, prepped to tackle Joselyn to the ground should she venture any further.

"Oh. Sorry, are you new here?"

Before the woman could answer Rosie rounded the corner. "Joselyn! We missed you the past few days. Where've you been?"

Snarly's mouth pinched into a hard line, but she resumed her post as the new warden of McKnight Grove.

"Long story. How is she?"

"It's not a real good day. But I'm sure she'll still be happy to see you. She asked about you yesterday, though. You know the drill by now." The crow's feet around the spunky, blonde nurse's eyes lent the impression that she was always smiling. But though they all did their part, this was not often a happy place.

Heart heavy, Joselyn reached out and squeezed Rosie's slim strong hand. "Thanks for taking care of her while I was away. You're her favorite, you know."

"The feeling is mutual. Now scoot. And don't worry about Brenda. She'll catch on soon enough." Rosie nudged Joselyn past the desk and the blistering glare of its new fire-breathing dragon. Joss shook off the singe of the stranger's hatred and strode her usual route through the halls before letting herself into the last suite.

Distant violet-blue eyes, so much like her own, locked in

on her and softened a fraction. Joselyn's spirits buoyed back to the surface. Maybe it wasn't a bad day after all.

"Good Morning, Yia-Yia. I've missed you." Leaning in Joselyn pressed a kiss to the papery wrinkles of her cheek, inhaled the combined fragrance of Trésor perfume and Aqua Net that had always been Yia-Yia's signature.

Confusion clouded her eyes, a teasing reprimand poured from her neatly penciled red lips. "Charisma, why are you calling me that?" She batted her hand at the foolishness.

"Yia-Yia, it's not Charisma, it's Joselyn." She tried a smile that wouldn't quite form. "I'm sorry I couldn't make it the past few days. How's the show coming along?"

"Joselyn?" Anxious confusion twisted the rare beauty of her aging face. "I don't know any Joselyn. You—You're Charisma, my daughter."

Her grandmother's Alzheimer's had progressed slowly. After years of flirting with forgetfulness she'd finally disappeared into a deep darkness about six months ago. The few good days with glimpses of memory were a gift Joselyn tried never to miss. The bad days were now the norm, sometimes graced with playful ignorance, other times with rage, yet always heartbreaking. Joselyn fought the inevitable despair of the bad days winning each daily battle, still foolishly clinging to hope she'd begun to realize was as naive as believing she wasn't completely alone in the world simply because she had relatives who were technically living.

"So, how's the show shaping up? I've got some new choreography for the dock scene. I think you're gonna love it." Joselyn infused as much enthusiasm into her voice as she could rally.

"I think the nurse said something about that this morning, Cassie. I'm not sure I feel up to doing much singing and dancing."

"That's okay. You can watch instead. But it's a lot of fun, and your friends Opal and Greta might try ousting you from the lead role. They've been pretty jealous about you being the star at all the practices. You're a natural."

Her eyebrows softened from their furrow, and she shrugged her petite shoulders. "I guess I could try it."

"That's my girl. So, we have about three weeks until showtime. I've been making up some fun costumes at my store from a few vintage pieces I found. You'll love them."

"Ooo, well, *'Dress shabbily and they remember the dress; dress impeccably and they remember the woman.'*" When she smiled, ten years melted off of her seventy-eight years. She was still a stunning woman, her beauty timeless, like a Greek spin on a classic like Doris Day. The silky drape of her silver hair still held more than a few threads of its original black.

The memory of her dark hair pulled Joselyn back in time. Playing dress up in the attic of the old house; long strands of pearls, lace gloves, and elaborate hats adorned with broaches. Clanking clumsily down the wooden stairs in her grandmother's retro pumps—they'd been the stars of their very own red carpet every Saturday night. The clothes had been both an escape and an adventure. In a way, they still were.

"What show are we doing?" Yia-Yia's question shattered Joselyn's happy memory. They'd been practicing for months. Every day. And nearly every day the same inquiry.

"We're doing *Mamma Mia!* for the Christmas musical this year, Yia-Yia. Remember?"

The response from her grandmother followed the now predictable script. "Oh! That's my favorite. You grew up in Greece, you know. So it's a bit like the story of us." Her hands fluttered with excitement. Today, Joselyn noticed, her fingernails were perfectly manicured fire-engine red.

Had to go there, didn't you. The association leapt from fire engine to firefighter in the flash of an idiotic synaptic misfire. And then of course she was thinking about Finn.

That stupid, cocky grin, those sneaky dimples, and that long, sun-bronzed surfer hair. He somehow managed to look effortless and yet seamlessly put together like a painstakingly vetted ensemble. His image droned on like a miserable first date. Her defenses must have taken a leave of absence because when she tried to rip the loose threads from her mind she found instead that she was sewn into the memory of his deep sea eyes and the inexplicably safe feeling of being in his strong arms … against his very warm, very solid ches—*Stop it!*

"Somebody's got a crush." Yia-Yia's eyes lit with mischief, the old wry smile showing a teasing glimpse of lucidity.

"Nooo! Uh-uh!" Joselyn protested.

"I know that look, Charisma," she giggled. "Oh, to be young and in love—"

"Whoa, Yia-Yia! I'm sorry to burst you're bubble but—"

She patted Joselyn's hand and winked. "It's all right, sugar, your secret's safe with me."

In her current state, the last thing Joselyn wanted to do was spend the afternoon with the perfect Carson clan. Their easy family dynamic rubbed salt in her dysfunctional, daddy-issued wounds. But after her unchaperoned field trip, she knew better than to push her luck.

At least she had her car back. It was a small consolation but she'd discovered her favorite pair of Old Gringo cowboy boots in the trunk, in addition to some extra clothes she'd packed to keep at work, and the crowning jewel—her mother's vintage pavé diamond locket. The clasp had broken the day before the fire at the nursing home during a vigorous rehearsal with the handsy male lead. Joselyn had stowed it in the center console of her car so she could drop it at the jeweler to be repaired. It meant more to her than anything she owned. Anything she could ever buy. And now, with every photograph and memento from her house destroyed, it was the only piece of her mother she had left.

Her nose tingled, and one warm tear escaped down her cheek—her daily allowance of mourning all she'd lost. So much more than just her mother.

Pulling into Sadie's lot, she was relieved to see that no one preceded her arrival. At least she'd have a few moments to herself before the verbal sparring with Finn ensued. A tension headache formed at her temples in anticipation of the long day ahead as she trudged the salt-sprinkled walkway to the condo and surrendered to the haven of heat behind Sadie's door.

Untangling her scarf and sliding from Sadie's borrowed green peacoat, she went to freshen up and changed from the formless long-sleeved tunic she'd thrown over her leggings into a lavender off-the-shoulder cashmere sweater to pass the time. The thin, luxuriant fabric skimmed over her hips to her upper thighs, the color a subtle contrast against her complexion yet made her pale skin look creamy and her eyes look nearly lavender to match. The clothes were her shield, and she needed all the confidence she could find to deflect the silent judgments about to lob her way.

When tinkering noises trickled down the hall and Sadie announced their arrival, Joselyn forced a deep breath and one last appraising glance before braving the Carsons. One in particular.

Lunch went by with minimal interaction. Finn's usual glare and scowl resumed possession of his face, giving her a break from his playful flirting from last night. If that's really what it was. It could've been crueler than that. Malicious, even. Joselyn knew from experience that he had it in him.

The clinking of a glass rescued Joselyn from slipping back into torturous high school memories. *Thank you, Archer.*

"Can I have your attention?" He glanced down at Sadie, his face glowing, and his smile so pure and uncontained the man was as radiant as sunshine.

Would anyone ever look at her that way?

"I have an announcement to make."

Sadie rose to stand with him, sharing a look before they blurted in unison, "We're getting married!"

Joselyn's couldn't help but squeal when Sadie extricated a stunning diamond ring from her pocket and waggled it proudly on her finger. Congratulations were passed around, although no one seemed surprised.

"You guys all knew already, didn't you?" Sadie chided. Titters of affirmation passed around as effortlessly as the salad bowl. "Even you, Finn?"

"Sis, you got yourself one smart man. Not only did he ask Dad's permission, he asked for mine too. You're welcome." Finn flashed a dimple-popping grin as his sister folded into his exuberant hug.

"Well, I didn't know." Joselyn stood and went to embrace her beautiful best friend before scoping out the rock. "Hot dang! Guess it's a good thing I didn't let you cancel last night, huh?"

Sadie sniffled back happy tears and nodded. "But I am sorry I had to leave you with Finn your first night here. I knew those boys were up to something when Archer and I left. I hope he behaved himself at least." Sadie shot Finn a teasing smirk before she made her way back into her fiancé's waiting arms.

Joselyn only meant to glance, but her eyes were swallowed up in Finn's intense gaze. Finn didn't look playful or amused. He looked … mad. *What now?* The man's strange bipolar temper kept her constantly guessing. Well, maybe not constantly. He did tend to default to the least pleasant option in her presence.

Luckily for Joselyn, the frivolity of the newsworthy moment distracted everyone's attention elsewhere while Finn's unabashed contempt aired in high-definition. Her skin prickled her unease, and since she was feeling like an outsider invading on a family moment, she thanked Sadie for lunch and then excused herself to her room under the guise of exhaustion. And that was no lie.

The man was exhausting.

Chapter 10

Finn Carson

"Is she doing all right? I can't image how scary this must be for her." Lorelei Carson's query forced his gaze from the phantom image of Joselyn's retreat down the hall. He was about to answer when Sadie jumped in. Foolishness warmed his face. His mom wouldn't have thought to direct her question at him as their long standing rivalry was no secret.

"I don't know, Mom. She's had a tough life. And she's always so strong. Too strong. It's like she worries about burdening anyone with her pain so she carries it all alone."

"Tough life?" The filter in his brain must have malfunctioned because before he could check himself he was spewing his ugly, careless thoughts out loud. "The girl's an entitled little brat—princess and sole heir to the Whyte Empire. Should we get some violins in here? How hard could it be?"

Oops.

"Finnegan Carson! Don't you break your mama's heart, making me think I didn't raise you right. The only person being a brat here today is you. Don't think we missed your little sideshow performance as Oscar the Grouch during lunch."

"I just meant—"

"You were *just* being a jerk." Sadie flicked his ear. "You have no idea what her life has been like. I guarantee you never bothered to ask. So get off your high horse and understand this: You mess with my girl, big brother, I'll kick your—"

"All right, you two. Cool it." Cal Carson was a man of few words. When he spoke, you listened. "There's enough strife in the world. Leave it there. It has no business in this family, you hear?"

Sufficiently chastised they each grumbled, "Yes, sir."

"And Finn," his stern voice held an authoritative warning not to be trifled with. "You best examine your heart, son. Because the next time that thoughtless garbage comes outta your mouth you better hope you brought your shovel to start digging your way out of that deep hole. I'm sure not gonna help you."

Monday marked the first official day of Finn's mandatory two-week sabbatical. After sleeping in and wasting away in front of the tube for two hours of mindless monotony, he had to get out of the house. When his phone rang, he welcomed the distraction and prayed the chief had a change of heart.

"Hello?"

"Finn. It's Archer."

"Hey, man. What's up?"

"I, uh, heard from Joselyn. She's meeting with the investigators from state at her place at two and an insurance adjuster after that. I've had a couple guys canvassing the neighborhood. See if we can catch a break. Maybe this guy's still trying to keep tabs on her."

"Okay? Sounds like a plan." Finn scratched his chest, working back a yawn.

"I'm gonna head over there a little early. About an hour. Thought maybe you should come too. To keep up appearances and hear more firsthand about what we are dealing with."

He sat a bit straighter. "Does Joselyn know you're asking me?"

"It's possible I may have failed to mention it."

"All right, fine. It'll probably mess with her. Might be fun."

Archer tsked. "Always an ulterior motive with you. Someday you'll have to tell me about this colorful history between you two. Story's bound to be a doozy."

"I hate to disappoint, but there's really not much to tell. It's a simple case of clashing personalities."

"Don't insult me. I read people for a living. And there's a whole lot more to this story. I'll get it outta you."

"Good luck with that."

"See you in an hour. And remember, as far as everyone is concerned, this is your girlfriend's house that burned down. No baiting her, no glaring, and absolutely no bickering. This guy could be anybody. And that means you've got to play the part."

Finn grumbled and hung up. *And we're off.*

With that thought, a rush of nervous energy clamored through him. He'd never been a great actor. Bluffing was a different story. Maybe he could channel his poker face and no one would see through to his disdain.

It was obvious Joselyn had some acting chops. It might be easier for him to fake it if she wasn't being her snooty self. *Here's hoping.*

A whimper pulled him out of his head. Soft paws propped on his knees, adoration swam in the dog's big brown eyes. "I've got this, right buddy?" He ruffled Dodger's ears setting the tempo of his feathery tail to a lively allegro.

Getting ready, Finn forwent shaving, leaving a healthy two days of stubble on his face. Throwing on his favorite pair of dark wash jeans, a gray henley, and his dark brown leather bomber jacket and boots, he headed out with Dodger for a short walk before driving the two miles to the devastated remains of Snow Whyte's home.

He'd known it was bad, but this … this was a new level of destruction.

Kirkwood was a charming and close-knit little town in St. Louis County. Quiet, tree-lined streets formed a grid surrounding the historic downtown area that hubbed around a beautiful old train station, a farmers market, and maybe a dozen novelty shops and cafes. And even more refreshing was that even though the wealthy suburb housed some of the most impressive plantation and Craftsman-style homes around, they often shared a lot line with modest, saltbox cottages and lacked the distinct air of pretension that could be found in surrounding suburbs of St. Louis.

All this to say that nothing burned for long without notice and prompt attention. Home fires were usually extinguished in time to preserve, at the very least, most of the exterior shell. What Finn saw when he pulled up to the deceased bungalow was nothing but bare bones.

Splinters of charred wood held up what was left of the sagging upstairs bedroom, minus the floor. The stairs Finn had risked climbing at nothing but divine prompting now contained a scorched handrail, three partial steps near the top, and a heap of crumpled pieces and soggy ashes.

Finn and Archer rummaged through what they could of the crime scene in perfect, stunned silence. There wasn't much to look at. The house was tiny. Couldn't be much more than 1,200 square feet on two floors.

Why would someone as wealthy as Joselyn live here? His own apartment, while only a one-bedroom loft, was at least as large. The billionaire entrepreneur's daughter lived in a shoebox? It didn't compute.

And yet, taking in the extent of the destruction, he felt his heart soften. She'd lost everything. Despite their past, that fact alone earned her some compassion.

Archer came around to the backyard, slipping a palm-sized notebook into his breast pocket. "Ground appears to have been too cold and hard to get a footprint. I don't see any pattern of broken branches or crushed leaves where he might have hidden out. The cement block foundation held up pretty well, but the cellar is littered with debris that fell through the floor. It's definitely not safe to go snooping around down there."

"Huh," Finn grunted in response. "What about the basement windows? A few of them looked like they were still intact. Any signs of forced entry with the latches?"

"Not that I can see. And because several of them were blown out it's hard to tell if anything but the fire caused that. I'm sure the fire unit has a few tricks up their sleeves."

"They do. Plus those accelerant dogs can pick up the tiniest trace of liquid residue. It's incredi—" The words slowed to mush on Finn's lips. Over Archer's shoulder Joselyn's lithe form strutted toward him in catwalk fashion. Cinematic slow motion played in his mind as her jet-black locks tossed in the faint wind, her hips swayed with a confident swagger, and long slender legs clad in tight jeans seemed to go on for miles. Her face was mostly hidden behind large stylish sunglasses, yet even without the addition of those exotic eyes, she was a knockout.

And he was down for the count.

Archer leaned in. "Dude, close your mouth. You're slobbering." And then he whacked Finn on the back, bringing everything back to rights. Archer turned and greeted Joselyn.

"What is *he* doing here?"

"*He* is here in support of his girlfriend." Archer nudged Joselyn toward Finn and then spoke through gritted teeth. "Dig deep, lovebirds. Cavalry's here."

Forcing himself to action Finn sidled up next to Joselyn, slipped his arm around her waist, molding her to his side. She stiffened but stayed in his possession while introductions were made.

"Thank you for meeting us here, Miss Whyte. I know this must be difficult, but we've been struggling with some of our findings and wanted to see if you might be able to help." The bomb and arson squad investigator, probably about thirty, like Finn, was tall and lanky with dark eyes that didn't seem to miss a thing. Including Joselyn's looks.

"I'll try. What have you found out so far?" Unlike when she barked at him, her voice was sweet as spun sugar.

"Well, that's the problem. We haven't found anything. The dogs seemed to sense an accelerant—"

"That's good. Helps to identify the origin and pattern of

the fire." Finn spoke close to Joselyn's ear, keeping his wits by enlightening her with a brief tutorial. That is, until that sugared mint fragrance of her windblown hair drew in with his breath, the delicate notes played in harmony with the crisp breeze to wrap around him like an intoxicating cyclone. *Witch.*

"Generally, yes." Joselyn's fan-boy continued. "But the issue is that the dogs sensed the accelerant virtually everywhere, on every surface, which would seem impossible. Then we ran tests." He shook his head. "We didn't find any ILRs."

"Ignitable liquid residues." Archer filled in the gaps since Finn's brain was temporarily out of commission.

"I'm sorry. What does that mean?" Joselyn asked.

"It means that the dogs found something we can't find. Either it's something unknown that we can't detect, or somehow the samples contain impossibly miniscule amounts that can't be tested. The other peculiar thing is the origin." The guy actually scratched his head. "We can't find that either." He motioned for them to follow, and Joselyn peeled away from Finn's side.

Her eyes were cloaked by the dark lenses, but Finn noticed the subtle strain of her brows as she took in the interior of her home, her teeth marring that pouty bottom lip.

"You all right, babe?" Finn's question gave her a start. Or maybe not the question so much as the endearment. He felt her heated gaze beneath her shades, but at least she stopped torturing that pretty lip before he did something stupid like soothe the bite with a stroke of his thumb. Or something else.

Okay, he really needed to focus on the scene of the fire. Once upon a time he'd burned for her. She'd left his heart in a pile of ashes no more recognizable than the place she called home.

Homeless. The reminder whispered through his chest.

A place or a feeling. Maybe they had more in common than he thought.

Chapter 11

Joselyn Whyte

"I'm just fine." Joselyn gritted out.

Did he think this was funny? The teasing glint in his eyes suggested the whole thing was a game to him.

Joselyn tamped down her irritation with her *boyfriend*, forcing her brain to make sense of the investigator's findings. Or rather, the lack thereof. Most of the spiel sailed straight over her head. The gist, she'd surmised, was that the entire first floor of the house ignited in one perfectly orchestrated flame by an undetectable accelerant. Like an explosion, only without the bang.

To be honest, she could scarcely concentrate on anything being said when her heart was breaking anew at the sight of her destroyed home and all of her possessions lost forever. But more than material loss, the house held her childhood. Her recovery. Her second chance. It had been her sanctuary from her father and his brutal rejection. And now it was a heap of ashes. Just like everything else.

At some point she'd switched onto autopilot. She hoped she'd provided helpful information for the investigator but couldn't seem to remember anything about the rest of their conversation other than his strange, probing eyes. When he was gone it was the insurance adjuster's turn, and he declared the home a total loss. Shocker.

Finn had played his part to a T. Doting, supportive, concerned. Every so often his arm would slip around her waist, his hand anchoring at her hip, and all her higher brain functioning vacating the premises like the world's most efficient fire drill. Frankly, it was absurd his touch had registered at all through the thick wool of her newly acquired Burberry belted trench coat.

"Fashion is the armor to survive the reality of everyday life." She murmured the old Bill Cunningham quote, wrapping her arms tightly around her new trench as if it might turn into a coat of arms, and then let herself take a mental health break from the scene to remember her retail therapy.

Despite the fact that Archer's partner had stalked her day's excursions—following her to the nursing home, her boutique, and to West County Mall—she found she hadn't at all resented the intrusion. For the first two stops Sal had remained in his car monitoring the surroundings from a discrete distance. For the third he'd let her bribe him with a venti caramel macchiato and a birthday cake pop from Starbuck's in exchange for his escort through the magical wonderland of Nordstrom for an hour of overindulgent retail bliss. It might seem shallow to some, but there was something so comforting about trying on the various styles and testing the decadent fabrics against her skin that she'd almost felt … *at home.* Which was delusional, but for a moment she'd been nearly weightless and unburdened, twirling in a dress Sal described as *"caliente"* and laughing at a dramatic retelling of one of his rookie bloopers as an FBI agent.

"… about your home, Miss Whyte."

"Huh?" She snapped back to the present, trying to grab a clue from the questioning faces around her as the stout, balding insurance adjuster packed up his briefcase. "Oh, uh … thank you, Mr. Franklin."

"We'll be in touch. Have a nice day." He showed himself out. Joselyn and her two bodyguards stepped gingerly in the marked off path toward the door as well.

"I have a question." Archer's voice, while kind, held an unmistakable edge of accusation.

She turned to encounter two sets of intense eyes. Archer's

unflinching honey-hued peepers would intimidate Al Capone, but it was Finn's jade stare that tied a noose around her airway. *Gulp.* "Shoot."

"Why didn't you tell me about your stalker when we went over possible suspects?" Archer's arms crossed over his dark suit, the bulky form of his muscled shoulders straining against the well-fitting coat.

"You have a stalker?" Finn crossed his arms to match. His height and width were an inch shy of the Archer's, though both men were unnervingly enormous. And so ridiculously good-looking if she didn't know better she'd say this was all scripted and she was secretly being punked. If only.

Joselyn sighed in defeat. "His name is Stuart Garber. He grew up in that yellow house next door. I didn't mention it because he's harmless. And he's been hassled enough by my father's muscle as it is. He has a little crush, that's all."

"A little crush? More like an obsessive infatuation."

"Archer, I think that's taking it a little far."

"Joselyn, in the past ten years the guy's been arrested three times for breaking into your house. And once for attacking you outside your store after work."

"I know. That's why I have a restraining order. But he didn't really *attack* me. He tripped and sort of fell on me. There may have been some inappropriate fondling when he refused to get up at first. I'd say it was more of an ill-executed come on. Not much worse than some of the blind dates I've had to endure, to be quite honest. Plus, I heard he's been in therapy."

Okay, blabbermouth. Insert foot anytime.

Archer pinned her with his intimidating FBI glare. One he must have practiced in front of a mirror for years because it was really *that* good. "Just because you've taken pity on this guy doesn't mean he's not dangerous. We can't protect you if you're keeping things from us. That means no more secrets. We clear?"

Joselyn swallowed the guilty lump in her throat, nodded, and looked away. The wind skipped a few brittle leaves past her feet, whistling as it raked through the naked, craggy branches of the unadorned trees like sad wooden wind chimes. The air was sharp and refreshing, hitting her lungs with a zing. No burned or bitter trace of the injustice she'd suffered remained, save the pathetic sight before her.

Archer cleared his throat and nodded once, as if satisfied with his lesson for the day. "Since it might not be *your* enemy we are dealing with here, we are looking into disgruntled ex-employees and are rooting through a massive list of layoffs from your father's companies from the last three months. It's gonna take some time."

An unfamiliar ringtone broke into the conversation. It took several moments for her to realize it was her purse that was jangling.

"Hello?"

"I see you got the new phone I ordered." No social niceties for Declan Whyte.

"It came this morning." When she realized both men were still watching her, she turned away. "What's up?"

"Leland is taxiing me in at Spirit Airport. I'd like you at dinner tonight." His voice, as always, a command, not a request.

"That's fine. What time?"

"An hour. Bring Finn with you."

Before a rebuttal could form on her tongue he was gone. She closed her eyes and took a deep yoga-type breath. It was worth a shot. Those people had relaxation down pat, right? "Oh, *muffin?*" She sing-songed and turned back around.

When the endearment registered, Finn's perpetual scowl went full pit bull. Sexy pit bull. The jerk. She tipped her shades down her nose. "We have dinner with my dad in an hour. We better get a move on."

"Wha—"

Archer's firm back slap severed Finn's protest. "Ahh, meeting the parents already. Good luck, buddy." He flashed a wave in Joselyn's direction and skirted to his car, tossing a wicked smirk over his shoulder. "Have fun, you two. No

PDA in front of the parentals."

Ignoring that, and the heat tinting her cheeks, she turned to Finn and rubbed her hands together connivingly. "Okay, you're not giving me much to work with here, but lucky for you I'm a miracle worker. Let's go fix you up. My father won't take you seriously in that man-boy getup, and seeing as I'm a giver, I won't feed you to the wolf." Actually, he looked like model Gabriel Aubry stepped off the pages of her archived *Vogues*, but it was more fun this way.

His inability to process manifested in a sort of paralysis, forcing Joselyn to close the gap between them, grip the front of his coat, and tug him along to their cars. "Come on, I'll follow you."

"Where?" He mumbled in a daze.

"To your place for a makeover, *muffin-puff*. Try to keep up." She patted his chest with satisfying condescension and smirked to herself as she slipped behind the wheel.

She loved that she'd thrown him, but not five minutes later when they pulled into the parking garage of Downtown Kirkwood's trendy new lofts she realized the joke was on her. Oh crap. Why had she insisted on coming to his place again? In her attempt to embarrass him she'd unwittingly lured herself into his den.

Okay. Get a grip. Same thing as before. Cool and confident. Prying her white-knuckled grip from the smooth woodgrain steering wheel, she stilled the nervous jitter of her fingers by mangling the soft leather of her petal-pink Valentino couture satchel. *Sorry pinkie, desperate times.* She issued the silent apology to the tortured tote, exited her SUV, and followed Finn to his door.

It wasn't the first time she'd been to his place, but it was the only time she'd been here alone, without her trusty ally, Sadie. As the door swung open her legs obeyed her cue to proceed ahead, depositing her behind enemy lines.

A bounding ball of grey and tan fur crashed with exuberance into her legs, excited paws clawing at her jeans and purse. "Well, you're new. Hi, pooch." She surrendered to the floor making kissing sounds while the pup lavished her with affection. She scratched his ears, beneath his chin, and then he rolled over for a belly rub. She obliged. The sweet pup was so content he was actually purring, his eyes rolling back, tongue lolling out to one side. Joselyn immediately fell in love. When she became aware of the silence she found Finn observing her from a few feet away. His eyes sparkled with amusement, yet his lips held a firm line.

"And who is this?" She couldn't hold his gaze, focusing her attention on the dog instead.

Taking a few steps forward, he squatted down next to her. "This is Dodger. He was abandoned. I took him in. Though, you might not want to get too attached seeing as how he mauled your purse."

Looking to Finn's hands she viewed the severed petals of one of the flower decals from her new bag. "It's no biggie. You didn't mean it, did you Dodge?"

She kept her eyes trained on the pooch, and her effort was rewarded with a lick to the nose.

"Must be nice. You can buy a new one without batting an eye."

The snarky edge in his voice snapped her head in his direction. She met his arrogant glower in a contest of wills. "Just because I have money, doesn't mean I value things any less." Mindlessly, her fingers clasped around the rectangular edge of her mother's priceless locket. "What's your problem with rich people, anyway? It's not like you ever wanted for anything in your life with your perfect little home and family. And this loft? So very Oliver Twist."

Dodger pranced to the threshold of the foot between them, volleying his attention back and forth before emitting a slight whine. The heartbreaking sound softened the fierce latch of her anger.

Finn opened his mouth to retort, his eyes ablaze. Without a thought she dashed her hand across the divide, covering his mouth gently with her palm. Simply too tired to go another round at the moment, she spoke softly, "Maybe we should call it a draw and move on."

After the second of shock skittered away, the angry bind of his brow softened. And she could have sworn she'd felt the slightest press of his lips on her palm as his fingers circled her wrist and pulled it away.

All vocal ability ceased in that moment. His eyes locked and loaded to stun. And she was. Stunned. Frozen. Hypnotized.

Look away. Self-preservation warned.

But then Dodger's bark erupted to fill the silence. Finn flinched and released the hand he was cradling in his own and set it on her lap.

"All right, babe. Different clothes is fine. But I draw the line well before guy-liner and hair gel." He nodded, throwing her with his light, unaffected tone. "Let's go find something that will impress Declan Whyte."

She shook her head, hoping to shake free whatever screw was loose in there. "Why, *babe?*"

Finn rose to stand and shrugged. "I dunno. *Sweetie* didn't seem to fit." He grinned in response to her playful sneer. "Why, *muffin?*" He challenged back.

"I was trying it out. There's always cuddle monkey or schmoopsy-poo, if you prefer. I might save those for a larger audience."

He laughed, and the sound seemed to ping around in her chest. "By all means, don't hold back. But remember, two can play that game, *sweet cheeks.*" He teased as she followed him up the stairs.

He hadn't seemed that way in high school, but for the past few years she'd known Finn to be a bit of a ladies' man. She wasn't sure how far that went, exactly, but he dated a lot of— let's call it flashy—women. Entering his bedroom—seeing it as other women did—felt disturbing, and oddly intriguing in a self-destructive, come-in-little-red-riding-hood kind of way. "So this is where the magic happens." *Oh flip, did I say that out loud?*

Too busy absorbing the simple, masculine decor and dark

wood furnishings, she collided against his back. *"Umph."* She teetered back on her wedge-heeled boots and blindly reached out to steady herself. She ended up yanking on his shirt with one hand and grabbing his waist with the other.

Only since she'd wrenched so hard on his the fabric that other hand was grabbing warm, muscled flesh. The sensation so unexpected it took a regrettably long time to unhand him. *Bad hand. Very bad.*

He swiveled around to view the no doubt splotchy heat of her embarrassment coloring her pale cheeks. Quirking a dangerous eyebrow over those eyes, emerald starbursts inside a deep blue ring, he slid behind a sly grin. "Care for a preview?"

Her pulse exploded in her chest. *Oh merciful Lord, steady my voice.* "Easy, Casanova. You might want to save that line for someone who actually likes you." She was pleased with the smooth delivery despite the mayhem within.

Unrelenting he inched forward until they were almost nose-to-nose, his fresh scent toying with her waning resolve.

"Oh, come on now, Joss. You like me a little. Admit it."

"So this is what your *game* looks like? A predatory saunter, a little hitch in your eyebrow, a come-hither smile, and I'm supposed to swoon like all the rest of your bimbos? Please."

She unleashed an arrogant smile of her own and leaned in to his ear. She left the faintest trace of her skin on his, intent on beating him at his own game. "You're gonna have to work a lot harder than that, honey." She almost didn't recognize the sultry whisper of the voice leaving her lips. Or maybe it had something to do with the way they grazed his ear when she spoke her sarcastic sweet nothings.

During their last few encounters, she was the one who'd given in, called a truce. He'd yet to relinquish his stubborn control, and all she seemed to be doing was folding.

Calling his bluff, she held her ground, completely unprepared when he snaked his arm around her waist and yanked her against him.

She stopped breathing. Just stopped. Fear and anticipation holding her lungs hostage.

His husky, whispering lips called her bluff right back. "You're messing with fire, Joselyn."

She shivered, hating how much she liked the foreign feeling of being held, even by Finn Carson. Even while it nearly scared her to death. "Good thing I'm cold as ice, right Finn?"

Chapter 12

Finn Carson

They were being followed.

The same older model sedan had tailed them at a distance from Kirkwood to the windy back roads leading to the Whyte's estate. Coincidence? Not likely.

Finn shot a discrete text to Archer, not wanting to cause unnecessary anxiety for Joselyn if it was only Sal or another FBI tail.

They made another turn, and the car still followed. Finn's eyes were glued to the side-view mirror of her luxurious Range Rover. The cool metal of his concealed .38 Special remained hidden against his low back, the firepower doing little to assuage his paranoia as he waited for confirmation from Archer.

After another two turns, his escalating nerves forced him to action. He made the call.

"Arch, tell me you have a tail on us." He kept his voice steady, but Joselyn's gaze darted to the rearview mirror. Her teeth tore at her bottom lip, a sure sign of the fear Finn had hoped to spare her.

"Negative. Where are you? I'm leaving now."

Finn rambled off a mailbox address as they passed it. "I can't see the license plate. He's hanging too far back. It looks like a late nineties Grand Prix. Dark green."

"We're almost to my dad's house. Sh-Should I keep driving or should I pull up to the gate?" Joselyn's voice wobbled.

"I radioed the local PD," Archer said. "They are

approaching from both directions. Tell Joselyn to call up to the house and have them open the gate. I want you guys out of harm's way."

The whole thing was orchestrated in a flash. Joselyn whipped her car into the long drive and tore through the gates with less than an inch to spare before the black spear-tipped metal jaws started to close again.

The Grand Prix had passed without pause, but something still didn't feel right. Finn ended the call with Archer who promised to call back when he had something to report.

"Nice driving, pumpkin. You okay?"

She nodded a little too enthusiastically. And the fact that she hadn't challenged him on the pet name spoke louder than words about her current state of mind as she drove silently up the mile-long entrance, around a marbled stone fountain to the cusp of the circle drive.

"Whoa." Finn knew he was gawking, even felt his jaw dislocate. Not only from the gorgeous view of a pewter Bond-issue Aston Martin, but also from the sight beyond it. The massive brick and stone structure couldn't be classified as a house. It was a castle. Sloping European roof lines, arched dormers with scrolled wrought iron terraces, and a flippin' turret were only a few details that made the Whyte Estate look like something out of a fairytale. The manicured grounds and picturesque rolling hills in wintery shades of muted green seemed to extend for miles to each side and were lined in the distance with a thick border of trees. The word was *wow*. It would seem Declan Whyte possessed the most beautiful things on earth.

He slipped the gun under the seat and stepped out of the car, but stood unblinking, awed anew. What would it be like to grow up in a place like this?

"Are you coming?"

He honed in on Joselyn's voice and found her looking back from the ornate fifteen-foot wood, iron, and glass entry doors.

"Yeah." Jogging to catch up, Finn met a salt-and-pepper-haired Ann Bancroft look-alike, Gloria, the housekeeper, who ushered him in and collected his coat.

Once inside, he couldn't help but let his eyes sample the grandeur. The gleaming wood floors were an exotic grain he'd never seen, arched doorways graced endlessly tall walls to ceilings adorned with carved beams and enormous chandeliers. Exquisite furnishings flanked every nook and cranny with an aesthetic elegance that reeked of class. He followed Joselyn into the great room and was greeted by three stories and about a hundred yards of windows overlooking the distant edge of a lake.

"Your father is on a conference call in the west den. Dinner will be in another thirty minutes or so. I'll call you when it's ready." Gloria turned to Joselyn and gave her arm an affectionate squeeze. "Glad you're home, Josie."

Joselyn watched Gloria's retreat with a stilted smile. And Finn watched Joselyn. Such an interesting peek into her world. Now that he'd breeched her fortress he was tempted to press her for some answers, delve a bit deeper into the mystery that was Snow Whyte. Yet something held him back.

Fear. The feeling slithered around him like a boa constrictor. He promptly shook off the absurd notion that he had anything to *fear* from Joselyn, but when that false pretense fell away too, it exposed the old scar he'd been tending for years.

Why reopen that wound? Nothing she could say would change the past. And history would not be repeating itself.

Then again, he wasn't entirely immune to his baser instincts. Nor could he forget the memory of Joselyn in his arms, the illicit thrill of skimming his fingertips over that silky skin. The faintest touch like a spark flirting with a stick of dynamite. And the white hot flare in her eyes, well …

The truth was they were both playing with fire. And as a firefighter, it defied every ounce of logic in his brain. Their mutual hatred teetered on the edge of something much more dangerous. Combustible.

It was a good thing Dodger had been there to douse the fire. Smart little pup had a knack for breaking the tension and keeping Finn from doing anything stupid—like kissing Joselyn in his bedroom. When Finn got home later, Dodger was getting an extra treat and a belly rub.

"So, are you gonna give me the tour?"

"Uhh, sure."

She began ushering him around the mansion like a docent guiding him through a museum, complete detachment in her tone as she pointed out her father's prized possessions. Among them a priceless Renoir painting Finn remembered seeing in his art history textbook in high school.

He and his best friend, Cody, thought it'd be a blow off class, but the more Finn learned, the more fascinated he became with the incredible beauty of not only the paintings, but with the object of his affection that sat across the table.

"I remember learning about Renoir from—"

"Our art history class," she interrupted, her eyes flashing with something he couldn't decipher—something like shyness. It was a look he hadn't seen on her face in over ten years. And it took him back in a way that was heartbreakingly familiar.

"I remember, Finn." Her voice shriveled to a wispy thread. The unspoken fragility of those memories stretched between them in the vast room, giving first breath to things long since smothered.

"Yeah. Me too." With a stranglehold on his composure, Finn dragged his eyes away from Joselyn and stuffed down those old reminders of his meager worth.

They finished perusing the first floor with minimal conversation and ventured up a large curved staircase. Finn kept his phone in hand, constantly checking for updates from Archer. Nothing. Nothing to distract him from the stupid trip down memory lane.

Aha! "What do we have here?" He forced open a door she'd intended to pass over—one with a theatrical dressing room star that bore her name.

The bedroom was bigger than his whole apartment. Finn counted eight windows at eye level, but the light coming from a loft area above, accessed by an iron spiral staircase in the corner, suggested more.

He whistled, turning in a circle. "Not a bad place to hang your hat." A king-sized sleigh bed was dwarfed by the enormity of the room. A white chaise graced a window cove near a large mirrored armoire. Purple and white floral decor gave the room its only youthful element. Lemon-scented furniture polish tinted the air and gleamed from every immaculate surface.

Joselyn followed him in, not masking the reluctance in her stride. She shrugged in response to his appraisal of the room, whether in agreement or ambivalence, he couldn't tell.

"Well, it's not giving me anything to work with." Finn lifted the lid of a small mirrored box on the dresser. Empty. "What a shame. I was hoping for some first place pony ribbons and awkward prepubescent photos of gangly legs and big teeth."

"Sorry. All my ribbons and evidence of braces are safely stowed—away from malicious intruding eyes."

"You mean you really rode horses?"

She nodded. "We have stables on the property. I still ride about twice a month."

"Seriously?" Finn stopped his search, absorbing the new tidbit. "I've never ridden."

"Oh, I would *love* to see you on a horse."

He preferred her sassy. That placid, empty expression she utilized so often made him want to shake her.

"Aww, come on. Look at me. I'd be a natural. Give me a Stetson and a belt buckle the size of a salad plate and I bet I could pass for a gen-u-wine cowboy." He threw in a twang and saw the corner of her lip twitch. "Can we go, please, Sally Mae? If ya teach me, I promise I'll help you get that burr out of yur britches." He winked, and her grin finally cracked enough to ease the tense bind of her shoulders.

Still she shook her head, the light reflecting off her shiny espresso hair. "It'll be too dark after we eat. But I'm sure we'll be forced to dine here again before this whole mess is over. I'll take you next time. Should be good for a laugh—as long as you don't get too cocky and wind up with a broken neck."

The woman was exhausting. He looked heavenward for patience and saw a spill of amber-colored light painting the ceiling. "What's upstairs?"

Her smirk froze and mirrored the sudden flicker of ice in her eyes. *Ooo, secrets.* Before she could manufacture a lie he darted across the room and started up the winding steps.

"Finn! Stop!" She was hot on his heels, grabbing at his legs as he raced to the top. Her cool touch seized his ankle and tripped him onto something spongy. Puzzled, he looked up from his sprawl on his stomach and took in the small room not much larger than the bed below, the floor as soft as a mattress, and dozens of purple and white throw pillows, all differing textures and fabrics, littered the floor. The pitched roof was low on each side rising to a standing height in the center. The walls below the slant were built-in book cases filled with novels, fashion magazines, and girly knickknacks. Though no pictures.

"This is sweet." Finn regained possession of his leg and stood. "It's like your secret sanctum."

"What is that? Sci-fi geek speak for my private space that you just invaded."

Ignoring her comment he perused the walls, gaining insight into a very complicated girl. "These are all chick books. *Pride and Prejudice, The Notebook, Shopaholic* something-or-other."

"In case you failed to notice, I am a chick." She crossed her arms and angled her body against a small door built low into the wall.

What was she hiding? It had to be something good. Time to push. "Trust me. I've noticed. How could I not, the way you keep practically prancing around naked to get my attention. Subtlety is not your forte, *Snow.* Luckily, a photographic memory is one of mine." He tapped his temple, as if reminding her it was all stored there.

A rush of red strangled her neck. "I have not! Could you be more repulsive?"

"I could try."

"Ehh! Tour's over. Let's go." She strode in a huff toward the staircase.

Oh, she played so nicely into his hand. Push her, and she ran. Exactly as he'd predicted. And riled as she was, she didn't seem to notice that while she was fleeing in her embarrassment, Finn was now opening the door she'd been trying to hide. Reaching his hand into the shadowed cubby, he gripped a leather-bound book and pulled out ... a diary.

Interesting. Leaning against the wall, he flipped it open and started reading little adolescent scribbles.

Dear Diary,

Today is my 10th birthday. Yia-Yia thought it would be fun to take some of the cupcakes we made up to my daddy's office. I am so excited! You see, I made a wish on a star last night. I wished my birthday would be special this year. And today THIS! So cool! Maybe wishes do come true. Maybe he got me a special present, you think? I'll report back later ... :)

Well, I'm back. And I learned something important. Wishing on stars is stupid. I'm sorry I'm crying on you Diary, but it didn't go good. At all. I'm so confused. When we got to daddy's work, there was a row of people in white coats in his office. All looking at their shoes except one. And daddy was yelling really loud. His cheeks got so red and his eyes looked crazy scary as he got in their faces like the bullies do at school. One guy's hands were balled up into fists, but he just stood and stared while daddy screamed. Those people must have done something really bad because daddy doesn't really ever yell. Or smile. Or really talk that much.

Well, to me anyways. And when daddy looked up and saw me he—

Finn was about to turn the page but stopped to grin at the overly dramatic retelling from a child's eyes. That, and the sad faces and broken hearts penciled in the margins. Poor thing. Declan Whyte probably had to buy her a pony to make up for it.

"And you know what?—" Joss turned back and gasped when she saw what he held. "Finn! Put that back!" Regaining the two steps from her descent back down the staircase, she barreled toward him in attack mode.

Finn darted away from her advances. "You're very predictable, Snow Whyte." Holding the diary above his head, he flipped to the middle. He couldn't read the scribble from the arm's length distance, but that didn't stop him from heckling her in a high-pitched imitation.

"*Dear Diary, Finn Carson is sooo dreamy! All the girls go wild when he smiles, including yours truly ...*"

"I'm not kidding. Give it!"

Finn was really starting to enjoy himself. She clawed at his arms, but he turned and slipped from her grip. She jumped as high as she could, but tall as she was she was no match for his six feet three inches. He blocked each attempt without much effort and continued his taunting. "*... I bet he's a good kisser. I wish he'd give me a big, fat smooch in front of the whole school ...*"

Attempting to climb his back proved to be the most effective in her progress until he abruptly sat and rolled forward, causing her to somersault onto the spongy floor.

The savage rage on her face fueled his fun. He laughed and saw something spark in her eyes as the slightest lift tugged at those stubborn lips, showing something she was trying to hide.

If he would've blinked he'd have missed it. But he'd seen it, all right.

She was having fun.

She was getting into the game now. A lioness hunting her prey, she circled around him, her eyes narrow and fierce, targeting him and her next course of action. Finn struggled to his feet, tilting on the mound of pillows sinking in the soft padding. She took her shot right then, gaining on him in a blink and knocking him down. He tucked the book behind his back as he fell deeper into the cushions.

"I am gonna kill you, Carson! Give it to me!" He detected the faint smile slipping through her heated words as she started flinging pillows and digging around his waist to pry at his tight grip.

"You're no match for me." He roared with villainous theatrics and writhed against her digging.

"Wanna bet?" Her eyebrows danced. A slow grin about knocked him cold a second before she dove over him, forcing his body to roll, exposing the diary. Her fingers grazed it, but not in time to gain full possession. "Ahhh!" Her high-pitched squeal tumbled into laughter as he slammed her right back, rolling over her, pinning her arm down with one hand, holding the diary high with the other.

She poked at him with her free hand, attempting distraction while she bent forward, straining against his weight, and threw her leg over his midsection, knocking him over and rolling him back again.

Losing his balance in the constant shift of wrestling in memory foam, he grabbed onto her back, his fingers curling into her shoulder blade. An explosion of laugher erupted, and her body went berserk. Wedging the diary back beneath him, his other hand joined forces with the first and went to town on her tickle spot.

Her hysterical laughter squeaked and hiccupped, and Finn had never heard a more endearing sound. But it was nothing compared to the look on her face. A carefree, all-access pass to the real Joselyn. Her smile wider and truer than he'd ever seen it.

He slowed his torment when her face was starting to resemble a radish and tears of laughter were streaming from the corners of her eyes. Playtime should probably be over, before it got any more out of control.

But the second he released his hands she amped the rivalry back to life by digging her fingers under his arms, exposing the one weakness in his tickle-proof armor.

"Stop it!" Thick belly laughs he hadn't shed in years poured forth from the work of her frantic prodding fingers. "Joss, I'm warning you!"

She giggled harder, sinking down until she'd pinned his hips beneath her thighs. "*Oh*, I'm shaking in my boots."

"You should be." He threw an arm around her shoulders and rolled over, trapping his forearm between her neck and the floor. She was completely caught up in the madness. But Finn, as he leaned forward onto her, stretching her arms above her head with his one free hand, finally felt the awareness sink in.

Her legs bucked playfully for a moment until it sank in for her too.

Their breaths heaving, smiles fading. Eyes searching. The gravity of it cementing in the sudden stillness.

Joselyn's plush pink lips parted, driving his eyes and his desire to the same place. His body sent a warning of their current position. His lips, inches from hers, drew closer, until their breaths intermingled and his brain shut down. Vanilla and peppermint invaded his senses, begging him to have a taste. Just one. Just once. Just … because he couldn't not.

She blinked, their labored breaths contradicting the seeming calm of the moment. Her eyes softened, her lids batting heavily before resting shut, granting permission.

Finn's hand relinquished hold of her wrists and skimmed down the length of her arm as he leaned in the last inch. His nose left the slightest brush on hers, his fingers guiding her delicate jaw, his lips coming in for contact, his eyes closing for the long awaited moment—

"—Josie, dinner!" Gloria's voice boomed from an intercom overhead.

Finn hurled his body off of her as if someone plucked him

up by his collar and tossed him on the floor.

Joselyn scrambled to her feet, and before he could even meet her gaze she was descending the stairs.

So close. Too close. He squeezed his eyes tight and raked both hands through his hair. *Have you lost your mind?* Bracing his palms on the floor to push himself up, he felt something crinkle under his fingers.

Joselyn's diary lay open in all the commotion. He knew he shouldn't read it again, but his eyes wandered of their own volition to the top of the open page dated April 29 – Prom. Fighting a battle against his conscience he closed the diary, but not before his eyes captured the first few lines.

This time starting with … *Dear Mom.*

Chapter 13
Joselyn Whyte

"Hey *Finn, come here.*" Sadie called out to the tall and lean surfer dude propped against the burnt-orange lockers. He raised his hand in greeting before rolling the pages of the comic book he'd been reading and shoving the tube into his back pocket. As he strode toward them he swiped a hank of shaggy blond hair from his forehead.

Sweet. Moses. Joselyn's breath tangled in her throat. His eyes were an unfathomable shade of turquoise. Crystal clear and swimmable. Stupid as it was, she was sinking like a brick.

"Hey. What's up?" His lips slipped into an easy smile, revealing stunning white teeth and heartbreaking dimples in each cheek.

Geez. Was this guy even real? Was he Sadie's boyfriend? She swallowed hard lest she start drooling over someone else's man and forced herself to duck away beneath the dark drape of her hair.

Joselyn had only met Sadie the day before, and so far she was the only person who had deigned to even speak to the new girl in school.

Mental note: Do not fantasize about my only friend's boyfriend.

"... –er, Finn. Finn, this is Joselyn. She's new." Sadie's introduction jarred her back.

Back to the boy's eyes she should not be swooning so

ridiculously over.

"Joselyn." Her name on his lips tickled her senses. "Nice to meet you." He extended his hand, his steady gaze holding hers. And then … contact. The warmth of his touch engulfed her completely. From her chronically cold hands to her frigid toes to the fire blazing in her cheeks she was practically a furnace. Charged particles they'd just learned about in chemistry came to life and zinged back and forth in the rowdy hallway, slowing everything but her galloping heart.

"You too." She let go and instantly felt a chill take hold once again.

"So, Joselyn and I were gonna run up to Smoothie King after school," Sadie said. "Thought, if you didn't have baseball practice you might wanna join. Ryan's coming too."

Joselyn slurped down a final glance before focusing on Sadie. Stunned by her odd reaction—something akin to love at first sight, though she knew that was ridiculous, not to mention impossible. Besides, what could a girl like her know about love anyway? Joselyn shook her head, chasing away the fanatical feeling.

"Umm, who's Ryan?"

"There he is. Ry!" Sadie beckoned over another nearly perfect male specimen.

Some girls have all the luck.

Finn leaned in, speaking unnecessarily close to Joselyn's ear. "Ryan is Sadie's BFF and our neighbor." A shiver descended her spine from his nearness. The fresh soapy scent that teased her nose didn't help either. This was bad. And completely unlike her. She really needed to rein it in.

"Wait, you live together?" Sadie didn't strike her as that kind of girl. But then again, Joselyn had never attended a public high school, let alone a coed one, and was unaccustomed to social norms.

His eyes crinkled with amusement. "One of the

downsides of being *siblings*. But I do get to go to college next year while she stays with the 'rents for two more years. We won't be living together then."

"Siblings." The word escaped from smiling lips as the realization bloomed like hope in her heart.

"Must have missed that part, huh?" His lips curled, her toes reacted in kind. "Now, tell me, what are your thoughts on drinkable fruit?"

The sound of Joselyn's alarm was the slap of reality she needed. She whacked blindly at the snooze button and buried her head beneath the pillow with a muffled sound of disgust. It had been years since she'd thought about the first time she met Finn and the asinine illusions of love that had sprouted out of loneliness, naivety, and yes, fine, attraction.

But she'd been on enough blind dates in the past few years to know for a fact that first impressions could be wildly off base. So could second and third. Her youthful infatuation with that boy a painful reminder of the untimely realization of his selfish arrogance—the consequences of which that had almost driven her to take her own life.

You should have.

The wicked whisper soaked all around her, permeating the doughy down comforter with a cold truth that had her shivering. It all came flooding back. The memories so dark, so chilling they dragged her under with the current, trapping her beneath the ice. Her breaths came faster. She squeezed her eyes tight, curled deeper under the covers into a quivering ball. "Stop."

The near silent command was met with a startling halt of the tormenting visions. And even more curious was a sudden swell of warmth in her chest. The mysterious tug-of-war was as unsettling as the dream. The cold paralyzing fear versus the fires of rebuke. Maybe there was something to be said for those years of coping mechanisms she'd had crammed down her throat.

But regardless of how far she'd come, the high-school flashback and the ensuing internal battle for her soul had her teetering on the fringes of sanity and it wasn't even eight o'clock.

She needed a fix.

Having been good the past week, even the past several days since her near kiss with Finn, her streak came to an end. Digging into the nightstand drawer she scavenged for the bag she'd hidden. Her secret shame. When the familiar crinkle signaled success, she tore it open, thrust in her hand and retrieved a fistful of heaven.

"*Ohhh*," she moaned. The peanut butter M&M's going down without a fight. Her eyes closed as she inhaled another handful. "*Ohhh, that's good.*"

"Cheese and rice! By the sound of things I thought you'd smuggled a guy in here." Sadie pushed through the door and plopped down on the bed next to Joselyn, digging in for a fix of her own. "*Oh my.* You might be onto something here. Keeping these bedside is dangerous, Joss. Brilliant, but dangerous. You've fallen off the wagon, and I'm here to, you know, save you from yourself and whatnot. So spill it before I confiscate the rest."

Oh, how she wanted to. But this was about Sadie's brother, not one of Joselyn's boring, impeccably vetted blind dates. It was too complicated, too … weird. The sad fact was she didn't have anyone else she could talk to. Except, maybe, Yia-Yia, though she hadn't had a lucid moment in days.

What a banner year. Yia-Yia's abrupt decline combined with a proverbial clown car of dating train wrecks. Not to mention the malicious media circus surrounding her father's campaign, and this just in, her attempted murder and newfound homelessness. A gut-wrenching combination of unsavory flavors all blended up and served with a cherry on top in the form of her mortal enemy, Finn Carson.

"There's … a lot going on right now. I'm a little stressed." Joselyn winced as she met Sadie's disbelieving glare and then sighed. "Fine. It might have something to do with your obnoxious brother, but that's all you're getting from me." She popped another few M&M's into her yapper, lest she be tempted to purge any further.

"Oh, boy. What'd he do this time?"

"Nothing." Joselyn chewed. Swallowed. "Everything. I dunno. I can't figure out why he'd volunteer for this, other than to torture me—which, by the way, seems to be his calling in life."

Sadie snorted. "You two are something else. All those years ago when I first introduced you I could have sworn there was something there. I never imagined it would be this."

Joselyn swallowed hard, forcing down the remaining slurry of chocolate and peanut butter. If only Sadie knew all the things Joselyn had kept from her. Protected her from. After Sadie lost Ryan, she didn't need any more graphic doses of reality.

"I will say one thing though." Sadie inhaled some more M&M's and continued to talk while she attacked the bag. "Finn is not the monster you've created in your head. I don't know what caused this rift, but I do know that, despite the arrogant front, he's a good man. We all make mistakes, Joss. I'm not making excuses for either of you, but at some point you are gonna have to talk this thing out. I can't keep running interference. It's not fair."

Joselyn opened her mouth in defense, but realization flooded in. All these years and she hadn't even considered that she'd put Sadie in the middle, pitting a family against each other. How much damage had she caused between the two siblings?

"Well, he, ah, did make a surprisingly good impression on my dad the other night." Although she'd refused to look at him for the remainder of the evening after their little tussle in her hideout. She didn't know what had possessed her to let her guard down. Over ten years of curiosity perhaps, but still.

Even the ride home had been stilted and silent. Maybe

more so from the fact that Archer had shown up and explained that the cops had lost the Grand Prix guy and were still scratching their heads about it. That sweet little morsel was coupled with the news about the Five-Alarm Arsonist fire that ravaged an abandoned warehouse in a neighboring suburb of Valley Park the same night her house burned down. Which fire had been the decoy? Had she been the target of the now infamous arsonist or were they looking for a different killer?

"… you okay, Joss?"

"Hmm? Oh, sorry. Lost in thought, I guess."

Sadie leaned over and rested her head on Joselyn's shoulder, found her hand, and laced their fingers in a firm clasp. "We're gonna get through this. You might not realize it yet, but there are greater forces at work here. A bigger plan we can't yet see. A good one."

Joselyn wasn't so sure, but she nodded anyways as tears burned her eyes. What would that kind of faith feel like? Would it fill the empty places in her lonely life or would it bestow short-lived but beautifully deluded false hope until it crash-landed into her reality?

Those greater forces had taken everything from her and left her without a family—without anyone to care about the stolen pieces of her life. She couldn't work out the kinks of how Sadie still believed after all she'd been through.

Because God, to Joselyn, was like that new Valentino purse. Exquisite. Perfect. A big starry-eyed wish. Until you let your guard down and realized too late that the claws still sink in—tearing apart that thing that seemed sturdy, reliable, and worth the high price of believing you could deserve something so special.

Like Declan Whyte, God may have spared her life, but then he'd walked away, left her in the cold to deal with the barrenness he'd brought upon her life. Left her to wade through the murky darkness alone again and again to a place that was neither warm nor welcoming. And would never be home.

She'd seen too many miracles to believe God simply didn't exist, but the truth of it was he was as much of a stranger as her own father.

After another colorful morning at the nursing home, rehearsing the simple and often seated choreography for *Mamma Mia!: The Geriatric Edition*, Joselyn stopped by her shop to go over invoices with Charisma's manager, Lacy, and sent in orders for the upcoming spring collection she'd hand selected from a variety of designers during fall fashion week. Having hung up her managerial hat six months prior, allowing more flexibility to spend time with Yia-Yia, Jocelyn was still having trouble giving up the reins to her baby.

She huddled over the white, shabby chic desk in her office, the cheeky glow of the dusty pink walls lifting her spirits as she spent several hours poring over the books. She'd come to love all the ins and outs of the business, even number crunching. Having attended the business program at Stanford for four miserable years, she was glad some good had come of her forced educational directive from Declan Whyte, the dictator.

It still irked her not knowing if she'd gotten in on her own academic merit. Her father had long arms of influence, and she wouldn't put anything past him.

And that made her think of Finn. The easy way he communicated with her father had aroused more suspicions about Finn's intentions for their "arrangement." He said early on that he didn't have to explain himself, but that only stirred up more doubts and insecurities.

Maybe he simply enjoyed toying with her emotions.

Not maybe. Definitely.

Or … maybe her father was paying him.

Her heart contracted at the thought. Not because it was Finn. Not really. But because it made her wonder if she would ever find someone who cared about her? Just her. Not her father's money, fame, and the power that gave the elite license to dispose of people like empty wrappers from her chocolate stash. Was there anyone without a selfish agenda? And did Finn really care about keeping her safe, or was this simply another power play?

She told herself not to care. His motives were irrelevant. She couldn't care less about Finn Carson. That was all in the past. She should stitch that into a T-shirt so she wouldn't forget.

A bit later, after bundling back up to brave the bitterness of a St. Louis winter, she bid Lacy farewell and deposited her fur-lined riding boots on the sidewalk of Downtown Kirkwood. The icy wind bit through the thick wool of her jacket and the flimsy barrier of her leggings. *Brr.* Hiking her purse on her shoulder, she pulled the drape of the hood low over her face and ducked into the bakery a few doors down from where she'd parked—where Sal's unmarked car reminded her that there was nothing ordinary about her day.

The hot green tea she ordered served dual purposes: soothing her nervous stomach and counteracting winter's assault on her bare fingers. As she stood in line to pay for her steaming confection her gaze landed on a glamour shot of the Kirkwood firehouse—reminding her that Finn, and the heroic men of the fire department, had saved her life.

"Only the tea, miss?" The cashier, a late sixties woman with a fine dusting of powdered sugar on the rounded center of her smock, smiled, her kind eyes crinkling down to fine slits.

"Hmm. No, I'd also like two dozen of these assorted pastries. Thank you."

Armed with goodies, Joselyn scurried through the cold to her SUV and drove the half a mile to the fire station to properly thank the firefighters who'd come to her rescue.

Well, some of them.

Chapter 14

Finn Carson

The prism of the late morning sunlight flashed a pattern beneath the slow-moving blades of the ceiling fan. The inanimate thing seemed to somehow badger him for his unproductive morning. Finn groaned in response to the unintentional message playing in tandem with the throbbing fist working his temple from the inside of his head. Sleep deprivation plus migraine equals misery.

But yet again, even with the cleansing wash of daylight and the anguished gray matter between his ears, her dark words rang with resounding clarity in his brain for the millionth time.

Dear Mom,

Something happened. I have no one, I've lost everything ... and nobody cares. I'm thinking I'd rather be with you.

It had been three days since he'd seen Joselyn.

Three long days reliving those few unguarded moments of fun. Remembering the sweet anticipation of her surrender. Rethinking the ominous admission from her most private thoughts.

Three days of no sleep. Not one wink.

On the bright side, he hadn't suffered any flashbacks from the Monroe fire, but at this point would consider trading in a few hours of nightmares for any amount of actual sleep. His feet found the floor and slumbered about like a dead man walking. The intercom redirected him from the bathroom down the stairs to the door.

He pressed the button. "Who is it?"

"Carson. It's Cody. I tried calling, but I guess your phone's off. Can I come up?"

"Yeah, sure thing, Largeman." The nickname was Cody's last name and an homage of sorts to his oversized ego and his family's grandiose wealth.

Opening the door, Finn's oldest friend slapped him on the shoulder and strode in like he owned the place. Dressed to the nines in a navy pin-striped suit tailored to his brawny five-foot-nine stature, Cody's presence and the potent sting of his cologne filled the room to excess.

"So, what's up? Haven't seen you in a while."

"I know, man. Been super busy helping my dad at the firm." Cody's father owned the largest, most prestigious law firm in St. Louis, and while Cody didn't possess a law degree, his dad made sure he was high on the payroll, doing … Finn didn't know what Cody's job entailed actually. But he'd always had that lawyer charm and could sweet talk his way into or out of anything. Came in handy with their childhood shenanigans. There'd been a lot of them.

"What about you?" Cody asked.

"You know, same old. Nothing major."

Cody smelled his bluff as evidenced by the sardonic grin twisting his mouth. "Anything else you've failed to mention?"

Finn exhaled a sigh. "Something specific you wanted to ask me, Large?"

Holding up his hands, Cody feigned innocence. "I might've heard something through the grapevine about you and Joselyn Whyte. I know how you feel about the little ice queen and wanted to help put the rumor to rest. Unless …"

He itched to confide in his oldest friend, but Declan Whyte's latest warning tamed the truth. "You heard right. Joss and I are seeing each other." He folded his arms over his chest. It wasn't technically a lie. They were seeing quite a bit of each other—some of which, Finn couldn't shake from his mind.

"Wow. I can't believe it. Needed to hear it firsthand,

though." Rubbing his jaw, Cody snorted out a humorless laugh. "So, scrounging my sloppy seconds, huh? What changed your mind about her?"

Finn's protective instincts fired, hot and fierce. Sloppy seconds? It's not like Joselyn had ever been Cody's girlfriend. And even after their one and only date Cody had done a thorough job of explaining why Joselyn had picked him over Finn. Seeing the petty and overt slander this time around made Finn question the validity of Cody's confessions all those years ago. He'd never given Finn any reason to doubt him. They were, after all, best friends since kindergarten, but the dark gleam in Cody's eyes gave him pause.

The accusations undoubtedly blazing from his eyes were unfounded so he bit his tongue and kept his cool. Until …

"Man, you've *still* got it bad." Cody mumbled.

"What'd you say?" Had he heard that right? Clenching his fists, the popping of Finn's knuckles pierced the heavy silence.

Finn caught the slight pull of a grimace before the aloof mask moved to cover Cody's slip. "Hmm?"

"Don't play dumb. It looks tacky with that suit." All these years he'd made excuses for Cody. *He didn't know how you felt about her … If you'd told him he wouldn't have stabbed you in the back.* They all crumbled when the phony look on his face exposed the outright betrayal from his spoiled friend.

Cody's thick brows pinched, and he managed to look contrite. "I … I was just looking out for you."

"Got a funny way of showing it."

"Listen. Okay, so I lied." He shrugged like it was no big deal. "I knew how you felt about her back then. I know you thought you were flying under the radar, but, dude, I know you better than anyone. It was pretty obvious."

"So you slid the blade in with your eyes wide open. That's good to know. You, who had girls all over your *radar* when I'd never even asked one out on a date, turned the only one I cared about into a conquest." It might seem like high-school drama to some, but to Finn, since this was his closest friend for the better part of three decades, it felt like the ultimate betrayal.

"I knew she didn't like you like that. She made this big deal about dating someone in her *class*. I dunno, man. I guess I figured if I took her out, you'd get over her without getting crushed by that cold heart of hers. At the time I thought I was doing you a favor. Sorry, bro. I really am."

Finn had known Cody forever, but he could be hard to read. Was that the whole truth or was that the Largeman spin? Large had always done pretty well with the ladies—gross amounts of money and cool cars to his advantage—but in everything else Finn tended to one-up Cody without even trying. Sports and school, and even their other friends seemed to show preferential treatment toward a more easygoing, less competitive Finn. But Cody's skin seemed so thick; Finn could never tell if something was bothering him.

Had he been jealous and honed in on Finn's weakness? Desperate for a win? Finn had battled his own insecurities but would never have taken down a friend to come out on top.

Finn's migraine was now at critical mass and his vision was starting to blur so he let it drop. For now. "Let's talk about something else."

"Whew." Cody's laugh grated. "Never been so grateful for all that faith and forgiveness crap you harp on and on about. Maybe there's something to it." He shoved playfully at Finn's shoulder like they hadn't just nearly come to blows.

"Yeah, you should try it out sometime." Finn forced a lightness into his voice he didn't feel and ushered Cody out. "I've got stuff to do. We'll catch up later." He slammed the door without waiting for a response.

After tugging on a hoodie and his Carhart coat, he leashed Dodger for a walk. The cold air was bound to temper the steam piping in his hot head. As he walked he prayed, trying to find some peace. Some direction. Feeling continually lost in the maze of his thoughts. When he finally looked up he realized maybe his compass hadn't been too far off the mark because he'd ended up exactly where he wanted to be.

The firehouse.

He missed it already. Something about the stately two-story brick and stone building was fortifying. It was where he felt grounded even when he was flailing.

The weight lifted off in increments with each step he took through the engine bay toward the office. The slight scuff of Dodger's nails on the concrete provided the only sound until he reached the main hall and something decidedly feminine infused the air—a sugary aroma and the twinkling sound of laughter. A lot of houses had female firefighters and paramedics, but not theirs. Not presently, anyways.

He heard it again, and the familiarity jacked his pulse up a notch. Oh, he'd know that giggle anywhere. He slinked silently down the hall until the voices were more distinguishable.

"… are so good, Miss Whyte. You didn't have to, but I'd never turn down any sweetness you have to offer." Jones called upon his usually disguised southern drawl, laying it on pretty thick to enhance his charm, no doubt.

"A small token of my appreciation."

Her sweetness? He leaned closer. What in the heck had she given him?

"So, you got plans for tonight?"

"All right Jones. Leave the nice lady alone. Besides, don't you have a girlfriend?"

Great. Bronson was an even bigger flirt than Jones.

"I, however, am currently single."

A smooch sound found Finn's ears, and he knew Bronson had laid one of his cheesy hand kisses on her smooth skin. There were some hushed words and another lyrical giggle. Squeezing his eyes shut, he stood out of sight, tormented by his interpretation of what he couldn't see.

"What'd I miss? Ooo, treats." Wally's snorting and gulping announced he was consuming something with savage intensity. "Oh. Oops. Hi, Miss Whyte." The muffled words escaped from a food-laden mouth. "Thanks for the pastries."

Finn fought back another cringe. Did they all have to make such fools of themselves?

"Wally, close your mouth. This here is a lady. A gorgeous one at that. But I bet you get that all the time."

He could picture the beefed-up Bronson pawing all over her. One by one the guys took turns buttering her up with praise. Joselyn rewarded them with modest deflection and timid giggles. It sounded like they were all vying for her attention like a bunch of half-starved dogs.

Speaking of dogs.

He looked down in time to see the looped end of Dodger's leash disappear around the corner. Seconds later Joselyn's silky voice greeted his pup. Busted. He'd planned on sneaking back out unseen after making sure Joselyn escaped his crew unharassed. Ship. Sailed.

Shrugging his shoulders and craning his neck, he slipped into character and made tracks toward his crew. *Here goes nothing.* "There's my girl."

Joselyn's eyes widened at the announcement.

Crossing the last few paces, Finn surprised himself when he tucked his arm around the slim curve of her waist and deposited a brief kiss on the satiny plane of her cheek before he nuzzled her ear. The heated scent right there slammed into him like a two-by-four between the eyes. *Danger. Danger!* He looked away before reading her expression, not sure he wanted to know and honestly a bit too dizzy to process it. At least he was until he met three other dumbfounded stares. "What's up, fellas?" It was then he realized he'd joined ranks of the hounds when he'd so brazenly marked his territory.

"Wait. You two are together?" This from a tanned and blond—both fake—Bronson, more often referred to as "Bravo" for his fixation with his own reflection and his likeness to the egotistical cartoon character Johnny Bravo.

Finn had already showed his hand, now he had to ride it out. Turning adoring eyes on Joselyn, he gave her waist a squeeze and she melded against his side. "You didn't tell them, babe?"

Her nervous giggle emerged in a stutter. "Guess I hadn't gotten there yet."

"Oh! Ha! Good one, Iron Man. Almost had me going there."

"Not joking, Jones." Finn relished in his cocky grin. *Read 'em and weep, boys.*

"But you don't date. I mean … you have dates, attractive ones, but—"

Finn held up his hand. "Don't help me, Jones."

"Sorry."

"When did this happen?" Bronson crossed his arms, flexing his muscles.

Finn had endured Declan's interrogation for an hour the other night. It was Joselyn's turn to be in the hot seat. He gave her the slightest pinch, and she startled. "Oh. Uh … Well, Finn and I have known each other for a long time, and, uh, after he rescued me he *begged* me to go out with him. Poor guy's had it bad for years. It was getting a little path—"

"She simply couldn't resist me any longer." Finn slid his hand down to her backside and gave it a little warning tap.

Keeping remarkably still, she reached discretely to his misbehaving hand, twisted his wrist, and bit her fingernails into his skin.

"Man! Why couldn't it have been me? Finn wasn't even supposed to be in there—after the trauma of the Monroe fire. Next time, I get to defy orders and save the girl, okay guys?" Wally's face shone with eagerness and innocence.

Finn stopped breathing. Joselyn released her punishing grip. The languishing silence spoke volumes about Finn's supposed secret. He drew in a brittle breath, hoping his words didn't sound as fragile as his emotions. "Well, guys, it was good catching up. See you after next week." He bent down and snagged the end of Dodger's leash, trying to breathe through the panic until the cold winter air hit his face.

They all knew about his PTSD? Had Ryker told them about the nightmares?

A cold sweat skated down his spine. He'd mounted extreme pressure on himself to keep it together in front of the guys. Didn't need everyone second-guessing him, treating him like some incompetent sad sack. If Wally knew, everyone knew. And now, due to Wally's verbal diarrhea, so did Joselyn.

Finn fled the building without looking back. Dodger trotted along, ignorant of Finn's escalating anxiety. Handling this on his own was one thing. Being scrutinized as some sort of weak, helpless loser was an option he would not accept. But what was he supposed to do now?

Something grazed his hand. When he turned Joselyn barreled into his chest. "Oomph." Stepping back, she searched his eyes. "Sorry. I keep bumping into you." Her lips quirked in a slight, teasing smile.

"Need something?" Over her shoulder he spotted Bronson peeking out the open bay.

She glanced back and then took a step closer. The soft pads of her fingers slipped across the skin of his palm, and she wove their hands together. "Can I drive you home?" Her teeth caught the corner of her bottom lip and held.

He swallowed a curse, hating feeling vulnerable with every fiber of his being. Her eyes were his undoing, so he glued his to the pavement as if there was something more fascinating in the slab of concrete than in the mystifying crystal-blue amethysts he'd gotten turned around in more than once. "I don't live far. I can walk."

"But it's so cold. Come on." Tugging at his hand, she towed him along to her SUV. He conceded silently. Dodger pranced across the backseat while they waited for a train to pass through Station Plaza without a word. A few minutes later he focused on the images hurtling past the window. "Uh, Joss? You passed my place."

"Yep."

"Fine. Sorry for my little love tap back there, but really, can you blame a guy?"

Her smiling lips remained forward.

"My family will come looking for me, you know?" he teased.

"I know."

"Uh, okay. Where are we going?"

"Ah, patience, Kemosabe. You'll see."

Chapter 15

Joselyn Whyte

Uncomfortable silence. How refreshing. Joselyn nibbled her lip until the skin felt raw, then finally risked a glance at Finn. His eyes were trained out the passenger window, looking sightlessly lost in the blur of barren trees.

What had Wally meant? Trauma? Defying orders? She wished she could rewind back and listen again, pay more attention. Instead she'd been squirmy, distracted. The faint trace of Finn's kiss burning a hole in her cheek and the dizzying effects of his hard body against hers was enough to demote her IQ a solid twenty points.

He obviously didn't want to talk about it, and it was driving her nutso. Another five minutes of perfect silence deemed too much to take. Joselyn pressed the power button on the steering column, counteracting the unbearable stuffiness with soft whining sounds of the local country station.

"She's trying to kill me." Finn craned his head back.

"Thought you were sleeping over there."

"As if anyone could sleep with this shrapnel slicing through their eardrums." He plucked Joselyn's cd case off the floor. "This oughtta be enlightening."

"It's not much farther."

"Another minute of this, and I'll need to have myself committed."

"Tempting."

Ignoring her, he turned down the volume and riffled through her collection. "Hey, Wednesday Addams, how about some music that doesn't require happy pills?"

"What? There's some good stuff in there."

"The Fray, Coldplay, Adele, Jason Mraz? We need to get you a proper musical education. Maybe Zeppelin, Clapton, and REO to get you started." He swore under his breath. "Evanescence, really?"

"Hey, now, there is nothing wrong with a little angsty girl rock. And Mraz is like the ultimate happy music. You're crazy."

"Whatever you say, Debbie Downer."

"Sweet. Let's get that in writing." She risked another glance and got ensnared in his gaze. *Moses*, her heart actually fluttered. So lame. Thankfully, she was driving and rerouted her eyes to the road.

"What's this Eli Young Band?"

"That's not their newest album, but they're amazing. Put it in."

Finn complied none the wiser. Joselyn skipped to track two. "One of my favorites."

It was like music therapy. The catchy tune for "Crazy Girl" slipped like liquid Xanax through her veins, loosening her tense muscles, helping her unwind. Belatedly, she realized she'd unwound too far. Managing to forget herself long enough to add her own sing-a-long harmony and an asinine jive of her head to the beat. Oh, the horror. She froze, clamped down on her lip so hard she might have tasted blood.

Silence met her from Finn's side of the car, and she felt his gaze like direct sunlight on already blistering cheeks.

Stupid girl was more like it.

She could hold her own, but she was no singer. Not like Sadie. Come to think of it, she was pretty sure Finn could sing too. She knew he played the guitar, but she'd never witnessed his talents firsthand.

Her thoughts careened from there down a very slippery slope that had her face heating even hotter. Curse her pasty skin!

"This song is like your anthem, crazy girl." Finn's fingers tugged a lock of her hair. "Better. Still country, though. Very sneaky."

She lifted her hands from their ten and two vice on the wheel and shrugged before returning them, her morbid clench on the smooth woodgrain a vain effort to restrain the humiliation still broadcasting in her blazing cheeks.

Before the song ended they'd pulled up to the back entrance of her father's property. Joselyn hopped out and unlocked the low metal gate, drove through, and repeated the act. Finn didn't seem to realize where they were as he scanned the endless equestrian fence and vast pasture until they pulled up to the stables.

When the car came to a stop, Finn angled toward her. "We gonna go for a ride?" He cocked an eyebrow.

"Well, I thought you could use a distraction. I always ride when I need to clear my head. And they say it's best to get back on the horse. Or in your case, just get on the horse."

A smile inched across his lips, his eyes, shadowed beneath a thick fringe of honey-highlighted lashes, filled with amusement. "You did something nice for me."

"No. I simply didn't want to deal with your sulky little tantrum. And—"

He grasped her chin, silencing her with the press of his thumb. "It's okay. I won't tell anyone." He winked and skimmed over her bottom lip before retracting his hand.

Oh ... oh, man.

Need. Oxygen. Joselyn sucked in a breath and of course that made him grin, all slow and knowing, completely aware of his effect on her.

Well, crap.

Not having any semblance of a comeback, she cracked the window for a snoring, belly-up Dodger before jerking open the door and fleeing the close quarters.

Deep purple ink spilled over the bleary horizon, bleeding lavender and periwinkle strokes onto the blanket of gray. The air had a frosty bite, mollified only slightly by her exhaled heat pumping out a ridiculously labored hazy white plume.

She told herself it was the late-afternoon breeze that sent a shudder to her bones and quickened breathlessly in her lungs. It had absolutely nothing to do with the muscle-bound tank of testosterone dogging her heels every step of the way. By the time she drew back the sliding door she was practically wheezing like an asthmatic. Chill pill. Stat! Of course Finn strode past, limber-legged, easy as you please, absorbing the top of the line stable with childlike wonder. Which she had to admit was a little bit adorable.

His wide starry eyes gleamed under the lights, the slight gape of his full lips lit into a boyish grin. "This is *awesome*. Which one do I get to take for a spin?"

"We'll put you on Odie." Joselyn pointed to the beautiful Tennessee Walker with a glossy bay coat.

"Aww, come on. That burnt red one with the black hair? He looks mean. In fact, I think he's glaring at me. I'm much better with the *ladies*."

"You're so delusional, it's cute. Odie's a good egg. He's strong and steady, great with first-timers, and has a real sweet disposition. Trust me. You get on that filly, LuLu, over there, she'll buck you right off. She might be a beauty, but she's a tough one to break."

"Tell me about it," Finn muttered, tucking his broad fingers into the front pockets of his low-slung jeans. "And who will you be riding? Unless you want to double with me. But I must warn you, I like to be the big spoon." He wagged his eyebrows suggestively.

Crossing her arms, she held her ground, not giving him anything this time. "It must be exhausting being so charming."

"It really is."

"And modest."

His throaty laugh rang out to the rafters, resounding like church bells. "Which horse, Joss?"

"I ride this Arabian next to Odie, Heston. He's my fella." Making her way to Heston's stall she swept her hand down his neck and nuzzled his face to her own, breathing in his loyal affection and strength.

"Heston?"

Pulling back she continued her loving stroke. Heston let out a soft nicker. "I had a thing for Charlton Heston growing up. Yia-Yia made me watch *The Ten Commandments*. I thought it was gonna be a drag, but Moses in that mini-skirt … totally hot." Heston dipped his head and nosed her waist. Reaching to the nearby bucket she offered up a carrot stick.

"Should I be jealous?"

She turned, tossing a smirk and a carrot over her shoulder toward Finn before she strode to get the saddles. "Eat your heart out."

After a brief tutorial they were on their way. Finn surprised her with his eagerness to learn and gentle approach with Odie, not to mention the rogue cowboy look he embodied on the back of the gelding. He'd already worked his way up to a decent cantering pace. They rode in companionable silence around the clearings and into the wooded trails before slowing to a walk.

"You doing all right?"

"Great. Thanks for doing this, Joss."

His candor caught her by surprise. Sarcastic bickering had been standard fare for each line of dialogue they'd exchanged for the past ten years. With this new breach of territory her heart felt ridiculously fluttery. Her stomach just as uneasy. But her eyes, yeah, those were steady. Steadily stuck on him like bugs on a glue board.

And of course he caught her staring. Those eyes turning midnight blue in the overcast illumination, their earnest expression yanking her back to that rare vulnerable moment in the firehouse where the arrogant lady-killer persona had seemed like a smoke screen.

"Finn?" She eased the reigns until they walked side-by-side, her voice measured and tender, knowing she was treading on thin ice. "What was Wally talking about today?"

With one blink, she lost him—all that was loose and easy between them zapped with tension, from the instantly rigid plane of his body to the locked hinge of his jaw. But it was the bleakness in his eyes that scared her the most.

"Listen, forget it. I'm sorry, it's none of my business." She had to look away or she feared she might cry from seeing him that way. Which was stupid and irrational. But everything was at once as fragile as the frost crushing beneath Heston's hooves.

It's not like he owed her an explanation. He wasn't really her boyfriend. This was all a ruse. Except now she'd caught a glimpse behind the curtain. And what she saw rattled the boards safeguarding her heart, somehow making them kindreds of a broken past, ashamed and desperate for redemption.

But before she let herself bond over their mutually concealed scars, a voice from the past stole her sympathy.

Oh, how easily you forget. You're broken because of him.

Chapter 16

That freaking guy was always with her. And if it wasn't the blonde meathead who was lusting all over her, it was that Hispanic FBI tail playing best gal pal. It was all so much more complicated now he wanted to burn them all, every last one of them, for stealing his moment of vindication again and again. He released his balled fists once he felt the blood wet his hands and then dug his nails in again—the self-inflicted wounds a physical outlet for his inner pain.

They'd all thought, because of the abuse he'd tolerated before, that he was harmless by nature. When the truth was, he'd become what they'd made him. A product of the deadly equation crammed down his throat. Each fraction of injustice had fueled the fire, layering on the rage until the weight of it would either crush him or detonate. The choice was obvious. Besides, watching things burn was fascinating. The way even an inanimate object seemed to curl inward as if seeking to hide within itself. He knew all about that. He'd hidden away in his own mind, tucking in to shield himself from the intensity of the grief and helplessness that burned away the skin of his humanity until all that remained was a twisted, bleeding heart on fire for vengeance.

Yes, someone had to burn for this. It was the only thing that made sense anymore. It was either him or her, and the agony festering within was enough torment for ten lifetimes. He would not be the only one infested with pain. She would suffer hers, a swift justice, and then the retribution would begin and the balance restored. Because if he couldn't have love, if his reason for living was all but a dying ember of stolen memories in his soul, she would have her burning grave.

Chapter 17

Finn Carson

He hated to admit it, but he was actually having a good time. A really good time. Riding Odie had been the distraction he needed. And while Joselyn's company kept him on the edge of his saddle in some ways—their past a proverbial wet blanket—she'd had him in stitches in spite of it all with her flirtatious quips and zany Yia-Yia stories.

Finn had never heard her talk so openly, and he'd never heard mention of her grandmother until today. The way she poked fun at herself bulldozed him with surprise. And when that girlie giggle snuck out he about lost his mind. Her presence more intoxicating than he'd ever remembered.

Come on, Carson. Don't go down this road again. You know better.

But his heart was already galloping faster than Odie. And though he tried to pull on the reigns, he wasn't sure it would do any good.

Dusk was settling in, night chasing away the light of day much too early in the winter months. Inhaling a frosty breath and releasing a huff of white steam, he relished in the serenity of the surroundings. The dips and veins of the land carving the intricate skeleton of a leaner hibernating season beneath the plod of hooves. The contented moments shared with his *"girlfriend"* warmed him to his core despite the blunt December chill.

A crunch of frigid twigs and leaves wove into his subconscious, intuition prickling against his neck. Whipping around, his eyes strained against the waning sunlight until he saw something. Someone. In a dark hunter's jacket and jeans, sprinting away through the thick brush.

"Hey!" Yanking the reins to his left and digging in his heels, the horse responded and took off. Finn gritted his teeth and grappled with the worn leather straps, fighting to hold on against the severe pounding and escalating speed. Well off the beaten path, Odie slammed against the uneven ground, jerking Finn's body in a wild bull ride.

"Finn! Pull back!" Hooves pounded behind him signaling Joselyn's pursuit.

"Easy boy." Finn's efforts did little to abort Odie's escapade, but at least he was still on the horse and still gaining on the runner. "Hey, you! Stop right there!" Odie chose that moment to halt.

And though the horse had stopped, Finn's body kept moving. Freaking laws of physics. Joselyn's scream shattered the stillness, the shrill vibration bounding off every rock and tree, and echoed back in his ears with piercing clarity.

Time slowed. His body weightlessly launching from the saddle and hurling toward a very big, very solid-looking tree trunk.

Oh, God. Help.

His knees tucked in self-preservation, the move forcing him into an airborne somersault of sorts. Coarse bark clipped his shoulder and redirected him to the ground right next to the trunk with a rolling crash landing ... on a surprisingly soft compost of leaves and mulch.

"Ow." Blinking up at the canopy of naked branches and the dusk-darkening sky, he fed in the breath that had been knocked from his chest. He took a quick inventory with an overall wiggle and assessed no immediate protest save the slight twinge at his shoulder.

Mercy. Plain and simple.

A swift blur registered to his left. The guy was getting away.

Not on Finn's watch.

Springing to his feet, he took off after the perp.

Adrenaline fed his pace, and he fell easily into his old sprinting stride from his high school track days. Icy hot zings of oxygen burned his lungs as he heaved in the glacial air. This guy was fast, but Finn was faster.

Ten more yards. Five more yards.

Gotcha!

Finn snagged the runner's hood and yanked. The horse-collar tackle sending the guy's back on a collision course with the hard earth as Finn skidded to a halt a few feet past. Points for resilience because after a mere instant on the ground he was darting in a different direction with impressive agility.

Finn cut back toward him. A pang nagging his side as he closed in again. *Almost there.* Springing forward, Finn hurled his body the last two feet. His arms wrapping around broad shoulders as his weight and gravity surrendered the guy in a tackle.

Brute strength battled back, rolling Finn over, giving him his first glimpse of a face. But instead of violent intent, he saw panic reflecting back from conflicted hazel eyes.

Bringing his legs up in a WWE worthy move, Finn wrapped them around the guy's midsection and whipped him onto his back. Fists flailed from below him, attempts Finn deflected until throwing a punch of his own that landed against a hard jaw with a crack.

The fight beneath Finn surrendered. And when the guy's hands pressed to his wounded chin, Finn clenched the runner's wrists in his hands, restraining any further backlash.

Joselyn was still perched atop Heston a mere ten feet away, frozen in horror. "Joss, call Archer or the cops."

"Here! FBI. Keep your hands where I can see 'em." Sal emerged from a clearing that exposed a back road, his Glock poised for a raid. Holstering his piece, Sal grabbed the moaning man off the ground and cuffed him. "Sorry guys. I followed you here, but I couldn't keep track while you were gallivanting around on horseback. I've got backup on the way."

Finn nodded, brushing away crushed leaves and cold powdery dirt as he pulled himself off the ground.

He looked up as Joselyn forcefully dismounted from her horse and propelled herself at him. She looked furious, so instinct should've had him girding up for a beating. But instead he opened his arms and caught her against his chest. Her face smooshed against his throat, her arms strangling his neck, revving his heart rate back to full throttle. Finn crushed her tighter, holding her like the strength of his arms alone could keep them safe.

Their displays of affection over the past week had been for show. Was she still acting now? Somehow it felt different.

He angled his head and inhaled a breath of her Christmas hair, mere seconds from pressing a kiss to her head when she brought her hands to his chest and pushed away. Hard. Shoved was a better word for it. The cocoon of fiery heat they'd conjured in the few short moments was instantly whisked away on winter's icy breath.

"What were you thinking? Taking off on Odie like that and chasing down some psycho in the woods. You were *thrown* off a horse. A few more inches to the right, and I'd be picking tree trunk out of your skull! Don't you realize you could have been killed?" She shoved again. "I wasn't joking when I said you could break your neck you kno—" The sparks of anger in her eyes died mid-sentence.

"Stuart?" Her voice cracked with tenderness. She crossed to the man in cuffs, leaving Finn shocked by her fresh tongue-lashing and her odd preferential treatment for the bad guy.

What the?

"Joselyn. Are you okay?" This from stalker boy, who, by the way, didn't look anything like Finn imaged would be a scrawny, pimple-faced weirdo with a hysterical crush.

This guy, *Stu*, was tall and muscled with dark, troubled eyes and a militant crop of brown hair. Intimidating, except for the gash now swelling on his granite jaw.

No wonder Finn's hand felt like he'd decked a brick wall.

Joselyn's voice emerged calm and velvety, not at all like she'd spoken to Finn. "Stuart. You're not supposed to be here. The restraining order, remember?"

"I wanted to make sure you were okay. I saw the house, and then *Fabio* here," his head jerked in Finn's direction, "started lurking around after the fire. I was worried about you."

"Yeah, that or you burned her house down and tried to kill her." Sal's no-nonsense blurt interrupted the strange scene. He prodded Stuart toward the back road. "Either way, you're under arrest for violating the restraining order and trespassing on private property. We'll get to the bottom of this, Joselyn."

"But, I would never hurt Joselyn. I love her. I was merely perched in my tree, never close enough to be in violation until that *linebacker* came after me."

All three sets of eyes—aside from Stuart's—looked up, scanning for the tree.

"What tree?" Sal asked.

Stuart huffed and ambled with his escort several hundred yards to a towering oak. Hammered rectangles of wood pierced the trunk in a make shift ladder to a small, fort-like merging of branches. A tripod braced on a large perpendicular limb and a plastic box rested in the crevice of the wide stump.

"What is this, Stuart? Have you been spying on me again?" Joselyn crossed her arms across her willowy frame, making her look both fierce and fragile at the same time.

Sal's incoming call severed Stu's grappling response. "Yeah Archer, what's your twenty? We need to take *super-stalker* downtown for questioning, and we need the team to check out his creepy hideout. And since we're all sufficiently wigged out," Sal smirked with his perpetual good humor, "is it cool if I rough him up a bit?"

"I don't care if they said we aren't going. We're going.

I'm going. You can do what you want." Joselyn stomped away from the retreating squad cars.

Stuart was on his way to the FBI, and the rest of the team had collected everything from Stu's lair as evidence. Joselyn was set on going to listen to the interrogation from behind the observation glass. Something in her demeanor showed a protective instinct for her stalker, and it didn't sit well with Finn.

"Where's Odie?" Finn viewed the clearing where he'd abandoned ship and saw no trace of his wild stallion. Not that he was eager to saddle up after Odie's joy ride, but now they only had one horse and were nowhere near the stable in Finn's estimation.

"He's a bit of a wanderer, but the property is entirely fenced. I'll tell Erwin when we get back. He'll track him down."

Finn questioned with a lift of his brow, and Joselyn filled in the gaps about the live-in house keeper/grounds keeper couple that see to everything while Declan Whyte is off on business.

"Do you know how far we are?" Finn scanned the endless acres of barren trees.

"Yeah, not too far. But if we walk it'll be pitch black before we get back."

His lips curled into a self-satisfied grin. "Guess we'll get to spoon after all."

Finn couldn't believe Joselyn had sweet talked her way into the observation room. She'd let him drop off Dodger at home first, and he had hoped to belay her intentions to subject them to a miserable viewing of the *Stuart Show*.

Didn't play out that way. The woman had a stubborn streak a mile wide. Surprise, surprise. A few pleading blinks of those pretty eyes and all the suits turned to putty.

Another prime example of rich kids and their entitlement issues.

What Finn wanted was to be anywhere but here, listening to this lunatic rave about his love for Joselyn. But guys like Finn didn't get what they wanted. It's true what they say. Nice guys finish last. High school, a bitter reminder of that fact.

At least they'd drummed up a viable suspect from the whole ordeal. The sooner they booked this nut job the sooner Finn would be out of Joselyn's life. Her rejection shelved once and for all.

The lab was already sorting through the contents of the tree fort. Mainly a camera with a telephoto lens and a bunch of empty protein shake containers. Long hours leering at Joselyn had necessitated meals on the go and apparently fueled quite the appetite. What a creep.

"Why don't you explain to me why you are so fixated with Miss Whyte?" Sal's interrogation hadn't revealed any gems so far, only some sonnets and fanatical raving about Finn's little ice princess who sat white-knuckled and motionless in the seat beside him. Finn, on the other hand, had raided the break room and was munching rather loudly. His slouched posture and propped feet seemed to aid in earning him a few peevish glares and snarls. So he kept on crunching and slouching for the sheer enjoyment of her aggravation.

"Stuart, I've got motive and a naughty little stack of evidence that puts you behind bars for a nice, long vacation." Sal leaned forward, drawing Stuart in, preying on his fears. "Someone—maybe it was you—tried to kill Joselyn last Friday night. You better get real honest with me real fast 'cause my patience is not so good, *comprende?*"

Stuart pinched the bridge of his nose and nodded.

"So let's go back to the beginning."

"Well, Joselyn and I grew up together. We were neighbors." Stu looked away, his fists clenching. "And when my old man sought an outlet for his anger, sh—she'd patch me up, or let me hide out till the storm blew over."

Finn eyed Joselyn from his peripheral vision. This

"guardian of the helpless" a side of her he'd never envisioned. She always seemed too self-involved to fit that bill.

"Our sophomore year in high school, she moved back to the estate and I was all alone. Helpless." Stuart dug his fingers into the short nap of his buzz cut, raked his nails into his scalp several times before pressing the heels of his hands into his eyes.

"I missed her. And I knew she was having a hard time adjusting to her new school so I decided I'd look out for her—like she did for me all those years." He shook his head, coming out of a trance of memory. "But I promise you, I would never hurt her."

"Where were you last Friday night between ten and one?"

"I was in my apartment, I swear. I've been trying to stay away from Joselyn, but she inspires me. The picture of perfection that I must capture. It's like everything's all wrong when I can't see her. Even if it's only from far away. Her beauty fills my soul. It stills the rage inside. She's my Sun and my symphony. She's *everything*."

Sal grunted, apparently as nauseated by Stu's Romeo act as Finn.

Stuart darted a glance to the glass. "Is she here? I need to see her. Joselyn!" He sprang from his chair, and Finn saw Joselyn flinch, her fingers reaching for an armrest that wasn't there.

On reflex Finn captured her hand, twining his fingers with hers and bringing them to his thigh. Her eyes made contact, swimming with a fearful sadness that made him ache all over. "It's okay. You're safe." *I won't let anyone hurt you.* The words he voiced crooned so soft he wasn't sure she'd heard him. But then, her arm relaxed, and she made no effort to retract her hand.

"I saw her with that guy. Who is he anyways? He's no good for her. I saw them wrestling in her room, made me sick the way he had his hands all over her. Trying to kiss her." Sal's cheek twitched, a foreboding grin tipping his mouth like he'd acquired some ammunition. But against Stu or Finn?

"He'll use you like all the rest of them. He'll never love you like I do!" Stu screamed, banging against the glass before Sal restrained him.

Joselyn's eyes widened, her hand clamping hard.

"Hey?" Finn touched her cheek, angling her face toward him. "You don't need to listen to this. Let me take you home. They'll fill us in on the highlights tomorrow." His unruly thumb stroked the graceful curve of her cheekbone. Her skin unbearably soft. And when a few silken strands of hair caressed the back of his hand he couldn't help but test the softness there to compare, rubbing a lock of minky black hair between his fingers before tucking it behind the delicate shell of her ear.

He was on sensory overload. Every touch was impossibly electric and explicitly transcribed from his fingertips to every aching cell in his body.

Not good. Finn was enjoying their arrangement too much. And in a way he'd never anticipated.

She nodded without a word. Keeping her hand fastened in his, he helped her from her chair, and ushered her out of the FBI building. But it got him thinking ... by the time this was all over, would it be as easy to get her out of his heart?

When he climbed in bed an hour later, he almost prayed for the same old nightmare, because if he dreamed about tonight he knew he'd eventually wake up with another broken heart.

And *that* would be more hell than he'd ever endured in a fire.

"Stand right there, okay sweetheart? Don't move. It's gonna be okay."

Was it? Finn's hands trembled as he set down the little girl, wrapped in her fuzzy pink blanket, in the narrow slice of her bedroom floor unravaged by fire. God, had she even heard his instruction over the roaring blaze?

There was no way out. An infernal wall barricaded the only doorway and a massive wooden hutch was obscuring most of the barred window in the tiny cluttered bedroom.

The girl's overdosed mother had already been rescued by Ryker. She was unconscious and being tended to by the paramedics while her maybe three-year-old daughter still risked being burned alive from her neglect.

Finn's pulse hammered against his temples with a sharp ache, his blood blazed through his veins like liquid fire. The scorching heat seeming to melt the rest of his skin to match the back of his burned neck. He blinked, the haze of heat whittled away visibility to a degree, but it was the overpowering pain that fed black blotches into his sweat-and-smoke-stung eyes.

Gripping the smooth handle of the ax he was praising God he'd grabbed, he went to work hacking at the loose board beneath his feet. Swinging with ferocity he didn't know he possessed, the floor opened up with only four nearly blind, yet miraculously placed, strikes. He swept the trembling child back into his arms and eased down to the hole he created in the burning floor.

Slithering tentacles of fire nipped at his flame-resistant pants. The little girl's slender arm flung out into the encroaching flames. Finn snatched it back, and she swayed in his arms, her eyelids drooping until the final flicker of her eyelashes veiled her tormented eyes. And like the old teddy bear she clutched to her chest, she went limp.

Chapter 18

Joselyn Whyte

"**W**hat are you doing? Are you coming in?" Since she was still a bit shaken, Finn had offered to drive her Rover home from the FBI. A thoughtful gesture that didn't fit his standard MO.

But now he was acting like the night wasn't over.

The silver glow of the moon illuminated the mischief in his shadowed eyes, turning them into mysterious orbs of moonlit magic.

"That an invitation?" His lips tugged in a sly smirk, tapping a dimple in his right cheek.

"Pfff. You wish."

His deep chuckle rang in her ears, surrounding her in a melodic haze. "Relax, Joss. I'm just walking you to the door."

Oh.

Before she'd even registered his absence he was opening her door, taking her hand like some Prince Charming to aid her exit, and then pressing a guiding hand to her back along the frost-encrusted path glittering like diamond dust.

On the porch he turned to face her. With one glance at those bedroom eyes the frantic chug of her heart came to a screeching halt.

It felt like a real date, only it wasn't.

Not many real dates end after leaving an FBI interrogation. Stuffing her hands into her coat pockets, she avoided his eyes. But, oh she could feel them. Probably reading right through her BS veneer.

"This is the part when I kiss you good night, Joss." His voice rumbled like a distant thunder, charges hung in the air ready to light up the sky with one word of compliance.

Her gaze jolted to his. "Not a chance." She'd meant to insert vehemence, but when the words wobbled she realized she'd gravely missed the mark.

He smiled. His eyes much too keen. "Might want to check your contract. You see, one of the perks of our little arrangement is that I get hands-on privileges. Gotta keep up appearances."

There was no contract. Was there? Her father might have made him sign something to keep him quiet. "I don't recall that section. Might have to confer with my lawyer and get back with you."

"Trust me, it's in the rider." He slipped his arms around her waist, levering her closer until their bodies almost touched. His minty breath both hot and cool, brightened in her sinuses, caressed her face with a potent sweetness. The strength in his grip made her want to lean in the rest of the way and surrender.

But this wasn't a real date. He was probably toying with her. And if she let him know how much she wanted him, there'd be no undoing the humiliation that would follow.

"W—Why kiss me? There's no one watching us." Was it possible he had real feelings for her?

"I think tonight proves that might not be true. You never know who's watching."

She shivered at the reminder. Could Stuart really have tried to kill her? Or was the real killer still out there? Watching. Waiting to strike again.

"You must really get your rocks off by messing with me." She draped her arms around his neck, crossing her wrists, and locking into his sexy stare.

Playing along. That's all you're doing.

That cocky grin unleashed his dimples. "There are worse ways to pass the time. Now shut up and let me kiss you."

"Fine. One kiss. But so help me if your lips so much as

part, or your hands wander to restricted areas—"

Finn cut off her words at the source. Warm lips covered hers, pressing gently, sweetly … perfectly. A tenderness in his kiss she'd never imagined he was capable of. Champagne bubbles flooded her veins and tingled down to her toes.

Wow. Her toes literally curled in her boots.

Joselyn inhaled a sharp and sweet breath of his manly spice—all Finn. Her lips relaxed against his gentle pressure. Her wrists unhooked from their passive pose, preparing to weave her fingers into his hair, caress his face, pull him closer, part his lips—

But his hands hadn't moved.

Not even a twitch.

She wished she hadn't run her mouth off and put so many restrictions on the kiss that she wanted too desperately to deepen. And then as suddenly as he laid it on her, he pulled away. Mere seconds of enticing bliss vanishing before the world's softest lip-lock could take flight.

"All right then, good night." He stepped off the porch, unfazed and not even looking at her, as headlights swung into the lot signaling Archer had arrived, fulfilling his promise to give Finn a ride home.

Dang it! Joselyn kicked off the covers, breathing hard, and practically bathing in yet another unseasonal hot flash.

How many times could she relive that moment from last night? Every time she woke—hourly—she was right back on the front porch, lost in that innocent kiss. It wasn't much more than a peck, yet it tortured her brain like it was some forbidden red-hot tryst.

Good grief. It hadn't even meant anything to him. He'd made that crystal clear.

Yet here she was, swooning like some love-struck sixth-grader over her first chaste kiss with a boy.

The real problem was if that PG kiss was turning her inside out, what would have happened if it had progressed to the real thing?

Never going to happen. Couldn't happen. It would push her past the point of no return. And Finn didn't feel that way about her. He just toyed with her emotions in his selfish little game. In that regard, he and Cody were the same. They were masters of manipulation, and she had been clay in their hands.

For years she'd invoked every therapeutic technique in the book to keep those memories at bay. But this constant contact with Finn had all those scraps of memory and all the bludgeoning emotions straining against the levee she'd painstakingly built.

You're all alone. The darkness whispered in her ear, and the film of sweat coating her body instantly chilled.

Joselyn rolled onto her side and drew her knees to her chest. The loneliness pressed all around her. Both vacant and suffocating, she felt it shackling her to those old fears she'd thought she'd banished for good.

"No!" Squeezing her eyes tight, she pressed her hands over her ears.

You are not a victim. You are strong. The past can't control you. She recited the psycho-babble mantra that had once rallied her diving spirits—encouraged her to keep on living past the pain and emptiness. The betrayal and abandonment.

But now the words felt as flimsy as the muscle definition in her spindly arms and as ill-equipped for the task of untangling the tragic mess of her life.

The twisted battle of depression still had a hold on her after all these years. But though the pull was strong, Joselyn was still fighting. Searching for something more. Something worth living for. Or maybe now … something worth dying for.

She'd been prescription free for years, but she shot up in bed and dug into the top drawer of the nightstand for the simplest pleasure she knew of that could boost her spirits. Her fingers rummaged the contents of Sadie's guest room drawer, knowing there'd been some left after the last binge.

Getting frustrated, she clicked on the bedside lamp. The smooth book her hand had grazed a dozen times in search of that sweet surrendering crinkle was a Bible. A now crumpled Post-it note still clung to the surface.

This works better, I promise!

Sadie's neatly scrawled handwriting proclaimed from the yellow square. *Oh, Sadie. I wish that were true.* Humoring her, Joselyn flipped open the cover. The inside housed another Post-it.

No, I did not steal your M&M's!
Stop plotting your revenge.
Look in the second drawer.
Love you!

Joselyn snickered, amazed at the calm overshadowing her despair with only a few words from a loving friend.

That or the mystical effects of this old book in her hands.

Worth a shot.

Deciding to play the lotto, she flipped open to somewhere in the middle. It's not like she was going to read the whole thing anyway, and the juicy stuff was always in the middle.

Isaiah. Okay. Here goes.

"Fear not for I am with you, be not dismayed for I am your God; I will strengthen you, yes I will help you. I will uphold you with my righteous right hand."

A blanket of heat snuggled around her, snuffing out the shivers that had grabbed hold moments before. The endorphin rush—or whatever it was—tiptoed through her like the wonderment of a child awakening and sneaking out of bed on Christmas Eve. Unsettled, she flipped ahead a few pages.

"Fear not, for I have redeemed you; I have summoned you by name; you are mine. When you pass through the waters, I will be with you; and when you pass through the rivers, they will not sweep over you. When you walk through the fire, you will not be burned; the flames will not—"

The air sucked from her lungs, severing her words. The

room seemed to glow with warmth, becoming a refuge from the despair and loneliness that had become her constant companions. The words echoing in her mind: *When you walk through the fire, you will not be burned; the flames will not set you ablaze.*

Her heart raced. What's going on? Fear clawed at the soft wave of comfort.

An illusion?

Was her sleep-deprived brain playing tricks on her?

She was always freezing so why did the room feel so warm and cozy all of a sudden?

Fear not.

Bold, beautiful words. But much like the recited mantra from her old therapist, they were just that. Words. How would they ever be enough to slay her dragons and free her from the captivity of her fears?

"Hey Sadie, do you know if Sal is waiting outside yet?" Joselyn hollered down the hall.

"Don't see him, but you know how he is—all *tuned in* and sneaky. I swear, the man could swindle some serious scratch as a psychic." Sadie called back.

Slipping on a short oatmeal-colored sweater dress with black faux-leather leggings and over-the-knee boots, Joselyn gave the full-length mirror a glance. Adding her mother's locket on an extra-long chain, she wandered out to meet Sadie in the kitchen. She had to squint against a vivid splash of sunshine, but after the long, restless night at least it served as a reminder that today was a new day.

"I know it's bright in here. It snowed last night, and the glare through this window is intense. I need to install a new shade." Sadie poured a cup of coffee for herself and a hot water with a China Green Tips tea bag for Joselyn. "Did you sleep all right? I think I saw your light on a couple times."

"Yeah. Just a lot on my mind." *Like the kiss I shared with your brother.* "And I was going over some last-minute choreography for today."

Sadie nodded innocently, though something in her eyes silently challenged the load of bull Joselyn dished out from behind her steaming mug. "Umm hmm. So what's on the agenda today?"

Keeping preoccupied, Joselyn pulled out a bowl and a box of Lucky Charms from the cupboard and started in on breakfast. "*Mamma Mia!* practice, dress fitting for the Christmas gala—oh, that reminds me. I haven't been able to get ahold of Finn today. He's not answering his phone, and my dad was going to send over a tailor to get measurements for his tux."

"It's Saturday, I'm pretty sure he's with Kendi."

"Kendi?"

Sadie clamped her hand over her mouth. And Joselyn knew that look. It was usually followed by Sadie's firm anti-gossip stance that went something like "If you wanna know, go to the source."

Most often it was the thing Joselyn admired most about her. Sadie was a rock. Completely trustworthy and never catty. But today she wanted to know who *Kendi* was and chances were Sadie would not be humoring her request for information.

Something odd squirmed in her stomach, turning her few bites of marshmallows and sugared oats into a bundle of nerves and nausea. "Come on, Sadie."

Her eyes, so like Finn's, answered before she did. Then she sighed. "Ask Finn about her, okay. It's not my place."

"Girl, if I didn't love you so much I sure wouldn't like you right now."

"Well then, it's a good thing I'm so loveable, because I need a favor." Sadie batted her lashes.

"Name it."

"Be my maid of honor?"

A high-pitched squeal burst from Joselyn's lips about the same time her spoon clanked against the glass bowl and splashed milk on the counter. "Yes! Of course. Have you set a date yet?"

The love shining on Sadie face was brighter than sunshine on fresh snow. "New Year's Eve."

"You mean New Year's Eve in like three weeks? Are you nuts? You know how long it takes to plan a wedding?"

The closest thing Sadie had to a giggle escaped her. "I don't care. We're keeping it simple. Family and close friends. And I honestly can't wait any longer."

"You and Archer haven't …?" Joselyn didn't know why she was curious, but the question slipped out before she thought better of propriety.

"Well that's not exactly what I meant by 'I just can't wait,' but I guess you're right about that too." She shrugged, so innocent and endearing Joselyn couldn't help but smile. "He's the one, you know? Because of Ryan my dating history hasn't exactly been normal for someone my age, but we both want to do this right. But you can't imagine how hard it is. I mean, have you seen Archer? The man makes breathing sexy. He exhales, and I want to swallow it down and maul his gorgeous face."

"Yes, I've been there for one of those. Not awkward or anything."

"Hey, when the urge strikes. But man, we have this insatiable appetite for each other. We're teetering on technicalities at this point, and you know I'm far from perfect, but I've waited this long. I want to give my husband this gift on our wedding day. I want him to know that it's only for him. Forsaking all others, and all that. So we decided we needed to expedite this wedding thing, before we lose our last shred of self-control."

Joselyn suspected as much. Sadie's faith had always been right out there in the open. The genuine article. Almost enough to make a believer out of someone as broken as Joselyn. Almost.

"Well, I happen to know this girl who comes with a lot of pull," Joss tapped her lips with her index finger. "She could probably help you pull this thing off in three weeks, easy."

"She sounds like a great resource. Maybe I should ask *her* to be my maid of honor?"

"We could work out a two-fer-one deal."

Sadie barreled in for a hug, and Joselyn held on to the one constant thing in her life.

Once Sadie was married everything would change. Mist filled Joselyn's eyes as she fought back a fading doubt about losing her best friend—about being completely and utterly alone in the world.

"Okay, well I better get going. Some of those old ladies start swinging canes if they think they might miss their soaps. That or the men get to whining about their swelling feet and that their double Velcro easy steppers are aggravating their bunions." Joselyn whipped her coat around her shoulders like a cape, and clamped her purse in the hinge of her elbow. "Such a glamourous life I lead." She smiled and eased the door open a crack. The frigid breath of Old Man Winter invaded the entry, breezing right through the wool of her coat as if it were a screen door.

"Oh, hey. I almost forgot to tell you."

Joselyn turned back. Sadie's shoulder was propped casually against the wall while she inspected her unpolished fingernails.

Not good.

"Archer installed a security camera on the front porch yesterday." She smirked, her eyes lifting and nailing Joselyn in place.

Definitely not good.

"They'll have twenty-four-hour surveillance for when they can't be here all night. Thought that might help you sleep better." Sadie's smile grew impossibly wide. "Of course if nothing else, at least you'll have footage of that kiss from last night to give your memory a break."

"That's a wrap for today. Great work everyone." Joselyn packed up her bag of props, glad to be done for the day.

Rehearsal had been a struggle. Several of her allies had joined the dark side, staging protests with a few of the regular biddies about not being front and center for the newest dance sequence. Such prima donnas.

Then, one of the men had distracted all the women when his pants snagged on Mrs. Cavanaugh's walker and wound up around his knees—giving the ladies of McKnight Grove something to talk about for a solid week until the next mishap soothed poor Gene's humiliation.

But her own scarred retinas weren't distraction enough to curb her waning concentration back on task. Because Sadie knew about the kiss. Joselyn couldn't stop thinking about the kiss. And whoever this Kendi chick was might be getting a kiss of her own right now.

Oh, for shame. Her traitorous mind wandering off unsupervised again. There was also the notion of that oddly appropriate Bible verse niggling somewhere in the back of her already overloaded mind.

And then, Yia-Yia. She'd missed practice today. The nurses said she'd been up all night with a violent bout of vomiting—an adverse reaction to a medication from the new drug trial.

Losing Yia-Yia piece by piece was the hardest blow Joselyn had been dealt so far. And that was saying a lot. Joselyn held her breath each time she strode through those doors, begging God, or whoever would listen, for another good day. And so far, each day, with the unexpected moods and side effects of the disease and the drugs, she seemed to edge closer and closer to the precipice of hopelessness.

Joselyn tapped on the door and entered Yia-Yia's suite. *Please. Let it be a good day.*

Chapter 12

Finn Carson

"Great idea, son. I haven't been to Forest Park in years, and I don't think any of those kids had ever been ice skating before." Cal Carson was a bit rusty on the skates, but he seemed to have enjoyed his time chaperoning the excursion.

"Thanks, Dad. I get all my best ideas from our adventures growing up. We always had a blast wiping out on that rink."

"Glad you invited me along. Sure was tough dropping them off back at the home though, you know? Don't suppose that gets any easier."

Shaking his head in answer, Finn kept his eyes trained out the windshield, trying not to lose his focus. His Saturday routine was something he looked forward to all week, but when it was time to head home guilt crept back in until it overwhelmed all the happiness he'd absorbed from sharing such simple joys with the kids. In those moments he was in that burning house again. The smoke and the pain blinding him from the truth of the only hope for salvation resting right beneath his feet but still somehow just out of reach.

"Everything all right?" His father, though a quiet man, was never one to mince words when he felt something needed to be said. "You know this is not about you right? Because those kids deserve better than being a salve to your guilt. And if you need to work out your demons, I'd hope you'd find a better outlet. I might not be the best with words, but last I checked my ears worked pretty good and my shoulder's still as strong as yours."

"It *is* about them." Finn bristled, keeping his eyes on the tire strips etched into the snow-packed road. "Well it's more about her than all of them, but I have a vested connection there. It's still hard, but trust me, I don't need a lecture."

"If you say so." He cleared his throat. "So how are things going with you and Joselyn?"

Now there was a subject Finn was even less inclined to discuss with his father. "What does it matter? It's only an arrangement to keep her safe, Dad." Finn touched the grafts on his neck, kneading his fingers into the tense muscles.

"Well that's a crock if I've ever heard one. You've always had a thing for that girl. You'd have to be blind, deaf, and dumb not to."

Finn huffed out a laugh at his father's absent filter. "Yes. Fine. She's beautiful. I'll admit it. But it's a little more complicated than that."

"This have something to do with that slimy best friend of yours?"

"You have something against Cody? News to me."

"Well, I doubt you'd find a soul in the bi-state area who'd argue any member of the Largeman dynasty is a pillar of integrity. Cody always struck me as the kind of guy who'd step on anyone who got in his way. I never understood how you two could be so close. Couldn't find a pair more opposite."

"Sure you could. Me and Joselyn."

"Still as stubborn as the day you were born, boy. And a little too proud, though you come by that honestly." Cal shook his head. "Now, I don't know the particulars, but I've heard enough to know Cody could color your perception with a few convincing words back then. You always were very trusting, but I wouldn't be too quick to trust someone who so completely lacks a conscience. Even little white lies can have disastrous consequences if you buy in. I might not have been the most vocal father, but I sure hope I raised you better." His words, tinged with pain, turned Finn's head. The lines on his father's face were deeper than he remembered, but they only seemed to soften his eyes, making them even more perceptive and caring despite the directness of his reprimand.

His father was his hero. His strength and integrity unmatched. The kind of man who could efficiently own and operate a successful chain of garages for over thirty-five years and still get greased up to his elbows beside his team, remember each of his employees' kids names, and have the time and energy to know and raise his three strong-willed children.

He was honest to a fault. His words so reliable and discerning you could cash them in to save your hide without question. And right now, Finn wanted him to be right. It would be easier to rationalize his feelings for Joselyn if the past wasn't quite so tainted. But Cody's words after prom were seared into Finn's memory. His father hadn't been there. Finn had seen and heard firsthand.

Who do I trust?

Maybe not even himself. His own part in the affair played on a sliding scale of shame.

Resolve in his father's voice tugged Finn from his teetering blame game. "Have you asked Joselyn about it?"

Finn smiled without mirth. "This isn't the kind of thing you can drop into polite conversation." The truth from her lips would be irrevocable. It would surely break him.

"Well then, if you can't even man up, you don't deserve the girl."

"Never said I wanted her."

"Ha! That's rich."

Biting his tongue, Finn steered his old truck through his parking garage and into the spot beside his father's pristine King Ranch, relieved that the awkward conversation would soon be over.

"You remember what I always asked you kids about the truth, growing up?"

Finn nodded. The words echoing in his mind like a trusty old hymn. "You'd say, 'What's the flip side of the story?' Always made us hash out the truth from each perspective."

"Seems to me you're casting judgment based on a half-truth. Maybe even a full deception. And trust me when I say that pride can be blinding, especially when it comes to matters of the heart. Food for thought. See you at church tomorrow."

And with that loaded provoke, his father exited the truck, leaving Finn to ponder his loyalties and the murky path to the truth.

Any motivation Finn had for the rest of the day deflated after that super encouraging pep talk. After leaving Sadie's last night, he and Archer had set up a meeting tonight to go over new leads on the case and reformulate. Finn supposed he should call Joselyn and let her know about that as it was fast approaching the afternoon hours, but for starters he was comfortably sprawled on his bed and didn't know where his phone was. Plus the last thing he wanted to do after his dad's guilt trip was call Joselyn and confront those demons.

Maybe if he closed his eyes, it would all fade away. The past, this harebrained scheme, all the flirty vibes between him and Joselyn the past week, that kiss ...

Helpless to the allure of the memory, Finn was there all over again. Holding Joselyn in his arms, touching those electric lips, fighting every inch of his being that wanted to pull her closer and throw caution to the wind.

"Get a grip, man." Finn tore the memory from his mind, ripping out the page that didn't belong. Falling for Joselyn again was the last thing he needed. The list of his priorities was full without the complication of some stuck-up heartbreaker.

First, he needed to pay his penance and patch up his leaky faith. Second, he needed to man up and move past all the PTSD nonsense. Then, things would return to normal, and he could do his job and date all the beautiful women he wanted. No strings attached; no messy emotions.

But what if that's not what you really want?

"Of course it is. Who wouldn't want that?" The second he

spoke out loud to that inner voice, he thought he might need some fresh air—or professional help.

No. What he needed was a fresh dose of the truth. Rolling toward his nightstand he grabbed on to the Word—his sword against the battling in his spirit. Slipping it open to the silky marker, his eyes roamed the highlighted passage in Jeremiah 33.

"Call to me and I will answer you and tell you great and unsearchable things you do not know." Squeezing his eyes shut, the simple words reminded him of his youth. Simpler times, simpler truths.

So he prayed for truth to be exposed, for wisdom to see through the cunning lies, even the ones he told himself, and as he surrendered his control, a calm settled over him. There was no still, small voice whispering the answer in his ear, but there was peace.

And then, like a premonition or call to duty, there was Joselyn—branded into his mind, as if the imprint she'd left all those years ago had never fully faded.

Was she the answer to his tangled quest for truth? And would the truth unite them or drive the final nail into the old wound. Maybe that was best. He'd lost her before, he could survive it again.

Or maybe this was about something else. Rescuing her from the faceless enemy. Fighting the danger that lurked in the fire. Vindicating the life he'd failed to save.

Yeah. He could do this and escape with his heart intact. Prove himself and regain his footing. He simply needed to play the part. But be sure to set limits.

Of all the women he'd dated before, he'd never been tempted to lose control. Why would this be any different? This wasn't about him. Much like his time with the kids wasn't about him. It was about being a servant to those in need. And that, he could do. He was, after all, a public servant and a man of faith.

Finn rolled onto his back and stared at the blank slate of the white ceiling.

Now, if he could only erase the feeling of Joselyn's lips from his memory. The silk-spun strands of her hair between his fingers, the curve of her body against his as they snuggled close on Heston, that sugary scent of her skin that begged him to succumb to a toothache.

He was a servant, not a slave, he reminded himself despite feeling completely enslaved by the woman he shouldn't—*couldn't* want.

A shower. That's what he needed.

A cold shower.

Chapter 20

Joselyn Whyte

"Open up, Finn. I saw your truck downstairs. I know you're in there." Joselyn banged on Finn's door one more time. At first she thought it had been luck that the delivery guy had held the door and let her in, giving her an edge of surprise to catch Finn breaking his end of the bargain.

Well, he wasn't answering, his phone or his door, and she was reduced to near lunacy, assuming the role of the woman scorned. Yep, she'd officially snapped. It was time to give up, let her frustration simmer before she made an even bigger fool of herself than her recent behavior had already revealed.

But then, right when she'd talked herself down, the door swung open.

Her jaw dislocated as her eyes traversed the length of him.

Wet hair sprinkled rivulets of water down his freshly shaven face, his powerful bare chest dripping with condensation to chiseled abs, and angular hip muscles peeking above a towel. *Hello, man candy.* Who knew that tall and lean surfer dude would turn into some sort of fitness Adonis?

"Up here, Joss." The big jerk was smiling like he'd won the lottery. And he had. The super-hot, genetic lottery.

Rein it in, Joselyn. You're losing it. "Catch you at a bad time?" She tilted her head and threw in a surprising amount of sass before she breezed past him.

"Not really." He closed the door and dogged her heels.

She whirled around to warn him to back off, but he'd left enough space for her hungry eyes to admire him once more.

"Do you mind?"

His lips tugged to one side, flashing one perfect dimple. "Not a bit. Might as well help yourself to another eyeful. Part of the package deal you're paying for." He winked and then propped his large hands at the culmination of towel and, well, muscle.

"Boy, am I paying for it." *Wait, am I?*

He was suddenly closer. Only a touch away, the scent of spicy man soap on his heated skin dissolved any semblance of capable dialogue into saliva.

Why are you here again?

Close your mouth.

Stop looking at him.

Snap out of it!

"Really. Could you please put some clothes on? This steroid freak show you've got going on is messing with my brain."

The tempting smile curling on his lips and the flirty intent of his stare fired off a warning flare. The warning should have read *Imminent danger: Run for your life!* Instead that translated to *Caution: Contents extremely hot!*

"As you wish, princess."

He made a swaggering retreat, and she noticed an angry web of scars smearing down from his neck to his very well-sculpted shoulders right before he disappeared into the laundry room.

Whew! That was close!

But moments later when the scuffle of his bare feet on the wood floor signaled his return, she turned back and was equally unprepared for the updated apparel.

"Gym shorts. That's it?"

He shrugged. "It's all I had down here. Deal with it."

Did that mean he wasn't wearing anything under those shorts?

Gah! Don't go there!

He stepped into her airspace, filling her lungs with his intoxicating aftershave. "There some reason you came by, or were you just missing me?" He tapped the end of her nose with his curled knuckle.

She swatted at the gesture that made her feel five years old. "I've been trying to get ahold of you all day. Hope I'm not interrupting your afternoon delight with *Kendi*. Which, by the way, would be a breach of contract. *If* there was one." She added, baiting him.

He didn't bite. His eyes were unreadable, his expression firmer than his biceps. In fact, it looked more like *he* was reading *her*.

She'd been very nearly drooling moments before but now she had to grate down a gulp of sand dune as she stepped away from his intimate closeness. "Anyway, my dad's tailor is going to have to reschedule a time to come by and fit you for your tux for next weekend. That is, if you can fit it into your endless parade of girlfriends banging down your door for couch time." She winced, not having meant to reveal quite that much.

And of course, the jerk was smiling again, and prowling toward her. "You're pretty cute when you're jealous."

Backing away, she bumped up against a wall. "I'm not jealous."

"No? Hmm …" He stopped an inch short of touching her and bracketed his hands on the wall around her shoulders. "I think you're running out of excuses, Joss."

It was too much. Too close, too revealing. Too … few layers of clothing. She ducked quickly under his arm, but he was hot on her tail again.

"Feisty." He darted in front of her. Before she knew it her hands had reached out to his chest and forced him away. "Ooo, and handsy."

"You best watch yourself, Finn. I might be the only woman alive immune to your charms. Which means I'm liable to knock that stupid grin right off that handsome face of yours if you keep this up." The confidence in her tone came out flawless. But then, out of habit, her teeth snatched her bottom lip.

His eyes lasered to that very spot. Laughter laced his words. "All right, Snow Whyte. Show me what you got?" He raised his fists, pumped his shoulders, and dared her with his sparkling eyes.

"Don't. Call me that." She dropped her purse to the floor and tore away her coat. Bringing her hands up for sparring, she delivered her first strike.

"Not bad." His block came easy, his taunt … effortless.

Fueled by the chance to deliver the blow she'd dreamt about for years, she circled around him, searching for signs of weakness. The kickboxing class she'd taken with Sadie a few years ago had been aerobic torture, but she thought she might remember a few moves. "It was you, wasn't it? Who coined my lovely nickname?" She threw a right hook.

He swiveled out of the way. "Seemed to fit the bill. Gorgeous, frosty attitude, your last name sealed the deal." Two more jabs, he dipped and ducked like a seasoned fighter.

Her heart went on a rampage. The name had mocked her for two years after he'd graduated. It still popped up in a tabloid now and then. How had she gotten herself mixed up with this guy? Finn freaking Carson. Her worst nightmare.

But, had he just said that she was gorgeous?

Before she could ponder that further, her left fist started its pursuit of his arrogant grin. The sudden blast of an old rock song sounded from the kitchen, turning his face into the crossfire of her line drive.

Contact loosed the grip of her fist, and his head snapped back. Joselyn's breath gasped from her lungs.

He stumbled backward, bracing against the front door before slinking down to the floor.

Oh crap! She scrambled to his side, wilting to her knees. "Finn? Are you all right?" Cupping his face, she removed his hands and roamed for the injury. "I'm so sorry. Where does it hurt?" Her fingers traced the spot near his mouth where she had been aiming, where a red blossom of color was blooming against his golden skin. His eyes tightened.

She flinched, but instead of retreating fully she detoured

and ended up stroking the hair that had fallen over his forehead, testing the texture for the first time. The damp strands were as soft and thick as they looked, and for some reason, it wasn't enough of a sample until she drenched her fingers in the lush waves.

The touch was meant to be soothing, to both her curiosity and his anguish, but with his eyes still closed in pain she instinctively leaned in and pressed a kiss to the corner of his mouth, the site of her assault.

The sharp intake of his breath set off a fire alarm in her nervous system. Fingers still tangled in his hair, she pulled away and found his open eyes. Smiling eyes. Not a hint of pain to be found.

"Sucker." His voice hummed low and gravelly.

Breathing out a laugh, she pinched her eyes shut, absorbing some of the shame of her impulsiveness in private. When she got up the nerve to peek at him, she let her hands drop. "All that for one measly little kiss?"

"It worked, didn't it?"

He'd caught her. Now what?

"Just needed to see how bad you wanted to kiss me." Long, lean fingers smoothed an errant strand of hair behind her ear, then brushed beneath her jaw to tip up her chin.

"I think you got that one a little backwards."

"No matter. You can still make it up to me?" A devious lift of his eyebrow left no question to his intention.

"And what exactly am I making up for?" she asked anyway. The close quarters of their huddle swallowed her ability to think, erased her memory, and left everything behind.

"That one measly kiss, remember?"

"Ahh, yes. However shall I repay you for such an inadequate gesture?"

Every trace of teasing faded from his face. "Nothing about it was inadequate, Joss." The rough pad of his thumb traced her cheek, stoking what was merely an ember to a roaring flame.

She swallowed down the heady desire to get lost in the moment, straining to focus on his words instead of the overwhelming urge to pacify her pathetic loneliness with his casual affections.

"W-What about Dodger?"

"He's passed out on the bed upstairs."

"What about Kendi?" She bit her lip, but it was too late to quell the insecurity that quivered on the thin thread of her voice.

He touched the corner of her mouth, his thumb stroking gently. "You don't need to worry about Kendi. *You*, Joselyn Whyte, are the only girl I'm seeing."

Her heart shook at the sincerity in his eyes. She might be a fool, but right in this moment she believed him. "But Finn?" The space between them closed to a sliver.

"Yes, Joselyn?" His reply grazed her lips.

"No one's watching." She closed her eyes, her forehead resting against his. Every cell in her body vibrating with need and anticipation. And fear.

His nose nuzzled against hers; his whisper rumbling against her skin like a warning thunder. "We'll call this one practice."

Finn Carson

This was *not* the plan. This was the furthest thing from the plan. But it was all he wanted. The only thing he could think about since the second he'd swung open that door.

He'd ruined it from the start. Went completely off script. And now this ... this was the consequence of his reckless flirting.

What a price to pay.

The draw was so strong he didn't dare fight it. Their lips brushed. Once. Twice. Three times. Finn's fingers swept over Joselyn's fine-boned jaw and locked behind her slender neck. Awakening with the strength and curiosity of each simple prod, he coaxed her lips apart.

Have mercy.

She was the sweetest thing he'd ever tasted. Her lips plush. The exploration soft. *Perfect.* Her dueling response somehow both passionate yet timid in the most unraveling way.

Something broke loose in his chest, expanding until the band of reserve that kept his armor in place finally snapped. Bit by bit, touch by touch, the weight of pretense fell away until no shield remained. Full contact. Being defenseless shouldn't feel so freeing.

She melted into him like hot wax. Her arms curled up under his with a reverent caress and her hands gripped his shoulders, the intensity in her touch setting his blood ablaze. Man on fire! The final shred of his restraint went up in flames.

He groaned into the kiss, holding nothing back, consumed by a need he never knew existed. She took it all and returned it with such fervor and tenderness he wanted to hold his breath to preserve the moment. A moment so surreal and fragile he feared if he stopped to exhale it might slip away like a wisp of smoke. So instead he breathed her in, prolonging the unbearable sweetness. Holding her tighter. Drinking in the desperation of her kiss and feeding his own. She shifted over him, squirming to get closer still and surprised him with a sharp nip of her teeth.

That was the moment he lost it.

His mind. His willpower. And every last conviction he carried. *Poof.*

As if a separate entity, his hand skimmed the smoking-hot stretch of leather over her slim thigh until he touched the warm satin skin of her waist, splayed his palm over the small of her back and worked his fingers beneath the band with a slight squeeze. The whimper of need that escaped her throat did nothing to douse the fire now raging out of control.

The second her cool hands settled on his stomach he—

What was that?

The bang on the door against his back barely registered at first. But it came again with more force, breaking the spell.

Their lips wrenched apart, the loss as agonizing as ripping off a patch of his own skin. Her labored breaths against his lips were nearly his undoing. And then, he saw her face. *Lord Almighty.* Desire pooled in her exotic eyes, wonder lit from beneath her creamy skin, and a coy sweetness touched her mouth before she folded in her freshly stung bottom lip.

He was mesmerized by the soft flesh he'd just claimed. The craving for more instant and so fierce his taste buds screamed for reunion like a dying flame gasping for oxygen. He traced his knuckles across her cheek, then let his thumb skim her perfect mouth. She drew breath around his touch, the shimmy of air around his skin flashed like glitter through his veins.

He was defeated. Done for. Even his heart was threatening

to expire in surrender, whooped harder than ever, even during his Combat Challenges.

But what was she feeling? Was this as one-sided as it had been before? Was it possible a kiss so full of honesty could be wrapped up in deception?

He searched her face for affirmation, and all his doubts crumbled. Her lavender-blue eyes softened, blinking languidly as he leaned in the last inch—

Another knock made her flinch before he reached paradise. Shifting back, a shiver of goose bumps became the only evidence of her intimate touch.

"Expecting someone?" she whispered. The words suggested a change of topic, but her eyes continued their current conversation.

The last thing he wanted was to relinquish the moment, the uncertainty of a repeat performance igniting his greedy desire to ignore the visitor and set the world on fire once more. But the killjoy persisted. "No, I'm not."

Finn helped her off the floor and took a deep breath—void of Joselyn's heady drug—to expel the lingering and reeling effects of their first real kiss. "Yeah, yeah. I'm coming!" He snapped and yanked open the door.

"Took you long enough. Some hot little number down the hall let me in. Have you hit that? Because I'm considering it."

Cody.

"Now's not a good time, Large."

But it was no use. Even though Finn blocked his entry, Cody had still shoved open the door. "What, you hiding a chick in there or som—Oh ... I see ... Hello, *Snow Whyte.*" With a pointed glance at Finn's bare chest Cody's eyes narrowed again on Joselyn with untamed hostility. "I see not much has changed."

Staying uncharacteristically silent, Joselyn shrank behind Finn's back.

Huh. He'd never seen Joselyn yield to anyone. And he hadn't exactly imagined the way this confrontation might someday play out, but something wasn't adding up. Now that he thought about it, he realized he hadn't seen Joselyn and Cody together, in the same room, since prom. In fact, Joselyn hadn't returned to school for the remainder of the school year after that night. The next time he'd seen her was with Sadie almost a year later when he'd come home from college on spring break and they were full into hating each other's guts.

Understanding of the situation had yet to unfold before his eyes. Based on the way iron bars seemed to slam down over her expression, something was missing from this story, and whatever it was, it was not a topic she would discuss lightly. If at all.

Their relationship might be changing, but that didn't mean she would trust him enough to fill in the gaps.

Did he trust her enough to let her see the scars that marred him? Would he ever be ready to open that vein and bleed out all his failures? Exposing the unworthiness that lived and breathed behind the smokescreen? He shook his head.

A playback of Cody's words resurrected from the time capsule in his mind. The echoing voice buzzed against the tight string of tension in the room.

"She said guys like you were beneath her. Can you believe that? That it was laughable you thought you might actually have a chance with someone like her. What a friggin' witch, huh?"

The simple dismissal had burrowed deeper and deeper for years, the beastly resentment growing with nowhere to claw but inward, turning the hurt boy into a scarred man he almost didn't recognize.

Had she even said those things back then? Cody's account of her cutting words didn't seem to fit now that he was getting to know her again.

But so what if she'd rejected him back then? That was ten years ago. She had just kissed him like he'd never been kissed in his life. And it was more than some flighty moment of attraction. It felt … significant. He restrained himself from touching his lips to reawaken the sensation. Instead he stole a glance over his shoulder.

Something broke through the solid ice in her eyes. One blink, and the fracture he'd seen froze back over. But that glimpse was unmistakable. And it was the last thing he'd expected to see elicited from an encounter with Cody. Not annoyance. Not anger. Or shame. Not any other thing that could fall an ounce short of … terror.

Slamming the door in Cody's face was the only thing that made sense. Wrapping Joselyn's trembling body in his arms was the only thing he wanted to do. So he did both—feeling like he was drawing a line in the same old sand and had finally chosen the right side.

He could only hope his instincts wouldn't fail him again. That maybe his dad's discerning legacy might begin to find solid ground in his son. Finn needed it now more than ever. Joselyn's life was in his hands, and Lord knew, that was a dangerous place to be.

As he held Joselyn, he realized he didn't have a clue who was trying to kill her or why she might be terrified of Cody. But he knew with a rising certainty that he wanted— *needed*—to protect her. And that his dad was right. There were two very different sides to this story.

He intended to find out exactly what they were.

"Joselyn?" Finn cradled her stiff body, trying to absorb her fear and assure her safety. But her arms didn't surround him, the rigid plank of her stance all but screamed, "Back off!" So he leaned back, searching her beautiful face for answers.

Looking up at him from dewy lashes, a shimmering trail of tears sparkled like stardust on her ivory skin. Gathering her face in his hands, he couldn't help himself. He drew her in and touched his lips to hers, his thumbs soothing away the tears he tasted.

Right when he thought he'd pushed too hard to comfort her, her body relaxed, surrendered, and her mouth fused with his.

Her hands skimmed up his chest until her arms encircled his neck, and then fueled by some sort of desperation, she pulled him tight.

And the fuse lit again. The charge of her lips frying his nervous system until white hot adrenaline flared from his racing heart. *Mine. Finally, mine.* He deepened the kiss, crushing her to him just as desperately, savoring the feel of her needing him, and realizing how much he needed her too.

Oh, Joss. Why did I wait so long to do this?

So he made up for lost time. Much too soon Joselyn jerked out of his arms. The regret in her eyes should have been sobering, but it only renewed the challenge. Nothing sounded more satisfying than drawing her back, replacing that haunted look with the dreamy, thoroughly ravished one she'd sent his way before Cody's interruption.

She touched her mouth, her eyes threatening more tears. "Finn ..." His name on her lips sounded like a plea.

Answering, he took a step toward her. But she backed away, her eyes burning into his.

"Stop. We can't. It's too—"

The ring of her cell phone severed her words. Clearly grasping for an escape, she lunged toward her purse. He circled her wrist before she answered the phone, speaking firmly over the jingle. "*Too* what, Joss?"

Turning away, she tugged her hand free to take the call. "Hello?"

Undeterred, he spun her around to face him. She lifted her gaze for a moment before fixating on the floor. Her eyes held a sadness he'd often mistaken for apathy. His quest for truth remained locked away behind those heavily guarded eyes, and he felt his window of opportunity closing by the second.

He was about to pluck the stupid thing from her ear when his own phone demanded his attention. With a huff, he snatched it up off the kitchen counter. "What?"

"Whoa. Wanted to see if you're gonna show up for our meeting sometime this century." Archer's smug tone pinched a nerve.

Finn checked the clock and squeezed his eyes shut. He was over thirty minutes late. How long had he been kissing Joselyn? It hadn't felt nearly long enough, but it appeared they'd slipped into a blissful black hole and burned more daylight than he'd realized.

His hope for enlightenment about Joselyn and Cody—and him and Joselyn, for that matter—had slipped through his fingers. He wouldn't be getting any answers tonight. At least not the ones he wanted.

Chapter 22

Joselyn Whyte

"**W**hat! Those little snakes!"

Her father's unfortunate news and misplaced blame almost made her forget about kissing Finn. Almost. The rampage also made her want to plunge her fist into someone's nose.

Finn was the only person present, and if she utilized him as an outlet for her violent urge, well, then she'd probably end up trying to make it all better, and in turn, make it worse. Again. Besides, he had a very nice nose. Nice lips. Nice … too many things she'd experienced quite thoroughly moments before.

As the blows kept coming from her father in the form of some fabricated media scandal she couldn't care less about, her trusty self-preservation instincts kicked in, muting his ranting, and instead, called upon the feel and taste of Finn's lips. Both tender and savage, she'd never felt more alive— and terrified. She wasn't sure where she'd found the strength to pull away but wished she had held on a few minutes longer.

Because if she could've stayed out of her head, for once, she might still be in his arms. But those arms were laced with deception of the most treacherous kind. Because although they felt like the safest, most enviable place in the world, Joselyn knew, tucked in Finn's powerful embrace, she was anything but safe.

Her emotions were spiraling, and there was too much baggage she hadn't yet sorted out. Too much history. Oh, her shrink would have a field day!

But it wasn't only the kiss—though she had to admit she'd never experienced anything quite like it. Something about him was drawing her in. She'd always had a weak spot for him, and yet she'd had no problems ignoring him for the past ten years. So this was different. Unsettling.

Nothing about Finn seemed to line up with the boy she'd known in high school. In Joselyn's experience, people didn't change for the better.

Sure, he'd adopted an irritatingly arrogant persona, but even that felt like a front.

And then Cody had shown up. A hot swirl of bile churned her stomach at the mere thought of him. How could *this* Finn still be friends with that jerk? The inconsistencies were dizzying. A sudden flood of doubts had hijacked her brain and made her retreat, when honestly, all she really wanted to do was succumb to ignorant bliss and fall into Finn's arms all over again. To feel wanted. Maybe even cherished. Even if only for a moment.

And wasn't that pathetic. She was a smart woman. She should know better than be swayed by the man's—possibly extraordinarily acted—affections. Having been wrong before, she knew the consequences were more destructive than a simple case of heartache.

"… Joselyn! You have to fix this!" Her father's voice boomed through the ear piece, the sheer volume of his command about knocked the phone from her hand.

"Uh, okay. How?" She curbed the default sarcasm begging to take more creative liberties with her response. Instead she folded an arm around herself, gripped the fabric at her waist, and awaited the verdict.

"You know how. Make a public appearance. Prove them wrong. I'll set it up. Monday night, the day after tomorrow. And Joselyn, you better sell it this time."

The metaphorical slamming from her father's end made her flinch. Like this was all her fault? The tabloid mongers could weave a web of lies at the drop of a hat, and *she* was responsible?

Sell it, he'd ordered. Those choice words wedged deeper, driving like an ice pick into her heart. As if she was nothing more than a call girl. A pawn. Declan Whyte had weighed his daughter's stock, cashed in the shares that suited his gains, and dumped the rest. The stab of his manipulation and neglect never ceased to hit their mark.

She lowered the phone, and as if looking into an oracle's glass ball of misfortune she could see it. Her future—however long or short it may be—controlled by the ruthless dictator.

"Come on." Finn tugged at her arm, snapping her out of the hellish vision. "We've got a meeting with Archer and Sal."

His voice slipped through her like warm syrup. That dreamy baritone held some mystical power, enslaving her to its commands. She followed like a mindless drone even when he scooped up her coat and eased it on from behind.

Was she a commodity to Finn too? Otherwise, why would he volunteer for this? And why would he kiss her like that? Did she dare hope that this was about something more? That maybe he really did care about her? Hope swelled in the vicinity of her heart.

Spinning her around as if helping a child, he buttoned her coat and tied the belt around her waist. She noticed he was now fully dressed—thank goodness—and without meeting her eyes he lead her out the door.

How long had she been zoned out?

She supposed it didn't matter. Time in Finn's presence seemed to defy the laws of nature. And she was not nearly loathe enough to note that with her new assignment, and the now intimate knowledge of his kiss, it was going to be more difficult than ever to avoid those lawless lips of his.

The atmosphere in the cab of Finn's truck was strange. Stilted and silent and strange. She couldn't take it anymore.

She needed something to fill the void. Anything to distract her from the alluring Finn-smell and the cloak of fog hugging the windows as if hiding them away in their own cozy cocoon.

"That was my dad who called."

"Okay. What'd he say?" His eyes flickered away from the road, and his hand came to rest over her anxiously knotted fingers.

She stared at the curious thing, inexplicably rough and gentle at the same time—kind of like his kiss. "Some photographer snapped a picture of us outside the firehouse the other day."

She remembered the agony on his face, still wishing she knew what had caused it, and knowing that the captured moment could've been interpreted any number of ways by the media. The thought of his pain displayed on some trashy tabloid for the whole world to see made her insides ache.

Without thinking, she turned over his warm hand and threaded her fingers through his. "Anyway, they, uh, spun this story about 'Trouble in paradise' and 'The Ice Princess drives another one away' and something about you 'Heating things up' with another woman." She shook her head, hating these intrusions into her life.

When her father had mentioned something about "another woman" it hadn't registered in her kissed-senseless brain. But now, she remembered those words all too well and the familiar doubts crept back in.

"But we weren't even fighting? That's all ridiculous."

"Doesn't matter. My father is livid, and he insists we do damage control."

Finn's wagged his eyebrows, his grin downright wolfish. "I think I like where this is headed."

Nothing could be done about her answering smile so she met his gaze and owned it. "I thought you might."

"Sorry we're late." Finn hurried her through the door of

Archer's office. Not one for sentimentality, Archer's professional space housed a commanding wooden desk, several tasteful and minimalist pieces of furniture, and two filing cabinets. There was a mess of papers tacked to one wall and a few stacks piled on the desk, but otherwise the space was clean, efficient.

Archer looked more amused than irritated by the delay, and she could have sworn she saw Finn blush as he slumped into a chair in front of the desk.

Sal lifted his feet from their propped position on the boxy leather sofa and offered Joselyn a seat. When she sat he sidled over and draped his arm across the cushion. "How you holding up, sweetness?"

"I'm fine."

Finn's glare absorbed her and Sal's proximity. Caveman.

"We did get some bad press though. That always stings. Honestly, I've never understood their interest. Makes no sense."

Sal squeezed her in a side-hug. "You're sensational, they just can't help themselves." He winked, stark white teeth flashed against tan skin in the form of a saucy grin. "You look amazing, by the way."

Sal was an affectionate person. It was his nature, so Joselyn didn't think anything of it. His time on her protective detail was making them fast friends.

And if that made Finn's fists clench and a slight growl come from his general direction, well, he'd have to deal.

Then there was Archer. His crap-eating grin so wide Joselyn thought he might split a lip or burst into laughter at any moment. It would appear he and Sal had cooked up the little ruse to toy with Finn. She didn't know why, exactly, nor why Finn was suddenly acting territorial, but it was pretty entertaining.

"Oh, you know what? You've got an eyelash." Sal's fingers brushed her cheek, his eyes flashing with secret amusement. "Your skin is like silk. Are you this soft all ov—"

"All right!" Finn erupted from his seat. "That … chair is really uncomfortable. Sal, switch me."

Sal and Archer cut up with laughter, and Finn rolled his eyes, awaiting Sal's removal from his new spot. "Can we start the meeting now?"

But before they could kick off, a woman popped her head in Archer's office. "Hey, Archer. You got a sec?" Sal stiffened next to her with a jolt, making Joss take a closer look. Whoa. She was secure enough to admit that this woman, with caramel skin and vibrant amber-colored eyes, was—for lack of a better word—*arresting*.

Sal leapt from the couch like his pants were on fire. "I'll get it." He nearly tripped over his feet but was out the door before anyone could blink.

Still chuckling, Archer shook his head, wiping the corner of his eye. "That's Candice, our new ME. Sal's got it bad. The poor dope."

Settling into Sal's vacated spot, Finn's thigh snuggled up against her leg and he leaned back, stretching his arm along the couch. Unlike Sal, Finn's contact was like a lightning rod. The awareness was so painfully acute, and absurd, she could feel the faint exhale of his breath brushing her skin. The beat of his heart pulsing against her side.

"I guess we should get started." Archer chimed into her thoughts, saving her from herself. "We sorted through the list of terminations from your father's companies from the past several months. Not a small list. I didn't know Whyte Enterprises had extended into so many different industries. I thought it was mainly manufacturing."

"It started out that way. But when that took off he started buying up other companies and slapped his name on them. I've lost track—other than the factories, the cable company, the chemical plants, a few laboratories, distributors, and a small chain of luxury hotels."

"Hotels, huh?" Finn nudged her leg with his. "I see perks in my future."

"I'm sure once my father wins his precious campaign he'll

be overcome with gratitude and toss you something for your trouble." She'd meant to joke, but as the words snowballed she was reminded that this was most likely a business transaction. Finn might be getting some big payout for pretending to like her.

Her spine went rigid.

"You two can plan your honeymoon later." Archer grinned at Finn, but Joss couldn't bring herself to look at him.

"Moving on. So far we're looking at these thirteen out of several hundred employees that were fired or laid off the past few months. They were the most disgruntled of the bunch, and we have confirmed the whereabouts of most of the others that drew red flags from the bureau physiatrist. Wanted to see if any of them look familiar." Crossing the room, Archer extended a file with eight-by-ten enlargements of old employee keycard photos from her father's various companies.

As Joselyn took the stack and flipped through, she started second-guessing every sliver of recognition she saw in the smiling faces.

One guy kind of looked like a clerk at her grocery store. Another reminded her of an excessively allergic blind date she'd been on six months prior. Poor guy could hardly get a word out. Shame too. He'd seemed nice. And cute. At least, from what she could tell between sneezes, which, with that much repetition, tended to make anyone's face pinched and red and unfortunately repugnant. But it all had proven her curse: She was "good-guy" repellent and catnip to dirt bags. It was hopeless.

Poring over the pictures again, she knew she'd over-analyzed their faces. These were not the same guys.

She shook her head and extended the file back to Archer, praying no one noticed how much the pages shook in her hand.

Finn started to reach out, but then pulled back and forked his broad fingers through his hair. "I, uh, just thought of something. Joss, you said your dad owned a few laboratories?"

"Yeah. Some of those were hit pretty hard by the economy, but they're surviving. Why, what is it?"

"Well, you were drugged. I don't know what type of labs, but is it possible that one of them has that Seco—whatever it's called—stuff? Maybe one of those red-flagged employees had access to it before they were terminated?"

"I don't think they're in the same vein, but I'll check it out." Archer scribbled on his notepad. "Oh, and the Five-Alarm Arsonist is off the table for now. The fires he started weren't nearly as destructive as yours and none of the other victims were drugged. In fact, none of them appeared to be targeted. More the wrong place at the wrong time.

"Plus, the fire team hasn't had any trouble identifying the accelerants and origins of the other fires. Since your case doesn't fit his profile, we're thinking whoever targeted you picked the date to throw us off."

Joselyn could only nod at first. "W-What about Stuart?" That drew a glare from Finn, one she ignored.

"Looks like he alibied out for the night of the fire. But we did confirm he was the one following you guys in the Grand Prix. Borrowed it from his landlord. The young lady, Cheryl Thomas, had quite the distaste for you, Joselyn. We looked into her, but she's clean. Other than her poor taste in men."

"I don't know any Cheryl Thomas. What's she got against me?"

"It would seem Stuart utilizes her company from time to time. She said he talks about you constantly ..." Archer paused, the look on his face said he didn't care to finish that thought, but he did, and Joselyn wished he hadn't. "Says he asked her to dye her hair black and that he, uh ... calls out your name."

"*Eww.*" She'd skipped lunch, but what remained of her breakfast threatened an encore.

"They're still holding Stuart for the other violations, and we're working to get more information. Personally, the guy gives me the creeps—and that's saying something." Propped against the desk, Archer looked ill at ease. His solid confidence and ruthless discipline were as dependable as Joselyn's chronic loneliness. That meant the restless vibe she sensed alluded to something he wasn't saying. Knowing Archer, she was fairly certain she wasn't ready to hear whatever it was.

Summoning the last of her nerve, Joselyn untied the belt from her coat and slipped it from her shoulders. Was she dressed right? Would her ensemble broadcast that she was an outsider like a glaring scarlet letter?

Having only attended a few staunch Masses while visiting her father's home in Scotland with her parents as a kid, she hadn't the slightest idea what to expect.

Yia-Yia had believed in God, but she wasn't the church-going type. And that suited Joselyn fine growing up. One less place she would be scrutinized for her family. Well, maybe family wasn't the right word. Name, wealth, notoriety, maybe.

Family *was* the right word for the thing she desired most, but for some reason, was deprived of time and again.

Sadie had assured her that jeans were acceptable, but it felt wrong. Sacrilegious or something. So Joselyn donned a long bohemian-styled smock dress and a black shrug from her store. Thinking it was still casual but more acceptable than jeans.

But being here now, walking through the church doors with Sadie and Archer, the breezy fabric felt like an iron vest, constricting its fashionably woven threads to wring the air from her lungs.

What if the shrinking material looked too tight? Showed too much cleavage? Pressing her hand to her chest, she felt her heart hammer beneath her palm. *Breathe.*

She wasn't overly busty, but she checked herself anyway, smoothed her fingers over the straight neckline to the empire waist, assuring the propriety of her attire. If nothing was hanging out, then why did she feel like she'd already made a spectacle of herself? *"People will stare, make it worth their while."* She remembered one of Yia-Yia's favorite Harry Winston quotes but couldn't rile any confidence. People *were* staring at her. They were smiling like she was a few frayed threads away from unraveling, and they couldn't wait to cash in on the next front-page exposé.

To confirm her paranoia she tugged on Sadie's non-Archer clad arm and spoke low through a plastered-on grin. "Are these people just inordinately friendly or have I already committed a cardinal sin?"

"Uh, I'd go with option number one." Sadie laughed and linked arms with Joselyn, steering their little trio toward another door opening to what Joselyn gathered was the chapel. Sanctuary? Whatever.

Someone was flagging Sadie down, so Joselyn untangled her lifeline from Sadie's arm and asked Archer for directions to the restroom.

Wandering the halls like a foreigner in a strange land, Joselyn came upon an opening for a child's play area. Squeals and giggles fragranced the air with an equally foreign but unimaginably sweet aroma of innocence that worked to sedate her nerves.

Watching the families, with babes clinging to their daddies' legs, something about the scene seemed peaceful. Normal. Joselyn couldn't recall the feeling but wished for it, wished back on every day of her lost childhood.

Absorbing the hum of chattering little voices was calming until a couple rounded the corner and Joselyn's breath hitched in her throat.

The young man was tall and blonde, average by all accounts. But it was his wife and daughter that completed the comparison. The woman had porcelain skin with inky-black hair and pale blue eyes—the little girl, a perfect carbon copy of her mother.

The man touched the small of the woman's back and

whispered something near her ear. Joselyn remembered her father's affinity for affection with her mother—as if the slightest contact was the joy and privilege of his life. It was clear he had loved Charisma Whyte. He had doted on her and looked on her with such adoration. And back then, Joselyn had felt loved by him too. If only as a reflection of his love for his wife, but it had been enough.

Freefalling into some vague fissure of memory, Joselyn remembered for a single fleeting moment what it felt like to have a family. To know you are loved as surely as the sun rises each morning.

The man plucked the little girl with outstretched arms from her mother. She wrapped her tiny hands around his neck, and he kissed the tip of her nose. "Love you, munchkin."

"Wuv you, Daddy." The timid little sound of love drifted to where Joselyn stood, and all she was missing came flooding back. Her mother, whose life was ripped away like one perfect, beautiful wave, crushed in an instant, and dragged back from the shores to oblivion. Her father, his love revoked when she'd needed it the most. And now Yia-Yia …

Drinking in the view of her past life for one more moment was all she could handle before she darted into the restroom, composed herself in the stall, and then headed back out to the sanctuary.

The music hadn't registered through her emotional fog until a rush of sound gave way from the doors. This was nothing like the Mass she remembered. The potent melody of a sort of rock ballad enveloped her, gluing her flats to the floor behind the last row of chairs.

And this time, no one was looking at her. Rather, they were immersed in this atmosphere of praise. Recklessly abandoned and pouring out their love. And though Joselyn didn't fully understand it, it was beautiful. Safe.

Free.

And then the words seeped into the barren places of her soul.

You unravel me, with a melody
You surround me with a song
Of deliverance, from my enemies
Till all my fears are gone.

A hand slipped into hers, and for a moment, she wasn't sure it was real or imagined. Dream or reality.

From my mother's womb
You have chosen me
Love has called my name.[1]

When she lifted her eyes, and saw the way he was looking at her, she still didn't have her answer.

---

[1] Bethel. "No Longer Slaves." By Brian Johnson, Jonathan David Helser, Joel Case. *We Will Not Be Shaken.* Bethel Music, 2014.

Chapter 23

Cold sweat stung his eyes as he wormed through the dank space. Here he was reduced to some lowly creature while she was out gallivanting around town like she didn't have a care in the world. She should never have had warning of her imminent death. But now that she had, he'd expected caution and cowering. When he'd recovered from the blind fury of his failed mission, something in him had looked forward to her languishing in the terrifying knowledge of what was coming. What was inescapable. And yet … she was going about life as usual. Shopping, running errands, attending *church*, and getting cozy with that effing firefighter who'd ruined it all.

His anger swelled in his throat, nearly choking him.

Maybe they should both pay for this.

If he timed it right, he might get twice the satisfaction in the finale. And there'd be no escaping this time. Pearls of icy water soaked through his sock cap. The plastic over his boots making a faint crunch in the dark, putrid slush.

The girl might not be as high maintenance as the tabloids would have people believe, but one thing she absolutely was—predictable. And that meant he would do what he does best and follow through with his plans.

He got into position and looked up. Perfect. He couldn't bring himself to smile, but the tension in his jaw waned, a sense of purpose like a charge of antifreeze snaking through veins long since devoid of warmth.

Oh yes, she was playing into his plans quite beautifully.

Chapter 24

Finn Carson

"What is she doing here?"

He probably should be asking himself the same question. Yes, he'd tailed Sal, who was tailing Joselyn. Tailed them, and lost them. And then Finn got to drive around for another thirty minutes trying to uncover the slip.

He'd almost given up until he turned into the private drive of an assisted living facility and spotted Sal's unmarked car about a hundred yards from Joselyn's Rover—parked in the first reserved spot.

The tailing exercise was a good gauge of Sal's competence, Finn rationalized. A test, if you will. But that wasn't why he'd done it.

Something about the familiar way Sal had put his hands on her the other day had Finn restless. They'd been poking the bear to rile a reaction, he got that, but it made him question all the time Joselyn and Sal were spending together. And how much of it was actually *together*.

Finn couldn't stand the possibility of getting duped all over again, so he was seeking out confirmation of where she was always sneaking off to with her undercover protection.

Finn could easily identify what he was feeling. Jealousy. It surged the exclusive and well-worn Joselyn-only path straight to his heart, just like it had ten years ago.

Why he was suddenly so possessive of Joselyn was a question with a more difficult answer, so he ignored the frightening implications his heart was sending to his brain.

He didn't consider himself a man that scared easily. Nor

did he consider himself easily fooled. But Joselyn was his Achilles' heel. Her hypnotic beauty a kind of rare kryptonite for his usually sharp instincts.

Yesterday at church he thought he'd breeched her defenses. She seemed … softer somehow. And when he'd utilized his "hands-on in public" privileges, she'd been a willing participant. Like when he'd held her hand, tucked her under his arm, whispered against her peppermint hair. Even now, the phantom smell of her sweet and spicy shampoo invaded his senses as if she were sitting right next to him.

He groaned at the stupidity of it. Had he learned nothing the first time around? He needed to snap out of it before he did something he might regret.

Like what you're doing right now?

After parking his truck what seemed a half a mile from the entrance—and Joselyn's VIP spot—he strode toward the door, stubbornly undeterred by his failing common sense.

The bitter wind stole though his Carhart, and the ripped edge of his dark jeans sluiced through the soggy remnants of melting snow. He shoved his hands in his pockets, shielding the exposed skin from the biting fragments of ice that hung in the air, and hastened his steps until he entered the building.

The reception wasn't much warmer. The hearty woman behind the counter had a scowl to rival a bulldog's. He hadn't been expecting a security checkpoint and felt a prickle of nerves kindle heat in his palms.

"Hi, my name is Finn Carson. I'm looking for Joselyn Whyte."

The middle-aged woman hocked up a disgusted grunt. Her dusty brown hair was pulled back in a nubby no-nonsense pony tail, which she tightened before she spoke. "Now *she's* getting visitors? You people must think you run the world."

Well then. Time to fight dirty. Finn dialed up the dimples.

"Not the world, no ma'am. The Almighty is on that one. Too big a job for lil' ol' me. These hands might be able to wield a Halligan and hose over at Kirkwood Station 1," he paused to wink, the woman's snarl softening when faint red splotches colored her jowls, "but their main job right now is taking care of the little handful that strutted through here not too long ago. Black hair, blue eyes, legs for days. That one's mine. She grows on you. Now, you're doing one heck of a fine job guarding this place. Top notch. But if you could point in the direction of my girlfriend I'd—"

"Joselyn's *boyfriend*?" Another woman emerged from behind the desk. She was about the same age but was wearing a smile and a sassy crop of blonde hair. The cranky one abruptly turned and stalked off.

"Yes, ma'am. Is she here?"

"Wow. Good for her. I'm Rosie, a friend of your girlfriend's." Rosie stuck out her hand, and Finn shook it, having to tug his fingers back when the woman held on too long. "Sorry, it's just Joselyn's never had a man come visit her here before. Let alone one that looks like you."

Finn's mind worked to make sense of it all. Had Joselyn had other visitors here, female ones? Was that what this woman was implying? Was Joselyn visiting someone here? Or perhaps the Whytes were benefactors or something? But then she'd mentioned something about her grandmother. But she hadn't said where she lived—or anything specific really.

"Go on back. They're in the common room. The rehearsal shouldn't last much longer. Have to keep 'em pretty short or we get some dozers."

He had no idea what the woman was talking about but thanked her and started down the hall. And then he heard something.

The further he walked, the more the swelling sound intrigued him. It was definitely music. It sounded like … show tunes? Finding his way in, no one noticed Finn settle into a seat near the back of the room.

He heard her before he saw her. She emerged from the right side of the cardboard set, an elderly woman linked with her arm, and they were singing. It sounded like Joselyn was helping the older lady remember her lines, but even through the clutter of noise, the sweet sound of her voice called out to him. He sat there grinning like a fool, and there wasn't a thing he could do to stop it. Sort of like when she accidently sang aloud in the car. He might as well have folded right then and there.

Dragging himself from the trance-like state of awe, he focused on her movements. She was dancing, simple steps—guiding a line of old folks with sparkling prop canes in the choreography she seemed to know quite well. It dawned on Finn then that Joselyn was running the show, and it was quite possibly the most adorable thing he'd ever seen.

The music stopped, and she crossed the stage to the male lead. "Okay, Harvey. Do you need a break, or are you ready to rehearse the next scene? The one where you dance with Helena."

The man hacked out a cough before he could muster any dialogue. "You mean I don't get to practice with you?" To Finn's surprise—and by the looks of it, Joselyn's too—the man stepped up and took Joselyn in a waltz stance, only his one hand strayed *way* south and grabbed a handful.

Joselyn yelped, jumping back, and Finn couldn't restrain a burst of laughter. She whipped her head around. Her eyes, even from a distance, seemed to bulge from their sockets. Turning back, she pulled at her shirt, brushing her hands over her hips, and clearing her throat to command the room and silence the heckling.

"Harv, I've warned you twice now. What was it you called it? T&A? *Yeah*, restricted areas, pal. One more strike, and I'm sending you back to knitting circle. If you'd like to continue to participate keep those hands to yourself, mister. Last chance."

The man simply shrugged, and a few of his silver-haired buddies were indiscreetly offering fist bumps.

"All right, everyone. Let's call it for today. Great job with the choreography. It's really coming along. Oh, and Greta, I'll have those costumes for you to hem here tomorrow."

She moved a few props out of the way and then helped a woman into a wheelchair, avoiding looking at him, which told him quite a bit about how much she appreciated his intrusion. And then, she was in pursuit, those violet-blue eyes blazing her trail.

She didn't say a word but grabbed his hand, yanked him up from his chair, and towed him out of the room.

"Sal is a dead man. He's not getting any more treats." She tugged her hand free and slapped her arms across her chest.

"What are you talking about?" He smiled at the stubborn set of her chin, making her gorgeous glaring eyes light with even more fire.

"Sal told you I was here."

Finn shook his head. "I followed you. Well, I got lost for a while too, but I was curious where you two kept sneaking off to. And now that I'm here, I'm not sure I fully understand."

"You followed us? Geez. You could have just asked, you little snoop!"

"Would you have told me?"

She huffed, and she looked so stubborn and cute Finn took a step forward and grinned down at her. "I rest my case. So what is all this?"

"*Mamma Mia!*"

Laughing a little, he shook his head. "Yeah, that part I got. What are *you* doing here?"

"I have a feeling this line of questioning might get tiring. I'll give you three."

"Three?"

"Questions."

"And you'll answer anything I ask?"

"Within reason."

"Okay. I'll try again. What are you doing here?"

"Directing the Christmas musical."

"Aww, come on. You gotta give me more than that."

"Hey, I answered your question. That's one." She propped her hands on slender hips hugged to perfection in painted-on denim. Finn fought the urge to thread his arms around to her back, crowd her closer, and perhaps pull a Harvey. She'd probably deck him again. He smiled at the memory. And all that followed.

Worth it.

"Fine. Why?" He quirked his brow.

"I do it every year. Yia-Yia used to love musicals."

"Yia-Yia?"

She nodded her head back toward the room.

"Yia-Yia lives here?"

"Yep, and that's three." Turning on her heels, she started back toward the common room, but Finn hooked her arm and dragged her back until she was nestled against him.

"I got gypped on that last one." He laced his finger at the small of her back, keeping her in place—though she didn't seem inclined to resist.

"I never said I'd be fair."

"And you might recall I don't like to share. You owe me one more for Harvey's trip to 'restricted areas.' Either that or I get my own helping to even the score." He'd never tire of teasing her.

Her face lit into an enigmatic smile that revved his engine while she primly waggled a finger like a schoolmarm scolding a naughty child.

Mixed signals left plenty of wiggle room so, without asking permission, he leaned in and pressed a slow, lingering kiss to her lips. Enough to distract her while he inched his hands down to claim a victorious handful, or two.

She caught on and pushed back. "Hey, now, *Frisky*. Same rules apply for you and Harvey." But again she smiled in a way that communicated something very different.

"What about Sal? Why does he get treats and not me?" Finn folded his empty arms.

"Oh, I think you're getting plenty of treats—and definitely more than cookies and coffee."

"Hmm. I guess you're right. My treats *are* sweeter."

A pretty shade of rose pinked her cheeks. Helpless, he reached out, tucking an impossibly soft lock of hair behind her ear, then stroked her elegant cheek with the backs of his knuckles. Just once. It wasn't nearly enough, but he couldn't seem to stop touching her. Finn had never once struggled with addiction. Did this count?

"Hey, Joss?"

Their eyes met, and she nodded. She was so close he could kiss her if he leaned down a few inches.

"I have several more questions I'd like you to say yes to." More than one of those would involve permission to touch her again.

"Pick one."

"Only one?"

"Which one is most important to you?" To his surprise, she slipped her arms beneath his coat, encircling his waist. A mere moment later a troupe of nurses shifted into sight and shuffled around them. Had Joselyn heard them coming? Was she playing up the ruse?

He decided he didn't care.

Her initiative, her nearness, tempted him to change his mind about which question she needed to say yes to. But his conscience whipped the scoundrel within into submission, regardless of how badly he wanted answers.

How badly he wanted lots of things.

He lifted his hands and cupped her face, the silky smooth skin beneath his touch begging to be explored. But he couldn't. Not here. So he pressed a soft kiss to her forehead, hearing the stuttering inhale of a shakily indrawn breath that was no steadier than his own.

"Will you … introduce me to your grandmother?"

After an hour of visiting with Yia-Yia, Finn decided he had never met anyone quite like her. She was fun and lively, quirky and honest. Above all, endearing. Even if a little forgetful.

Why was she living here? She didn't seem to have a great deal of physical limitations beyond the standard slow and cautious movements afflicting most aging folks.

In perfect and not-so-contented silence, Joselyn walked

beside him through the maze of sage green hallways. The place looked like a resort but smelled like a hospital—a strange mix of sterilizing agents, latex gloves, and stale bread. When they got to the double glass doors at the exit, she stopped and fished around in her purse.

"Hey." He nudged her arm, and her search stopped, their eyes connecting in that way that forged a bond they could neither deny nor explain.

"What's wrong with Yia-Yia?"

Her gaze flicked away, her hand resuming her search in her fancy purse. "Alzheimer's."

He didn't know what he was expecting, but that wasn't it. "Oh. I'm sorry I didn't think it … I shouldn't have—"

"It's okay. I don't usually offer up the information. I don't like talking about it … or thinking about it." Extracting her keys, she absently thumbed through, inspecting each trinket. "Today was a good day though. They're becoming a rarity."

"You come here every day?" He touched her shoulder, rubbing his thumb over the coarse wool of her coat.

She looked up. The vibrancy that usually sparkled in her eyes was merely an ember.

"*Oh,* sweetie." He stepped in front of her, hoping she might seek refuge in his arms.

Instead she quirked a halfhearted smile. "I thought you said *sweetie* didn't suit me?"

He grinned, admiring her strength. "I'm warming up to it."

Exhaling a wisp of a laugh, she glanced again at her keys. "Speaking of warming up, I'm gonna remote start my car— get it all toasty before I venture out into the arctic out there. You don't have to wait for me.

"But don't forget," She nudged the toe of her boot against his, the return of her megawatt smile like a shaft of dazzling light cutting through the gray haze of winter. "My dad planned our super romantic date for tonight. Sure to have paparazzi in tow. You might want to prepare yourself. It's bound to be over the top and atrociously snobby. Think you'll survive it?"

"I get to spend the evening with you. Couldn't be *that* bad." He winked. "Plus, you can put those adoring glances you practiced to good use."

She giggled, and he loved that he was responsible for the sound. "Smooth, Carson. Real smooth." Nibbling the corner of her smile, she looked down at the remote starter for her car, her thumb flexing over the ignition button.

Thunder shook the ground beneath his feet a split second before the glass doors exploded at his back. He didn't have time to plan, could scarcely react. But like a freeze frame in his mind, he saw the explicit terror in her eyes as a horizontal rain of glass and inertia propelled him forward.

For one helplessly prolonged moment they were suspended amid the wreckage, sailing on a burst of heat. Then as if catapulted into real time, Finn's body collided with hers, his arms somehow snatching around her. And though he should have expected they would land eventually, the blow came hard and fast, the tile floor rising beneath them like a tidal wave, jarring through them both, and ripping the breath from his lungs.

Feeling the full, violent force of his weight crash-landing atop her frail body and hearing the sickening sound of her skull slapping the floor, took ten years off his life in an instant. "Joss!" He dragged his crushing weight off of her and pulled to his knees, not wanting to move her until he assessed her condition. "Joselyn. Open your eyes, honey." He bent over, listening for breath sounds and checking her pulse. Rapid and weak.

"Babe, can you hear me?" He brushed away the glass near her face, the needle-fine shards embedding in his hand not even registering.

Her eyes flickered. Slits of lavender peeked through heavy lids. "Finn." His name exhaled on a flimsy breath. "My head."

Lush black lashes batted once more before shuttering her glassy gaze. He touched her face. "Joss, please." But got no response.

All his training abandoned him, and all he could think to do was shout, "Call 911!"

Chapter 25
Joselyn Whyte

"Sadie, I didn't know you played the guitar." Joselyn picked up the Ibanez 6-string acoustic and threaded the stitched leather strap over her shoulder.

"I don't. That's Finn's. I only play piano." Sadie wandered over to a shiny black upright in the music room. The Carsons had converted a spare bedroom in their homey traditional two-story into a sort of music sanctuary. There were rock 'n' roll posters framed on each wall, countless retro vinyls in a stacked multicolored assortment of milk crates, a turntable, a red and white electric Fender Strat, and a tall stack of speakers among the eclectic collection of instruments and odds and ends.

What Joselyn liked about the Carson house was that every room was lived in. Useful. Not a pretentious gallery of priceless artifacts like her father's estate. Whyte Manor felt like living in a museum. She was surprised there weren't signs designating what she was forbidden to touch.

Joselyn had only been over to Sadie's a few times, but it felt like a real home. And the Carsons felt like the perfect mold for a family. They encouraged and respected one another. Prayed together. Talked. It was amazing that such elementary things were so difficult to find.

The last time Joselyn had tried to talk to her father, she'd asked him about finding a better place for Yia-Yia to live, and he'd cut her off twenty seconds into the conversation, saying he had an urgent call. It was about ten seconds longer than their obligatory once-monthly conversations growing up. Now that she was living at the estate she felt hopeful that she might get to spend some time with him. Get to know him again.

"Coming!" Sadie hollered and rolled her eyes. "Hang on a sec, Joss. My mom is calling me." The half-wit literally trudged out of the room as if dreading a confrontation with her mother.

Sadie so didn't get it. Joselyn should really shake some sense into that girl.

Okay, so maybe Mrs. Carson was a bit over the top. So what? She was present, and she loved her daughter. Unquestionably.

It was Joselyn's greatest dream. A simple and yet unattainable dream, to have someone love her who might actually stick around long enough to prove it.

Joselyn plopped down on the loveseat. Only knowing a few basic chords her fingers awkwardly gripped the neck of the guitar, the buzz of the strings cluttering an already clumsy riff.

Closing her eyes, she strained to remember the next progression for her mother's song—the one she sang before Joselyn's bedtime as a little girl. The smooth and velvety timber of her mother's voice was such a distant memory she could scarcely recall the faintest trace of it. But she missed it. She missed everything.

"Not bad."

Her eyes shot open, and there he was, leaning against the door frame, looking at her with those irresistible turquoise eyes. His lips quirked with that boyish grin she saw in some of those dreams. *Sigh.* When your crush catches you by surprise your heart does strange things, becoming a joyously inebriated klutz dancing around in your chest. His presence was the trigger. Or maybe it was his smile. Whatever it was, it worked instantly in dumbing down her years of cool refinement. Sucking away her poise as well as all the oxygen in the room until she was breathing only him and was quite pleasantly dizzy with it. One could not be held responsible for any impending foolish behavior with an intoxicated heart like hers.

A foolish heart that all but melted into a smitten little puddle at the mere sound of his husky voice. Not the voice of a high school boy. But then again, nothing about Finn was ordinary. He was perfect, at least in her eyes. Funny, considerate, kind, and to say he was easy on the eyes would be like saying Coco Chanel probably kinda liked clothes.

Her fingers stopped strumming, and she felt herself beam like an idiot. "Hey, Finn. I thought you had practice today."

He shoved off the door and headed her way. She saw him every other day in their art history class, but she could never seem to tamp down her excitement when he was near. "It's raining, so coach called it. I didn't know you played." Folding into the love seat next to her his leg brushed hers, and she thought her heart might burn out from sheer exhaustion if he stayed there for long.

"I—I don't really. I only know a few chords. I didn't know *you* played." She risked a glance at him.

"I, uh, I get really nervous. So I don't play in front of other people." He smirked and shrugged his shoulders. "Here. Let me show you something." To Joselyn's utter delight and nerve-imploding pleasure, Finn scooted over until the whole side of his body hugged against hers. His arm stretched around behind her, and his warm fingers repositioned her cold ones on the fret. When he was done, he left them there, resting atop hers like it was where they belonged.

She couldn't think. Couldn't breathe. How could she possibly will her hand to strum at a time like this?

Turning her head, she found his face an inch away and froze. Wanting nothing more than to close the gap she tempted fate and held her position.

She had no idea what he was thinking, but if she didn't breathe soon she'd faint before she found out.

His hand fell away, the tickly touch of his fingers skimmed down her back as he brought his hand to rest on the seat of the couch behind her. His gaze never wavered.

Kiss me, she willed the thought into action. *Or say something. Anything.* But he held his position. Hesitating for an unbearably long moment. *Ask me to prom.* She wished. It felt like a wishing kind of moment, a suspension of reality, a dream teetering on the edge of her fragile hopes.

His friend Cody had been working on getting Finn to see that she was interested in him. Prom was the perfect segue. Surely, any day now Finn would ask. Right? How could he not know? Or maybe he knew but didn't know how to let her down easy.

Joselyn had virtually no experience in the dating world. She'd attended an all-girl school her whole life. But it seemed like Finn's current position, and the look in his eyes, were a mirror image of her feelings. Maybe he was as scared as she was.

The stare down continued. Swallowed up with desire she lost herself and leaned forward.

"Joselyn." The words rumbled so close the vibration tickled her skin.

"Yes, Finn." Their breaths tangled, his lips not even a whisper away. *This is it.*

"I—"

"Hey, Joss? Do you want anything from the kitchen before I come back up?" Sadie's holler jerked Finn away. The look on his face fired straight to the tenderest part of her long-neglected heart. A direct hit. The pain gushed forth.

Her hand instinctively went to cover the wound.

It was a look she knew well, always gifted from the other man who was supposed to love her but somehow … wouldn't. Finn was *ashamed*. And he couldn't get away fast enough, practically leaving a trail of dust as he shot out of the room, tossing a casual, "Catch ya later" over his shoulder.

Panting to resuscitate her low oxygen saturation, she fought back the burning tears of yet another rejection. Could she have misunderstood? Was she foolish to believe she'd read that wrong? There was only one week left until the prom. And then he'd be headed off to college. Time was running out, and the last flicker of hope was a dying ember.

She sure hoped that Cody had something up his sleeve to seal the deal, and soon.

When Joselyn's eyes blinked open, an opaque blur sloshed in unison with the contents of her stomach. Oh barf. She needed to … to …

Wait … Was she in bed? It seemed she was lying down, but it also felt like she was moving. A stale, blue-ish light made her wince, and she felt something flex against her face.

Where was she?

The cobwebs receded, and she recognized the roof of a van—an ambulance! Why was she in an ambulance?

Tearing away the oxygen mask and jerking upright, the world spun around like the Highland Fling. Nausea squirmed in her belly. "Ooo, stop spinning." She squeezed her eyes shut, cottony bells chimed in her ears, clogging up her senses while her body swayed against her attempts at equilibrium.

When she opened her eyes again a menacingly dark pair returned her stare. A cone of light struck her pupils until she saw nothing but floating spots, and then dabbled with another urge to retch out the contents of her stomach.

"Lie back down." The man's gravelly voice sent a strange shiver over her skin, resonated and rattled in her ears like a gong.

When the world slowed to a stop, she blinked her focus back and discovered the large, dark-haired man was inspecting her. A bristly unkempt overgrowth of facial hair webbed down onto his neck to the collar of his EMT uniform. He pulled a pad from the shelf to his right and attempted to guide her head back down to rest. It seemed like he was trying to help, but everything about this man—from the anger brewing in his eyes to the tense plane of his body—insinuated something else.

Ow, it hurt to think. Her head was throbbing, her pulse in her ears only stirring her nausea. Where had she been today?

The nursing home.

The answer came quick, as if someone was trying to tell her something.

Finn.

"Where's Finn?" Something happened. She couldn't fill in the blanks. But Finn would know. Why wasn't he here with her? Was he hurt? "Excuse me, where's Finn?"

The EMT pressed her back onto the gurney. "He's fine. Didn't want him in my ambulance distracting me."

"*You* didn't want him in *your* ambulance? And distracting you from what? I'm just laying here, I'm not going toward the light." She didn't wait for him to respond, her motion sickness and prickle of anxiety joining to manifest in some sort of verbal vomiting. "Did you even consider that it might be a little frightening for a woman to wake up to a scary Grizzly Adams in the back of a van?"

"Settle down. Nothing you can do about it now."

The driver called back from the front seat. "I know you wanted to head the other way, but there's an accident so we'll have to take a detour. But we've got an escort from Ms. Whyte's friend from the FBI. He radioed over. We'll be there shortly."

The EMT's midnight eyes narrowed, scanning the cabin

of the ambulance. More than merely disoriented, Joselyn felt unease slither around her like a tangle of vines.

She was in an ambulance, so she should be feeling safe. But she didn't. If any more nervous energy was coursing through her body the hairs on her head would stand on end. Shaking it off was the only thing to do.

And well, she *had* been pretty rude just now. Perhaps he was simply trying to avoid another encounter with the crazy chick who'd spewed her venom all over him. She could see the tabloid now. "*Heartless Snow Whyte harasses man trying to save her life.*"

"Look. I'm really sorry. I didn't mean to yell at you and call you scary. I must be a little out of sorts, but, nevertheless, I apologize."

He didn't respond, but she couldn't muster up any more conversation anyway. Every word from her mouth rebounded back a shrill jolt to her throbbing head. Knowing that Sal was now caravanning her safely to the hospital, she let herself relax against the stiff gurney, her body freely jostling with each turn and bump in the road. And before she knew it, the gentle lull of movement had coaxed her to sleep.

"Well, I'll be doggoned. It's nice to see you again—not under the circumstances, but still a pleasure, Miss Joselyn."

Dragging her groggy brain out a daze, she connected with a familiar face. Not one she was expecting, but a pleasant one, at least.

"Hi, Shelby. How long have I been out?" The nurse stood at Joselyn's bedside examining the monitor attached to the blood pressure cuff that was now sucking the life out of her arm. Movement beyond the shifting curtain meant Joselyn was still in the ER.

"Only a few minutes. We've been trying to wake you up. That EMT should have known better than to let you snooze with a concussion." Shelby's soft hands cocooned Joselyn's. "How're you feeling, my dear?"

"Umm, I'm fine. My head hurts a little, but other than that." *Other than the pickax going to town on my skull, and the fact that I'm once again in the hospital alone, I'm grand.*

"Uh, huh. Nice try. Listen, we don't always do a CT for a concussion but the Doc said because of the force of the explosion, he'd rather be safe than sorry." Her lips pulled in a slight smile, the fine lines around her eyes imprinting deeper with empathy. "How are you doing, really? And not only the headache stuff. This has all gotta be a lot to take."

The maternal concern swirling in Shelby's kind blue eyes made Joselyn's heart leapfrog into her throat. What if she let someone in? Should she lean on Shelby?

And what if she got used to leaning on someone and was then forced back into the same old solitude? Would she be strong enough to keep from getting sucked down to that dark, desperate place she never wanted to find herself again? "I don't even know what happened today. I can't begin to process it all without some information." Joselyn searched the blank space in her memory bank.

"Well, as far as I know there will be some more investigatin'. But it appears someone blew up your vehicle."

"What!" Dread dumped like toxic waste into her blood steam. The instant poison shook every cell, every fiber down to the icy core. "Someone tried to kill me, again?" Burying her face in her numb hands, she smothered the tears that surged forth, shaking with the renewed terror that wouldn't let go in the face of the truth. It hadn't been a fluke before. Someone was still after her. And they wanted her dead.

The bed shifted from Shelby's weight, and she pulled Joselyn to her ample chest. "It's gonna be all right. You're not alone. That much is for certain."

That brought Joselyn's head up.

"Would you mind if I pray for you?" Shelby asked.

Joselyn considered telling her to not waste her time, but something shone in Shelby's eyes that changed her mind— peace and strength braided together with an undeniable authority over the dark tentacles slithering away at the suggestion. Because it was a look she'd seen so often in Sadie, it immediately unarmed her defenses.

"Sure, why not." Besides, it was one of those pat sayings people threw out while pretending to care. The busy nurse would probably forget anyways, so Joselyn supposed it didn't really matter.

But then, to her surprise, Shelby clasped Joselyn's hand and bowed her head.

Now? She's gonna pray right now?

Something like panic, or was it anticipation, rent from her chest; the fraudulent feelings making a riot of her senses. The room came alive. The curtain swayed, and someone barking orders alongside a creaking gurney siphoned away Joselyn's focus. The beeps of the monitors, the whooshes of the nearby breathing machines, the soft grinding of an inflating blood pressure cuff all wove into her mind, stealing away the moment.

Shelby's prayer. The thought warred for the top spot, breaking through the chaos and grabbing on tight. Joselyn closed her eyes and grappled for the lifeline.

"… and we thank you for watching over Joselyn today. We sure don't know what is going on here, but we know that only you can turn this around for good. We pray for continued protection and peace over this special young woman. Hold her in your arms and don't let go …"

A fresh batch of emotion spilled over from Shelby's sweet and simple supplication. Wasn't there a certain protocol for prayers? Could you really just talk to God like a friend?

The words fell over her like armor, heavy, solid, and secure. But what about before? When she'd needed protection the most? Why was it only people like Sadie, or Shelby, and those lucky ones with families and support systems, people whose hearts had been nurtured in their faith, who had access to that kind of security? Blind as it may be?

With every ounce of brokenness she possessed, she wished for it. Wished for the kind of hope to believe that somebody out there—anybody really—might show up to fight for her. Protect her from loneliness and fear and … fire. After all these years she was still casting pieces of her heart into that empty wishing well. And yet, the answer couldn't be plainer. Nothing at present forecasted the kind of future where she'd find someone patient enough to thaw her heart and grant her wish. In fact, the thought resounded in her aching head; there was no forecast for a future at all.

Chapter 26

Finn Carson

More waiting. And it was driving him crazy.

It all started when that grungy EMT wouldn't let Finn ride along. Even after he'd pulled his credentials. And since Joselyn was still unconscious when they'd loaded her up, she hadn't been able to vouch for him.

He'd been further delayed when a different incompetent and annoyingly googly-eyed medic took her sweet time extracting the splinters of glass from his hands with all the finesse of an epileptic with ADHD. That is until he plucked the darn thing from her hand and finished the job himself. And when he finally managed to get away from the crime scene to head toward the hospital he got stuck in traffic for an hour.

Of course, that still wasn't the worst of it. Sal was in the waiting room when Finn finally arrived. In his hot-headed, helpless panic, Finn hurled a barrage of accusations at Sal for not noticing someone planting a bomb in Joselyn's car.

Sal looked as distraught as Finn felt and didn't even try to defend himself, which meant Finn got to feel like a royal jerk for endless snail-paced minutes that rolled into eternally long hours.

When the doctor came in after the longest two hours of Finn's life, he and Sal both erupted from their seats and pounced on the poor guy for answers.

Once the Doogie Howser doppelganger could get in a word edgewise, he informed them one visitor could be admitted back to Joselyn's room. Finn was prepared to fight for those visitation rights, but Sal graciously relinquished his bid.

When Finn was halfway out the door, Sal blurted. "I'm sorry, man, I didn't know."

Finn's mind was already racing down the hall to Joselyn's room. But he turned back and saw clearly the weight of guilt the other man was carrying. Man, he might as well be looking in a mirror.

"And I sure as heck didn't know how deeply you felt about her, or I wouldn't have messed with you the other day." Sal's gaze was earnest, and far too perceptive for Finn to attempt a convincing denial.

He tipped his head to acknowledge Sal's apology and then ran. Ran past incensed staff members and gawking patients until he reached Joselyn's room, barely restraining himself from crashing through the door. "*Joss.*" Her name, broken and breathlessly uttered, betrayed the calm he'd wanted to portray. But since he'd already shown his hand, he took the room in two strides, collapsed to the bed, and pulled her gently to his chest, fighting back the choking emotion now flooding in his eyes. "Thank God, you're okay."

Breathing deeply from her hair, he felt his nerves back away from the ledge. She let him hold her like that for a long, long time. He didn't trust himself to speak. Wasn't ready to identify or voice the jumble of feelings tearing through his heart, nor was he ready to relive the past few hours and give her answers—many of which he still couldn't make sense of.

So he held on, only allowing his mind to settle on the miraculous way her life had been spared. Again.

"Sakes alive!" The strange expression was delivered on a gasp of a southern drawl and served to revoke Joselyn from his arms. She turned her face, smearing away the glint of moisture from her cheeks as the nurse he remembered from last time bounced into the room.

"Joselyn, girl, you done snagged yourself that sexy hero after all. My, my." She fanned herself with the clipboard in her possession. And paying no heed to the surge of crimson edging up Joselyn's neck, the woman prattled on, "You know, I was thinking I might write one of them romance novels. Maybe I could base the story on you two? This is some good material. Oops, sorry. Don't pay me any mind. Never could stop my silly words once they started. Slippery little suckers.

"I came in here to tell you that an Agent Hayes and another pretty little gal, uh, Sadie, are here to see you. You're not s'posed to have too many visitors, but I'm sure they need to go over some important things with you. So when you're ready," she stopped and winked at Finn, "I'll send 'em in."

Joselyn cleared her throat, still not looking at him. "Ready or not."

"… was detonated by your ignition." All of Archer and Sal's words started to pound together in his head. Finn pressed his thumb and forefinger against his eyebrows until the bones ached; the concentrated pain helping to bank his fury and rein his focus.

The look on Joselyn's face didn't help matters. She was an ice sculpture. A beautiful, catatonic display of shock and fear.

"Wait, detonated by the ignition? That sounds familiar. Isn't that in a movie?" Sadie scrunched her nose, mulling it over to herself while the guys continued their detail of the CSU's findings from the scene.

They'd also contacted the U.S. Marshals to see if they could beef up security.

"One thing's for sure. This guy definitely wants to see her burn. Oww!" A right hook came from Sadie and connected with Sal's shoulder. "What, Sadie? *Ay dios mio*, that hurt!" While rubbing his wound, Sal's mood lightened and he smirked at Archer. "Lucky dog. This one's a firecracker."

Chuckling, Archer pulled Finn's sister into his arms. "You're telling me." Undeterred by their audience, the macho FBI agent turned to putty. He leaned down and stole a kiss.

And though he had to look away because it was pretty repulsive to see his sister and Archer kissing, it tempted Finn to partake in a little PDA of his own. If for no other reason than to put some color back in Joss's cheeks.

Finn's extraordinarily loud throat clear ended the nauseating display and brought everyone back on point. "O-kay, thank you for that," he shivered, "but let's get back to the attempted murder, shall we? Arsonists tend to be fascinated by their creations. Obsessed even. Might want to have a chat with some of the first responders and onlookers to see if anyone struck them as suspicious. It's possible this guy doubled back to view his handy work."

"Well, somebody played cops growing up." Archer smirked, "I'm on it," and started tapping something into his phone.

"And how are we on evidence?" Finn decided he might as well lead the meeting since Archer's mental faculties were on vacation in Sadieland and Sal looked about as helpless and sad as a lost puppy. "If anything survived the fire this time maybe we can track the supplies used to make the bomb. There's gotta be something left that will generate a lead, right?"

"That's what we're hoping. Until we get the report back from the bomb and arson unit, and likely ATF as well, we won't have a lot to go on because I didn't see anything. Not sure how he got in and out without me noticing." Sal tunneled his fingers into his hair.

"This is not your fault, Sal." Joselyn reached out her hand, and Sal took it. Finn could see her knuckles flush white with reassurance, unable to squelch the sliver of envy when the handholding persisted longer than seemed necessary.

He needed to get a grip. Stat.

Archer's cell phone chimed in, and the scene scattered. Finn itched to fold in next to Joselyn, but because the only people in the room were already privy to the arrangement there was no need for show. So he hung back, not wanting to give the boys any more ammunition.

"Okay. Keep me apprised." Archer ended the call. "Got some bad news, guys. There's a storm drain under Joselyn's VIP parking spot at McKnight Grove. Must be how this guy rigged the explosives without being seen."

"*The Pelican Brief!*" Sadie shouted in a sort of "aha moment." Her enthusiasm faded when she seemed to remember they were in the middle of something more important than her movie trivia. "Uh, sorry. Got caught up."

"It's okay, Sherlock." Archer winked, snuggled Sadie to his side, and resumed his recap of the phone call. "We've got guys down in the sewer system trying to track him. So far it looks like he got away clean, so we're not gonna get much help there. But it appears he's familiar with Joselyn's routine, and he's smart. These strikes are well calculated, and each scene is meticulously devoid of useable evidence. Might not be an ex-employee, might be a pro, but this seems personal. All I know for sure is that I don't like it. Not one bit."

"Me neither." Finn's heart clenched, barricading all that felt fleshy and vulnerable. The discussion of the case continued around him, but he couldn't bear to hear any more.

The events of the afternoon cemented the fact that the threat still loomed. Only now they knew this guy wouldn't stop until he completed his mission. Which meant eminent danger lurked around every corner, hid in every shadow. Dread pooled in the pit of his stomach, knowing how close they'd come to being blown up today.

On every account it seemed that Finn was failing. Failing to keep Joselyn safe. Failing to protect his heart. And failing to trust his instincts. It dug up every old fear he'd been trying to hide, poked at the open wounds from the Monroe fire, and resurrected every doubt and inadequacy about his ability to be a hero.

Maybe it should have been Sal—or someone else less likely to get Joselyn killed—to protect her. He'd thought this assignment would be an easy way to rebuild what he'd lost, but somehow he was still failing, and each failure stripped away another piece of Finn's armor. Before long, he would be rushing into battle empty-handed.

Uncertainty weighed on him from every side until it felt like his whole body might implode from the pressure. But there was one thing he knew for certain and it gripped him with an odd combination of foreboding and anticipation.

This thing with Joselyn was far from over.

Archer and Sal had insisted on seeing Joselyn and Sadie home before they headed back to the bureau to do some late-night digging. In their stead they had patrol cars cruising the area and two undercover agents stationed outside.

Feeling left out of the group, Finn made a quick stop to pick up some supplies and ventured over to see Joselyn. He hadn't gotten any time alone with her after Shelby had walked in. He wanted—no *needed*—to make sure she was okay.

He called his sister to inform her that he would be sleeping on the couch as an added security measure and got clearance to bypass the guards. When Sadie let him in, she promptly returned to her spot on the couch beside Joselyn, staking claim to the only place Finn wanted to be.

He felt like sulking. In fact, he probably was sulking when he trudged to the media console, inserted the movie he'd picked up on his way over, and sat by his lonesome on the cold leather chair in the corner.

"*Pride and Prejudice*? Really? Wow, Finn. That's Joselyn's favorite." Sadie's eyes slanted with scrutiny—her x-ray glare digging to uncover his motive.

Finn looked at Joselyn instead. Her eyes magnetized with his, the corner of her pretty lips lifting as if she too was remembering their little wrestling match in her room when he'd first glimpsed her secret stash of romance novels. The hours enduring the chick flick would be well worth it now.

"I had a hunch." He shrugged, grinning boldly back at Joselyn from across the room, and belatedly remiss to note

Sadie had unleashed a fully loaded grin of her own.

Trouble, that one. Finn restrained his huff of exasperation. Sisters were exhausting at every age. He watched Joselyn nibble at her luscious lip and amended that assessment. Women. Women were exhausting. And unfortunately, he was just restless enough to never tire of one in particular.

After an hour and a half of what Joselyn informed them was "Regency-Era English" and the, yes, *exhausting* antics of the Bennett sisters, Finn was ready to pass out. Joselyn had been sleeping for the last thirty minutes, and Sadie looked about ready to nod off on the couch herself.

With a yawn, his sister raised the remote and clicked off the TV. Finn rose from his isolated corner and crossed the room. The stark silence in the condo would make the quest for sleep excruciating. White noise seemed the best defense against nightmares lurking in the deafening silence, but the only sound softening the brunt of the stillness was the brush of his feet against the wood floor.

He scooped Joselyn off the couch. With a slight stir, she relaxed her head against his shoulder and released a deep, restful shudder as he carried her to her room. She felt so small in his arms, but when he laid her down the loss felt too big.

Stroking the hair off her face, he leaned down and pressed his mouth to her forehead, a silent prayer of gratitude for her safety overwhelming the jumble of emotions wrestling within him.

But the tension in his chest made him realize that killer or not, he was anything but safe. As a firefighter, it had become instinctual to put others first. And as a man of faith, death didn't scare him. He wouldn't hesitate to give his life to protect Joselyn or anyone else, for that matter.

Giving his heart, on the other hand, was truly terrifying. And judging by the reaction of his pulse to the melting ice princess, the danger was already here.

"No, please. Stop." Bathed in moonlight, her slim form thrashed beneath the covers. *"Don't."* Having released him from his own sleeping torment, the whimpering cry had propelled him to action. Many who suffered night terrors woke with no recollection of the nightmare. Finn knew that wasn't the case for either of them.

He knelt on the empty side of the bed. With a hand that still trembled from visions of fire and agony, he rubbed her arm. "Joselyn."

"No!" Her panic spiked.

"Joss, it's Finn. Wake up." With a bit more force, he shook her.

Without warning, she jolted up, her arms flailing, her breaths racing near hysteria. She lunged at him. It was too dark to fully prepare himself—and the last thing he wanted to do was scare or hurt her—but her arms swung frantically in the shadows until the flat of her palm connected with his cheek. Then fingernails raked over his neck. A hank of hair was ripped from the root. Swipes of her fists became glancing blows he struggled to restrain.

Though he had stars in his eyes—and not the good kind—he managed to pin her arms down and shake her one last time. "Joselyn, wake up!"

Chapter 27

Joselyn Whyte

"Finn?" Joselyn ripped her arms loose from his biting grip and flipped on the bedside lamp. The scarce illumination wasn't much more than a night light, but it brought everything into focus—her nightmare, her tingling palm, her safety. She exhaled the panic screaming in her lungs.

And when she saw his face, so sweet and caring—despite her crazed and misplaced abuse—and disarmingly handsome with the soft pour of moonlight draping over him from the window, she had no choice. Okay, maybe she had a choice. What she lacked in this instance was control.

She launched into his arms. Again. This time for entirely different reasons. He adjusted against the impact to keep them from toppling over, and she burrowed her face into the warm pocket of his neck, breathed in soap and spice and comfort. Helpless to the need that was all-consuming, she parted her lips to taste him.

With a catch of his breath, he nudged her with his chin and then let his lips do the talking. Slow, hungry wordlessness from behind her ear, over her jaw, across her cheek …

He pulled her onto his lap, and she wrapped her legs around him, turning his lips to align like the stars that must be shining down on this bit of madness as he kissed the living daylights out of her.

Sinking one hand into her hair, and the other at the base of her spine, he used the strength of his arms to stitch them together in a seamless fit. His wild and sure ministrations scattered the last bit of sense in her head. It was too much. And not nearly enough. So she dove in, abandoning herself in the kiss that filled her love-starved heart to overflowing. *Finn.*

She must have moaned his name into the kiss because he returned the sentiment, revving her to the redline. Her heart took off, a frenzy of tangled emotions shook and trembled from within like a dismantling rocket fighting for orbit. She changed the angle to further deepen the kiss, a searing frisson of electric heat setting her blood on fire at his eager response. She couldn't breathe, couldn't think. Was she frightened or elated, she didn't know? Driven by a mindless instinct, she could do nothing but rub shamelessly against him, practically begging to drown in his bewitching kiss.

He didn't disappoint. His warmth seeped into every pore on her skin, freeing her from her frozen wasteland. Nothing had ever felt like this. Nothing.

The truth of that fact was so dizzying her head started to spin, and she felt the room tilt around them. Some sort of logic suggested that the earth-moving kiss might not be solely responsible for the vertigo. But she didn't want to stop. Didn't care to breathe anything but the air she drew from his lungs. This was happening. After all this time. And she couldn't … she couldn't …

She pried her lips away, surrendering to the nauseating effects of the concussion. An excuse. A safe one. And though she was now sitting on the bed next to him, she could still feel his body heat lingering on every inch of her skin beneath her pajamas.

She was still breathless when she spoke. "You *really* have to stop rescuing me."

His chest heaved in sync with hers, and the dazed look on his face melted into a wicked grin. "I'm finding I have new motivation."

"I'm serious." She couldn't help but smile, contradicting her words.

"Well somebody's gotta do it. And if this is the reward, it

better not be anyone but me."

Without thinking, she reached out and touched his cheek. "I'm sorry I hit you again. You're always sneaking up on me." *Drat, must stop touching him!*

She tried to draw back, but he caught her hand and pressed each of her fingertips to his lips.

Oh my. "W-Why are you in my be—my room?"

"Doctor's orders. I need to rouse you to consciousness every couple of hours."

"Hmm, you just prescribed yourself into my bed. Pretty crafty, Carson. Unfortunately, I think your medication gave me a fever."

Still in possession of her hand, he tugged her forward, his eyes smoldering. "I can help you with that."

She managed to pull her hand back and stay several inches away—baffled by how it was both too close and too far at the same time. "How, by setting the sheets on fire?"

He wagged his eyebrows in response. And while the thought of "burning up the sheets" should have given her a hellish flashback to her burning bedroom, she instead flashed forward to a different kind of burn entirely. A heat she knew she couldn't stand. For several reasons.

She delicately cleared her throat and went for a diversion. "But really, you need to stop taking care of me. A girl could get used to this, and then what?"

"I'd think you'd be plenty used to being waited on by now."

Burn. And there it was—his opinion of her. It still hadn't changed. "You don't know me as well as you think." She crossed her arms.

"I know your daddy already sent over a shiny new Mercedes Benz G-Class SUV. Keys were on the counter, and the in-your-face pretentious tank was on display outside when I got here last night. Couldn't be all that tough having everything handed over on a silver platter."

After the smack had landed, his face went slack, like he couldn't believe his mouth had dumped out his thoughtless words without permission.

But that didn't ease the sting, much. And she was tempted to slap him all over again and return the favor.

Finn was a jerk. And a player. How could she keep forgetting? A heated look from those drowning eyes, a hard physique, a skilled tongue, and a morsel of attention, and she'd fallen like every other vapid little hose hussy. Or was it badge bunny? *Gah!* Either way, she was disgusted with herself.

"I couldn't care less about the stupid car—you know what? Forget it. I refuse to sit here and justify myself to you when you certainly never did that for me. I don't know what I was thinking. Temporary insanity. But your mind is obviously made up, so go ahead and show yourself out." She flung her hand toward the door, but he caught it again and firmly cradled it in both of his.

"Prove me wrong." His eyes pleaded—daring her to spill it all. As if he concocted this whole ruse in her moment of weakness to wheedle out the missing pieces of the puzzle.

Fury boiled below the surface, ready to erupt and leave him a pile of ashes. Tugging at her captive hand, she attempted to clear the mess he seemed to make of her senses with a simple touch.

But he was way ahead of her. Keeping a stern grip with one hand, he used the other to tuck away a rebellious clump of hair behind her ear. Trapping her face with his palm, holding her gaze hostage, the rough pad of his thumb skimming her cheek, tracing tantalizing circles of unwelcome desire on her skin.

Shuddering from his touch, her anger simmered. And then feeling easily manipulated, it fired back up again and she jerked back.

She thought better of defending herself and giving him exactly what he wanted, but before she could boot him from her room, her lips started unloading against her will.

"You wanna know about my life, Mr. Perfect? Fine. Yia-Yia raised me. I grew up in that house that burned to the ground. My father decided he wanted nothing to do with me after we both watched my mother die. I saw him maybe once a year around Christmastime.

"And when I was about twelve, Yia-Yia started forgetting things. How to work the stove. Where she'd parked at the mall. She'd walk down the street and forget her way home. So I'd spend hours searching the dark streets by myself to find her sitting by the tracks, watching the trains roll through the station. That's when my childhood ended and I started taking care of her full time, which was better than any alterative.

"I was in high school by the time my father finally caught on to my living situation. He tore me away from the only home I'd ever known and locked me up in his cold, isolated castle. Now that I'm older and less of a burden he *uses* me as political ammunition in whatever 'happy family' farce he's cooked up for the media. I'm a trophy daughter. The extent of his 'generosity' with these over-the-top cars and gifts I couldn't care less about is more about power than about affection of any kind. And there isn't a luxury in the world he could buy with his billions that he could barter for pain of his abandonment."

Fueled by the angry rush, she jabbed him in the chest with her finger. "So you think my life is easy because my father has a bunch of money in a trust for me somewhere. I don't care. I don't want it. It feels like blood money, for all it cost me. I make my own living—made plenty of money all on my own. Bought Yia-Yia's house and have been working ever since to get her the help she needs.

"The only money I have touched from my inheritance was used to fund the rest of the nursing home she lives in that I couldn't afford on my own. So get over yourself. *You* are the spoiled brat as far as I'm concerned. I've never had a family, or a childhood, or anything that really matters. And the last thing I need is a lecture from some arrogant playboy who gets everything he wants and has never known my kind of loss."

Tears burned her eyes, and she wished she could pull back every one of those words when she saw shock and pity in the eyes of the man she loved.

Yes, she loved him.

She supposed she always had—from that very first moment. But that was her problem—on top of everything else—she was stupid. An idiot, really. To let herself love someone she could never have. Their past was too tainted to overcome, and yet here she was—a fool—kissing and falling back in love with her enemy.

Good grief, Joselyn, will you ever learn?

The emotion swimming in Finn's eyes was too confusing. Everything about him was confusing.

Loving him at the top of that list.

So she resorted to staying angry. It was her only hope for getting out of this alive.

"There you have it, hotshot. I even left out some of the more gory details for your peace of mind. Now leave me alone." The last word caught on a poorly stifled sob. Oh, if only the earth would open and swallow her whole. She was so weak. She'd let him past the barricade of her heart, past the emotionless mask and the placating niceties.

Tears, so many stupid tears escaped from the purge of her *stupid* confession, so she shoved him. She was already stupid, might as well tack on irrational and impulsive to make a miserable trifecta. It was sheer torture being all exposed—letting him view the tragic wreckage of her life like some drive-by gawker.

Even more painful was seeing him so distraught that he couldn't even speak. It made her long to comfort *him*. Crawl back onto his lap and kiss away *his* sorrows.

And that's when she knew it was official. She was the biggest idiot on the planet.

Couldn't he yell at her and storm off? Call her Snow Whyte or a spoiled brat? That would be easier to deal with than his renegade tear and his heartbreaking helpless paralysis.

"Please go." The words sounded flimsy and pathetic through her stupid tears. *Stupid!*

"No," he said, quiet, but firm. He slipped his arms around her back and pulled her into him, leaning back so she was snuggled against his iron chest.

She tried to resist, but he held tight, combating her best efforts until she relaxed into him. The steady drum of his heart beneath her ear and the masculine musk of his skin drawing in with each breath lulled her into complete compliance and contentment—so much so she was really starting to hate herself.

"Joss." He breathed her name like a solemn vow and then made a promise she knew would shatter her heart. "I'm not going anywhere."

Winter white sunshine billowed into the room like a fog of heaven. Joselyn's eyes were heavy, but the warmth of the light pressed all around her. She felt rested and peaceful, the air drawn into her lungs was laced with something tantalizing. And though she was still trapped in some sort of sleepy haze, it felt like a waking dream. Warm and cozy and perfect.

Blinking away the last of the euphoric smog, she discovered the reality of that dream still in play when she eased her head away from a well-muscled chest and found she'd fallen asleep in Finn's arms.

It would seem she'd gone fetal at some point, curled against him like a baby, and maybe even cried herself to sleep.

Still leaning against a slant of pillows propped up at the headboard, Finn was asleep. That's when it hit her. She'd slept with Finn! No, not with. Near. Against maybe. Because for as much as the man liked to push the limits with his hands-on liberties, he hadn't made a move on her all night.

Every shiver and knot of stress had left her body while she watched him sleep. And really, since she was pinned in place by his strong arms, she had few options. *Darn.* So she stayed, and it was no hardship.

As if drawn by a magnet, her hand skimmed up his shirt and faintly touched his cheek. The feel of the coarse, shimmering stubble beneath her fingertips was more satisfying than any consumed amount of peanut butter M&M's.

Amazing how she hadn't needed any since that first kiss. And all those kisses since had started filling the emptiness of a life devoid of affection. Chocolate was a poor substitute, and the awakening of her need for touch—even the simple comfort of a friendly embrace—made her realize all she'd missed out on in her life.

Yia-Yia was never much into hugs. Her alcoholic husband hadn't been an affectionate man—or so Joselyn had been told. He'd left Yia-Yia and Joselyn's mother, Charisma, when Charisma was five years old, broke poor Helena Verraros's heart, and left her bitter and sworn off of men for life.

The man's legacy was not a fine tribute to the word "family," and Joselyn's own father—though no blood relation to Demetrios Verraros—followed in those same callous footsteps.

And while Joselyn knew her mother had been warm and caring when she was alive, she could only vaguely remember being swaddled in her arms. The years had wiped away any tangible memory.

Now, in Finn's solid arms, she felt something so foreign it was like a drug—altering her brain chemistry to the point of desperation for another fix. And that was the scariest thing of all.

Realizing she wanted to stay right where she was, forever.

A piercing array of blues and greens peeked out from sleepy lids. Snatching her hand away, she attempted to right herself, but his arms tightened around her back. A slow, lazy grin etched disarming dimples into his handsome face. "Hi."

Her stomach flip-flopped in response to the rumble from

his chest. Or maybe the grin and the dimples. Or all of the above. Tough to say.

"Hi." Feeling uncharacteristically demure, she tilted her lips in a shy smile, her hand settling on his chest.

Holding his stare, it felt like he could see straight into her battered heart and wasn't repulsed by what he saw. Not yet, at least. It was as if no one and nothing else existed in the world. She'd never been the center of anyone's anything. It was heady stuff.

"Now that you've said your hellos, maybe you guys could get up." The illusion was ripped away in an instant. Standing in the doorway was Sadie. With hands propped on her enviably curvy hips, she looked like mama bear coming to protect her cub. Or maybe both cubs. From themselves.

Finn and Joselyn jumped up from the bed, untangling their embrace in record time under the watchful eye of the warden. "Finn, I don't recall bunking being part of the deal when I agreed to let you check on her." There was a slight twist in her lips and a glimmer of a teasing twinkle in her eye, but she stood her ground for an explanation.

"Pfff, Sadie, please. Nothing happened." Finn looked a little nervous, like he didn't feel that was entirely true. Even though it was.

Well, nothing beyond the scorching make-out fest and the all-night cuddle.

So Joselyn came to his rescue. Clearing her throat with extra pizzazz, she said, "I do believe you and Archer," lifting her hands to use quotations, "'shared a bed' when that seedy motel in Kansas only had one room left." Joselyn cocked an eyebrow, knowing she'd hit her mark.

Sadie's mouth gaped open for a soundless moment before she clamped it shut and scowled. "That was an extenuating circumstance—a man was dying. And we fell asleep, okay, nothing happened."

Joselyn shrugged. "Same here."

Sadie crossed her arms. "Okay, fine. But my brother's making breakfast. *And* doing the dishes for his defiance of house rules."

Scrambling out of the room from the sparring women, Finn smirked back at Joselyn, "A small price to pay. I'll take it."

Chapter 28

Finn Carson

Had he ever felt this good? It was worth pondering. Last night, with Joselyn in his arms—her kisses still searing into his lips—it was better than every dream he had the whole senior year he'd spent pining away for her.

After prom, any dreams involving Joselyn were either nonexistent or mercilessly cruel. And as of late, there hadn't been any dreaming. Only nightmares. But last night was the first in months that he'd slept peacefully.

Flipping the chocolate chip pancakes in the skillet, he withdrew four perfectly golden rounds, scraped four more sizeable dollops from the mixing bowl into the pan and relived the glorious moments before he became a first-class jerk and raging idiot.

They say old habits die hard, but nothing had been harder than witnessing the look on Joselyn's face when she'd unloaded the loneliness of her past. All because Finn's bitterness—stockpiled from the past ten years—kept spilling over.

Please, forgive me for acting like an arrogant fool.

No wonder Joselyn had been so frosty in high school. She was all alone, having been uprooted from her home and Yia-Yia and her school to live in a virtual ivory tower—deprived of love from the one person she wanted it from the most.

Distracted with his growing contempt against Declan Whyte, Finn failed to flip the batch of pancakes before the first side got cast iron crispy. He'd choke down the burned ones.

It made more sense that she'd had fallen for Cody. She'd been so desperate for attention—something Cody gave freely to each and every attractive female within shouting distance—and maybe she thought, with his family situation, he might be able to relate.

Something soured in his gut, something sick and jealous when he thought of them together. Even now, the whole night was crystal clear.

"Ooo, Finn, I love this song. Let's dance." Renee Ross's fake nails clawed at Finn's hand as she attempted to drag him from his seat.

Finn growled his response of "No thanks" to the painfully annoying prom date Cody had set him up with. But she either wasn't smart enough to pay attention or she refused to read the blatant revulsion for her written across his face and tugged at his hand once again.

"Aww, come on. We haven't even danced, and the night's almost over. She pinned him with an evil glare, and he begrudgingly let himself be dragged to the dance floor.

"One dance," he snapped. This had obviously been a huge mistake. Renee was more Cody's type of girl—skimpy dress, even skimpier brain power, and a reputation that wasn't skimpy at all.

Why on earth had he agreed to this?

The answer was clear. The very thought of Joselyn made his choice to come along on this charade of a revenge date worth it.

His date's cackling hyena laugh struck his eardrum even over the blaring music, and Finn remedied his momentary lapse of judgment. *Almost* worth it.

Renee's moves were quite possibly too explicit to witness, so Finn turned away and preoccupied himself by bopping along to the stupid rap song that was about a hundred decibels too loud.

Finn's head was throbbing from the incessant grating noise, and he hadn't caught a glimpse of Joselyn all night. And his eyes had been glued to the dance floor for that very reason.

He knew it was a form of torture to come along and see her here with him. But up until now he'd never even seen them talking. Or together. During class, the only times Joselyn spoke it was to the teacher or to Finn.

Cody's relay of her rejection echoed in his mind. *"She said guys like you were beneath her. Can you believe that? That it was laughable you thought you might actually have a chance with someone like her."*

And after he'd escaped the close-encounter with the impromptu guitar lesson/almost kiss, he'd accidentally overheard her and Sadie talking about prom. He'd never forget the laugh she'd forced out when he heard her say, "Puh-lease. As if I would go with *him*. I'm holding out for a better offer."

He sucked in a breath upon remembering the sting of those words. How they'd tunneled down into his deepest insecurities and built a nest.

The song died off, and Finn was ready to bolt. From the dance floor. From the prom. From this whole stupid mess. It was time to move on.

But when he turned to go, he saw her. His heart stalled out. She was a vision, almost angelic, as every light in the room seemed to spotlight her in a perfectly incandescent glow.

Man, it hurt to look at her. She was breathtaking. The ethereal white dress shimmied mercilessly over her slight curves, but that wasn't where he was looking. What he couldn't seem to tear his eyes away from was her face.

Radiant with her sparkling eyes, dewy pink lips, and a silky pile of black curls gracefully swept up, framing her elegant features.

He pried his gaze away and saw Cody leading Joselyn out onto the dance floor. He was trying to say something in her ear, but she seemed to be preoccupied looking for someone until … her gaze found Finn's, and everything crashed all around him, leaving his foolish eyes for her alone.

Cody tugged on her arm, and she stumbled against him. His hands clamped possessively around her lower back. Then he turned her, and Cody's dark eyes met Finn's across the expanse of the dance floor where couples were drawing together for the last slow dance.

It was that moment when Renee crashed into him. "One slow dance, cranky. And then we can go back to my hotel room, and I'll turn that frown upside down," she cackled in Finn's ear. He was so disgusted he about turned away … but then Joselyn swiveled back into view.

So Finn got even. Grabbing hold of his awful date, he held Joselyn's gaze to remind her of everything she had passed on. Okay, so maybe not passed exactly. But he'd all but blurted his love for her in grand sonnets every time she was near. Dropping hints and flirting every way he knew how to prepare for the moment he'd been dreaming about since the day he'd first laid eyes on her.

But before he'd gotten his chance—or maybe worked up the nerve—she'd stomped his heart and his self-worth beneath her designer shoes.

He struggled to keep a hardened look on his face as he watched her. Not wanting to give her the satisfaction of witnessing his pitiful infatuation.

But she didn't look happy. And she wasn't smiling. Even still, the whole thing was like salt in his wounds. Well good riddance. He hoped she had a terrible time tonight.

By the look on her face, it seemed that wish was coming true.

Mindlessly flipping another burned batch, Finn came out of his agonizing flashback, making a note to himself not to meander down memory lane while making pancakes—especially when preparing them for others.

After dumping a few of the worst ones, and scraping the charcoal from the others, he emerged from the kitchen with the stack and some maple syrup, and joined the girls at the table.

"Sorry ladies. But if you ask a man to do a woman's job you gotta prepare yourself for the consequ—Ow! Sadie, you have got to stop punching people!"

His feisty little sister smirked and stabbed at the top pancake with her fork. "I'll stop punching people when you men stop staying asinine things that justify a beating. Deal?"

"Relax, Cujo. Just a bit of sarcasm." Finn was getting his hide handed to him left and right between these two. While he had his hot buttons like anyone else, he was generally easy-going. Though admittedly his sarcastic talents hadn't fully developed until after prom night.

Finn's dad always claimed sarcasm was the lowest form of wit. He said Finn used it as a defense mechanism, but Finn didn't much buy into all that psychobabble and embraced his new identity as a man of confidence. Even arrogance if that meant no longer being the nice guy who finished last.

Joselyn cut into his thoughts. "Oh, Finn. I forgot to thank you for the flowers. Though, you should know now—since we're dating," she fluttered her lashes teasingly, "that my favorite flowers are daisies, not lilies. But still, it was very thoughtful."

Finn's chewing slowed, and he spoke around a syrup-drenched briquette. "Sorry, what are you talking about?"

Her smile went cockeyed, and she jabbed her thumb over

her shoulder to a grandiose bouquet of big white blooms. Lilies, she'd said. As if Finn knew the slightest thing about flowers.

"The flowers you sent me."

Great, she'd probably gotten flowers from one of her many admirers. Now Finn was going to look like a jerk. Again. Why hadn't he thought to get her flowers? *Idiot!*

"Uh, Joss, I didn't send you those."

She furled her brow, looking at him as if he'd been dealt a short stack between his ears. "But the card said it was from you."

They all sat in silence for an extended moment, looking to each other for a simple explanation.

"Wait. Didn't you get a similar bouquet after the fire?" Sadie set her fork down, that sleuthing look sparking in her eyes.

Finn's stomach lurched, and air crawled sluggishly through his lungs as he too set the now bent fork in his hand down on his plate.

"Well, yes. I assumed they were from my dad. White lilies are his flowers of choice. At least, for funerals. Needless to say, the gesture didn't exactly give me the warm fuzzies." Joselyn sprang up from the chair and retrieved the card attached with the flowers, with Finn following right behind her.

I hope I am always there to rescue you. Get well soon.
Love, Finn

A growl emerged from Finn's throat, and he used every ounce of his restraint to keep from ripping the note from her hand. "Sounds like a threat. To both of us." He could scarcely articulate those words with the angry bind of his jaw grinding it shut.

"Hey, hey! Be careful with that." Ever prepared, Sadie rushed to their side, Zip Lock and tweezers ready. "That's evidence." Bagging the note, she set it on the table.

Finn snatched up Sadie's phone and dialed out.

"Morning, gorgeous. Missing me already?"

"Oh, yes, terribly." Finn grunted, and Archer barked a laugh at the mix up. But Finn didn't much feel like laughing at the moment.

"Arch, you better get over here."

"I want every available hand tracking down where these flowers came from. That means local florists, grocery stores, online orders, anything you can think of. You find out where they came from we might get a description, a bank account number, or maybe a surveillance video. Don't come back until you have something for me, we clear?" Archer's orders were clipped and efficient, true to form for the ex-military sergeant he was. And with their assignments, the agents he'd brought with him scattered like ants, the local PDs on speakerphone chorused their agreement and signed off.

"Can I do anything?" Joselyn's face blanched, her fingers clasping nervously in front of her stomach.

The thin fabric of her form-fitting sleep shirt had inched up around her waist, exposing a slice of smooth, creamy skin. Several of the agents that had been present a few moments ago hadn't bothered to veil their appreciation for her figure, nearly tempting Finn to flare his nostrils and paw at the ground in warning.

Now only Archer remained and he only had eyes for Sadie, so the little peek of alabaster skin was for Finn alone.

Without lifting his eyes from his notepad Archer asked. "You don't happen to still have those other flowers and the note, do you?"

Joselyn shook her head. "No. I guess I left them in the hospital room last week when I was released."

"What'd the note say?"

She wrapped her slim arms around herself as if retreating into her shell. "It said 'Sorry for your loss.'" The tension on the fabric from her hands fisting at her sides pulled at the hem of her shirt even more until Finn could see her tiny belly button.

He swallowed back a groan, and probably some drool, and forced his eyes away, trying to stay focused on the case and the very real threat of danger that should be front and center in his mind. But even with his best intentions, and his eyes occupied elsewhere, he couldn't help but think about how beautiful and perfect she was to him—almost too intimidating to look at. Even now, with her hair still matted from sleeping against his chest and not an ounce of makeup, she was flawless.

And that made each of his own flaws all the more repulsive in his eyes.

What did she see when she looked at him? Did she see the angry burned skin at the back of his neck from the Monroe fire? Or did she see the scarring that went far deeper?

Did she see an honorable man fighting to protect her or an arrogant punk she'd once rejected toying with her mind?

Finn supposed he'd been a bit of each of those things. But he desperately hoped to prove he was bigger than the man who'd manipulated her into tears last night. That he wasn't going to keep holding a grudge, keeping one foot in the past to remind her what he'd thought of her all those years ago and all the years since.

He knew he needed to let it go. Needed to surrender all that rejection and hurt. And not only about Joselyn and how she'd once ripped his heart to shreds. But about all of it. Everything else that robbed him of becoming the man he needed to become to be worthy of her.

And worthy of grace for all his senseless mistakes.

Crossing the space between them, Finn stopped directly in front of Joselyn. Her eyes were weighted with worry, and she'd once again trapped her bottom lip between her teeth. Her arms wrapping ever tighter around her slender frame seeking comfort. He smiled down at her lovely face to put her at ease. She could use a distraction and he could think of a perfect way to do exactly that.

Though sadly, not with Archer and Sadie still talking flowers and strategy in the room.

He stood close enough to breath in the sweet and minty elixir that seemed to diffuse from her skin, filling his senses with something so much more tempting than revenge. After he glanced over his shoulder to check their audience, he touched his hands to her hips, barely breathing when his fingers treasured the forbidden boundary of the petal-soft skin before he gently righted the rising hemline.

Her arms loosened around her but stayed in place, and for several long moments Finn's mouth wouldn't cooperate. He wanted to kiss her. Hold her. Reassure her it would all be okay. That he'd keep her safe no matter what.

Instead, he pried his hands away from their newfound addiction and tried to smile. Might have even tried to wink, to lighten the mood the way he did best.

"I told you I don't like to share." Except, his voice shook when the truth in his sarcasm threatened to give him away completely. It was far too soon to lay all his cards on the table, but he was tempted to do just that.

"That's a little possessive for a guy who's only pretending." He saw the challenge in her eyes. Too fierce for simple curiosity.

Leaning in until his lips brushed her ear, he whispered, "Who said I was pretending?"

"So … there's nothing in this for you?" she whispered too and then leaned away to read the truth from his face.

The words were out before he thought better of them, so he wagged his eyebrows and covered with a smile. "I wouldn't put it that way."

Chapter 29

Joselyn Whyte

"So, you're sure?"

Despite the seriousness of the task, Joselyn couldn't help but snort a laugh. "Archer, are you kidding? I can't see a thing from this. That could be anybody."

After a full twenty-four hours of zero progress on the flowers, the eighteenth endless surveillance video proved her breaking point.

The grainy man on the screen—who may or may not be a killer—looked like any plain old average Joe. Like the last thirty or so guys on tape, from more than a dozen stores, that had bought lilies in that past two weeks. And that was only scratching the surface of the videos yet to be sorted through—or even come in.

Not to mention all the places that didn't have surveillance. Or all the men that had placed orders online or by phone, or who didn't walk out with a nice telling white bouquet, or whose faces had managed to elude the video feed. Like the man who had dropped the first arrangement at the information desk at the hospital, who'd worn a flu mask and had found a hole in the hospital's security coverage.

The flowers could have been shipped in from anywhere. All they knew at present was that this guy in the video from Schnuck's grocery store bought white lilies similar to the arrangements Joselyn had received around the same time—designating him as a new suspect.

"Facial recognition picked up this one." Archer angled his pen at the screen. "Works for Parkway School District so we had him on file."

Thus the poor guy was being picked up by Sal and brought in for questioning, while she sat scrutinizing the fuzzy images of strangers who might end up on the losing end of the lotto today. Dozens had already been questioned and dismissed. It seemed like a true needle-in-a-haystack impossibility, but Joselyn stuck it out—wanting to show her appreciation for the FBI's diligence.

"I'll stick around and see if I recognize him in person. But this all seems kinda crazy. I mean, we looked through all those order forms, but any one of those could be a fake name, right?"

Before Archer could answer, her worries started snowballing. "Didn't most of those places say they don't even make customers fill out forms with personal information? And so what if I don't recognize him? It's quite possible I've never seen my attacker before. And what makes us think this guy will slip up after creating a bafflingly brilliant, evidence-free house fire, car bomb, and whatever genius plan he has to roast me alive next? Like he's gonna waltz right into the florist, look directly at the camera, and hand over his credit card?"

She shook her head, her heart anchoring to hopelessness and sinking faster and faster into a dark, drowning abyss. "Thank you for everything you're doing, but I feel like I'm wasting everyone's time." *Dang it, don't you dare cry.* She sniffled back a few tears and thought seriously about surrendering to her fate.

This guy was too smart. Too fixated. And despite his fiery signature, too unpredictable.

The words from the bouquet from "Finn" rushed back to her. She shivered. What if something happened to him? Or Sadie, Archer, or Sal?

Even the thought made her consider going rogue and sacrificing herself on the burning alter. While they chased down one dead end after another they became puppets in his little game. Would this next time end it all?

Every thought turned morbid and paranoid. She hated constantly looking over her shoulder, but she also knew that Archer wouldn't give up on this even if she begged him to. Which, she didn't think she possessed the nerve to do.

"The safe house is still on the table."

"No, Archer. He's motivated. And I can't hide forever. We'll lose any chance we have at tracking him down if I fall off the grid."

They'd weighed the pros and cons already. Numerous times.

His hard hand came to rest on her arm, and she looked up into his eyes—eyes with deadly resolve. "We're gonna nail this guy, Joss. I know it seems like a long shot, but you gotta trust. And let me do my job."

Of course, he was right. The panic was very persuasive, but if she gave in to fear it would suck away what could possibly be the last days or weeks of her life. "You're right. And I trust you."

"Not me, Joss. I'm darn good at my job, but I'm not God." Somehow this solid brute of a man seemed to fortify even more with his next words. "Most things are bigger than you and me. But you're in good hands. Of that, I have no doubt."

Joselyn drew in a deep breath, willing Archer's words to absorb into her heart.

He had no doubts.

Well, that made one of them.

"Hi, Yia-Yia. How're you feeling today?" In her attempts to avoid any discussion of the boarded entry of McKnight Grove and the nightmarish highlight reel of the car bombing incident looping in her mind, Joselyn's voice emerged a bit too energized, catching Yia-Yia with a startle.

"Sorry, didn't mean to scare you, just stopping in for a little visit." Softening her voice, she searched her grandmother's vacant eyes for any sign of recognition.

"Well, I suppose I wouldn't mind a little distraction from

this ridiculous knitting nonsense." Abandoning the knitting needles to her lap, she rolled her crystal-blue eyes. "They're trying to bore me to death. That or maybe I'd turn one of those big needles on myself. Gave it a thought. Much rather play some hold 'em. Difficult game to play by oneself." She lifted a manicured brow. "You know how to play poker, young lady?"

With a sinking heart, Joselyn lowered herself to the chair beside the woman who'd raised her, who taught her everything she knew—including how to play Texas hold 'em.

Today was not a day Joselyn could handle duking out the truth, so playing along would have to do. Striving to keep her voice unwavering in her disappointment, she said, "Yes, ma'am. My grandmother taught me. Great game. Shall I fetch some cards?"

Yia-Yia's face lit up; the lines around her eyes and mouth crinkling with delight. Scooping up the knitting needles, she dropped them into a small trash can and dusted off her hands. "Ah, yes, my dear." Batting her hand at the discarded scarf, she flashed Joselyn a sassy smirk and winked, "Sweet Moses, that was boring! You saved me. I will be forever indebted." Placing her hand on her heart, she dipped her head in an amusing bow.

Now, there was the Yia-Yia Joselyn remembered. And though she didn't seem to recognize her own flesh and blood, sharing some quality time with someone she loved was enough for today.

Jogging out to the supply room, Joselyn scrounged up a sleeve of poker chips and a deck of playing cards and went back to shuffle and deal to the card shark herself.

Yia-Yia had always loved a good poker game. Games of all kinds, really. Her friends would come over, and Joselyn would sit enrapt by all the strategies and rules of Yia-Yia's weekly bridge, hold 'em, or bunko tournaments with a bunch of crazy old gamblers.

"So, what's your name, sugar?" Yia-Yia left her cards on

the table and lifted the edges—her face trained and perfectly aloof. Years of observing her grandmother's poker face had helped Joselyn develop and fine tune her own defense mechanism—something that was slipping with the intoxicating charms and devilish good looks of one high school nemesis.

"Joselyn." Her throat tightened.

"Oh, my, what a beautiful name. Then again, it would have to be to suit such a lovely girl." Tossing in two chips, Yia-Yia waited for Joselyn to kick in and then motioned for the flop. "So tell me about your fella?"

Joselyn felt her eyes spring wide. "Pardon me?"

With a smirk, Yia-Yia upped the ante. "I'm an old bitty, so I obviously wasn't born yesterday. Plus, I can see from the storm behind your eyes that something's on your mind. A matter of the heart, perhaps?"

The clarity of her speech alone was miraculous. Joselyn was tempted to page Rosie to get a read on this but feared she'd lose the moment if she broke this connection. She should also change the subject, but she hesitated long enough to think it over. There was so much weighing on her heart about Finn, about their past. Things she had never told Yia-Yia because it would hurt her too much. But while the woman in front of her was her grandmother, she was also a stranger.

On the turn—the fourth card dealt face up—Yia-Yia threw in a few more chips as well as some gentle prodding. "I'm a great listener. And I tend to be forgetful, so your secrets are safe with me."

Releasing a heavy-laden breath—easing the burden of what she was about to say— Joselyn took a moment to pray that she'd made the right decision and then started at the beginning.

Meeting Finn in the hallway, falling for him a little more each day—the abbreviated version of the events leading up to the prom. "And that's when his best friend, Cody, approached me about prom. After I turned him down—and he guessed the reason why—he said he could help Finn realize that I was interested so he would ask me. Said Finn was shy and needed some coaxing."

And finally Joselyn turned over the river. Round one went to Yia-Yia with two pair. No surprise there.

With a practiced sweep of her hand, Yia-Yia collected her winnings while Joselyn got to shuffling—like old times. Joselyn smiled at the parade of memories. Thankful that she had some good ones she could call upon for a rainy day.

"Go on, dear."

Oh, boy. Here goes. "But then prom came, and Finn had already asked someone else. Cody showed up at my door that night and offered to take me. And since I already had the dress, I went, barely arriving before the last song of the night."

While she spoke about the dance, Joselyn continued shuffling and dealing, glad that something was occupying her hands that started to tremble as the stress of the tumbling words made every part of her ache.

"... since we'd only made the end of the actual dance, Cody insisted that I accompany him to the after-party at his parents' house." Though the Largeman family wasn't nearly as wealthy as Joselyn's father, their house was expansive. That had been part of the problem. Too secluded. Sound proof.

Suddenly, what Joselyn feared most took hold of her. She spoke through the daze as she drifted off on the memory.

Why did she agree to this?

Wandering around Cody's parents' mansion, amidst a sea of inebriated faces and deafening music, Joselyn wished she could close her eyes and be back at home. Only home at Yia-Yia's, not at her father's estate. And since her father wasn't answering his phone, and she couldn't seem to find Cody anywhere, she didn't have a ride home. And calling a cab would be an open invitation for the driver to fabricate some misdeed and make a pretty penny with the tabloids. Happened before which was how she knew the ensuing fallout with her father would be particularly unpalatable. So she did the only thing she could think to do at her helpless juncture. Closed her eyes and wished.

Only a moment passed until someone crushed her. Literally. Her body crumpling when a tremendous weight squashed her onto the lavish marble floor. Darkness bled through her eyes as the drunken oaf peeled himself off of her and shouted, "Stage dive! That was awesome! Who's next?"

Spots of color and light slowly crept back into her vision. Her head was now throbbing from something other than the noise. She winced again as the room stayed on the merry-go-round for another long moment of nauseous agony.

"You okay?"

Her heart turned over. She knew that voice. Peeking open one eye, she saw a broad hand extended, and beyond it, a scowling Finn.

As he came into focus, she noticed his hair was mussed beyond its usual beachy waves, his tie gone, and his shirt unbuttoned at the collar. Reaching out for help, his warm hand swallowed all the cold in her body with a single touch as he hefted her off the ground.

How could he have asked that Renee Ross girl? She was a viper. Mean and predatory, and unapologetically so. Was that Finn's type? Did Joselyn even know him at all?

The room did another tumultuous turn, and she felt her body sway before another bumper car drunk collided with her backside and shoved her into Finn's arms. Clinging to him kept her from reuniting with the cold, hard floor. He steadied her, looking down with those deep sea eyes that held her captive day and night.

His expression softened for a flicker of a moment, and then the glint in his eyes returned them to steel. "Come on. Let's get you outta this mess." He led her through several rooms packed with people until he found a less populous area.

Everything was blurry, and she struggled to concentrate on anything but Finn's hand in hers. "Finn?"

"What?" His tone was sharper than she'd ever heard it. He tugged his hand away.

"I want to go home. And I haven't seen Cody in an hour. He was acting really weird after we got here." Feeling like she needed to close her eyes again to concentrate on her words, she let them fall shut, relieved to be able to hide from Finn's surly look of disdain. What was his problem anyway? "Would you please take me home?"

Silence stretched longer than seemed natural, so she opened her eyes. The light pierced her skull with a profound pain, and she felt another bout of dizziness swing her around again.

"Why don't I track down your date Cody for you? Wouldn't want to miss out on any end-of-the-date rituals, now would you?"

With the spinning in her head, she could barely make sense of his words. "I'd really rather just go now. Please? Don't you have an old truck, or something?" She loved old trucks. She'd learned how to drive in Yia-Yia's classic cherry red 1966 Ford F100.

Taking in the strain of his magnificent features, her moment of nostalgia faded. He was angry about something. She about reached up to smooth the lines knotting his eyebrows together, but he spoke before she got the chance. And based on his words, saved her the embarrassment.

"Too lowly for a princess. And, hey, you held out for better, so we'll get you your carriage." Grabbing her arm, he tugged her along with him.

Scarcely keeping up, her heel caught the raised edge of the threshold transitioning the floor from tile to carpet and she stumbled forward like a rag doll. Only she didn't land on the floor. She was instantly swept up in Finn's arms. And she decided—despite the venomous glare and the scowl—it was a pretty nice place to be.

The brushing cadence of his steps on the plush surface and the soft sway of her body in his arms made her feel a bit sleepy, so she relaxed against his chest and shielded her eyes from the pain-inducing light. "Are you taking me home now?" The words pressed into his shirt and she snuggled a little closer—breathing in that tantalizing musk of a guy that didn't need cologne to smell like fresh spice and warm leather.

His steps quickened.

"Why are you so grumpy?" she thought she heard herself murmur. But as the music behind them faded, the sound they approached swelled with equal intensity and irritation.

And then Finn stopped, one arm stretching out from beneath the cradle under her knees to rap on a door.

She didn't need to see that the door had swung open, or who was standing behind it, the artificial man smell rushed on the movement of air and stung her nose.

Cody.

The thumping music rocked her eardrums so hard she swore they must have shaken loose. And when she felt another swirl of air rush around her she peeled her tired eyes open and saw several guys leaving a room. A few of them coughing and laughing, one of them as droopy eyed as Joselyn. Cody stepped out into the hall.

She looked away and glanced up at Finn who looked intent on ignoring her, which must have taken quite the effort considering he was holding her tight against his chest.

"Finn, please." Something felt wrong. And she didn't know what was going on here, but she felt like a loose thread was exposed somewhere and one pull would unravel all the safety she felt here in Finn's moody arms.

Tightening her grip on his neck, she inched up closer to his ear to compensate for the overbearing noise. "Finn, please. Take me home."

But he still wouldn't look at her. Instead, he pried her away from his chest and dumped her in Cody's arms.

She couldn't be sure, but when his voice broke through the thundering bass line it sounded something like, "Here you go, man. She's all yours." And before the door closed, the last thing she saw was his arrogant swagger, striding away after depositing her at the threshold of Cody's lair. The doorway to her own personal Hades.

Those self-preservation techniques kicked in just in time. Unfurling her mind from the wicked memory, she blinked back the tears.

And then she saw Yia-Yia—eyes so earnest and kind, swimming with an understanding that made Joselyn regret taking her along for the ride.

"That's not the end of the story, is it?" Yia-Yia's voice was muggy, her gaze too keen despite the missing pieces of memory.

Joselyn couldn't lie, yet she couldn't quite gather up the nerve to purge the rest of the truth at the moment. Either way it felt like she was taking advantage. Instead of confirming, she moved on. "But now this guy, Finn, is back in my life. And it seems like he's changed." Joselyn shook her head, hating that tug of vulnerability, and calling to trial her foolish heart versus her sensibly stoic brain over one particular doozy of a question.

Can people really change?

"Hmm." Yia-Yia cleared her throat and tapped her lips with her Barbie-pink fingernail. "Do you still love him?"

Joselyn didn't need to mull it over to produce an answer, but she gave it a moment regardless. "Yes. But I wish I didn't. Everything seems tainted by the past. And I'm not convinced I'm strong enough to get over it."

"Love is the strongest force in this world, Joselyn. Just think about that man on the cross."

Joselyn's brain screeched to a halt.

Something about Yia-Yia had always bent toward the spiritual or whimsical, but she'd held those deeply personal convictions close to the cuff. There had been a quiet strength to her faith that Joselyn hadn't been able to decide was more admirable or confusing. Regardless, she'd never been this frank with Joselyn in the past. Granted, a lot of baggage was just unloaded and Yia-Yia might simply be reacting in an effort to console the damaged young woman who'd spilled her guts to a stranger.

"Oh, fiddlesticks. I chipped a nail."

And just like that—with one blink—Yia-Yia's eyes changed and the slate was wiped clean.

If that was mercy pouring over her poor grandmother, Joselyn would take it,

"You there, nurse. Would you grab my nail polish?" She muttered incoherent babble and something like, "I look like a *schlemiel.*"

So Joselyn stayed and preoccupied herself by fixing Yia-Yia's manicure, feeling mildly unburdened that she'd shared at least a part of her story with an actual person, instead of a journal to her dead mother.

And it wasn't until later that Joselyn remembered the warm wave of peace that had invaded her body and soul when she'd stepped outside her grief and let someone else carry it. Peace that followed her the rest of the day.

Chapter 30

Finn Carson

Ribbons of golden sunshine wove in through the flimsy shades of Finn's bedroom window, adequately announcing the arrival of the day and a time well past suitable for lazing around in bed. But sleep had been a stubborn target last night, and more than nightmares were to blame.

Joselyn had occupied his fitful mind well into the wee hours of the morning—and not because of her fantasy-worthy allure. It was something else. Something had changed in a single day, and that veneer had gone up again, masking all the progress they'd made in the past few weeks.

What had happened at the nursing home yesterday? Was something wrong with Yia-Yia?

Naturally when he'd asked her about it she'd shrugged it off. The Future Mr. & Mrs. Archer Hayes had been hovering more than usual and then Finn's parents had stopped by after their date night, squashing any possibility of alone time for Finn to dig any deeper.

Finn had even offered to pull couch duty again, but Archer had staked a claim and in doing so shared a secret smile with Sadie, triggering an expedient departure from the big brother who did not want to know.

Dodger huffed out a snort of air and wiggled a little tighter against Finn's leg. Having kept him company in his hours of unrest, the pup deserved a little mattress time for his faithful companionship. Finn dug his fingers into the mutt's fluff and rewarded him further with a nice long scratch behind the ears. "What do you think, Dodge, time to get up?"

Dodger froze mid-stretch, legs jutting perpendicular to Finn's, and then hurled himself off the bed. Engaging in a little dance and turn at the top of the stairs, the dog signaled his owner's neglect of the call of nature until Finn untangled his weary limbs from the sheets, tossed on a hoodie and some pajama pants, and ventured down the stairs to let the dog do his business.

When they got back inside Finn's cell phone was rocking out from the coffee table. Closing the distance quickly he scooped it up and answered without a glance at the caller ID.

"Hello?"

"Please hold for Declan Whyte." The woman's voice was as pinched and irritating as the request.

A bland, jazzy elevator mix played over the line while Finn waited. And waited. Right when he was about to throw in the towel, that signature Scottish burr piped in.

"Finn, my boy. We'll need to make this quick, I have a conference call in a few minutes."

"Fine. Fire away." Finn tried not to wince at his word choice.

"Unfortunately, since you and Joselyn missed your date the other night the press has gone wild with accusations again. Now, I was able to keep the car bombing under wraps, but the circus has only begun with the speculation about your breakup."

"Sir, I hardly think the public's opinion about our relationship is important right now. Joselyn and I were almost killed." *You narcissistic pig!*

He found the unspoken insult helped to curb his anger.

"Well I realize it seems trivial, but the weight of the campaign is bearing down and we have to keep up appearances when we can. So, I have issued a leak about Joselyn feeling under the weather and rescheduled your date for Friday night. Same place and time. Security will be firm."

The man breathed commands. It seemed it was the only language Declan Whyte knew.

"Fine. But with all due respect, sir, have you even gone to

see Joselyn? She was understandably shaken up. I'm sure she could use a little more support from you."

"Ahh," the native grunt reduced the man to a grizzly. "She's a tough lass. She'll be fine."

Finn gritted his teeth so hard his jaw clicked. "This is bigger than your precious campaign, Mr. Whyte. This is about the safety of your daughter. Remember her? A living, breathing person, not a pawn to score you points in the polls."

"Watch your tone, lad, I am not to be trifled with. You'd do well to remember our agreement."

He clenched his fists until crescent moons cut into his palms. Declan Whyte was a self-serving egomaniac, and he didn't deserve her.

Thinking of Princess Joselyn in her lonely, ivory tower stole the steam from his mounting fury. He wouldn't trade all the wealth in the world for the life she'd endured because of this cold, callus man. "I feel sorry for you, sir. You're missing out on something with immeasurably more value than your precious career. Open your eyes. Your daughter needs her dad. And since you refuse to be a decent human being, let alone a passable father, I'll be there. I'll be the one she can count on. But know this—I don't work for you. You couldn't pay me any amount of money to stay away from your daughter—"

"That's enough!" The razor-edged rebuke forewarned the force of his retaliation. But Finn couldn't care less. The man was the lowest of the low. Abandoned and manipulated his daughter to suit his ego-driven gain, deceptively dangling love and affection he had no intention of giving for her compliance.

"If you so much as cross me, boy—" He cut off with a grunt. "The conference call. I shall spare you with this one warning—play your part Friday night. I will not have another slip up. Consider yourself lucky I won't make you pay for that little tantrum."

"I am lucky, sir. But it has nothing to do with your

sparing me and everything to do with your amazing daughter. *You'd* do well to remember *that.*"

Finn wished for simpler times where he could actually slam down the phone. Severing the connection with the resolute jab on a touch screen didn't seem to satisfy the violent urges blazing in his blood.

So he started pacing, grumbling the unspoken frustrations under his breath.

Soft scraping followed his ranting, and he looked down to see the faithful Dodger warring out the anger march to match. Of course, the wagging tail and lapping pink tongue didn't much mirror Finn's tense simmering rage, but he appreciated the support.

He'd finally wrestled down the last remnants of fury when his phone rang.

Private caller.

"What now?" He snapped, expecting Declan Whyte's retaliation from being hung up on.

"I'm sorry, Finn. This is Trisha Bollivar, from the group home. Is now a bad time for a visit? I'm afraid I have some news."

Switching gears, his anger melted away and equal concern filled in its place. "I'll be right there."

With each step the weathered boards groaned the swan song of the weary, aging house. The aching sound beneath Finn's feet resounded yet another failure as it shuddered through him.

Why hadn't he replaced that loose, splintered board before the winter weather settled in? Someone could get hurt. And that wobbling banister was certainly not up to code. There was so much to do. So much need. And Finn was certainly no hero.

The house served as a reminder of that.

The gutters were constantly spilling over from the clogging remnants of autumn leaves. A dusty black shutter had slipped loose during a storm and hung diagonally across an opaque window. And the roof, well, Finn had done some patching to remedy a few leaky spots but the whole thing needed to go. Everything about the house seemed to sag—as if it were a vestibule for the forgotten.

The screen door whined, the sound trailing away on the bitter wind. Finn rapped on the next peeling red door. And when *that* door echoed a wail on its equally rusty, old hinges it revealed a compassionate Trisha Bollivar—looking as stressed and pained as the old, moaning house.

The middle-aged woman had started the group home over twenty years ago, after losing her husband and newborn son to carbon monoxide poisoning while she worked the night shift as a nurse, turning her tragedy into a purpose.

Trisha stepped back to let him in, and he noticed the tight strain of her tired gray eyes shadowed under the new entry light Finn had installed last month. "How is she?"

She shook her head, the chestnut brown of her wispy hair now overrun with an overgrowth of coarse white making her fifty years seem more like seventy. The woman looked overworked and undernourished, but she did the best she could to give these kids a stable intermediate home before they could be permanently placed, or in some cases, reunited with their parents.

"I tried to explain it, but I'm afraid she didn't quite understand. She's pretty upset and wouldn't stop asking for you."

He tipped his head toward the hallway. "She in her room?"

With a sad smile, Trisha nodded. "I was thinking maybe you could take her out if you're not too busy. Chrissy has a visit from a couple who are working toward her adoption in an hour. Probably be best if lil' miss isn't here for that."

"Sure, I'd be happy to take her. It's still early, so I'll have all day to cheer her up. What time is naptime again?"

"Around two o'clock. But she hasn't been sleeping well the past week." The woman wrung her frail hands together—

hands that somehow managed to carry all the pain and worry for the six young girls under her care.

Finn touched her shoulder. "I'll bring her back before bedtime. Give you a little break."

As he started down the hallway he allowed a miniscule touch of pride. Contrary to the abysmal exterior, the little improvements he'd made to the interior of the run-down Victorian house over the past few months had really made it feel like a home. A slap of fresh paint in a pale, friendly yellow made the rooms glow with warmth and cheer. New overhead light fixtures chased away the dim casts of spooky shadows from previously drab, lamp-lighted rooms.

The floors were newly refinished and glossy, tested by Finn and the girls upon completion to be sock-slideable. The plumbing was now functional, and the musky old air that had plumed from the gritty vents newly filtered and healthy since he'd cleaned out the ducts.

The efforts weren't enough to turn the home into a showpiece, but compared to the wreck he'd stumbled upon almost five months ago, it was becoming a place where a kid could flourish under a nurturing hand.

The soles of his Converse squeaked on the smooth surface as he traversed the hall. When he got to the right door it flew open.

"Finn! You came!"

And his heart melted right there, as the little girl, so innocent and forgiving, launched into his arms and refused to let go.

Chapter 31

Joselyn Whyte

"**Y**ou have one unheard message. First unheard message," the prim voicemail lady announced as Joselyn sat at the coffee shop in Downtown Kirkwood, lazing over a steaming Zen tea after having spent a few hours at her shop.

The day might have seemed commonplace thus far, but a normal day wouldn't have her under the guard of several menacing shadows. One in the form of a behemoth U.S. Marshal poised a few tables away. Two incognito FBI agents stationed outside the building. And an additional two squad cars patrolling the area.

She wasn't sure if her father had some influence over the excessive protective measures or if the well-meaning overkill was courtesy of her new friends at the FBI, but she wasn't about to balk at feeling smothered.

Unease raked over her skin at the mere thought of being watched, preyed upon, but why hide away? Having almost been cremated in her bed, and then narrowly escaping being blown to bits in her state-of-the-art secured vehicle, it seemed nowhere was particularly safe.

"*Hey, Joss, it's me.*"

Nowhere.

Her heart quickened. The trill of his voice feathering down her spine. *It's me.* They'd developed a familiarity in two short weeks of make believe that made her crave something just like it, only real.

"*I'll be a little tied up to—*" Cut off by a crash in the background, his voice muffled words for someone else—

something not meant for Joselyn's ears. Something that sounded suspiciously like, *"Are you okay, sweetheart?"*

Whatever came next was more adequately muted by Finn's hand. His words from before came unbidden, calling her a fool. *You, Joselyn Whyte, are the only girl I'm seeing.*

Kicking back in at full volume, he stuttered, fumbling for words through a scatter of "ums" and "uhs"—like he knew he was busted. *"Anyways, Archer assured me you were well covered for today. And as I'm sure your father informed you, we have round two of our first date Friday night. Can't wait. I'll call you tomorrow."* He hesitated.

Was he feeling guilty for lying through his teeth? And what must this *sweetheart* be thinking about his tactless plans for a date with another woman right in front of her?

"Stay safe, okay, princess?"

And that was it. But it didn't make sense. They'd been spending all their time together. Well, almost. Except Saturdays.

And then, like the ever popular light bulb analogy, a name illuminated from the corner of her mind.

Kendi.

Uncontrollable indignation raged in her chest. The calming effects of her brew overrun with her heated scorn. *Zen tea, my eye.*

Rising with resolve to sort out the truth of this—no longer only—tabloid hearsay, Joselyn marched out of the café, conveniently located below Finn's apartment, and went to go catch him red-handed.

The gun-toting marshal on her heels might come in handy should she find Finn in a compromising position with the little minx.

The thought of his betrayal, although fake, felt so real she had the fleeting inclination to run. Run to protect her heart from the ugly truth behind his door. But she was tired of running. Tired of letting other people dictate who she needed to be.

Make me strong.

The prayer slipped from her soul on an effortless breath and was instantly forgotten.

Doing her best to calm the spasms she'd worked up in her chest, she raised her hand to the door and froze. Did she really have a right to come barging into his life?

He certainly didn't mind barging into yours.

She thought of all the ways he'd been leading her to believe that he cared—and not only when people were watching.

The surge of warm fuzzies from the memories died when she heard the TV sound from behind his door. She hadn't even bothered to check for his truck outside, and since a woman was leaving when Joselyn and her hulk had entered the building she hadn't needed to buzz up to confirm. But he was definitely here.

Breathing in a lungful of courage, she knocked.

"Hang tight, I'll get the door and grab the popco—" The crescendo of his voice met an abrupt end. She could feel his presence just beyond the door.

Slowly, the door inched open enough to allow Joselyn a tall drink of a gorgeous and … guilty man.

"What are you doing here?" Pulling the door tight against his side, Finn's eyes shifted, taking in the mammoth bodyguard a few feet behind her.

She crossed her arms and let her glare do the talking.

"Joss, I … uhh …" The silence was thick enough to braid. His eyes were so conflicted she about caved and walked away, letting him keep whatever secret was tormenting his conscience.

But the long-ignored hurt rapped against her breastbone, so she grabbed her gumption by the boots—er, heels. "Thought you *couldn't wait* to see me." Raising an eyebrow, she pinned him in place with her stare, needing the truth, no matter how painful.

The cornered rat released a helpless sigh, his broad shoulders collapsing in surrender, and then he checked open the door with a bump of his shoulder. "Come on in."

With confidence that felt as plastic as brunette Barbie, Joselyn prompted her legs to strut through the door like she belonged. The glittering sound of the Disney introduction "When You Wish Upon a Star" filtered through the room drawing Joselyn's eyes to the couch where she saw ... a little girl?

What?

Unable to move, she stared as the adorable little toddler—maybe three years old—slid off the cushion, scurried on Hello Kitty socks across the room, and hid behind Finn's legs. Tiny fingers gripped his track pants and luminous pale blue eyes, fearful and round as saucers, peered around his thigh for a split second before she buried her face again.

Joselyn darted a glance between the two. Was this Kendi? Was she—*gulp*—Finn's daughter? Just when she thought she might be warming to him, she felt the cold settle back in—freezing over the parts of her heart Finn had kindled to life.

Why had he never mentioned her? The shame on his face and the air of secrecy made her sick with memories of her childhood. Her father's neglect. The way he hid her from the world as if he were ashamed to have her for a daughter. A shiny layer of deceit coating every word and deed to bolster his ego and greed.

Maybe Finn and Declan had more in common than she thought.

Waiting for an explanation, Joselyn conveyed her furious questions across the divide with the hardest look she could uncover. His lack of a response was quickly rectifying the old barrier between them. And that space, while only a few feet, might as well have been the Grand Canyon for the lonely echo of her heart.

How could she have been so blind? What a fool she was to purge the truth to him when he'd fed her only lies. Was any of this real?

Of course it wasn't. *Stupid!* This whole thing was a farce. And so far the only one who was buying it was her.

An awkward grating noise emerged from Finn's throat

before he spoke. "This is Kendi." Right, as if that explained everything.

The little angel-faced toddler stuck her head out to steal another glance at the strange mute woman who had barged in, probably scaring the little girl senseless.

Joselyn's fiery scorn simmered with one glance. Never had she seen a more beautiful and enchanting little girl. Big blue eyes, tiny little button nose, and the most adorable sandy-colored puff of tight and frizzy curls.

But she didn't much look like Finn. If he was indeed her father, the child's mother must be at least part black—the bronze, honeyed tint of her skin contradicted the rest of her coloring.

Shooting one last questioning glance at Finn to fess up proved useless. So she crouched down, avoiding his eyes all together. Maybe for good. It would certainly help in regaining her sanity.

"Hi, Kendi. My name is Joselyn, I'm a … uh … friend of your …"

What was he to her? Sperm donor, friend, Brownie leader? What? I mean, the man could perhaps take a moment to explain himself. He certainly wasn't shy about flapping his gums most of the time. And yet somehow, *now* was when the big dumb ox finally found his filter. Perfect timing.

"A friend of *his*," she amended, extending her hand and a sincere smile.

Kendi shrank back behind his leg, her slender little arms, encased in a neon pink shirt, clung to him.

"It's okay, sweetheart." The familiar way Finn's hand reached back and brushed over the little girl's curls made Joselyn love him and hate him all the more. Manually loosing Kendi's arms, he bent down and hugged her to his side. "Kendi, this is my *very* special friend, Joselyn. She came over to meet you." His eyes locked with Joselyn's, pleading something unspoken and much too loaded to fully comprehend.

Joselyn held on to his gaze as long as she could, trying to

piece it all together. But then a tiny hand stretched out to meet her so Joselyn gave Kendi her full attention.

"It's a pleasure to meet you, Kendi. My, what a pretty little girl you are. Whatcha watching?" Joselyn angled her head toward the TV, and the little girl lit into a shy grin.

"*Cinderella*." The meek and heartbreakingly sweet sound about made Joselyn cry.

Smiling, Joselyn revved up her excitement. "Cinderella! She's my favorite fairytale princess."

"Me too!" Kendi squeaked.

"Not Snow White?" Finn smirked.

Oh, now he's got something to say.

Joselyn ignored him. "Oh, look. I love this part. There's Gus Gus."

Kendi nodded in agreement and smiled as the stout little mouse on screen was fitted with a red shirt and booties.

Joselyn could feel Finn's eyes devouring her, but she refused to look at him. "Would you mind if I watch a little bit with you? I've got some hot pink nail polish in my purse that would match your pretty shirt perfectly. We could paint our nails?"

Her heart soared when Kendi's little face came alive, pixie dust sparkling in her bright eyes.

"Okay!" Dainty little fingers wrapped around Joselyn's hand, and Kendi led her to the couch where they sat and played beauty shop. Joselyn got to be the fairy godmother to princess Kendirella. The play on words made the little girl giggle every time she said it.

They watched the lovelorn girl fall for the handsome prince and live happily ever after, and Joselyn did everything in her power to fight back a cynical—and far too unladylike—snort that might shatter a young girl's dreams of fairytale endings.

The heat radiating from Finn's gaze was too intense to ignore as the two lovebirds rode off in the wedding carriage on screen. So she dug deep for her courage and met his gaze for the first time since the movie had started, pouring all her hurt from his distrust and his lies into her eyes.

Kendi stirred on her lap with a sniffle and tell-tale eye rub before flopping back into the crook of Joselyn's now tingling arm. The movement effectively cut the tie that had been rebuilding a bridge between them without her permission. Kendi's long lashes came to rest on her cherubic cheeks, and unable to deny the small affection, Joselyn swept the pad of her thumb over that downy skin, love tugging at her so hard a piece of her heart pulled away.

"Nap time," Finn whispered.

They both rose, and Finn closed the space, pressing against them to gather Kendi from Joselyn's arms. The exchange of the sleeping angel tangled their arms. When Joselyn looked up time slowed and the deep chug of her pulse thundered in her ears.

More passed between them than seemed possible without words.

Feeling her shield of anger falling away, she unwound her arms and deposited the Sleeping Beauty in his possession.

"I want Josh-wyn put me to bed." Sleepy eyes batting, Kendi rested her head on Finn's shoulder but reached out a limp arm to Joselyn.

"How about I carry you up, and Joss will tuck you in?" His eyes softened in question, begging Joselyn to trust him.

Kendi's only response was a yawn. So Joselyn followed Finn up the stairs to his bedroom, helplessly drawn to the memory of the last time she'd been here, bluffing her way around her attraction and yes, playing with fire.

Something she knew she'd been toying with ever since.

While Finn eased Kendi down atop his made bed, Joselyn went to retrieve a spare blanket draped over an armchair and brought it to cover the teensy little body.

The expanse of the king-sized bed and the ocean of blankets surrounding the small child tempted Joselyn to climb in and snuggle away any loneliness Kendi might feel.

But Finn's hand enveloped hers and persuaded her toward the stairs. Ready for answers, she let him tug her along until—

"Josh-wyn, do you know a bedtime sto-we?"

Joselyn slipped her hand free of Finn's and whispered, "I'll be down in a minute."

Finn Carson

Finn stalled near the top of the stairs, out of sight.

"Bedtime story, hmm ... I could make one up *or* I think I might remember a song my mom used to sing to me before bed."

Kendi must have nodded her response because Joselyn voice was the only reply. "All right, the song it is."

Unable to help himself, he inched forward so he could peer around the corner to take in the scene. The sugary sweetness in Joselyn's voice struck the center of his chest like a battering ram.

"Sweetie-baby close your eyes, dream of daisy lullabies.
Snuggle close and make the most of dreaming sunshine in the night.
Sweetie-baby starry eyed, love you to the moon so bright
Cuddle closer, warm and just a kiss, my dear, sleep tight, goodnight."

To a tune reminiscent of "Old Lang Sine," the slow and tender melody on Joselyn's honeyed voice unraveled the binds over his tortured heart.

The back of her head, cascading with minky, midnight locks halfway to her waist, was all he could see. He wished desperately to have witnessed the unguarded moment on her face.

She bent forward, touching a kiss to Kendi's forehead, and lifted gingerly from beside the sleeping child on his bed. Tiptoeing away, she caught him, her wide eyes betraying her embarrassment before she brushed past and vaulted down the stairs.

He followed, still entranced by the tender moment, until she spun back and propped her fists on her hips.

"Speak."

Ruff! Dodger's tags jingled as he trotted from his daybed. Sitting at her feet, he lifted his front legs and pawed at the air.

The scowl on her pretty face subsided when she glanced down at Dodger. "Not you, Dodge."

Stepping closer to fill his lungs with her festive fragrance, he brushed his knuckles over her cheek and snatched back her attention. "You're incredible, you know that?"

She swatted his hand away as the frown returned. "This isn't something you can smooth over with your sweet-talking lies."

"I'm not lying." He risked it and snaked an arm around her waist, levering her toward him. "You're mesmerizing."

This time she stayed, and Finn thanked his lucky stars. That is, until she spoke. "Yeah, well, talk is cheap, baby. If you're not even gonna try to come up with an excuse for lying to me, I'm afraid we're done here." There was a cold resolve in her eyes, but it couldn't hide the hurt engraved in the ice.

But could he really stand to let her see his monumental failure? To expose his scars and let her see how weak and wounded he was?

He owed her the truth, but the words building in his throat burned like hot acid—nearly as painful as the spill of fire that had devoured the back of his neck. And that recurrent nightmare still torturing him day and night since the Monroe fire seized him anew, this time with a paralyzing fear of losing the girl he loved all over again.

"Good-bye, Finn." She leaned in, her lips touched his cheek with a feathery-light kiss, and she turned to leave.

He caught her wrist, feeling his pathetic weakness building behind his eyes. He had to take a chance. Had to face his demons and let someone in. Then she could decide for herself that he wasn't worthy of her.

Weaving his fingers through hers he nodded and silently led her to the couch. She sat next to him, back stiff, and perched on the edge ready to flee.

Closing his eyes, he summoned help from on high for enough nerve to make it through to the end. When he opened his mouth the words scraped out coarse and quivering. "You remember Wally saying something about the Monroe fire?"

The distress in her eyes laced through him, webbing in his chest until he almost couldn't breathe. She nodded.

"It was about five months ago. Right before Sadie's neighbor was killed. When we got to the house, it was a bit like yours. Devastated. Consumed. Too dangerous to run in blind."

The infernal images flashed in his mind. A melding of the hellish nightmares of the Monroe fire and Joselyn's came together, sending a jolt of remembrance through him that felt more like electrocution than a daydream. He flinched, every muscle tightening.

Oh God, help.

"It looked abandoned," he continued, "and it was literally crumbling before our eyes. We worked as hard and fast as we could from the outside. Normally there are a lot of onlookers, concerned neighbors. But the house was in a pretty sketchy area. I guess no one wanted to risk a brush with the law. Needless to say, there was no one to alert us if anyone currently lived there.

"But as I worked my way around to the back of the house with the hose, I spotted a little pink tricycle." Finn swallowed, perspiration prickling his brow. His voice steeled low, his gaze reaching through the empty space, staring at nothing, yet every horrifying memory paraded in front of his eyes.

"My buddy Ryker and I went in. It felt like a suicide mission. In the kitchen he found a woman crumpled on the floor, badly burned. He got her out while I went to search the bedrooms."

The heat from that moment in purgatory swelled around him, lost in the memory, he could scarcely force his lips to continue. "I—I tried to search what was left of the house. Chunks of ceiling were collapsing around me, but I made it and found a little girl huddled in the only square foot of her room—maybe of the whole house—that wasn't on fire. Before I got to her a big piece on the roof came down on top of me."

Finn reached back and touched the raised, angry skin he thanked God he couldn't see when he looked in the mirror. Yes, he'd survived. And the scar was evidence of that act of mercy on his behalf.

But it was also a mocking reminder of the life he failed to save. He didn't need any more reminders of that. He felt the loss every day, every moment. And the guilt had become an enemy within.

Silky soft fingers covered the ones he had on his neck. Stroking his fingertips away, she let hers balm over the ugliness. The gentle way she touched the puckered skin soothed to the depths of his soul where the wounds would never scar but lay festering and open. He latched on to the kindness in her eyes, and somehow, was able to keep going.

"The falling roof smashed my helmet and my mask, but I emerged from the rubble, burned but alive. And so was she. But there was no feasible escape at that point." The sound of the crushed Legos hadn't been discernible over the fire's furious roar, but he heard them in his nightmares, accompanied by the scream of a slow suffering death.

"I kicked aside the charred remains of a dollhouse and some … Legos." *Lord, why hadn't I noticed.*

"And I axed through the floor. When I swept up the little girl, she reached out into the fire." His eyes clouded with tears that teetered on the edge and then spilled over. "I didn't know why, so I snatched her hand back to protect her and lowered us through the floor in the nick of time—before something ignited and an explosion shuddered through the house. I was able to drag her out from the crawlspace."

Pent up anguish flowed out through his tears. He scrubbed his palms over his eyes and dropped his chin, sniffling back the weakness.

Finn felt the tender assurance of her presence when her fingers swept at the hair draping over his forehead. The whispered touch made him want to forget the rest and pull her into his arms. Distract himself from the cruelty of the truth.

"You're a hero, Finn. Not only did you save that little girl, you saved me." She tipped his chin, forcing him to meet her eyes.

"No." The admission cut deep, more tears bled down his face. "No, I'm not."

Breathe … "The little girl had a twin brother. He was hiding in a wooden hutch." The unspoken words burned in his throat—it was now or never. "He burned to death. I didn't save him."

Tears gleamed in her eyes. "You couldn't have known—"

"The Legos. Boy Legos. I saw them. Right by the dollhouse. And I didn't even think to look for another child. And …" Tearing to his feet, he strode away and then turned back, battling with his self-loathing. "She tried to tell me. She reached out for her brother, and I left him there to die."

He swallowed the knot in his throat; a hollowness settled into his stomach. "The little girl is Kendi. She wouldn't let go of me after the fire. I stayed with her in the ambulance and at the hospital for three days while her burns and smoke inhalation were treated." Lowering his voice, he added, "And my own."

Finn cleared his throat, reaching for a handhold as he sank down further into the suffocating memories. "I try to spend time with her every weekend. She's living in a group home. It's a temporary situation, but the place needs a lot of work, so I've been helping out with that too."

Joselyn nodded, seeming to digest the information. "What about Kendi's mother? Did she survive?"

"Yeah, she survived. But after she'd been treated—for the

burns and the drug overdose—she was sent to jail to serve out a sentence for possession of meth. She'd been cooking some up that night—it's what caused the fire."

He shook his head in disgust, chasing away the hateful thoughts about the woman whose selfish choices resulted in the death of her son and the abandonment of her sweet, beautiful daughter.

"So, if she's in jail, what happens to Kendi? Foster care? Do they send her back to her mother when she's released?"

"Well, I had been talking to—" Cody. Finn didn't dare say his name. "… to a lawyer, to feel this thing out and fight it if necessary. But the lady that runs the home called me today and said that Desiree Monroe signed away the rights to her daughter. Said that once she got out she didn't want to be a mother anymore. Kendi found out today that her mommy's never coming back for her."

Joselyn's eyes seemed to absorb too much. As if she could steal away the thoughts he'd left unspoken. "Maybe that's best. Maybe she'll be adopted. My father gave full custody to Yia-Yia the day he was released from the hospital after the car accident. Threw me away without a care. But honestly, as much as it still hurts that he could dispose of me so easily, especially after everything I'd already lost, I thank God he did it. Saved my life."

He lowered back down to the couch beside her. "Your father doesn't deserve you." He reached over and squeezed her cold, delicate hand. "And Kendi's mother certainly didn't deserve such a precious child.

"But I worry. This is all pretty traumatic for a four-and-a-half-year-old. I don't think she's coping very well."

"She's almost five? Finn, she looks three. Barely. She's so tiny."

He knew what she was thinking—the child was frighteningly underweight. Another instance of neglect, in addition to the meth that had seeped into Kendi by default. A meth lab home was usually coated with the stuff—it was a miracle Kendi hadn't suffered more symptoms of withdrawal. Malnourishment, exposure, it all compounded the reasons Finn needed to make sure Desiree Monroe never got custody of Kendi again.

And in light of her decision today, she wouldn't. It might be the kindest cruel thing she would ever do for her daughter.

"She's too small, I know. And fragile. She wouldn't speak to anyone but me for two months after the fire. She's finally starting to come out of her shell, and even still, she barely interacts with others."

Something warm tingled in his stomach when he thought about the last two hours they'd all spent together. "She seemed quite taken with you."

A sad smile tipped her lips. "The feeling is mutual. Plus, I ... uh, sort of ... thought she might be your daughter."

"My daughter?" That explained the intent behind those probing glances. "I don't have any kids, Joss. That's not to say that I wouldn't love to have her, but it's a complicated process."

She nodded, and silence thickened the air between them. In the still, quiet moment, the balm of her words rushed back to him.

You're a hero, Finn. Not only did you save that little girl, you saved me.

If only he could believe that. But as much as he wanted to, the guilt was stronger. He simply couldn't forgive himself. Couldn't forget the cost of his failure.

Why couldn't you have helped me save him? Why must I live with his blood on my hands?

And why, when he reached out for what had already been freely given, did forgiveness keep slipping from his grasp?

Having laid the truth of his failings out for her to see, he searched her eyes for the disgust, or the pity. Instead, he saw a flicker of something he'd seen once before, the moment she'd come crashing into his arms the night of the fire. Something peaceful. Like she'd surrendered to the end. The panic that had ignited from that look had somehow propelled him through a dangerous maze of destruction with inexplicable choreography and timing. He'd gotten her out. Yes, maybe even saved her.

But this wasn't over. The hounds of hell kept coming back. With his faulty instincts and his confidence gone, it was only a matter of time before the fire bested him again. And the thought of Joselyn dying at his hand, well, that was something he knew he couldn't live with. Time to face reality.

"Joss, I'm afraid I'm not the best person to protect you. Maybe someone like Sal could make sure you're safe. I know they're all watching but I still feel responsible, and I fear that if I fail at this, I-I'll never recover." And there it was. Plain and simple. He was weak. Useless. Bailing out felt like the only means of survival.

A war of doubts raged in his head. But he silenced them the best he could. Silenced Joselyn's attempts to change his mind as well.

The tragic death of Kameron Monroe was enough to torment the night. If anything happened to Joselyn, he knew the devastation would blot out the sun forever.

Chapter 33

Joselyn Whyte

"**S**o, you're *not* going tonight? I don't understand." Sadie stood beside Joselyn in front of the mirror, dusting bronzer over her cheeks, conversing via reflection.

Joselyn studied their faces side-by-side. So different. Sadie had elegant features and wavy platinum blonde locks. Sort of all-American. While Joselyn's raven, poker-straight hair, and nearly clear and strange slanted eyes bent toward a more unconventional look.

The eclectic amalgam of her Greek and Scottish heritage was distinctive. And the more she settled into her skin as she grew up, the more she remembered her mother's face—saw her as she was, staring back at Joselyn from the mirror of the past.

Sadie passed over the bronzer, and Joselyn went to work faking a subtle glow. Neither of them had an ounce of color left by wintertime.

The obscure thought reminded her of Kendi. The beautiful caramel of her skin, the sandy blonde frizz of her springy little curls sticking out in every direction—she sparkled despite her circumstances. And maybe it was those circumstances, though notably different from her own, that had formed the instant kinship between them. Their shared loss and neglect.

It made Joselyn want to be in Kendi's life. To be someone like Yia-Yia, who could turn the tragedy of the hand she'd been dealt into something sweet. To give Kendi a sense of belonging like Joselyn had felt with Yia-Yia, for a time.

But then again, with the target on her back and her days numbered, she'd better not.

"Hey, are you okay? It's only been two days since this whole fake breakup, but you've been in a funk ever since."

"Yeah." Joselyn shook her head to nix any pointless plans for the future. "I mean, no. I'm not going tonight."

Her brain had been stubbornly stuck on Finn Carson. Story of her life. She'd tried to comfort him, show him that he wasn't to blame. But it all seemed to bead off of that tough skin. His torment was a difficult thing to witness in such a strong man, and despite her efforts to combat his self-sabotage, he seemed intent on burning away with guilt, dying slowly … like Kendi's brother.

She should have seen it coming, but she'd been blindsided when he'd pulled out on their arrangement. The resolve on his face almost frightening. She knew right then, she'd lost him.

Again.

There was nothing else to say but good-bye. When the words left her lips there was something in his eyes that transported her back to that last glance on prom night.

She shuddered with the helpless plague of misery that forced her to that dark place, remembering the long walk home on that barren road. Despair and pain so deep she thought she might die—wanted to die—as she'd clutched the shreds of her dress and the dead and useless cell phone in her frostbit fingers. The unusual chill of that early spring morning knifed through her skin and leached into her bones. But the vicious nip of the air had nothing on the cold that had encased her heart.

Joselyn jerked herself from the ruthless pull of depression, still feeling the slither of deception lying in wait. "It's for the best, Sadie. There's a history between Finn and I that I've never told you about. And trust me—dragging out those skeletons will not be a fun anatomy lesson." *More like an autopsy.* "Better if we move on before this gets more complicated than it already is."

Her fingers dabbed concealer on the dark circles beneath her eyes. The words had emerged with flawless conviction. They sounded right, but they felt all wrong.

Until she pictured Finn in that fiery house—fighting to save a little girl's life. Joselyn knew she needed to walk away, if for no other reason than to spare him. And not simply his conscience. His life.

A warm hand touched the frigid plane of her arm. She could feel the cold taking over again. As if Finn had taken all of her warmth with him.

"You really care about him, don't you?"

Tears prickled behind her eyes but managed to stay put. She felt like tossing a carefree smile Sadie's way and saying it was all in the past.

But Joselyn's defenses had failed her. Her denial cluttered in her throat, and even if she could force the words from her lips, no one would believe them. Least of all Sadie, with her wise, discerning eyes and tender heart, Joselyn feared she knew more than had ever been uttered.

The memories from that night had never been put to rest. The past, in all its haunting forms, still lurked around every corner. And not only for Joselyn, for Finn too.

Clearing her throat, she changed the subject, praying Sadie wouldn't push it any further. "So, I guess you're stuck with me tonight. She plucked a brush out of Sadie's hand and awakened her pale cheeks with a pink shimmer of blush. "It feels like a cheat night. Some ice cream, brownies, maybe? Oh, and I hear there's a Christmas movie marathon on TV. Maybe we could catch *It's a Wonderful Life.* It's almost a week until Christmas, and I need a little boost of holiday cheer."

Sadie grabbed a palette of eye shadow and worked a smoky streak across Joselyn's lids.

Before Joselyn fully appraised the makeover, she caught Sadie's eyes, so keenly attuned to everything Joselyn was trying to hide.

In them, she saw Finn looking back at her. Her friend's

eyes were so like his they made her ache for him. Physically ache. As if she didn't already grasp the full meaning of the term "love hurts" by now.

A somber smile tipped Sadie's lips. "Of course we can do a girls' night. But if you eat any more sugar I'm afraid you might slip into a diabetic coma. We'll have to get some real food—and for Pete's sake, some meat on your bones. I don't know how you can eat candy all day and still fit in a size four. Never met anyone as addicted to chocolate and allergic to exercise as you. It's not fair. How on earth are we friends?" Sadie's playful sneer a valiant attempt to lighten the mood.

"Oh, puh-lease. You wear the same size as me." Though Joselyn knew she was more of a shapeless stick figure and Sadie was enviably curvy and athletic.

"Yeah, right. I stretch a six until the seams are one wrong move away from rupture, and you'd could string both of my stunted legs end to end to match one of your runway gams. What I wouldn't do for long legs. And as a bonus, I have to run my brownie-lovin' bootie off every day to afford our weekly binges and still be able to pour into my pants."

Joselyn could only roll her eyes.

Sadie withdrew a tube of lip gloss and slicked over Joselyn's lips. "We're getting real food for your skinny butt, and that's final. Let me make a quick call. Be right back." Smoothing some flyaway hairs, she arranged Joselyn's locks over her shoulder and left the room.

Joselyn appreciated Sadie's angle for flattery and distraction, but her mind was immediately elsewhere. "It's for the best." Studying her reflection, Joselyn recited the words she'd proclaimed about the "breakup" and begged them to take root in her heart.

She'd simply have to endure tonight, and the company Christmas banquet tomorrow night. Then, she could forget all about Finn and concentrate on staying safe until the authorities figured this whole mess out.

Okay, so forgetting all about him might not be such an

easy task; ten years of practice and she was still hopeless. But, she might be able to manipulate that love into hate again. She'd done it before. She could do it again, right?

Just two more days.

"Ooo, how about this one?" Sadie held up a newly acquired piece Joselyn had picked up from her store. A fitted three-quarter-sleeved minidress. The sexy little number with a tight hem in smooth black cashmere was way too dressy for grabbing a pizza. But she heard Yia-Yia's voice in her head, *"In the words of Karl Lagerfeld, 'One is never over-dressed or under-dressed with a Little Black Dress.'"*

Still. "I thought you said you wanted to go to JJ Twig's. Isn't that like a bar and grill kinda place?"

Sal and Archer were among the guard post on watch tonight. Sadie had called Archer to make sure they had an escort for girls' night. The boys expressed some concern but were swayed with the promise of leftovers for their stake out. And though Joselyn had voiced her intention to stay in, Sadie persisted with the planning.

"But we're all primped and made up. Might as well dress to match. You can dress it down with these plum-colored tights and those cute ankle boots." Shoving the clothes at Joselyn, Sadie discarded another fail onto the growing pile of misses at her feet and plucked an off-the-shoulder top off a hanger. She slipped it over her head and gave a shrug, deciding that it paired with her skinny jeans and knee-high boots.

Joselyn issued her reluctance once more with a sigh and a blatant eye roll before she shucked off her zip hoodie and yoga pants and wormed her way into the snug dress and tights.

She stood in front of the full-length mirror and saw that her fingertips hung further down than her skirt. Though the top of the dress was perfectly modest. And the whole thing was a bit snug. According to Yia-Yia—and famed costume designer Edith Head—*"Your dresses should be tight enough to show you're a woman and loose enough to show you're a lady."* Man, she was full of those tonight. And this dress, well, it was all woman.

At least she had dark tights on—somehow tricking the eye into assuming there was more to the skirt than there actually was. But the four-inch heels made her legs look like stilts regardless.

Sadie whistled. "Wow, girl. I might have to borrow that dress sometime. Archer would lose his mind. Then again, perhaps I should wait until after the wedding. No need to fuel the fire." She winked and draped Joselyn's mother's locket around her neck. "Okay, you ready?"

"Are you sure we can't stay in tonight?" Joselyn felt like sulking around anyways, and if she pouted, Sadie might give in. Maybe.

"Come on. You have been miserable for forty-eight hours. You haven't left the house. And to be honest, you are lucky to have me because if I hadn't kicked your butt into the shower, you'd still have that two-day-old bedhead and smell like Oreos and peanut butter M&M's. We need some sustenance and fresh air. Trust me."

Huffing, Joselyn trudged to the door and slipped into her Burberry coat that hid essentially every ounce of her dress—scandalously alluding to nothing underneath but the deep burgundy tights encasing her legs.

She was usually more modest, but today she didn't care. Might as well create a stir. Her father had been calling all afternoon. Probably to give her a list of dos and don'ts for dinner, but she couldn't face him—didn't want to deal with the backlash. He'd probably soil his kilt if he saw her dress. Even the thought tickled her rebellious side with satisfaction. "Let's get outta here. I think you're right. I could use some fresh air."

A knock sounded on the door right when Joselyn pulled on the knob.

Everything stopped, including her heart.

Looking devastating in a charcoal suit and starchy white shirt open at the collar, she stared into the eyes that had hijacked her dreams. *Finn.*

Some malfunction in her brain made it impossible to form any semblance of speech at that moment. But she could scarcely breathe, so wordlessness wasn't her only problem.

"Hi, Joss." The rumbly timber of his voice caught on the cold winter air and shivered through her coat with inexplicable warmth. He didn't smile, but the gleam in his eyes was enough to have her completely undone in two seconds flat.

Snap out of it!

Her brain kicked back in and scolded her pathetic swooning heart.

"What are you doing here?" She hiked her purse up onto her shoulder and managed to fold her arms around herself instead of launching into his.

He glanced at something beyond her, and following his line of sight she caught Sadie ducking around a corner.

Unbelievable. Sold out by her best friend. "I'll get you, my pretty." Joselyn called over her shoulder. No wonder Sadie had forced her to get all dressed up.

"Joss, I—"

"Listen, I don't know what you think you're doing, showing up like I've been pining for you, but I have plans, so if you'll excuse me—"

"Oh, you have plans all right. With me." His eyes hardened over. That cocky grin he loved so much fell back into place.

"I seem to remember you backing out. What makes you think you can just waltz on over here and pick up where you left off without so much as a—"

His hand covered her mouth—it was becoming a thing for them. "Zip those hot lips, and I'll explain myself."

It was insulting—and she seriously considered unleashing her teeth into his hand—but she bit her lip beneath and glared her impatience.

He pulled away, but not before his thumb traced her lips over and back. *Why must he torment me?*

"I wanted to come here and tell you I was wrong." His eyes bore into hers. She searched them for his ever present sarcasm and yet not a hint of teasing could be found.

She felt her jaw dislocate. Had she heard him right?

"I—I guess I panicked. I don't know what to say other than I was an idiot and I'm sorry. I'm not going anywhere. I promise."

Oh, how she wished she could believe that. Surrendering would be so easy. Easy, but stupid. And she'd already concluded that when it came to Finn, she was about as dumb as they come.

Come on, Joselyn. Stay strong.

"You were right to walk away. This is too dangerous. I know now what it cost you to run into that fire to save me. I won't ask that of you again."

"You're not asking. I'm here. Whether you like it or not."

She wished she could read his face. His words bespoke obligation. Like he'd been coerced. Even the strongest will could be swayed by Declan Whyte. She'd seen it time and again without fail. But this was about more than protecting her life and her father's reputation.

There was something much more fragile at stake.

"Finn ..." The word pleaded with a vulnerability she'd meant to disguise. "This isn't a good idea. I know what it's like to live in a nightmare. I don't want to become another one for you. Let's cut our losses and call it a day. I can't keep doing this." Retreating backward, she started to close the door, but the stubborn idiot couldn't let it go.

His hand slapped against the door, something wild and rebellious blazing in his eyes. "I told you I wasn't asking permission. I'm yours. And though I appreciate your concern, I'm a big boy, I can handle it." Those eyes dared her to disagree, to deem him weak.

And though he wasn't a violent man, that determined expression on his face scared her. Like this was about more than simply protecting her and putting on a show for her father's campaign.

It had become a quest for Finn to prove himself.

A very bad feeling quivered to her core, alerting her senses to an approaching storm. If they failed—and the odds were definitely swaying that way—more than only *her* life would be destroyed.

Joselyn knew her life was a mess to begin with, and she had next to nothing to live for. But Finn was, in fact, a hero. His life meant something. He had faith and family and a purpose.

She wanted that too. All of it. A place to belong, here or beyond, where love was true and steadfast. Unconditional.

"Let's go. We've got reservations at seven." He tossed in an arrogant smile and a ridiculous shrug of his eyebrows, as if they hadn't spent the last five minutes in a standoff.

Joselyn sighed again. It was all she could think to do at the moment. The man was stubborn as an ox. "Fine. One more night. Don't forget to smile pretty for the cameras." Tossing over a sassy sneer of her own, she stepped out onto the porch and locked up.

He extended his arm as if he were a perfect gentleman, she took it with another huff as they walked out into the frigid black wind—the stalking darkness a constant reminder of who might be plotting her death in the shadows. Her grip tightened, a prickling sensation raked over her skin.

"I, for one, plan on doing a whole lot more than smiling."

"Huh?" She quit scanning for signs of trouble and looked up at Finn, searching for meaning in his eyes as he opened the passenger door. His large hands wrapped nearly all the way around her waist as he hefted her up into his truck like some helpless damsel in distress. Which she had to admit, she kind of was. The thought pinched, but something tingled in her belly that had nothing to do with shame or fear.

Finn winked, and before he closed the door he brought clarity to his comment. One that left little room for doubts.

"Though what I have in mind definitely requires lips and

is bound to make me smile for a long, long time."

Finn Carson

Despite the arctic blast battering the old Ford and the flakes of frost kissing the windshield, it was smoking hot in Finn's truck. Heat burned the tips of his ears. A slick of sweat dampened the steering wheel beneath his palm.

This was their first date.

Maybe contrived and manipulated, but still.

The pressure of the moment mounded on his chest, and his heart beat harder to combat the strain. He felt the yips nipping at his heels, and he could almost envision everything going wrong. The date had barely started, and already it wasn't going so great.

The silence seemed to mock him.

And the heat! Good Lord, the heat!

He dialed down the air flow and redirected the vents, but right then Joselyn crossed one of her long, shapely legs. The heater might as well have been on full blast and one hundred degrees in the cab for the swell of fire suddenly breathed upon his neck.

It didn't help matters that Finn couldn't tell what Joselyn was wearing underneath that trench coat, so his mind ran wild with what might be revealed in the hour to come.

"Okay, you really need to loosen up. You're making me nervous. Where's all the sarcasm, even the innuendo. I'll take anything at this point."

Finn rolled to a stop to wait for the light to change and took the opportunity to look over at his date. Man, she was gorgeous. Undeniably and uniquely jaw-dropping.

In fact ...

He clamped his mouth shut.

The stubborn jut of her chin and the glare in those hypnotic eyes told him he was blowing it.

"Sorry. I was lost in thought." *Thank God she can't read my thoughts.* "Oh, here, I got you something." Steadying the jitter of his fingers against the hard case, he passed it over and studied her reaction.

The corners of her almond shaped eyes crinkled adorably from the full force of the megawatt smile that about stopped his heart. "Eli Young Band. You remembered my favorite song?" Dang. The way she was looking at him made Finn decide his life's mission should be to make her smile like that every day.

His lips couldn't help but curve to match hers, and he nodded. "Mmm-hmm. We lost yours; thought you might like a new car-warming present."

"Wow. That was amazingly thoughtful. You're making it difficult to stay mad at you." Her eyes teased, and her smile held. And he may have lapsed into cardiac arrest. "Can we put it in?" She bounced in the seat.

"No can do, babe. This is a country-free zone." He patted the dash of his trusty old truck and felt slightly self-conscious about the simple accommodations compared to what she was used to. It was well-maintained, clean, and rust-free, but it still seemed a little rudimentary.

Someone honked behind him. The light was green. *Oops.* He stepped on the gas and lit out under the soft, starry lamplight of the sleepy suburban streets. "I could be persuaded if you agree to sing along, crazy girl." He peeked at her from the corner of his eye and tried his best to remember how to flirt.

"Nice try. I've sang enough for you, you little sneak. How about you sing something for me?"

Shaking his head, he refused to meet her gaze. "I don't sing for other people."

"I remember."

The words were low, the memory an elephant sandwiched between them, and the heat in the cab spiked another couple degrees. Remembering that moment, all those years ago, when he'd almost kissed her for the first time made him want to pull over and take the liberty simply because he could. Was that what she was remembering too?

"I do too, Joss. I don't think I could ever forget."

Dinner was painfully unimpressive, and Finn found he kept closing his eyes to pray for a do over.

No such luck.

Ornate molded ceilings and an extravagant glittering chandelier canopied over their secluded booth. Everything was shiny and pristine, draped in sweeping textures of whites and creams. And scarcely a sip of his water would go down before someone came to replenish the loss.

But while the service was exceptional, if a bit overbearing, and the opulent aesthetic quite pleasant—especially with the most stunning woman he'd ever laid eyes on mere inches away—the date was … quiet. Boring.

And that wasn't even the worst of it. The pretentious five-star restaurant was crawling with leeches. Several of whom had wormed over to Finn and Joselyn's private table and expressed their support for Joselyn's father's campaign.

Finn could barely restrain the urge to erupt on the bottom-dwelling swine that kept popping in and stilting their conversation.

The extent of the media frenzy had been unexpectedly overwhelming too. The stunning view of Joselyn's face had been obstructed by an array of black spots for five minutes after their intensive photography session from the truck to the door of the restaurant. And even now, though the maître d' had assured discretion, a shuttering sound would occasionally weave into Finn's ear. Prying eyes were everywhere, and it only seemed to squelch the romance.

As the courses strung along, Finn concluded that this was

the last place he would have picked to take Joselyn on their first date. Though it appeared he had no choice but to hang on for the—rather dull—ride.

When the time came for the sauntering meal to finally come to an end, Finn had been cut off at the knees, emasculated further by Declan Whyte's preemptive payment for the absurdly overpriced food for mice.

"Are you ready to go?" he asked.

Joselyn smiled, a sigh of relief slipping from her pretty pink lips. "Yes. I thought you'd never ask."

Helping her up from their c-shaped booth, Finn eased Joselyn's coat over the little black dress that, as he'd suspected, induced a sweltering fever and about made him salivate all over the pristine table cloth.

Guiding her toward the rear exit, he pressed his hand at the small of her back and leaned into her ear. "You ready to give 'em an eyeful?"

Her head whipped around, and her eyes unleashed their venom, a waft of her peppermint hair teasing his nose. "Don't get any ideas. I do everything in my power to avoid the spotlight, because it's not just a light. It's a microscope. A really cruel, unflattering magnifier of half-truths and outright lies sensationalized for maximum destruction. We're going out back. Hopefully they won't catch on until we get to your truck. In the meantime, just behave yourself."

He allowed a few moments for her to witness his slow, mischievous grin for her edification and was rewarded when a subtle flush of color filled her cheeks. Then he leaned in, humming his words against her ear. "But I don't wanna behave myself. I'm thinking we should misbehave together. Plus, this will get your father off your back. And the paparazzi will think they snuck up on us, and they'll write all about our fiery romance, putting all the rumors to rest. Win-win."

Finn held open the door, his heart twitching with anticipation he could hardly contain. Scrutinizing his intention, her eyes drew their bead on him and she stood planted in place. What was sure to be a play at intimidation evoked something else entirely. He tugged her outside and almost dragged her down the back alley, around to the sidewalk several doors down.

"Finally." Turning her to face him, he stepped closer and cradled her face in both hands.

"Finn, what the heck are you do—"

Cutting off her protest at the source, Finn closed the distance between their lips.

She was immediately inching back, her body resisting the magnetism. Her lips, on the other hand, had no qualms about the intrusion and eagerly parted to introduce one of her own. Yet she was still pulling away until the space between them widened enough to break the kiss—much too early for Finn's liking.

Finn indulged the game of cat and mouse, stalking slowly forward until the heels she wore brought them almost nose to nose.

"What are you doing?" She licked her lips, and he tracked the movement before watching her gaze dart to the photographers still oblivious to their slip.

"This is called kissing, Joss. You do it quite well. Now stop stalling and give me something to smile about." He loved having an excuse to do this. Backing her against a brick store front, he leaned his body flush against hers in a way that was none too innocent, aligning them from their shaking knees to their racing hearts. Their breaths billowed white in the night air as he breathed her in, hovering a skin-tingling whisper away before her hands tentatively touched his chest. Game over. He captured her lips again.

This time, she surrendered. Her touch lit a trail of fire on his skin. The flame skittered up his chest, over his jaw, and into his hair where her fingers gripped hard. She arched her back, allowing his arms to surround her and hold her tighter.

A tiny moan of pleasure escaped from her throat, and the clicking and flashing of approaching press faded away leaving nothing but Finn and Joselyn—their lips, their souls intertwined, lighting up the dark world with the kiss of a lifetime.

He groaned and crushed her, savoring every stolen second. She tasted so sweet, like the Italian crème dessert they'd sampled after dinner had lined her mouth with silken sugar.

His appetite was suddenly ravenous, and any semblance of restraint obliterated. Breaking from her lips, he let his kiss do the talking for how beautiful she was, how precious and desirable. How loved. All while indulging in the skin of her neck, her cheeks, her eyelids, her ear. Her candied breath warmed his skin as he explored the satiny planes of her flawless face.

"Finn."

His name ached out on a breathless sigh that unraveled his brain, sent his God-fearing mind to a dangerous place. A place where her kiss leveraged his very existence, her touch more vital than the oxygen she siphoned from his lungs.

It was only then—with that abrupt and absurd realization—he remembered that the film was rolling on this moment. The pictures, relentless. And the reporters weren't simply observing they were barking questions, slinging accusations about politics and appearances. And payment.

Gently, he pulled back, dragging a regrettably crisp breath past his lips. Joselyn blinked languidly at first, as if she too had lost herself in their kiss. A more lucid blink, and a grimace tightened each one of her lovely features as the crude slander snatched away their perfect moment.

Reaching up, he ignored the chaos surrounding them and smoothed the hair away from Joselyn's face—soft, glossy, perfect hair he was solely responsible for ruining with his wild, untamable affections.

"Let's get outta here." He tipped his head toward his truck, curled her hand into his, and parted the pack of wolves still hunting for a story. They'd given them more than enough to satisfy their rabid hunger—and Joselyn's father's need for a newsworthy romance—but these vultures were ruthless in their quest to expose.

Finn hadn't expected the pummeling cruelty. Each blow cheap and dirty. Finn's alleged infidelity, Declan Whyte's bribery, and worst of all, Joselyn's cold and heartless talent for keeping men at bay.

Feeling her fingers tremble in his, he lifted her frozen hand and pressed it to his lips.

The scavengers were still scrounging for scraps when Archer slipped from cover and sidled next to Finn. Amid the bustle of too many bodies, Finn doubted anyone noticed Archer speak low and firm into Finn's ear.

"Get Joselyn out of here. Now. The area's not secure." Archer seamlessly ambled away as if he hadn't dropped a bomb.

Finn thought about calling out, getting more than the abbreviated warning, but instead he went onto autopilot, boosting Joselyn into his truck, sprinting to the other side, and tearing away from the flashing frenzy.

Joselyn looked shaken. It was her eyes that gave her away. What had been a white-hot flame of desire was now as cold and vacant as tundra. She couldn't have heard Archer, but he knew she'd seen him.

And if Finn thought the date had been loaded with pressure, it was nothing compared to the mountain-sized task of protecting her from a cunning and obsessive lunatic.

Finn thumbed to Archer's number and wedged his phone against his shoulder.

"Hayes." The edge in that one curt word wasn't exactly reassuring.

"Dude, what's going on?" Without looking, Finn reached over and snatched up Joselyn's hand. Somehow, simply holding on made the possibility of losing her less threatening.

"Patrols spotted a man with a military rifle ducking into an alley about 300 yards from the restaurant. They spooked him and are scouring the area. Sal thinks he's got a trail, so we're gonna go. I need you to take Joselyn someplace safe. Maybe the Whyte Estate. It's not far, and they have good security. Go now. Lay low. I'll send someone over."

The call disconnected before Finn could get a word out. Urgency rammed his foot down on the gas as he tore through the windy back roads toward Declan Whyte's mansion. The pristine white winterscape a deceptively peaceful counterpoint to the dangers lurking around each black ice-riddled bend. The heavy duty tires continually fought for traction, carrying them to the Whyte refuge that had been Joselyn's prison.

It was the unsettling polarity of it all that tweaked his unease, making it feel like they were heading straight into the eye of the storm. And that nothing was quite what it seemed.

"Is no one here?" Declan Whyte's castle loomed all around them with an unnerving silence and an eerie cast of moving shadows. They'd let themselves in, and while Joselyn disarmed the alarm for their entrance, Finn shed both his overcoat and suitcoat and draped them over the round marble-topped table gracing the center of the giant rotunda that was the foyer.

"Well, my dad's rarely here. Gloria and Erwin are usually early to retire to their house on the west edge of the property." Continuing to tinker with the touch screen embedded in the wall, she didn't bother to raise her eyes.

"Gotcha. Need some help?"

She continued to tap on the screen. "Something's up with the security system. It's not showing if it's armed right now or not."

"Are all the doors locked?" It seemed simple enough to Finn. Lock the doors. Stay inside.

She turned, clearly annoyed which was a little bit cute. She shucked off her coat with a single frustrated jerk and chucked it at him. "There are over twenty entry doors into this house."

Turning her eyes back to task, she tried again. "Ehhh, stupid thing!" She hung her head. "I guess we should probably go check the doors, to be safe. If we split up, it should only take us about fifteen minutes."

"I don't think so. I'm not letting you out of my sight. And not only because you look so *fine* in that dress."

A slight, spreading grin couldn't be contained by the soft bite of her lip, nor her shoddy effort to scowl. "I demand to know what's going on." She crossed her arms, no doubt aiming for cold and prim, but paired with the scorching hot dress the dichotomy was fascinating. And quite possibly the sexiest thing he'd ever seen.

He shook his head, needing to get ahold of himself, which she mistook for his refusal and haughtily stomped her foot in protest. He couldn't help but grin. The sassy show of defiance only uncovered another inexplicably cute and sexy side of Joss he found irresistible.

Great focus, Iron Man.

She tapped her foot impatiently as he moved closer. Though he despised the thought of scaring her for no reason, he wouldn't lie to her. "There, uh … there was someone with a gun near the restaurant."

She went stock still, her teeth clamping hard on her lip until the peachy skin turned white.

He kept moving forward. "We don't know if it has anything to do with you. We're being care—"

Beep! Beep! Beep!

The low whine of a siren called out and stopped Finn in his tracks. Joselyn whipped around; the LCD screen over her shoulder flashing red.

"Finn." The tremor in her voice fired a ripple of dread through his body. She turned slowly and looked him dead in the eye. "Someone's in the house."

Chapter 3.5
Joselyn Whyte

Don't panic.

A thread of terror zip-lined through her system. Her thoughts splintering. Someone with a gun. Someone trying to kill her. Someone inside this massive house. Run. Hide. *Move*.

Self-preservation instincts had apparently booted her brain out of the driver's seat because she found herself running down the hall, jerking Finn behind her.

"Joselyn, stop. Where are we going? I need to—" Not knowing where the oomph came from to tug along a resistant 200-pound tower of brawn and stubbornness, she hauled Finn into the east den to the third bookcase on the left. With quick precision, she located and levered down Milton's *Paradise Lost* and then shoved Finn behind the hidden door.

The lock clicked behind them, and Joselyn activated the screen to the right.

"Wow. That was unexpected." From the corner of her eye she could sense his anxiety pulsing in time with the spastic rhythm of his chest. Knowing she would come completely unglued if she saw that panic reflected in his eyes, she studied the screen, attempting to make sense of the defunct security system.

"Joss." The heat from his hands seeped through the fabric of her sleeves as he gripped her shoulders and turned her to face him.

She kept her eyes low to conceal her doubts, but she suspected he could feel the palpable current of fear skittering through her body.

"Look at me." His fingers tightened on her arms. She lifted her gaze. "I want you to stay here, lock the door behind me, and call 911." His eyes said so much more as they lingered a moment longer.

Turning away, he jerked at the door. But it didn't budge.

"Joss, open the door." He spoke into the door, the tense line of his shoulders seeming to coil like a snake about to strike.

"I can't," she whispered.

"I'm going out there. I'm not gonna sit around and cower behind a locked door until help arrives. This guy could get away, and we still don't know who he is. This has to end. Now disarm the door." He was still facing the exit, as if he couldn't stand for her to see his face. With his voice skating on the razor's edge of menace, she wasn't sure she wanted to.

"I can't." And she was relieved she couldn't.

He whirred around. "What do you mean you can't?" he roared. His eyes were glazed with fire, a violence in them she'd never seen before.

Had she just thought she was relieved? Scratch that.

She took a step back. Then another. Putting distance between them. Her heart a panicked bird in a cage, the frigid outpouring of that old terror bathed her skin with goosebumps and wracked her whole body with tremors. "I— It's—ah—p—panic room. There's a timer, but the security system isn't working right. We're l—locked in here." *Together.*

Finn wouldn't hurt her, would he? The wild rage in his eyes drew upon her every fear until she was immersed back in those torturous moments when her instincts had failed her.

Finn took a step forward, his eyes softening. But she'd already jumped back, bumping into a shelf on the wall.

Seeming just as startled, he raised his hands and eased forward. "I didn't mean to scare you."

Not trusting her voice, she could only nod her acceptance. But the paralyzing fear held on.

He kept closing in, and she had no place to run. With aching tenderness he surrounded her with his arms and breathed the soothing words into her hair. *"Baby, I'm so sorry."*

Without even knowing it, her heart started to settle, her breaths evened out. And somehow her arms were around his waist, her face nuzzling into his chest.

Oh, her traitorous heart was so easily won.

"It's fine." She pulled away, sniffling back embarrassing tears.

Finn took in their surroundings. "So, now what?"

Joselyn's father had always been paranoid about others being out to get him, stealing his wealth, taking what was his. She supposed it was why the estate had two vaults, or panic rooms. One in the west wing, one in the east.

Only they sort of looked like walk-in closets—as if the house were lacking storage space. Everything from winter coats, bottled water, a card table and folding chairs, to some innocuous boxes and a stack of blankets lined the shelves of the maybe twelve-by-twelve room. Though not much of that was inherently visible due to the black walls and the single canned light in the middle of the room that suggested the receding darkness was endless. It felt like one of those interrogation rooms on *CSI*.

"I guess we wait," Joselyn said. "Wait until either the timer runs out or the authorities arrive. Hopefully the alarm is functioning enough to trigger a call out because I left my purse by the front door."

Finn patted his pockets and groaned. "And my phone is in my jacket on the table. I hate feeling this helpless."

The last of her unease about Finn's presence wicked away. The intensity he'd shown was his protective instinct urging him to fight for her. The thought now warmed her clear down to her toes.

The shaft of light glinted off the golden threads of his hair and spilled over the planes of his face, etching the angles with a fierce sort of strength.

And then he smiled, a little bit of mischief slipping through the sultry tip of his lips, making all traces of danger seem like a silly dream. "You know, we're still technically on our date. It's about time we had a little privacy. Don't you think?"

Heat pinched her cheeks. Hopefully the shadows concealed the way the thought tempted her. "Stop looking at me like I'm a tasty snack."

"But you are a tasty snack. And after that *Happy Meal* appetizer for the paparazzi, I'm finding I'm suddenly famished."

Strangely emboldened, she stepped up to meet him under the light and patted his washboard stomach. Bad idea. Terrible. She snatched her hand back as if burned. "Poor little fella. Unfortunately, *I* am not on the menu tonight."

What were they going to do, make out in the closet until someone found them? Based on the heat they could conjure up without even touching, they could get carried away a little too easily.

And one of them had to be the sensible one here, right?
Right?

Finn's eyes blazed with hunger, that heady musk of strength and spice laid waste to the inches between them, making her burn. As if grasping fistfuls of sun-scorched sand, she felt her willpower sift through her fingers.

In the only act of self-preservation she could find, she turned back, pretending to peruse the shelves for a distraction yet still feeling the singe of his stare.

"Hard to get, huh? Yeah, that's kinda hot. I can work with that. But mark my words, you'll never last. By the end of the night, you'll be begging for these lips on yours."

Oh, yeah. There was the old Finn. "Wanna bet?" She whipped around, feeling shielded by the dim light until she realized he'd followed her into the shadow.

"Oh, babe, you don't know who you're dealing with. You don't stand a chance. In fact, let's make it official." Another bold step brought him into her air space.

"Okay, what's the wager?" She stared up through the whispered streams of light, catching that cocky smile he loved so much.

An idea took root in her mind. Joselyn couldn't help but smirk. "I know, how about a little performance?"

He leaned down and stole a quick kiss she couldn't have dodged if she wanted to. Which, she didn't. "Performance. Now we're talking." The devilment in his grin made him look like a fallen angel in the haloed glow. "What'd you have in mind?"

She shrugged, struggling to contain her grin. "Just a song. Choreography optional."

"Is clothing optional too? Because I could get on board with that?"

"Ha!" Oh, he was all bluster. She could see the sweat sprouting on his brow at the idea.

Well, both ideas.

Her lips still tingling, she gave his chest a little shove. "What makes you think *that's* a good idea?"

"Actually, I think it's the best idea I've had in quite some time." He wagged his eyebrows.

With a rueful shake of her head, she laughed. "Dream on. The original bet stands. I resist your kiss for the rest of the night, and you give me a serenade."

"Does anyone win in this scenario?"

"I guess that depends on if you brought your A game."

"Oh, I'm never without my A game. The question is … can you handle the heat?"

And therein lay the problem. She wasn't sure she could.

Chapter 36

Finn Carson

Worst. Bet. Ever.

Why on earth had he agreed to this? In his desperation to protect her, his belligerence had left her frightened. Having her all twitchy and nervous wouldn't help her keep a level head in this situation. He'd been looking for a way to ease the tension.

So he teased her. Which used to have her spitting icicles. Instead, she'd flipped the tables on him. Beating him at his own arrogant game.

An arrogant façade, he realized, that was sinking in too deep—becoming a little too automatic. What he once viewed as protection was instead stirring up more trouble than he could handle. Because while his crassness was meant to intentionally provoke her, what he'd provoked instead was his desire for this woman who had—until recently—always been untouchable.

And it was the one thing he couldn't seem to stop doing. The physical liberties that accompanied the public exhibition of their arrangement had him barreling past the warnings— past the boundaries he'd set to keep his affections in check— to make up for all those lost years without her.

Yes, he talked a big game, but he wasn't the guy who took advantage. No one would guess it but he was, in fact, the guy who never let anything go too far. At least, he was until now.

Finn fiddled with the poker chip he'd kept in his pocket since the hospital, contemplating his next move. Perhaps his luck had run out. *Hmm.* Then again, maybe it was just beginning.

Bracing his hands on the shelf, he caged her in and bent his head to trace the tip of his nose along the fragile tendon of her neck, drinking deeply from the sweet wintery scent of her skin, her hair, and the softly exhaled mint of her breath. "What song will you sing for me, Joss?"

"Little presumptuous." She sighed the words. He felt the quiver pulse over her, her head tilting back, her resolve already fraying. He smiled against her neck and laid a chaste kiss over her heartbeat. Another near her earlobe, before skimming his lips over the tender shell.

She tried to turn away, but he grasped her shoulders and twisted her back around. Regretting it the instant he felt her tense.

"Joss? Joselyn, look at me. These hands …" which he rubbed gently down her arms, "will never hurt you."

She swallowed and nodded. The shadows in her eyes lifting like a cloud of smoke, bringing an immediate sense of relief and a ballooning host of unanswered questions about who hurt her and who he needed to pulverize.

And then, well … then she was folding into him too easily, as if the space between his arms was for her alone.

"Ask me to kiss you, Joss."

She drew her hands up and rested them on his chest, leaning into him as she raised up to her tiptoes. "Never," she whispered so close he could taste her kiss already. Her eyes challenging him to forfeit their bet, the miniscule distance between their lips …

And both of their bluffs.

The faintest beeping sounds wove through his subconscious, but somehow in not thinking this through, he'd made up his mind to allow a few more minutes of reckless behavior before he cut his rampant desire off at the knees. And walked away with the win.

He tightened his grip around her low back. Her hands slipped up around his neck, her fingers tickling the damaged skin and threading into his hair.

Screw the win. The real prize was right here. The banter. Their budding friendship. The magic of her kiss …

Yes, back to that.

He leaned down the last inch, simultaneously lifting her to meet his expectant lips—

"Well, well, would you look at that, Archer?"

Sal's voice stomped out the flames, reducing the sensual sparring match to some kind of awkward, teenage basement grope fest. And they hadn't even been kissing, yet. Or groping. But in light of their position and the kiss that was a millisecond of enjoyment away from Finn's lips, they had no choice but to jerk apart, reacting with the shame of being caught red-handed. And red-faced.

"I'm glad to see you guys were keeping busy and not runaway with panic." Archer grinned, all superior like he hadn't also crossed the line when he'd thought Sadie was a murder suspect and went and fell in love with her anyway.

As much as Finn tried to form a comeback to that effect, nothing came. The stilted silence beside him meant Joselyn went blank too.

"Conveniently locked in this tiny room with a beautiful woman. Finn, you scoundrel, did you plan—"

"All right, all right. We get it, you caught us." Finn interrupted Sal's jest. "What's important right now is did you catch the gunner?"

"Yes and no." Archer finally stowed the infuriating smile. "We caught the guy with the rifle, but we're pretty sure he's not involved with the other attempts on Joselyn's life. His name's Donnie Fuller. He was released from a psychiatric facility two days ago and was apparently staked out in protest of Joselyn's father's support for the war. His brother was recently killed in Afghanistan. He'd assumed Declan Whyte would be in the restaurant since the reservation was under his name."

"We're not entirely sure how he found out where Mr. Whyte would be dining," Sal tagged in, "but your father has been pushing this thing with you two pretty hard, and we figure with the publicity Donnie got confused. Not too difficult considering the man is a loony toon. Anyway, when Declan never showed, Donnie split. He confessed his intent to kill."

"Okay, then why did he follow us here?" Finn folded his arms, knowing full well he looked defensive.

"He didn't."

"What do you mean?" He felt a chill rake over his skin.

"We caught him right after you guys split. It was only a half-hour ago that we were informed there was a security breach here." Shrugging, Sal wedged his hands in his pockets and rocked back on his heels. "Turns out, the groundskeeper, Edwin—"

"Erwin," Joselyn interrupted.

Sal's gaze landed on Joselyn, a smile crept over his lips. "*Erwin*, came back over to the house to get his wife's sleeping pills she left over here during the day. The alarm went off, and he forgot the code. It was recently switched, but the real problem was that the system hasn't been working right for days."

Archer cleared his throat. "Someone from the security company was supposed to come fix it today. Gloria said they never showed. Then when we couldn't find you, Gloria suggested we check the safe rooms. We tracked down your father to figure out how to override the lock, and there you have it. You're all caught up."

"So, what you're really saying is you still don't have a suspect." Finn could feel the heat on his cheeks, felt the frustration and embarrassment hitting all the telltale markers.

"Unfortunately, no. No suspect." Archer agreed, looking equally frustrated for at least *some* of the same reasons.

"Fantastic." Finn pushed past Archer and Sal and spoke over his shoulder, "Come on, Joss. Let's get you home."

If at all possible, Finn was more on edge than before. Not knowing who the predator was or when he might strike was enough to screw with anyone's mind. The force of his anxiety drummed against his skull.

Glancing over at Joselyn, he could see it was getting to her too. The stiff line of her body held none of its usual grace.

And even though they had a security detail on their tail and a team back at Sadie's condo sweeping the area, a grim feeling overshadowed their every move. Like they might, at any moment, encounter the wrath of a faceless enemy.

Unnerved by the helplessness, he itched to do something—*anything*—to be a hero. But the only thing he could think to do was lighten the mood. He was good at that.

"So what'd you think of our first date?"

"Scintillating." Her eyes didn't stray from the fogged window, or the dark smog blurring the passing landscape beyond it.

Okay, well, that didn't work.

"You mean you're not gonna go home and scribble in your diary that I fulfilled all of your deep-seated fantasies about me from high school?"

Her head whipped back, the soft flutter of her hair fanned out and draped around her shoulders like a silk scarf. But instead of the amusement or playful annoyance he was expecting, daggers beamed across the bench seat and struck him perplexed.

"Doesn't that get old? Can't you ever be serious? I know tonight was a false alarm, but this is scary. It can't be smoothed over with your sarcasm and your ass-backwards charm. Someone is trying to kill me. Someone might kill you too! And you think you can keep badgering me because I was in love with you in high school? You think that gives you license to taunt me forever? To play all these mind games, stringing me along. Grow up, Finn. " Her voice broke, and she turned away.

All the air stole out of his lungs. He tore his gaze back to the road for safety's sake, but although he was looking, he wasn't seeing yellow lines … he was seeing red.

Was she messing with him? Fair game, Finn supposed, because he'd been doing his share of that too, but this jab hit hard. Harder than the fist she'd planted in his jaw days ago.

He eased on the brake and pulled the truck onto the slim shoulder of the two-lane road. In the distance their entourage followed suit.

"What did you say?" He managed to tamp down his temper, but the words still growled from his throat.

She turned back to him, the slightest sheen glowing from her eyes. "Why did you pull over?"

"Don't change the subject."

Pained silence settled over them, and he saw it again, that little flicker of enlightenment. Then panic. "This is a really dangerous place to stop."

"So then start talking," he hissed.

"Why? It's not like it will change anyth—"

"Were you or were you not in love with me in high school?" He interrupted, not able to wait for her to finally get back to the topic at hand.

In the dim glow cast from the dash, he saw her swallow, her eyes riveted on her hands in her lap. Her words growled right back. "As if you didn't know."

"How would I have known? All I knew was that you'd said I wasn't good enough to breathe the same air as you." His heart hammered in his ears. If she was messing with him now he'd never forgive her.

"How thick could you possibly be? From the first moment we met I hung on your every word. I practically begged you to kiss me in the music room when you sprinted away like I had leprosy, and then Cody was trying to get you to see the light and ask me to prom, but *no*, you kept treating me like some pathetic groupie. Well, not anymore. I'm through being under your spell."

"Joselyn, I was in love with you too."

"*Oh*, that's rich. You know, I was right. You really are a jerk! Take me home. I'm officially done with this."

"No! I was crazy about you! Obsessed, even!" And now

he was yelling at her, feeling very close to being full-tilt crazy again. "But I was so insecure I didn't think you felt the same."

"Finn, I know you. If that were true, you would have pursued me. Asked me out. I don't know why you are doing this, but we can't undo the past." The brokenness in her voice about shattered his heart.

He unlatched his seatbelt and slid across the bench to her side. Cupping her face, he saw the truth shining in her eyes. "We were manipulated. Both buying into a lie." Finn's father's words flooded back to him. *Seems to me you're casting judgment based on a half-truth. Maybe even a full deception.*

Oh, how had he not seen it back then? Cody's jealousy. His lies. The beautiful beacon of Joselyn's love. "Imagine how different things might have been for us had we only known this sooner."

A tear slipped down her cheek. She tried to turn away, but Finn held on, stroking the glistening trail off her velvety-smooth skin. She drew in a shaky breath and slowly lifted her eyes. "Don't you see? The damage is done."

"*Ahhh!*" A rap on her window made her scramble out of her seat with a panicked squeak. She landed on Finn's lap, and for the briefest moment she clung like ivy.

Looking over her shoulder, Finn's eyes connected with the steely glare from Joselyn's titan U.S. Marshal.

Before Finn could react, Joselyn was somehow slipping off his lap and out the door, replaced by a rush of glacial air, and a cold, hard knot in his chest.

The passing prism of headlights illuminated her swimming eyes before she left the parting comment he knew was coming, "Go home, Finn. It's over," and slammed the door.

Chapter 367
Joselyn Whyte

Three fifteen.

Joselyn reached down beside the bed and snatched up the little black dress she'd left balled up on the floor. Then with a lazy toss, used it to obstruct the nagging view of her clock—an obnoxious reminder that she was obviously not sleeping. Miserable hours had tarried by, laughing as each minute turned with the monotony of an hour.

The moonlight was muted in a cloudy web of shadows. And Joselyn's heart felt as dark and empty as the endless night.

Imagine how different things might have been ...

Squeezing her eyes shut, Joselyn let Finn's words wash over her like a wish from the collective broken shards of her heart—praying that *what if* into existence. That somehow, God might mercifully rewind the clock and erase the pain—the betrayal—of the past.

Praying?

Really?

Strange enough, it had become part of her routine. Thinking back on the past week, Joselyn realized she'd reached beyond herself for the first time, uttering inaudible prayers on an exhaled breath. All the while some tiny seed had bloomed in her chest.

How was it even possible? And did she really believe?

Maybe she did, just a little. Or maybe she simply hoped she did.

It felt foolish to overlook all the ways she'd been robbed

as a child, but somehow, she wasn't angry anymore. She hadn't made a conscious decision about it, but when she'd caught herself praying, she felt this confident calm soak into her pores. And an insurgence of warmth would wrap around her.

If I ever stop running and really surrender, could I really be loved? Accepted? Flaws and all?

Joselyn heard a tap on the door. Pulling her restless bones up in bed, she flicked on the bedside lamp and called out, "Yeah?"

Sadie slipped into the room and crawled onto the bed. "I couldn't sleep, and I had a feeling you were up." Her expression was kind, but Joselyn knew what she looked like. Having tied her hair up several combative hours ago, the knot had slumped to one side. Eyes puffy from hours of tears and likely demon red. And since she hadn't bothered to wash her face—and was risking a constellation of zits tomorrow—she was sure the Picasso print displayed there was a swirly mess of colors reminiscent of a child's finger painting.

She'd thrown on one of Sadie's cut up, *Flash Dance* inspired sweatshirts and ridiculously loud blue and green pajama pants with an ice cream sundae print. But even with the layers of clothes and covers, Joselyn felt cold. Frozen, all the way through to her heart.

She leaned back and rested her head on Sadie's shoulder. Maybe some of that great faith would absorb through osmosis.

"He finally gave up a few hours ago and went home," Sadie whispered.

Joselyn had heard the racket outside when Marshal Raglan wouldn't let Finn near the door per her request. She couldn't think clearly when he was around. With the complications of the past and the looming danger of the present, it was easier to push him away and protect him than try to unearth every mountain that stood in the way.

And as much as she wanted to explore the possibility of a fresh start, she was afraid there was nothing left of her deeply damaged heart to give.

What would happen when he found out how desolate she was? How might he torture himself when he realized what he'd done? Joselyn figured she was far beyond repair, but maybe she could protect Finn from the ugly truth of the past.

And the murderous criminal in their present.

"He won't give up, you know."

And Joselyn knew that too. It was who he was. Strong and steady. Giving and heroic. Why would he even want someone like her?

I was in love with you too.

Was, past tense.

So maybe he didn't really want her now. Maybe it really was about their arrangement. But the thought wouldn't take root.

She felt so weak. Knowing if she'd heard him out tonight she'd tell him how much she still loved him. How she would do anything to be his, for however much time she had left.

And the scariest thing of all was that she was sure he would find a way into the Whyte Christmas gala tomorrow night, despite her attempts to cut him off tonight. He and Archer were probably formulating a plan right now.

Tonight had felt like a sort of noble sacrifice. Tomorrow foreshadowed a complete cave-in.

And once that happened, she'd be a goner. No doubt about it.

"I know. But I wish he would give up just this once."

"Liar." Sadie wrapped her arm around Joselyn and cocooned her with her unwavering strength until hope welled up so bright Joselyn could believe that almost anything was possible.

Isn't it written somewhere that all things are possible? If that's true, and if it's not too much to ask, I'm in need of a miracle. I'm just not quite sure what it is yet.

Chapter 38

Why wouldn't she die?

If ever a person had nine lives and fireproof skin, he'd found her. It'd make an interesting study if it wasn't so maddening. So cruelly unjust. How some people, sturdy, strong, and vital could be snatched away against all odds, while other feeble, fragile souls just wouldn't die no matter how much brimstone you threw at them.

Well, hell was coming. And this time there was no stopping it.

Chapter 39

Finn Carson

Inhaling a deep, fortifying breath, Finn slipped out the back door of the surveillance truck and scanned the perimeter. Craning his neck and adjusting the cuffs of his magnificently tailored Armani tux, his pregame jitters manifested in countless other nervous ticks he couldn't quite shake. Dang it, he was no sleuth. And he definitely wasn't as smooth as he pretended to be. Mooning over Joselyn the past few weeks had hardly been the farce he'd originally signed on for, but this ... this was a whole new playing field.

He turned toward his entry point, tugging at his lapels, needlessly tweaking his attire. One of the security guards at the Chase Park Plaza Hotel had agreed to give Finn clearance to enter the Whyte company Christmas affair via a back door at the request of the FBI. Finn got to avoid the assault of the media, and hopefully if Sir Burns-A Lot was spectating, he would think Joselyn was attending alone.

Maybe this could all end tonight.

The slightest scuff sound caught on the thin breeze. Finn jerked around, nearly crouching for his trusty .38 Special holstered at his ankle. He didn't like it there, out of reach, but it was discretely stowed for the occasion.

"Hey, you all right?" Archer stepped down from the truck.

Finn raked in another calming breath to soothe away the start Archer had given him. "Yeah, I guess I'm a little edgy."

"I think we are all on edge since the whole world knows where Joselyn will be tonight. But I'm sensing there's more." Archer used that probing interrogation stare. Finn cracked a respectable eight seconds in.

"What if something happens to her? What if I can't stop it?" He jammed his hand through his hair, a power grid of nervous energy humming through his veins. "Lord knows my control when it comes to that woman is miniscule at best. As much as I want to help protect her she is far too distracting for me to pledge to you my A game. I mean you saw us in the safe room when we thought the killer was in the house. I can't help myself. I get all heart and hormones."

Archer's hand clamped on Finn's shoulder. "Finn, we have half a dozen undercover agents in that building. We have uniforms at every exit. Eyes and ears inside. We are all working together to get this guy. I know it feels like this is all on your shoulders, but that's a burden you were never meant to carry. Not in this. Not in anything."

Archer literally shook him as if to jar something loose. "If you need me to go over the emergency plan again, I will, but maybe you should let go. You're not Superman, pal. You can't save everyone. But we are all doing everything in our power to keep you both safe. You can take that to the bank, brother."

Finn's nerves abated slightly. He knew Archer was right, but then again, knowledge and acceptance were miles apart in Finn's mind.

Like the Monroe fire. He could delve over every detail again and justify his actions. Had he known about and tried to rescue Kameron Monroe, it was likely they all would have died in the explosion instead of only Kendi's brother. But accepting that heavy-laden truth was next to impossible when a boy had died in a burning coffin, scared and alone, on Finn's watch.

Archer's appraisal stripped through the fancy suit and all the bravado Finn possessed, exposing his greatest weakness.

Finn shrugged off the supporting hand and let his eyes wander the darkened alley behind the elegant hotel.

The succession of street lights reflected off the rain-doused pavement illuminating a path to the entrance.

Sloshing sounds of tires cutting through pocks of slushy water on the road provided the only soundtrack for the still, dark night.

That and the thunderous pounding of his heart in his ears.

"Okay, I'm ready." Finn turned, his stiff shoes grinding the salt crystals to powder. Billows of ashen exhaust plumed from the vents of surrounding buildings, as if the streets of the Central West End had become a little slice of the Big Apple.

"Hey."

Stopping in his tracks, Finn spun back to his friend—the heroic Special Agent in Charge for the St. Louis FBI, and soon to be his brother-in-law.

"When you meet the right girl, I'll admit, there's a definite war for control." Archer lifted a dark brow to leave no question to what he was referring.

"Ugh. So not cool, man." Finn shivered.

A deep laugh echoed off the stone walls. "What can I say, your sister really lights my fire."

"Do you have a point? I really don't want to throw up on this suit that could fund world missions. Though I suppose smelling like vomit might kill some of the chemistry tonight."

Archer chuckled again. "Sorry, you're so squeamish I couldn't resist. What I mean is, it's not easy, but it's not impossible. Comes with the territory, protecting her. And it's worth it."

Deep down, beneath the emotions that boiled so hot, Finn felt honor-bound to do right by her. But the hauntingly personal knowledge of her past held a piece of his heart hostage. He wanted letting it go to be easy. It wasn't. What he wanted still didn't seem to matter.

"I know what you're thinking." Archer shrugged like the answer was so simple. "Grace, man. There's no statute of limitations on it. No one is beyond redemption. Including you. Don't forget, you're no perfect prize either."

"Gee, thanks for the ego boost."

"Like you need one." Archer drawled. "Now, go get 'er, tiger."

Vibrant colors and textures swirled all around him as if he'd fallen down the rabbit hole and entered into some twisted dreamland. The ritzy ballroom held hundreds of people dressed to the nines in elaborate gowns and sleek designer tuxedos like the one Finn was wearing. The one Finn was wearing that Declan Whyte had paid for, and for that reason, felt itchy and tainted.

Finn curled a finger around the collar of his shirt, tugged at his tie, and wormed through the tight spaces between guests.

Snippets of conversation about business ventures, vacation homes, and market shares were the talk of the day as he shouldered through the upper crust of all conglomerates of Whyte Enterprises.

Instead of chandeliers, modern light fixtures threaded like a tapestry of branches with small twinkling lights across the expanse of ceiling, as if a blanket of stars hung over the room.

And Finn actually spotted a few stars. Celebrities, rather. To prove how important a man like Declan Whyte was in the world.

Muted whispers of recognition tapped into his ears, dubbing him "Joselyn's man."

He decided he liked the sound of that.

A stocky man with a Teddy Roosevelt-esque stache hurled his thunderous voice over the noise. "… can't believe you ever let Tobin go. Heard he really lost it after what happened to his family. But he *was* our most valuable asset in R&D. And that paper tubing he invented showed real promise for several of our industrial plants."

"What about those twin blonde receptionists he canned? If you weren't so successful I'd question your judgment on the exceptionally low company quota of attractive females. Not a lot to look at, am I right, Walt?" Another robust counterpart jumped in on the heckling.

"—Finn." A man in the group spun around. Declan Whyte, in the flesh. And he was none too amused evidenced by the way his thick brogue growled Finn's name.

His meaty hand extended between them, though not in a way that meant the Scottish giant was welcoming Finn into his posse of associates. Thank God.

As tall as Finn, and solid, if not slightly overindulged, the man gripped Finn's hand with an apparent intent to crush it to show the power was an extension of his very being.

Meeting the challenge in the stormy gray eyes that matched his distinguished crop of silver hair, Finn reciprocated the crushing shake with vigor, taming a smirk at the man's almost imperceptible wince of pain.

"Mr. Whyte."

"It's about time you arrived. Perhaps you should run along and find Joselyn." His eyes hardened with an unspoken warning, a vein of displeasure pulsing at his temple. "I think I last saw her near the dance floor."

Finn bit his tongue and with a terse nod, pushed past the group of men now curious to his every move. He scanned the vast array of unfamiliar faces, desperate to land on the one that could stun.

It had only been a day. The strength with which he missed her should have been alarming but instead buoyed a bit of happiness in his chest. He turned toward the sound of a familiar feminine giggle, his pulse leaping with anticipation. A crowd of men shifted to accommodate a passing waiter, and Finn caught his first glance. At that moment, somehow, she saw him too. Every last detail he'd catalogued from the room faded in an instant, leaving her.

Only her.

The breath-stealing beauty in a killer red dress. Subtly provocative but yet exquisitely elegant, the crimson confection poured ever so perfectly over her chest, melted over her curves, flaring below her knees to the floor. She glistened like the only diamond in a sea of pearls from the tiniest straps of her dress encrusted with sparkle, to the starry glimmer in her eyes.

Without realizing it, he was parting the crowd, fixed by the beckon of her gaze. He shrugged past the mob of suitors surrounding her and closed in, slipping his hands around her waist, and ever so gently tasting her ripe cherry lips.

"I thought I told you it was over," she whispered against his mouth, and the contestants vying for the fair Joselyn started to disperse.

"I wasn't convinced."

She shivered, the little shimmy of contact testing the metal filings in his veins fighting the pull to magnetize against her every lovely curve.

"Are you cold?" He loosed his hands from her back and rubbed her bare arms, keeping his forehead pressed to hers. "Because you look insanely hot."

That earned him a slight smile and a self-conscious shrug. You know what they say, *"When in doubt, wear red."*

"I'm serious. There are lots of pretty things in this room, Joss, but as exceptional as you are on the surface, and I mean, *wow*. There is more beauty hidden in here than in any other place on earth." He moved his fingertips against the delicate thread of her collarbone over her heart before bringing his palm up to cup her face. "I see you, Joselyn. And what I see is so beautiful it hurts."

She gasped softly, then leaned into his touch. "You're not so bad yourself. But it's not safe. You should've stayed away."

"I can't."

The dulcet strains of the twelve-piece band hummed something slow and melodic, and Finn stepped forward, flush against the exotic beauty in the fiery red dress, and held her against him. "Dance with me." He breathed into her ear, nuzzling her neck.

With a shaky exhale, she relaxed into him, her head snuggling against his chest.

And heaven came to earth for the three songs that followed. Joselyn tucked in his arms, soft and yielding, trusting him with her life, her heart, as they swayed amid the bustle as if no one and nothing else existed.

Finn felt her lips graze his neck, a spiral of fire rained down his spine. "Joselyn." Her head came up, vulnerability adrift in those luminous eyes. "I know this didn't start out right, but I want you. I want … *us*." *Forever.* "Tell me it's not too late."

He couldn't tell if it was hope or heartache, but her eyes glowed with the faintest dew of tears. The slender column of her throat came alive, betraying the surging of her heart.

"This is really about us? Not about money or anything else?" her voice emerged so fragile, so insecure.

He stroked her cheek with his thumb. "What more could I want?"

"Finn, I—"

A burly guest with a crew cut and a solid black suit barged through the quiet moment. "There's been a breach in security. You gotta move, now." The thick vibrato of the threat stalled the blood in Finn's brain.

Alarm stole the warm glow from Joselyn's face, vacated the life from her eyes as her hands slipped from around Finn's collar and curled together against her chest.

Without a beat of hesitation, Finn snatched her hand and fled the ballroom.

All tenderness vanished in that moment, and the assaulting panic had him tugging her along to the stairwell. Finn could tell she was trying her best to keep up, but the shackles of her formfitting dress and the struggling clack of her heels on each concrete step slowed their progress.

And then a wave of terror seized his chest.

Footsteps.

Someone was following them and gaining *fast*.

Finn hauled Joselyn up in his arms. For a fleeting moment, he flashed back to prom night, the anguish he'd felt dumping Joselyn into Cody's arms. Immediately shaking free, he vaulted up each flight of stairs.

All of his training, the Combat Challenges, prepared him for this moment. But somehow, that did nothing to calm the frantic fear clawing at his back.

Please protect us.

Hard scraping echoed up from the floor below, and Finn risked a glance over the open railing.

There were two men—big men—wrapped in black clothes. Finn couldn't glimpse their faces, but their matching skin heads and their thunderous approach did little to negate the nefarious threat.

Pulling ahead and reaching the eleventh floor, Finn slowed momentarily, easing open the door to provide a soundless escape. The sound of the thugs on their six seemed far away, but Finn knew, from the foreboding shiver of dread prickling the back of his neck, they were still coming.

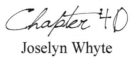

Chapter 40

Joselyn Whyte

"**W**here is she? He's going to kill us if we lose her!"

"She couldn't have gotten far." The other man wheezed. "Check that way."

Why did their voices sound familiar?

Joselyn's breathing stalled, the bludgeoning force of her pulse beating her lungs to a bloody pulp.

Silence and the labyrinth halls of the Chase Park Plaza Hotel were their only allies, so she clamped down on her lip, drawing insufficient breaths through her nose, and curled tighter into Finn's chest.

He set her down, dug into his pocket, and unearthed a room key. His fingers slipped before fitting the key card into the door she realized they were now standing in front of.

Once inside the soft click of the lock granted a gasp of renewed oxygen like a fairy godmother's wish. But even then anxiety crashed like a riptide against her curdling stomach, yanking the bottom out from under her. Numb and motionless, Joselyn stood by the door, her knees threatening to release her body to the floor—or maybe just the contents of her stomach.

Finn, on the other hand, was moving enough for the both of them—pacing the length of the room, checking his cell, and double-checking the hotel phone in the process. The pendulum effect of his rapid movements did nothing to assuage her vertigo.

Then, out of nowhere, he calmed. Stripped off his tux jacket, then bent down and pulled a gun—a gun!—from his pant leg and set it on the nightstand. "You should sit; you look a little faint." He leaned back onto the bed and crossed his ankles.

Oh yeah, sure, let's just take a load off. Pretend there aren't people right outside the door hunting for her. Pretend Finn didn't just whip out a gun!

As if reading her mind, he said, "Relax, okay. This is part of Archer's emergency plan. This room is reinforced, reserved for politicians and dignitaries. No one is getting through that door. We're safe." His voice lowered. "*For now.*"

It felt like she was nodding in agreement, but everything in the room seemed to be spinning. Or maybe the room was still and Joselyn's mind was on the tilt-a-whirl. It was hard to tell.

Before she came to, she went weightless again. Finn had risen and scooped her up like a limp noodle, moving to set her on the bed. But for some reason she couldn't signal her arms to let go.

"Here you go, man. She's all yours." His voice from the past echoed in her mind, tearing her back to the first time she'd been someone else's prey.

"No!" Joselyn's arms tightened around his neck when he made to move away, a convoluted mixture of past and present toying with her mind. "Please don't leave me." The words ached from her throat, cold seeping in from all around her.

The mattress shifted, and she had to reach through the closing darkness to remind herself that this was not prom night. She was twenty-seven, not seventeen. The man now cradling her in his arms was not, and would never be, Cody.

"Shh." Easing down beside her, the tension from that horrible night was steadily stroked away with each tender brush of Finn's hand through her hair.

And then his hand stilled.

She saw his Adam's apple bob in his throat, a glossy gleam reflecting from his smooth, clean-shaven jaw.

Uncertainty hovering in his gemstone eyes.

Joselyn wasn't sure who made the first move, but suddenly they were close enough to share air. Her heart skipped as his coarse fingers traced over her jawbone and locked behind her neck.

Their eyes held with an intimacy that should have scared her, even as, with slow and steady deliberation, he crossed the boundary between them and brought her lips to paradise.

The kiss started slow and savory. Thick with meaning and a riveting transparency, it rent a cry from the deepest part of her that longed to be known and loved. But a handful of heartbeats later her body quickened, responding as if every tickling nerve ignited at once.

Kind of like the fire that started it all.

A tentative touch turned into something fueled by desperation. The floodgates broke loose, and it was hotter than the fiery inferno of her house. Desire and panic surged back and forth from his charged body and lips to hers in a delicious duel.

He tucked her beneath him, the weight of this strong, beautiful man awakening her in ways beyond her wildest dreams.

What are you doing?

Something niggled in the back of her mind but was quickly overrun by the intensity of the moment. The urgency of each gentle caress exchanged like a flawless symphony of wanting.

Oh, she wanted this man. In a way she never wanted anything in her life.

But almost as much as that, she felt wanted in return. Needed. It was rapidly filling a loveless, lonely void.

When her fingers skimmed up the muscular crevice of his spine she was only distantly aware that she'd felt his skin, not his shirt.

An alarm went off in her head. Fear began wrestling for dominance.

Don't overthink it. Don't go to that place.

His grip tightened on bare skin previously covered. She flushed hot and cold. She couldn't think. Could barely breathe. Blotches of black danced in her eyes before she squeezed them shut.

His lips broke away, trailing down her neck …

Don't freak out. Don't be a freak. He's not going to hurt you.

His hands coasted up the backs of her thighs, the press of his body pinning her like a butterfly. Trapped. It felt amazing, and yet the passion ripped from her grasp.

"No!"

She'd meant to speak, but the word hadn't come from her lips. The chill of his sudden absence was a slap of sanity. Part of her was relieved, the other part almost desperate to pull him back down and finish what they started, if only to prove the past didn't have a hold on her. That she wasn't some frigid basket case who freaked when a man so much as touched her. But he was scrambling off the bed, his eyes darkening with a startling burst of anger. "I'm not like you."

The knife of his words wedged deep. Somewhere between a clavicle and a rib, an imaginary blade struck to the hilt. Pain, unlike anything she'd ever felt, sliced through her chest.

I'm not like you.

Her first impulse was to dissolve into tears. Give in to the heartbreaking conclusion of his words.

He would never accept her. She was stained. Used.

Unworthy.

But before the tears could break free, the words came back for a second go-around.

I'm not like you?

This time, she felt another emotion.

Joselyn called it pissed.

"No, you're not. You're worse!" Shooting up from the bed, she caught and righted the delicate straps of her dress that had fallen, groped for the zipper open at her back.

Finn's shirt hung open, untucked and wrinkled, his

muscles rippling with each breathless pant.

Joselyn struggled with her own breath but managed to unleash her fury with ease. "Not like me, huh? And what am I, exactly?"

With a tortured wince, the jerk now managed to look contrite.

"That came out wrong. I didn't mean it like that. I got carried away, and I was trying to do the right thing." His eyes wandered, as if the act of looking at her made him feel dirty.

Is this the same Finn who'd dated every bimbo this side of the Mississippi?

Tunneling his hands through the hair she had personally mussed, he heaved out a sigh. The words that came next seemed to cause him pain. "Look, I know you slept with Cody."

Slept? He didn't know the half of it.

Self-righteous coward.

Tears brimmed to the edge and poured over without consideration of her humiliation. Joselyn shook her head. "I can't believe I could've been so stupid. They say love is blind, but my eyes are wide open, and all I can see clearly is that—I'm a fool. A fool to open my heart to someone as selfish as you. A fool to think I could trust you again after what you did to me." A sob broke the words, but she was beyond caring.

"A fool to believe you might actually love me back."

He took a step forward. She jerked back out of reach. "And finally, a fool to let my guard down in that bed tonight. Thank God nothing happened. Lord knows you'd probably turn it into another thing you could torture yourself about. Pile it onto your mountain of egomaniacal martyrdom. But rest assured, you did the *right* thing."

"Joss." He looked so broken. Confused. "I didn't mean it like—"

"Cody raped me, Finn." she blurted before she could stop it, not even certain he would believe her. Her own father hadn't. Simply threw a high-priced shrink her way and told her to get over it. "And not just once. All night, after you refused to take me home and delivered me to his room." Joselyn choked back the vile images flashing in her eyes. Immeasurable pain. And loss.

It seemed, it was her destiny.

Finn froze. His skin drained so sickly white she thought he might faint.

She couldn't look at him any longer. But somehow the rest tumbled out, the memories rushing back with excruciating clarity. "He'd obviously taken something. High on some sort of sadistic rage. And the more I fought him, the more violent things got."

Forcing down the acid now coating her throat, her voice wobbled, but she forged on. "What may or may not have been the last time ... I—I can vaguely remember him bashing my head into the bedpost. When I woke up it was morning. And I'd been discarded on the front porch steps." Her skin scrubbed raw and reeking of disinfectant.

Breathing deeply, she said, "So, you see, you're right about me. I'm damaged goods. Inside and out. I have nothing left to give." Without stopping for her shoes, or her clutch, she threw the lock and got to be the one to walk away. Out of Finn's life.

This time, for good.

Joselyn jabbed the button for the lobby and collapsed to the elevator floor. Blinded by tears anyway, she drew up her knees and folded her face under the shadow of her arms.

Her sobs echoed all around her as if four other women were unleashing their sorrows in cannon. The metal box closed in on her, seeming to solder all the hurt together, crushing her chest and the remnants of her heart into a million little icicles.

A ding sound preceded the opening of the door, exposing the pitiful wreckage of Billionaire Heiress Joselyn Whyte's life. Managing to rise from the floor of the elevator, she peered around the open door. Vultures were still camping out in the lobby, ravenous for their next exposé.

She couldn't very well get her SUV from the valet looking the way she did—the press would be ruthless and her father would never forgive her—but she had to leave.

Then she remembered the FBI surveillance truck out back. Sal would take her home.

But how would she get outside undetected?

At that moment, as if by divine intervention, a bellhop cart bounced by, affording Joselyn cover to a nearby hallway. Creeping down the hall, her vagabond feet under the custom-made Roberto Cavalli gown stung against the chilled travertine tile. With each step, a frigid nip snaked up her legs until the real and imagined cold encased her in a protective layer of ice. Snow Whyte had returned.

Shoving open the back exit she tumbled out into the street, a rumpled and barefoot Cinderella fleeing the ball.

But there was no guard at the door. Wasn't there supposed to be security at every exit? The slice of winter air sobered her instantly, exposing the rashness of her actions right when a dark shadow stalked through the billows of hot air venting from the buildings. Oh crap. She was about to become a statistic. Her chest convulsed in spasm before she could even eke out a scream.

"Joselyn?" The form picked up speed and emerged from the mist writhing through the dark alley.

"Sal." His name released on an exhale, and Joselyn, unable to think through the dense scramble of emotion and relief, vaulted into the strong, capable arms of Agent Dorian Salivas. The slick icy pavement dropped out beneath her feet. She pressed her lips hard against his cheek. "Please, can you get me out of here?"

Easing her back down, he cupped her face, "Joss, what happened? Where's Finn?" Sal's fingers swiped at the relentless downpour of tears before his sharp, assessing eyes took inventory.

And then, as if showing solidarity, the sky opened up and

shed tears of frozen rain. The ping of sleet swelled in seconds, masked only by the faint purr of a nearing engine. *"Oh, Sal,"* Joselyn fell into his deep, hazelnut eyes, "Why couldn't it have been you?"

Sniffling back the mess that was leaking from her face, she wondered if he had any clue what she meant or what had just happened.

Finn was the only one that could leave her this broken. She should have never let him back into her life. Sal would have been the safer, more sensible choice. Why hadn't she listened to reason?

"Hey, now, shhh." He tipped up her chin with a curled knuckle. "Don't go filling my head with that kinda fancy, you hear? An aimless bachelor like me would jump at the chance to settle down with someone like you." The teasing in his eyes faded, his brows knotted together and he gripped her arms. "Did Finn try something? Oh, I'll kill him myself, the little twerp. Did he hurt you, Joselyn?" He searched her eyes with an intensity she'd never seen from the wise-cracking Sal.

But she couldn't form the right words. Wasn't sure there were any. And in the span of a heartbeat, his eyes widened as if enlightened with the truth. "Let's go."

He withdrew the arms that seemed to have been holding her together, and she felt the jumble of her insides threaten another meltdown. Taking her hand, he started toward the truck parked at the end of the street.

Sal mumbled under his breath, *"I'm gonna beat the living—"*

An explosion of ultraviolet light blasted from the ground—the blinding supernova sent them stumbling back onto the dank pavement.

"What the—" Sal's curse scattered into the sound of a gunned engine.

Joselyn groped the ground, the slushy compost seeping through her dress. When she righted herself a world of mocking darkness toyed with her senses as her eyes continued to absorb the shock of the blast.

Rubber screamed on the water to her right, she bolted to her left.

"Joselyn, hit the ground, I can't see!" Sal roared with authority that literally loosed her knees and sent her colliding again with the road. A spray of gunfire ricocheted off the walls, bounding the piercing sound back from every direction. But the spitting bullets rained on, pelting metal and glass on the approaching vehicle.

The charge of the engine tickled the fine hairs on the back of her neck as if it was passing over her. Hugging the asphalt, Joselyn jerked her hands up to cover her head, wishing she could see something.

Oh, God. I'm going to die.

"Run!"

Joselyn's heart crashed as the undeniable sound of the battle between man and automobile ended with a thud and a life-releasing grunt.

No! A breathless scream choked in her throat. Overrun with a jolt of terror, she leapt to her feet.

Sal was dead. She sensed his life slipping away as if she were holding his heart in her hands.

Honoring his last request, she ran. Aimlessly. Miniscule blips of her surroundings crept into the corners of her blinded eyes. The engine noise revived from its idle.

And when she felt the heat of the engine, it was as if the devil himself breathed on her neck. She knew it was all going to end any second.

Oh, God, please. I don't know why but somehow this is about me. Don't let Sal die. Forgiv—

Whack! Black ink bled back into her eyes as something landed with a crack against her skull. Receding into a pit of emptiness, she fell into someone's arms.

But unlike the peace she'd felt in the arms of her rescuer that first night in the fire, these arms felt like fury. Like pain and hopelessness.

Like a kiss of certain death.

Chapter 41

Finn Carson

Cody *raped me, Finn.*

For as long as he lived, Finn would never hear words that could dismantle him as much as these. He couldn't untangle his mind from her words, couldn't shake away the catatonic shock that gripped him when her confession delivered the fatal blow in his quest for redemption. This was a prison of guilt he would never escape.

Something cruel and vicious on Cody's face from prom night looped back on the live feed in Finn's head, tipping him off about ten years too late.

Cody. Finn's best friend since kindergarten. Who'd been as close as a brother.

Cody had raped and assaulted Joselyn. Practically bragged to Finn's face about how easily she'd come on to him for weeks after that night, slamming her character and her performance with crude frankness until Finn begged him to stop.

How could he have been so blind?

"It's all my fault." Not only was he *not* a hero, he was the villain. He'd hand delivered her to the enemy.

He felt sick.

He needed to sit, except ...

In an instant, the past clicked back into its place, and Joselyn's absence from the hotel room registered with a spurt of panic. He cursed his stupidity.

Cramming his feet into his shoes, Finn left everything but his gun. Swiping it off the nightstand, he tucked the pistol into his waistband at his back and bolted from the room.

His open shirt flapped like wings as he sprinted to the elevator. The screen adorning each door showed that one car had passed the eleventh floor and was continuing its ascent and the other was in the lobby.

Scrambling to the stairwell, Finn vaulted down each flight of stairs, shooting his gaze down the open spiral core for any glimpse of movement.

Where were those men that had been chasing them?

More importantly, where was Joselyn?

Dammit!

As he made his descent to the ground level, time slowed—taunting his too-little, too-late effort to save the day, again.

First he tries to save the girl. In all his runaway passion he almost takes advantage of her at the worst possible time. And then in his knee-jerk reaction to do right by her, he insults her in the most tactless way imaginable.

I'm not like you? Could he have conjured worse words in that moment?

Oh, and the hurt etched into that beautiful face. Not only from his thoughtless words but from her heartbreaking confession.

Finn couldn't erase it from his mind. Those bright amethyst eyes turning gray and lifeless. The carefully cool mask she wore to hide the hurt he'd caused all those years ago.

It all made sense. Her reaction to Cody in Finn's apartment, her trepidation to Finn's anger when they were locked in the panic room—she had been attacked, imprisoned, abused for a night of emotional and physical torture.

And Finn, being a proud and dense jerk, had not only put her there but had bought in to every line of Cody's masterful deceit.

How different things might have been had Finn only heeded his father's advice about the truth? How different

Joselyn's life might be without having suffered such a defining act of violence?

Dear Mom,

Something happened. I have no one, I've lost everything ... and nobody cares. I'm thinking I'd rather be with you.

The words from Joselyn's diary wrapped like fingers around his neck and shook him to the bone.

She was haunted still. Might have even tried to take her own life. Something that traumatic couldn't easily be erased or reconciled.

"Joselyn, forgive me." He breathed the words into existence. Praying she might somehow be able overcome the devastating consequences of his stupidity. Yes, Cody's violence had caused this. But knowing Finn could have prevented it brought his every inadequacy to the surface.

If he could have one more chance, Finn would stop at nothing to earn her trust, protect her, and show her exactly how much he'd always loved her.

Would it be enough?

Well, he'd been trying to barter for forgiveness for all his mistakes so far and that wasn't going so well.

But with that thought, something invaded Finn's spirit. Some awakening that was nearly impossible to explain but irrefutable nonetheless.

He needed saving.

Not only today in this crisis, but every moment of every day.

All his life he'd been trying to prove himself worthy, but the truth was, he'd been found worthy all along. It wasn't about being brave enough or strong enough, because when it came right down to it, it wasn't about him at all. *When I am weak, you are strong.* The words nestled into his most vulnerable places, packing into the wounds that had robbed him of his true strength and now readied him for battle. He was made for this. To be a warrior. To stand strong against whatever giants stood in his path and keep on fighting.

And that was exactly what he intended to do. He'd fight it

all. The doubt, the fears, the failures. The enemies, in his head and in the flesh. Because somehow he knew, though the battle was just beginning, the war was already won.

The ballroom, the restrooms, the lobby with all those reporters—Joselyn was nowhere to be found.

He must look like a lunatic, but he didn't care. Joselyn's safety was the only thing that mattered. So where was she?

Realizing it should have been his first line of defense, he slipped into a quiet hallway lined with small offices and placed a call to Archer.

Not even a full ring later, Archer answered, shouting, "Finn! What happened?"

Burning hot sweat prickled his skin, "I—I—Where's Joselyn?"

The distinct sound of a stretcher retched in the background, muffled sounds of medical jargon crept through the speaker.

"She's gone, Finn!" Archer barked his fury, which, to Finn, only meant one thing.

Gone? As in …

He couldn't force himself to fill in the blanks. His mind shrunk back, retreated to someplace safe. Numb, but safe. The only thought he could muster was a cry from the depths of his soul.

God, please.

"—And Sal is fighting for his life! I need some answers. Get out here, now!"

The door that now dumped Finn into a waking nightmare was the very point of inception for the promising evening.

Crime scene precautions were in full orchestration, the bustle of activity had awakened the dank and sleepy alley. Spotlights from patrol cars and a nauseous rotation of reds and blues strobed out through the narrow space, casting long, dreary shadows in places of darkness.

Scanning the figures in the crowd, Finn found the outline of a beast of a man towering over every other silhouette. Archer.

From sheer determination of will, Finn managed to push past a protesting uniform setting up a perimeter to slide under the crime scene tape.

"Archer," Finn charged into the huddle with more confidence than he felt. The armor he'd rallied inside the hotel felt like shavings of chainmail shedding from his skin with each step toward the answers he needed but feared all the same.

Continuing to bark orders, Archer held up his hand to Finn. "… all of these buildings searched. I want no stone left unturned, you copy? Someone had to have seen something, and since Sal's vision was compromised we've got nothing on the vehicle. We're pulling the feed from the traffic cams, but without any leads, we don't know what we're looking for.

"This guy's smart. And highly dangerous. These homemade flash grenades we found hidden near every entrance tell us we need to be on guard for anything. He was ready for us. And now, the only assurance we have that she is alive is that there's no body. The clock is ticking. This is everyone's first priority. Even the smallest blip, I want to be contacted immediately. You all have your orders. Go!"

Archer whirred around, his dark eyes menacing. "What the hell happened? How'd you get sep—"

"What do you mean gone?"

A flicker of sympathy softened Archer's hard glare. "Taken."

Taken. That one small word packed enough punch to level him. Keeping his legs steady enough to stand on was nothing short of a miracle. And the only reason he could rationalize that he was still breathing was because Joselyn wasn't dead—though they couldn't be sure of that without evidence.

But something—maybe hope—dug its heels into Finn's gut. Call it a premonition, or perhaps wishful thinking, but Finn could feel her heart beating as if he were still holding her in his arms.

She's alive. He knew it as sure as he knew he loved her.

"Are you sure it's her? It's only been a couple of minutes. Maybe she's headed home. I—"

"We found her diamond earring right over there" Archer pointed. "About thirty feet further there is a trace amount of blood in the slush. We are waiting for confirmation that it's Joselyn's, but Sal's word is enough for me."

"Sal? What did Sal say? And how could he not see anything? How could—" Finn's mind raced ahead with too many questions. It was too much talk, too little action.

"Sal found Joselyn in the alley. He was manning the truck when he noticed one of the guards walk out onto the street about a hundred yards east from his station. Called it in right after we were alerted to the breach on the inside, so all our men were covering the ballroom. Sal went to check out the unguarded entrance. It's my understanding that that's when Joselyn tumbled out."

Lowering his eyes, Archer shook his head. "Sal started losing consciousness again when he got to that part. The paramedics are taking him down the street to Barnes-Jewish Hospital. I've given strict orders for someone to call me as soon as he's lucid again. Hopefully he'll remember something."

Finn fought to tamp down the hysteria accelerating in his veins and ripping his heart to shreds. "God, we have to find her. *Now.* He's gonna kill her." He raked his fingernails into his scalp, pinched his eyes shut like it might all be a bad dream. "I messed up. It's all my fault."

Archer took a step forward and lowered his voice. "Keep it together. We're gonna find her. Now, go home, Finn. I've got work to do."

"Absolutely not. I can control myself. I want to help." And like the flip of a switch, Finn sensed his composure click back into place. Felt that fireproof shield he'd once carried rise up and surround him. He might stumble his way through this transformation, but he wouldn't rest until he got it right.

Archer's eyes burned into his, discerning Finn's unwavering resolve. "Fine," he growled. "You can come. But before you go off and do anything stupid ..." He clapped a hand on Finn's shoulder and closed his eyes for a beat.

"What are you doing?"

"Praying that agreeing to let you help wasn't a giant mistake."

Finn shrugged off his hand. "Dude, if you're gonna pray you better be aiming those favors at finding Joselyn."

"Already got it covered."

Chapter 42

Joselyn Whyte

Y*ou unravel me, with a melody*

A soft reassurance wove into Joselyn's subconscious.

You surround me with a song

It sounded like a chorus of angels singing, the words latching deep into her heart. Like a song she didn't know but had heard somewhere was tuned to a frequency in her head.

Of deliverance, from my enemies, till all my fears are gone.

The sweet sound unfurled some deep, abiding peace that was only counteracted by an interval of breath-stealing sharpness hammering nails into her temples.

Something jarred her from the trance of the lullaby. She went airborne for a suspended moment, and then the music severed on the gasp that ripped from her lungs as her body crashed back down to earth.

Her head landed with a thud. Pain exploded behind her eyes, and a spark of lightning fractured the darkness before it settled back to black with a blink.

Her eyes were open, weren't they? Why couldn't she see anything?

The vibration beneath her ceased for a moment and then changed pitch, rolling her body forward.

Jerking her arms out was instinctual, but something pinched at her wrists. One arm was trapped beneath her, the other tethered to the first, leaving her helpless to brace for impact.

She splayed her legs to impose some sense of stability, but

it was too late. Her skull banked hard against the wall, a hot rush of pain tugged at her consciousness. Sedation fell over her like a smothering blanket.

But then an engine revved, shocking her back to life when her heart mimicked the acceleration.

An engine! The rumble that shook her body was mutually exclusive to the tremors of panic that rattled her bones.

Her head hadn't hit a wall. A trunk! She was in the trunk of a car—which explained why the scrap of wool exfoliating her face smelled like a sweaty gym bag.

A slithering cold caressed her skin as it all came flooding back. The gala. Finn. The alley. The flash. The car. Sal.

Oh, Sal! Joselyn felt a trickle of warmth crest her cheek and sting in her nose. Had he survived?

Would she?

The car slowed and started to veer. Joselyn was able to anticipate the tumble of her body and braced her legs against the far end of the dark, empty space.

She strained to remember the last few minutes before blacking out. Had anyone seen her get taken? Did she even want to know where she was headed?

And could she escape the clutches of death again without Finn protecting her?

Finn. She allowed herself only a moment of reflection to review the highs and lows of the evening. Those perfect moments in his arms could nearly erase all the devastation he left in his wake. Almost.

Man, she was a mess for that boy. A brainless, pathetic mess.

Oh Lord, why him? Why do I love a man I shouldn't? And how is it possible, after all the ways he's hurt me, that I still ache for him?

Catching herself mid-prayer, Joselyn couldn't shake the feeling that God was, in fact, listening. That maybe He *did* care. She'd spent the better part of her life hurt and bitter, blaming him for the cruel and unrelenting losses that robbed her of her family, her childhood, her innocence … But in spite of all that, for the first time in her life, here on this final ride, she'd reached a place of surrender. She finally felt *worthy* of love. Not because she'd earned her stripes, but because of the one who had taken them for her.

The car pulled hard to the right and caught her off guard. Forcing her onto her back, the pin turn shoved her head toward the side, but since her arms, while still bound at the wrist, were now free from the trappings of her body, she managed to shield her skull from another hard blow.

Slowing on what she gathered was a gravel road, the spitting clank of rocks shot up and pelted the underside of the car.

A gulp of air turned sour in her stomach.

They were almost there–wherever her final destination would be. Full-blown hysteria was ready to pounce, and she could feel the terror tightening its binds to render her defenseless against the predator.

There was nothing to be seen in the dark, so she closed her eyes.

She could see ... her mother. Clear as the crystalline blue of her irises. With an easy smile, and a light of glory in her eyes, Joselyn could sense her complete joy. She felt herself reach out, but her mother was vanishing, flecks of light and color scattering like ants.

Her breathing shuddered and then eased, filling her lungs with strength. There was nothing but darkness, but Joselyn felt enlightened and ready to claim her life. Maybe she was meant for more than mourning. More than merely surviving. Seeing that vision of her mother, she knew it was time to let the ghosts of the past rest and really live.

Not real great timing for that particular revelation, but she still had a chance.

A hasty minute later she had formulated the only semblance of a plan she could think of. Coiling up into a ball, she lifted the fabric of her dress and untangled her legs. Poised and ready to strike, she closed her eyes, and lay as still and lifeless as she could manage.

The barrage of kicked up stones made a marked decrease in frequency. The gentle whine of the brakes squealed what sounded like an inch below her ear.

This is it.

Her heart rate hitched up a notch, but she combated the assuaging panic with unuttered prayers and a final deep breath as the slam of the driver's side door signaled the end of the ride. The haunting crunch of the gravel planted images of charred and crushed bones beneath the murderer's feet.

Her lungs constricted, battening down for the storm, as if the last moments of safety afforded by the sealed walls of the trunk were winding down to zero.

Fear not for I am with you ...

At that moment, the first verse she'd read from Sadie's Bible dangled like a lifeline, the words grabbing on before the terror could pull her under.

The slipping sound of fitting metal sheared at the lock, and the door lifted away.

Still as death, Joselyn didn't dare open her eyes and lose her only advantage of surprise. One second of distraction could be the difference between life and death.

She could hear nothing but the muted breaths of her attacker, but it was enough to approximate a location.

Please, God. Let this work.

Allowing only a moment to distract him with the indecently exposed length of her leg to the scant fabric of her panties, she cracked her eyes and locked on to her target as he bent forward.

Now! Joselyn snapped her leg like a striking cobra. Those kick-boxing classes had been worth their weight in peanut butter M&M's.

The kick caught him by surprise, but he managed to rear back, her foot only glancing off his chin. But her heel did manage to clip his neck. From the croaking sound that escaped the man, his windpipe.

Throwing her legs over the lip of the trunk, Joselyn's feet slammed down on a tundra of rocks. She bit back a gasp.

Clutching the hem of her dress in one hand, she grasped the wheezing man's shoulder and jerked him toward the thrust of her knee.

He wailed his distress and cupped his groin.

Joselyn dropped her skirt, gripped the man's coat front with both hands and yanked his face down toward the open truck. She shoved against his backside, trying to force him in and feel for his keys at the same time.

Come on! Grinding her teeth, she grunted, hefting the enormous man with all of her might, and then some.

Only problem was, he didn't fit.

The compact trunk space of the old blue Civic would not accommodate his bulky frame.

Hope slipped loose like a tendril of her hair on the wayward wind. The sound of their struggle like reverb intruding upon the crisp winter silence.

Her attacker tried to jerk back, but she saw it coming and slammed the trunk atop his head, momentarily collapsing him back down. Her mind washed of any reasonable defense.

Without knowing any other course of action Joselyn slammed the door down once, twice, three times more to buy some time and ran.

The frozen stones, seemingly sharpened to arrowheads, cut into her tender feet. Tearing at the flesh, her feet grew slick with each agonizing step, the shooting pain catapulted up her legs and weakened her knees.

Scanning the long, deserted drive, Joselyn's heart collapsed. There was nowhere to run. No one would see her. Or hear her.

She forged on, racing toward the cover of trees that never seemed to get any closer.

Her breaths came heavy, and through the huff of white air and the sorrow spilling from her eyes mourning her wasted life, she saw only a tiny peek of the waning moon—a reminder of hope pouring out over the bleak and sinister night.

Joselyn felt her pursuer more than heard him. The

crunching rocks should have given it away, but the adrenaline pounding in her ears drowned out all other noise.

It told her all she needed to know. Her heart was still beating. That meant, if only for the moment, she was still alive.

Chapter 43

Finn Carson

"That stupid jerk! No one stands up Missy Rollins! Wait until that little twerp sees what I write on Facebook, he'll be ruined."

The artificial redheaded basket case couldn't seem to stay on point. Finn was more than tempted to slap her.

Thankfully Archer intervened. "Miss Rollins, we know you're upset about your date, but this is important. After you saw the flash of light from your window you said you saw a car."

Missy nodded, and as if suddenly aware of her male company, she adjusted her top and smoothed a hand over her hair before pulling out a flirtatious smile.

Finn's hand twitched. Lord, help him, he would not strike a woman.

"Yeah, I saw a navy blue car. Not sure what kind. I only saw it from the top when I was checking my window for Lance. That pig!" She snarled. "I mean. My date. Just my date, not my boyfriend or anything." The phony smile was back. "I'm single." Her lashes batted.

Was that Archer's teeth grinding or Finn's?

"Even if you can't give us make or model, what about size. Midsize sedan, coupe? Anything you remember would be helpful."

The aloof witness smacked her gum and gave a poor imitation of a thoughtful pose. "I think it was small, Agent Hayes. Yes, definitely small. Like a little two-door. And it looked like the paint was peeling off the roof because there was like some silver and rusty metal showing through."

There was a knock at the door, and the uniform that caught the lead went to answer. When the door swung open it revealed a spiffed up meathead with a quizzical brow and a bouquet of pink roses.

"Uh … Hi, Officer." The guy's gulp was loud enough to hear from across the room. "I'm here for my date with Missy, sir."

"Lance!" The flighty redhead must have forgotten her peeve and rushed to the door to receive her bounty.

"Sorry I'm late. I was only running a few minutes behind, but then the cops wouldn't let me in." Looking as nervous as a schoolboy, Lance woodenly thrust out the flowers. "Here. I got you flowers."

Flowers. Flowers. Something wormed around in Finn's brain. Something other than the scent of fresh cut blooms and first date awkwardness.

"Flowers!" Finn blurted as the first tentative pieces clicked together.

Archer turned, his eyes narrowed from the strange outburst. "What about 'em?"

"Joselyn kept saying something about the flowers and how she thought they'd come from her dad. Something about white lilies is significant." And something was warning him not to shrug off his hunch that the flowers were somehow linked to Joselyn's father. He looked to Archer to produce some sort of a connection, and bless Archer for his discernment, he went with it.

They bolted from Missy Rollins's loft with the lovely view of the alley and went to facedown the bulldog himself.

"Well, what's he saying?" Finn fidgeted in the passenger seat of Archer's Suburban. His anxiety manifesting in a manic restlessness that had him uncrossing and recrossing his legs and arms more than a dozen times during the maybe three-minute phone call between Archer and Declan Whyte.

Archer held up a finger. "Umm-hmm. I understand that, sir, but I'll decide what is and isn't relevant at this point."

Come on! Come on!

"Mr. Whyte, we will keep you apprised. But if you ever interfere with an FBI investigation again I'll charge you with obstruction of justice, are we clear?"

Dang.

While the anticipation was excruciating, Finn had to admit he felt a smidgen of satisfaction that someone had put the mighty Declan Whyte in his place.

"We'll be in touch." Archer signed off. Heaving out a burdened breath, he stalled one second too long for Finn's liking.

"Archer, you spit it out this second, or heaven help me—"

"Okay, okay. You were right about the flowers. Declan's flower of choice for his bereaved employees is white lilies."

"What, you mean like he sends them to his workers' funerals?"

Archer nodded. "And their families. Company courtesy for the loss of a loved one. Now we've got something to go on." Plucking his cell phone from his pocket, Archer dialed out and barked a slew of orders to someone at the FBI while weaving with a sort of maniacal precision through downtown traffic toward the FBI building.

"The breach in security was Declan Whyte's fault." Archer slammed his fist down on the steering wheel, the deadly growl of his words so low Finn strained to hear him over the heavy hush of rain and sleet. "All that money, and the man can't even buy a lick of sense.

"He paid off the guard to allow his own henchmen in undetected. Told the guy at the back to walk away from the door and let those Gill and Royce clowns in for a little added protection." The laugh that emerged was anything but comical. "They were the ones that chased you guys up to the safe room. His taking matters into his own hands left us vulnerable for attack."

Finn ground his teeth to keep from swearing. "But how

did the kidnapper know Joselyn would leave from that door specifically?"

"He didn't. He had those homemade flash grenades hidden at every entrance. He sat around and waited. Probably had some of his own surveillance set up so he'd know which one to trigger if he got the chance.

"It guess it didn't matter if the guard was there or not. I trust Sal over any one of those uniforms, and even he couldn't stop him. The real problem was the diversion of those giant Scottish goons that pulled all of our resources inside. Even this psychopath couldn't have anticipated that kind of luck."

Within minutes they were bursting through the door of the FBI office. Activity hummed in the bullpen. Several agents rushed at Archer, all seeming to talk at once.

While they wove though the hive to Archer's office, Finn understood that some of the agents were running all the plates from the vehicles that popped up on the traffic cams. Others were compiling a list of past and current Whyte employees and family members that had received a bouquet of white lilies per the company records released by Joselyn's father.

Archer seemed to have gleaned more from the chaos than Finn and bossed a bunch more people around. All of whom scurried away to do his bidding without the slightest hesitance.

If anything ever happened to Finn, he'd want Archer heading up the investigation. The man was a machine.

The spate of activity was keeping Finn's mind from wandering to a dark place. Silent prayers looped on an unspoken and almost mindless repetition, somehow keeping the anarchy clawing at his insides from cutting him to ribbons.

"I'd wager anything he took that exit there." Archer pointed to the DOT schematic on the white board in his office, talking more to himself than Finn. "He's too smart— too prepared—to risk being caught on camera, and that

Forest Park cut through is the only one that avoids every traffic cam in the area." Archer stormed around to his desk.

Finn followed and looked over Archer's shoulder at the lists emerging on his computer. "So ... you're *not* going to look at these traffic cam photos?"

"It's a dead end. I can feel it. I've got a few people on it, but we can't afford to waste any more time."

Finn dropped the folder and fought the urge to pace. "Okay, then what's our next move?"

Archer snatched a stack of sheets spitting out of the printer and shoved roughly half of them at Finn. "Let's start looking over these employee records. Don't seem to be more than a hundred deaths for employees or family members for the last two years, so let's get through these. There has to be a link here."

Dropping to the chair in front of Archer's desk, Finn started poring over the depressing files of factory mishaps and heart attacks, cancers and car accidents. Archer did the same. They worked in silence for no more than five minutes when Finn caught a break.

Tobin Devore. "Bingo! This has gotta be him." Finn scanned the page detailing the man's loss. Losses. His stomach jammed up in his throat.

Archer was instantly at Finn's side. "Oh, man. Not good. And look at the date. It was never a decoy. He set Joselyn's house on fire on the one-year anniversary." With a whispered curse, Archer slipped back behind his desk and hammered the information against the keyboard. With the whip of his finger, a posse of agents returned to retask.

Excruciating minutes passed while Archer and the team scrounged for the whereabouts of the ghost of a man. The flurry of agents bounded in from the bullpen with updates on their search. All of which led nowhere. And all of which made Finn feel about as useful as a garden gnome.

All they had was a name. A former address. A former occupation with Whyte Enterprises as a scientist/inventor in research and development. Brilliant, not only from the looks of the file, but the orchestration of the elaborate revenge.

The information they managed to obtain over the next half hour was useless. Everything else came back blank. No credit cards. No active DMV records. No current residence. No next of kin. It was as if the man liquidated his life and disappeared.

Something in Finn snapped. Without a word he fled Archer's office. The fear pinched around his neck, hopelessness rising up to drown him. He needed air.

He rounded the corner to the exit and collided with a woman. The files she'd been carrying scattered to the floor.

"Sorry," he muttered and bent down to help retrieve the mess. He froze.

Laid out before him was a moment in time he'd never forget—the moment in the loft of Joselyn's bedroom, his first unguarded glimpse of the heiress he'd loved and loathed from afar.

Except it wasn't a dream. He was actually seeing it. The surprisingly artful photography of Joselyn's peeping Tom, Stuart, now lay before him.

Clinging to something, anything to feel close to her, Finn raked up the rest of the photos and refreshed his mind with the sweet memories of the night the tide had turned for them. Or for him, at least.

Oh man, that's it! Finn pushed the pictures at the woman and ripped another sheet of paper from her hand.

Stuart.

These pictures were only from that one night. There had to be more.

Maybe Joselyn having a stalker would be the key. With Stuart being so dedicated to all things Joselyn, maybe he had unwittingly caught Tobin Devore on camera. Or captured some clue to where he might've taken Joselyn. His heart buoyed with the possibility, fresh adrenaline charging through his veins.

Declan Whyte's stuffy business partner's words from hours earlier came hurtling back.

"... can't believe you ever let Tobin go. Heard he really lost it after what happened to his family."

The man lost his family, his home, and his job, all at the hands of Declan Whyte.

And now, Finn feared, he was out to even the score.

"Stuart!" The force of Finn's fist splintered the door panel. "Open the door, now!" he roared.

Having pilfered Stuart's home address from the spilled contents of the file and the keys to Sal's Dodge Challenger from his desk—*sorry, bro*—Finn left to get answers, by any means necessary. He'd called Archer while he was en route and may have promised that he would wait until Archer arrived to confront Stuart about his "surveillance" photos.

But time was of the essence, and he didn't want to tap dance around any bureaucratic red tape. He wouldn't put Archer in that position when every minute that passed could be Joselyn's last.

And now that he knew *why* this guy had a taste for fire, his skin prickled, and his neck heated, recalling the agonizing touch of the flames. Knowing Joselyn could be burning alive at this very moment was incinerating him from the inside out.

Finn shuddered and set his fist to the door again. He'd walk through fire again and again to be the hero she needed. And not because he had something to prove to himself anymore. He could see now who he was and where his strength came from. Helluva time for that to finally sink in. But this time he had something to prove to *her*. Love had cost her too much and brought her nothing but pain. And it was time for that to change.

"You can stop yelling at me. I know I should have waited, but there's nothing we can do about it now, so let's get on with it."

Finn sat in the interrogation room with Archer roughly forty minutes later. The man was fuming, but at least Finn's initiative had paid off. Archer would get over it; he simply wasn't used to people defying his orders. And since he was about to acquire an obstinate wife in a few short weeks, it was good practice, Finn thought wryly, surprised he could find anything even remotely amusing at a time like this.

"I *am* trying to get on with it. The kid will be here any minute. Agent Mackenzie, you know, the one you stole Stuart's address from? She's bringing him in. But apparently the roads are in bad shape due to the weather."

Archer assured him things were coming together quickly. It had only been two hours since they'd left the crime scene. At this point the clock was irrelevant. The countdown was racing down to zero in his chest, each heartbeat of waiting an eternity of imagining life without her. But sitting in this tiny room waiting for, what they hoped would be, the final piece of the puzzle, proved to be the longest fifteen minutes of Finn's life.

"Did they at least get a BOLO out on the car now that I got the license plate?"

"Yeah. We've got everyone on it. Don't worry, Finn, we're close." Archer's ire softened to something much more frightening. Sympathy. As if it might already be too late.

It couldn't be.

Finn clung to the smallest hope. Just over an hour ago a divine whisper had propelled him out that door on a collision course with the information they needed. For the first time in far too long, Finn felt like he'd surrendered the burden of his own expectations. He couldn't control everything. But he was poised to be the ready weapon in the hands of the warrior who could fight the battles he couldn't win alone.

It was as if the blinders had been lifted from his eyes. How else would he have sensed that the flowers were significant? Or zeroed in on Tobin's file in that massive stack within minutes of searching?

Good things came in threes because the hat trick was

complete when Stuart finally opened the door to his apartment.

His stalker-den had been plastered with pictures of Joselyn. Candid and hauntingly beautiful shots of her being surveilled serving as wallpaper, sparing no inch of blank space.

Of course, Stuart hadn't exactly rolled out the welcome mat, but a few aggressive shoves, and a quick rundown of the evening had granted Finn access to Stu's "security detail" of Joselyn's street in the days leading up to the fire.

And that's when Finn struck gold. Or rather a battered and rusty navy blue Honda Civic. The car had appeared down the street from Joselyn's every day that week, each time in front of a different house.

Finn had snatched up the photos and rushed to leave, but a firm grip on his arm had stopped him at the door.

"I can see that you love each other." Stuart had produced a picture of Finn and Joselyn from outside the restaurant on their first date.

Big surprise, Stu had been there to document it.

Finn had hesitated long enough to drink in the captured moment, once again ensnared by the memories. Joselyn was nestled in his embrace, their eyes locked. Their emotions so transparent they'd been almost too easy to miss up close but from a distance seemed ironically magnified with perfect acuity.

The moment from the image came alive in his mind. The silk of her hair beneath his fingertips. The sweetness of her mouth millimeters from his but still imprinted on his lips. That look in her eyes he hadn't been able to decipher until now. *Love.*

"It's up to you now to keep her safe." Stuart's words had brought him back to reality. And Finn had eyed the resigned man who loved Joselyn too—in his own hopeless way. He couldn't condone the guy's methods, but Finn supposed he could relate to being totally gone over Joselyn Whyte.

Finn had accepted his mandate with a terse nod and had

set off again, phoning Archer—who'd still been en route to Stuart's and consequently on the other side of town from the registered owner of the blue Civic. Crappy cards on that score, but he had the ace in his pocket.

So now they waited. And waited. Until finally, sixteen-year-old Billy Levenworth stumbled into the interrogation room.

The gangly teen in a hoodie boasting Spock and the words *"Trek yourself before you wreck yourself"* sat warily in the metal chair, his tawny brown eyes darting with confusion under the sloppy mess of his curly dark mop-top.

"Billy, I'm Special Agent Archer Hayes. I need to ask you some questions, and it's really important you're completely honest with me. Understand?" Archer's tone, while calm and collected, could strip a coating of paint off a steel beam.

The young boy's gulp echoed through the small room, and his pencil neck bobbed his head in compliance.

Archer laid a print from Stuart's collection on the frigid metal table and slid it across to Billy's laced, white-knuckled hands. "Billy, is this your car?"

"Y-yes, sir."

"About three weeks ago, do you remember parking your car on North Harrison Avenue in Kirkwood every day around noon," Archer produced another picture, "near this house."

The boy's bushy eyebrows pulled together despite the lack of distinction between them. A bead of sweat dripped from beneath the matting of bangs down the slope of his nose.

"N-no, sir. I have perfect attendance at school. And I don't have a parking pass so my car is at home during the day. I've had to ride the stupid bus for the past month while my parents are on their European cruise. What's going on? Why was my car there?"

Archer ignored the questions and pressed on. "Do you know a man named Tobin Devore?"

His brows disappeared further beneath his bangs. "My uncle Toby took my car?"

"Uncle? I thought Devore didn't have any living

relatives," Finn interrupted.

Billy nodded, "That's because he's not technically my uncle. My mom and Toby grew up in the system. They lived in the same foster home for four years. After the fire—and even more so after that Declan Whyte d-bag fired him a month later—Uncle Toby kinda snapped. Stopped going to church with us. Grew this gnarly beard. Sold all his stuff and moved into this nasty old hunting cabin in the middle of East Jesus. I mean there's no electricity, or running water, or anything. It's like a shack.

"Anyways, my mom's been really worried about him so she asked him to come and stay with us for a while. Plus, she needed someone to keep an eye on me while they were on their cruise. Lotta good that did because I've only seen him twice in three weeks. And one of those times he was dressed up as an EMT. I swear, he's totally lost touch with reality. Outer limits, for sure. He's battling some serious demons. Like Luke verses Darth stuff. And there's like this ... deadness to his eyes. When I look too deep I can feel the dark battle of all that spiritual warfare. I know you don't believe me, but it's freaky."

"Where is this hunting cabin?" Archer stood, economy and urgency in his movements.

"Leasburg, Missouri, I think? Somewhere near those campgrounds off of I-44. I'm not even sure there's an address. He paid some guy off the books a tiny hunk of cash for it. Like I said, it's not much of a house. I only saw it once in a picture."

Finn and Archer darted out the room. Finn flashed a parting Vulcan 'live long and prosper' symbol for the poor kid with a perplexed look on his face.

They were approaching the Suburban some twenty seconds later, and Archer was already ending a clipped phone conversation. "Leasburg is about fifty miles west. We'll head that way. I've got a chopper and local backup en route. I think it's safe to say Devore is planning on setting his cabin on fire with Joselyn in it. Not sure where the cabin is located, but hopefully they'll find it before we do. Or before we see the smoke."

They slipped into the car, and Archer tore away, tires screaming over the icy pavement.

Finn braced himself as his body lurched with the violent jerk of the car.

"Better buckle up, Finn. And keep praying we're not too late."

Chapter 44

Joselyn Whyte

It felt like she was floating. Swaying. Dancing. Whatever the reality was, Joselyn knew she wanted to remain blissfully ignorant of it as long as possible. With her eyes closed she could almost grasp the memory of Finn's embrace. Cradled in his arms, the music had all but faded as she swayed with the rhythm of his heart.

But this … this was different than that. So very different.

Nature's fury rained down above her. Pelting sounds of ice and rain warred against a strange surge of peace that entranced her mind. But the increasing violence of the hail on the roof above pinched stray nerves in her head, ricocheting random sparks of pain through her throbbing skull. The splitting headache and slick of blood seeping into her eye suggested another blow to the head. But that couldn't touch the agony that radiated from her shoulder. The only explanation she could warrant was someone had ripped her arm from her body.

Straining against the weight tearing at the joint, her body swayed too much. A rush of delirious pain shook a gasp from her throat. Without summons, tears washed the blood from her eye and the pain threatened to steal her questionable consciousness.

Stay awake! Open your eyes. Open them!

She winced, fighting for strength to both open her eyes and hold back the curtain of darkness pressing heavily from the pain. *Oh. Oh God.* The meager tentacles of lantern light in the dilapidated shed produced enough light to arouse a fair amount of panic.

What kind of *Sling Blade* horror movie had she been cast in? Rusty blades of all shapes and sizes hung from hooks on the walls. A blood-soaked wooden table against one wall held the lantern and a length of chain. The place reeked of rotting carcasses. But animal or human, she couldn't say.

When she was done scanning what could only be described as a butcher shed, she blinked up and saw the source of her pain.

She was the next animal to be slaughtered, it would appear. Her hands were strung above her head. Suspended from the beam that traversed the pitched ceiling of the fifteen-by-fifteen death lair, she hung from bound wrists, one of which craned at an awkward angle and was surely broken. The other wrist appeared intact, but as she let her eyes slip the length of her arm, she saw that this arm was much longer than the other. Almost as if her shoulder no longer connected her arm to her body.

The agony was unlike any she'd ever felt. The physical pain could match and possibly surpass the emotional devastation of her tragic life. Each torturous moment felt like an eternity of suffering. Each breath a desperate hold on consciousness.

And yet, even as the delirium threatened to steal what she assumed would be her last waking moments on earth, she felt warm, unafraid. The drafty shed was no match for the hostility of the December wind, and the insulation of her designer gown wasn't much warmer than a slip, but somehow, when Old Man Winter's icy fingers raked over her skin, the chill that should have frozen her bone deep was overcome by a strange hug of heat.

"I'm not alone." She closed her eyes to erase the surrounding threat. "You're here, aren't you?"

Her breath emerged shaky, a wellspring of hope bubbled up in her chest. "I can feel you." Her lips formed a tremulous smile. Tears coursed down her face. "I don't understand this. I don't understand a lot of things, really, but I've been so lost and alone for as long as I can remember. I wanted ... *needed* someone to love me. And now you're here. Just in time to carry me home."

Beloved.

Love whispered, possibly a mirage born of delirium, but as sure as the pain ravaging her body. In the stillness, it came again.

Beloved, I have held you in your darkest moments. Carried you to safety. Fought for you and won. I have loved you from the very beginning.

As if viewing a highlight reel, Joselyn was back on the icy road that fractured her family, seeing the explosive flames pass over without touching her. She was then wandering the streets for Yia-Yia, somehow knowing exactly where to turn to bring her home to safety. And then still, about to swallow a handful of Gloria's sleeping pills after prom, when Erwin came in from the stables early with heartburn. And finally, she was resigned to die in a fiery prison when Finn came to her rescue.

"Oh, God." She closed her eyes and prayed, the locks breaking open and the words in her heart the sweetest surrender.

"He's not gonna save you."

Joselyn's eyes shot open. The door that slammed behind her killer made her flinch—sending another circuit of misery through her body.

Shaking the pellets of ice from his derelict onyx hair, he tossed aside a dripping sheet of gray tarp and what looked like a spool of ribbon.

"Already has." The pain was no more manageable, but an unlikely peace ascended on her and took the edge off enough to clear the haze from her eyes.

He looked familiar, but she struggled to place him. His midnight hair and unruly beard hinted at a rugged lifestyle, but it was the untamed fury in his wild, obsidian eyes that made him belong here in this horrifying shack.

"Wrong. You're gonna die today." His eyes flashed hot

with rage. "Soon as the rain stops and I remove the tarp keeping this place dry. I'm not taking any chances this time. Guess you can thank your precious *God* for the storm delaying your inevitable fate."

"It doesn't matter." She felt strong. More confident than she'd ever felt. Even in the face of certain death, she was no longer afraid. "I'll be home. You, on the other hand, will rot in prison for the murderer that you are, or you will live haunted by the life you robbed from me. But it's not too late."

"I am not a murderer! I am a servant of justice. Your life is the price to be paid for retribution. An eye for an eye. Even *God* himself knows about that one." The man pumped his hands into fists at his sides. It was an odd gesture, but it triggered a memory.

"Vengeance, huh? That's what this is all about?" Something clicked. "Wait, I do know you. Tobin, right? You used to work for my father." And though he was harrier, and lined with stress not from advancing age but from despair, she could see the man who'd been her father's prodigy. The brilliant young inventor who would usher Whyte Enterprises into the brass ring—the cutting edge of technology. She remembered him when she'd once dropped in on her father at work on her birthday bearing cupcakes and a foolish hope that she might get a morsel of his time.

But there'd been nothing sweet or special about that day. Instead of the moment of connection she'd craved, she'd witnessed her father tearing apart a team of young scientists in lab coats, one absently squeezing his hands into fists while he received the brunt of the lashing. When they'd been thoroughly dressed down and demoralized she'd watched them leave. One woman had tears in her eyes. Several other faces had been lined with distress. But one, the man with the white-knuckled fists in rapidly clenching hands, had walked past and looked directly at her. His eyes unfathomably cold and empty, she remembered feeling the chill in them sweep through her like a winter wind.

Then her father had come to the open door of his office, and everything in her shook from the uncertainty she felt squishing around in her tummy. Fear. Longing. And a spark of hope that died when he looked on her with annoyance and said, "I don't want you here. Leave." before he slammed the door in her face, not hearing her sniffle and whisper, "But it's my birthday."

The headline came to her mind next. *"Family of Whyte's head of R&D, Dr. Tobin Devore, dies tragically in their Chesterfield home."*

The man was broken. Just like she had been. Joselyn's voice softened, and though her physical misery was powerful enough, her heart began to ache for this man. "Your wife and your four-year-old daughter. I remember. I'm so sorry for your loss."

Her father was known for overworking his employees. Guilting or threatening them into excessive overtime. Slinging money at roadblocks and problems as if it could solve anything.

Because he was a man of incalculable influence, she'd often pondered the potential domino effect of her father's greed. Rather, she wondered how exactly it affected others. She knew all too well how it affected her.

But then last year after Devore's family died in a house fire while he worked late into the night, she'd seen the depth of her father's cruelty. About a month after the accident that robbed Tobin Devore of his family, a major project he'd been working on had fallen apart, and Declan Whyte had fired him. It was heartless. Unconscionable.

Her life would now serve as the ultimate repercussion of her father's selfishness.

An eye for an eye, Devore said. He'd lost his wife and daughter. Now Declan Whyte would too. And the worst of it was, he wouldn't care.

Devore worked in silence, unrolling the white ribbon and scattering it in the room.

"This isn't going to heal your pain, Tobin. Nothing can.

Nothing but love. And not the kind that can be lost in the fire. It's not too late." The truth swelled within her, resurrected from the deep recesses of her mind. And then the verse from Isaiah unfurled from her heart like a captive being set free.

"Fear not, for I have redeemed you; I have summoned you by name; you are mine … When you walk through the fire, you will not be burned; the flames will not set you ablaze."

"Stop!" Tobin hissed on a ragged breath. Flinging down the last of the ribbon, he stormed to where Joselyn hung from the beam and withdrew a gun.

The barrel stared Joselyn down, point blank. She swallowed down a tremor. "D-Don't y-you s-see? Even if you d-do this, you can't escape it. You're already redeemed by blood that won't wash away with your mistakes, even this one. I know you're hurting, but this won't bring your family back. Nothing you do to me will erase the pain of losing them. Just like, in all my lonely years, nothing I did could bring back my mother or win my father's love."

The gun shook in Tobin's hand. Heaving hot white air into the frigid space between them, his jaw jutted to one side, his eyes filling with barely leashed emotion.

"But you're not alone, Tobin. And if you think back, past the heartache, you might realize you never were."

Backing away, Tobin's eyes were unseeing, looking through Joselyn as if he'd already made her a ghost. The gun still absently trained on her head.

Oh help. I don't know what else to say.

Just then Tobin's retreating backside collided with the bloody table. The lantern crashed to the floor, and before the faint flicker of darkness settled, the floor ignited, the snaking pattern of ribbon erecting walls of blinding white fire all at once.

Like an explosion, without the bang.

Too numb with the shock of pain to move, Joselyn heard her own scream sail over the villainous roar of the flames eating up the empty spaces, teasing the flesh of her bare feet, slithering over the beam that held her from the instant inferno below.

The heat consumed her—her eyes stinging from the smoke and sweat pooling in her pores. And she knew with certainty, there was no escape.

This is it. Finn will never know that I've forgiven him. That he is so much stronger than he realizes. And, that despite my efforts to hate him ... I really, truly loved him like crazy.

Satan's hands reached up from hell, his fiery talons clawed at her feet. Through the burning wreckage, Joselyn saw Tobin pressed against the only portion of wall relatively untouched by fire. The door was only a few steps to his right, but he remained in place. His eyes coated with the drunken daze of the smoke. He squeezed them tight, uttered something she couldn't hear or read through the wild dance of the flames consuming the shack.

And then he raised his gun. Aimed at her.

Pulled the trigger.

The split of the round silenced the hiss of the flames for a mere moment before the hellish inferno rose from beneath her dangling feet. She had a fraction of a second to recognize that the bullet must have severed the rope before crash-landing onto the molten floor. Immeasurable agony flared out to each offending limb. The falling catch of air in her dress huffed away a scant scrap of flames now more eager to backtrack and devour her.

Like Devore's mystical arson ribbon, the full force of the pain exploded through her body tenfold. The scorch of each kiss of fire on her skin manifested in a blood-boiling scream that choked from her throat over and over.

Reenacting her fight to survive from the fire that started it all, Joselyn struggled to stand, the blazing board beneath her feet rapidly disintegrating to ash. She leapt forward. The searing heat melted through her dress, each layer of flames lapping at her skin. The smothering scent of smoke and burning flesh called her to death, mocking her coming defeat.

And yet, something pressed her forward. The fabric burned at her feet, but she was almost to the door. The air was useless, but she couldn't remember breathing. A flash of gun metal to her right caught her eye. The snub nose poised where it would do the most damage.

Tobin's face streaked with sweat, soot, and tears.

"NO!" Joselyn lunged at him.

But it was too late.

Chapter 45

Finn Carson

"There!"

The winding back roads were a labyrinth of dead ends and deserted hunting cabins. Even though they'd made record time, they were still wandering around blind.

The chopper had yet to report a sighting of fire, which meant maybe they weren't too late.

A small break in the trees revealed a ghostly funnel of smoke winding up to mingle with the night sky. One blink, and then it was gone, but the call of the fire was strong, beckoning him to the heart of the flame. Joselyn was there.

"Are you sure? I didn't see anything." Archer asked the question but whipped onto the gravel road before Finn could respond. The thick wall of towering pines blocked what lay ahead.

Dispatch kicked in over the sound of rocks spraying like a gunfight. "We've located the fire." The precise location followed.

This is it. Anticipation and terror raged in his chest.

Archer stomped his foot down on the accelerator, and a torch of vibrant light began to peek out through the dense trees otherwise shrouded in darkness. Finn unlatched his seatbelt and grasped the door handle, ready to charge. They drove as far as the road would allow until they were blocked by the swell of the forest.

Before the car came to a complete stop near the Honda, Finn had tumbled out and was in an all-out sprint toward the burning shack some 300 yards ahead.

"Finn!" Archer's scream was muted by the descending whir of helicopter blades.

He had no doubts Archer was in pursuit, but Finn's adrenaline enhanced his stride, leaving everyone behind.

The heat sliced through the icy air, spiking with each step until the heat of the sun crashed into him. He charged ahead driven by a reckless kind of love. The kind that could move mountains, part seas, sacrifice it all.

"Come on. Come on." Finn chanted to himself, the sound of his words siphoning away as the taunting flames screamed with laughter.

And then he heard it, piercing through the night air, shattering the hope rising within him.

A gunshot.

"Joselyn!" His scream was wasted as the roar of the fire snatched away his panicked cry.

But for the first time since the Monroe fire, Finn found that his courage hadn't left him. There was no hesitance. No fear of the fire. His armor held strong—stronger than ever.

His heart, however, was crumbling fast.

Launching up the three steps, Finn kicked down the burning scrap of the door. The splintered wood disappeared into the consumed shack like a scrap of paper lost in an instant to the blaze.

Before his shoe could cross the threshold into the fiery hell, something lunged at him. He stumbled back, his heel teetering on the edge of the small burning stoop.

And like an angel cutting through the curtain of Hades, Joselyn barreled into him.

Despite the torment of the fire on his face and the blistering touch of his prize, his relief was so great that he let them fall.

Before he could take inventory, he swept Joselyn up, cradled her to his chest, and ran like the fire might chase after them.

When he was sure they were safe, he let his pace slow and looked down to the soot-stained beauty in his arms.

"Joselyn." Leaning down he pressed his mouth to her cheek. "Joss, wake up!"

Taking a moment to look over her still and lifeless form, his blood became sluggish, and nausea washed over him until his legs nearly buckled.

Crimson red blood—the exact hue of her dress—drenched one side of her face and neck, yet he couldn't discern a bullet wound. The arm not pressed against his chest was covered in ash.

"Help!" The dehydrated word croaked from his throat, and even before emerging in its entirety, someone was snatching Joselyn from his arms and spreading her on a stretcher. It was then he saw the awkward angle of her wrist and the sagging joint of her dislocated shoulder that had been crushed into him.

His body shook when he thought about how much he must have hurt her by merely touching her.

Finn stepped toward the stretcher, but one of the medics forced him away, each of them working methodically to tend to her injuries, or keep her alive. Finn couldn't compute what was happening.

He needed answers. Right now. But no one would talk to him. Helpless, he took a few steps back to let the medics work and saw Archer step away from the team setting out to scour the area for Devore. Archer marched over to Finn, pulled him into a tough hug, and held him for a long moment. Then slapping his back, he set Finn an arm's-length away and let his hands rest on Finn's shoulders. "You got her, buddy. It's over."

Archer's eyes didn't miss a thing. They were assessing Finn's stability, weighing his thoughts on wiretap in his FBI brain, and calculating the actions bubbling up through Finn's firefighter rationale.

Finn released a pent up-breath, dragged a cool, cleansing breath of oxygen into his stricken lungs, and willed his heart to reboot.

Archer was right, he got her. But with Joselyn being

carried away on the stretcher, it still seemed far from over. Faced with a momentary decision, Finn shrugged out from Archer's grasp and ran full out to catch up with the retreating medics.

"Wait!" He sprinted until he caught up with the chopper. "Let me ride along. Please." Without a thought, he reached out and covered Joselyn's cold, little hand. It moved, and his heart frogged to his throat when her fingers curled around his.

"Oh, sweetie, I'm here." The oxygen mask hid her mouth, but her eyes slivered open and seemed to almost smile. "I thought I lost you."

Tears of relief and joy poured down Finn's face. He was a mess, but he didn't care who saw. Joselyn's thumb stroked his hand, and he knew everything would be all right.

"Okay, fine. One ride along," the medic said.

"Then it's going to be me." The accented voice cut in a moment before the whirring blades of the helicopter thumped out an ascending rhythm.

Declan Whyte.

"No way. I'm not leaving." Finn shouted his challenge and slid in beside Joselyn.

Joselyn's father was not easily deterred. Against the medic's protest, Declan shoved through the door. Joselyn's fingers tightened on Finn's hand, strengthening his resolve to stay, though he had no need for additional persuasion.

"Listen, Finn, you did your job. Your check will be in the mail tomorrow. Now please, let me be with my daughter." What might have been a smirk played across Declan Whyte's mouth.

Joselyn's eyes widened. He sensed her body tense, but her fingers grew lax in Finn's hand.

"Joss, it's not what you think."

The sound of the blades intensified. Tears slipped from the corners of her beautiful pale blue eyes, smearing a white line through the smudge of soot coating her temples. Her hand pulled away.

"The money. I can explain." Finn tried not to yell over the roar, he reached for her hand again. The pain in her eyes ripped a hole through his chest. "It's not—"

"Which one's it gonna be?" The medic shouted; the pilot anxious to lift off.

Turning away, her head angled toward her father. Though her eyes rested shut, the medic took that as her decision. It was plain enough that in spite of everything, Declan was her choice. Which wouldn't have shredded him if her father had been anyone else. Or if there'd been even a flicker of faith in him in her eyes after Declan played that cheap hand.

Only moments later, Finn stood alone, bereft, watching his future lift away without him. Knowing the most important thing right now was getting her to the hospital didn't dull the pain of her doubt. And his need to set the record straight. The funneling winds of the chopper faded until all that was left was the bitter chill of the December night, and the frozen wasteland of his empty heart resounding with an odd sense that he'd just lost her all over again.

"Come on, Sadie, you have to help me." Finn pleaded his case. It had been four days since the rescue, and he'd yet to see Joselyn. Her father had her room in the hospital on lockdown for the first night, and then the next day he had her transferred to the estate with his own private concierge physician keeping watch twenty-four hours a day.

Finn hated everything all broken and unresolved. If she would only listen to him, give him a chance to explain about the payment, she would see that it was all a big misunderstanding. After all, it hadn't been his idea. Declan Whyte had insisted that no one does something for nothing.

What was Finn supposed to do, tell the man he'd been in love with his daughter since high school? At that point, Finn hadn't known that those feelings had survived ten years of perfected disdain. He'd been trying to protect his sister from losing another best friend and resurrect his courage in the process.

The money wasn't important. And the solution had been perfect.

But as each day stretched between them, Finn wasn't sure his motives would ever be heard. Of if they'd even make a difference.

"Finn, you should've been honest with her. I'll do what I can, but she's pretty upset. One way or another, people have treated her like she could be bought and sold because of who her father is. Money was all they saw."

"I'm upset too. Don't you see how her father manipulated the situation?" He heaved a sigh, spoke to himself, "I can't believe this is happening again."

Finn raked his hand through his damp hair, amazed still that he'd taken the opportunity to shower given the distress of the past few days. He'd pretty much stalked the hospital and Declan Whyte's estate every waking moment until today. Desperate to see her, to tell her the truth, he'd foregone sustenance, sanitation, and sanity until it became pathetic, and quite frankly hazardous to his health, to keep camping out on her lawn.

"Give her some time." Sadie seemed torn, and Finn hoped he could wear down her defenses in light of the lovey daze of her upcoming nuptials. In less than a week Finn's baby sister would be married.

"She's hiding out, hasn't left her room, and even cancelled *Mamma Mia!* But she *will* be at the wedding." Finn didn't need to see his sister to see the wheels turning in her head over the phone. "Perhaps it would be a good time to, uh, you know … bare your soul."

The beginnings of a plan started to take shape in his head. Oh, yes. The idea had promise. A gamble for sure, and his track record gambling with Joselyn wasn't all that comforting. But love was worth the risk.

"Are you sure you don't mind? It is your big day. I wouldn't want to steal your thunder." Even the thought of what he was planning made him break out into a cold sweat.

But if he was going to win a prize like Joselyn, he had to go big or go home.

Sadie laughed. "If it will get you to stop bugging me, and make two of my favorite people happy, I'm all for it. What did you have in mind?"

Chapter 46

Joselyn Whyte

"**A**ll right, almost finished. Hang in there, Your Highness."

The crooked smile that had once seemed charming now made her want to kick his teeth in. But that would hurt worse than enduring another hour of mindless small talk about medical conventions and the downfall of great American medicine.

Joselyn gritted her teeth and rested her head back on the pillow. Maybe if she looked away from the blinding white grin that was oblivious not only to her agony but also the intense irritation that his presence elicited, the violent urges would subside.

Max droned on and on while he debrided and rewrapped each one of her feet with all the speed of the "underground" walker races Yia-Yia used to run in the closed wing of the nursing home.

Frustration scratched beneath her skin. Her nervous system wasn't only revolting from the excruciating tenderness of the second-to third-degree burns on the soles of her feet—you know, the ones the good doctor was very casually scraping with his medieval torture devices—it was also on high alert because her father was up to something.

First with that comment about Finn's payment in the chopper. Even in her dazed state of monumental pain she still saw the twisted glint of satisfaction in her dad's eyes as he outed Finn.

No doubt the master manipulator received some sort of

sick pleasure in hurting them both with his ill-timed words. The man was cruel when it suited him. In this instance, she didn't get his angle. What would motivate him to do that right then? Sure, she knew very well what motivated Declan Whyte to bribery. He liked lording his wealth over others like a trump card of superiority and power. But choosing to hurt her in that moment was an undeniably low blow.

After that, the suspicious activity continued when he hired a private physician to dote on her during her recovery. And of all the docs in all the world he handpicks Max Dickensen, Joselyn's former next-door neighbor and one-date wonder.

The man he likened to a Girl Scout, if Joselyn recalled correctly.

"I guess taking you dancing on our next date is out of the question, huh?" Max interrupted her thoughts.

If only he knew what she'd been thinking he wouldn't have that cocky grin plastered on his face. Nor would he have winked as if that line were solid gold and he'd cashed it in and scored an heiress.

Three days of trying to be polite, be subtle, and let him down easy was proving fruitless—and it was plain torture. And she now had a whole new appreciation for what that word actually meant.

Time to switch it up.

"Listen, Max, there isn't going to be a next date." She poured as much compassion as she could muster into her words. Everything still hurt like she'd been flattened by a steam roller and then set on fire; it was all she could do to not tell him to get over himself. That or close her eyes and let her silence do the rejecting. She'd considered both, but didn't want to be rude.

A suave, dark eyebrow curved downward. The grin lilted on one side but held firmly on the other, as if this Harvey Dent was now emboldened by a game of cat and mouse. "Don't worry, Joselyn." He set her foot down and rounded the bed. "I don't make a habit out of dating my patients, but there's nothing unethical about what we're doing here." Lowering beside her, he braced his hand on the bed near her hip and leaned in with that wicked smile of his.

Seriously, what had she seen in this guy? He wasn't charming. He didn't make her laugh, or even smile. And not a single fiber of her being longed for his touch.

Her mind drifted to someone else she did long for. Someone strong and funny and warm. Someone who made her forget about everything broken in her life. Someone who made her feel perfectly beautiful in her skin. And whose touch lit her up with the only form of fire she ever wanted to feel again.

The same someone who used and lied to you.

Severed from the fantasy of Finn, Joselyn looked up to find Max closing in. Only, from the look in his eyes, he had moved past innocent flirting. He was going to lay one on her.

Of all the brazen—her hand shot out from the sling in time and cut off his clammy kiss. She winced as the backlash of her abrupt action sent a strong message of protest through her body.

Shocked but somehow not enlightened by her blatant rejection, he leaned back and held on to the stupid smile. "You don't need to play hard to get with me—"

"Max!" This was getting ridiculous. Curling her fingers to wipe the sticky mess of his kiss from her palm, she decided lies, even little white ones, had the power to destroy lives. Honesty was the way to go.

And for someone as thick as Max—brutal honesty was the only way to go. "I'm perfectly serious. There will be no more dates. And furthermore, I think it's best we part ways now. I can have Gloria tend to my injuries from here on out. Your services are no longer needed. I'm sorry."

With one arm in a sling from having her shoulder dislocated, the broken wrist on the other in a splint, and some bandages on her arms she couldn't very well produce a look that was at all intimidating. But she gave it her best shot.

Annoyance flickered across his face, tightened every

aristocratic feature into a scowl. "Pfff." Pushing up off the bed Max started to stalk away but then changed his mind and reared back to have the last word.

Joselyn fought back the eye roll that was itching to let loose and braced herself. *Here it comes.*

"Fine. But just so we're clear, I was never really interested in you. I was only doing your psychotic brother a favor by taking you out that night, and I—"

"Brother?" she interrupted his rant. "Max, I don't have a brother."

"Yeah, right. Some random stranger waltzed into the hospital spouting all sorts of sob stories about your sad life and his concern for his poor isolated sister needing to be taken out on her birthday. Well, it's true what they say about you, *Snow Whyte*. You're a frigid little witch. Good luck finding your own dates from now on."

Joselyn flinched, those words were so constant she should be immune to them, and yet they still managed to cut each time they breached her skin. Steeling her composure, she felt her spine tighten, endowing her with several more inches from her seated position.

"I'm only going to say this once more so pay attention. I don't have a brother. And that day, our first date, was not my birthday."

Although a doctor, she wasn't sure the doofus was smart enough to put the pieces together.

"Congratulations, Max. You're an accessory to attempted murder. I'd bet good money that that man, my *brother*, was the one who burned my house down and nearly killed me the other night before he pulled the trigger on himself. He needed me out of the house so he could set his trap. Perhaps next time you should read up on the facts, not the gossip, doc."

Max's mouth gaped open, and no words escaped the man for the first time. Silence in his presence was a beautiful thing.

"We're done here. Now leave before I arrange for a large,

angry FBI agent to perform a complimentary cavity search before escorting you from the premises and into a holding cell with other men who like to play doctor."

Without another word, little Max tucked his tail and ran.

Her shoulders collapsed, the tension draining from her body as she slumped back into bed. She wanted to get up. Get out. Anywhere. Despite the enormity of the room, the walls seemed to close in on her. Her only escape had been when she read some books Sadie dropped off. Not much else she could do confined to the bed.

The pain meds took the edge off, but her shoulder was still sore, her wrist submitting a protest every now and again, and her arms had both seen and felt better days. But neither compared to the chronic pulse of misery that clawed up her legs with each surge of blood to her toes.

Miraculously—though not so mysterious knowing the source—she had escaped the cabin without any serious burns other than the ones that ate away the skin on the bottom of her feet from her short stint as a fire walker. Neither the medics nor the doctors bought her explanation, but she knew what had happened in that fire.

She'd been shielded from the worst and meant for something more.

The knock that sounded on the door across the room seemed to echo through the vastness of space. She hadn't had many visitors, hadn't felt up to it. Sadie had come twice and Mrs. Carson once, but that was all she could take of the Carson clan.

Joselyn had yet to sort out the hurt of Finn's deceit, but it was the last thing she wanted to think about. If she let herself go there, she was sure she'd close the door on him for good. And something in her heart wasn't ready for that.

If she ignored it, then the small shard of hope still clung to existence, struggling against the crushing weight of the past, but still fighting for a chance. Facing it head on meant realizing there was simply too much for them to overcome. Their entire relationship was infested with open wounds and scar tissue. They both had marks to prove it. It was a heartbreaking truth that kept her in denial and avoidance of all things Finn Carson.

Except for the rare occurrence when he would, *occasionally*, slip into her dreams. In the waking moments that followed, she could bask in the delusional—and undeniably delicious—possibility that everything might work out for them. That they might be able to wipe the slate clean and have their own fairy-tale ending. The handsome hero awakening Snow Whyte from sleepwalking through life.

The whimsical thought lost traction when the door swung open and the formidable Declan Whyte approached her bedside.

"Gloria informed me that Dr. Dickensen is no longer with us." It was as if a storm cloud blew into the room. His presence was oppressive. Gray. Gray suit, gray hair, steely gray glare. It all seemed to match the gloom within.

Joselyn bared her teeth in her best imitation of a smile. "To what do I owe the honor of your visit, Mr. Whyte?"

It was the first time in four days he had bothered to enter her room. She wanted to be genuinely gracious for the attention. But the hurt of her father's neglect ran deep, and Rome wasn't built in a day.

"I'm leaving for a few weeks. Going to see if I can salvage what is left of my campaign after the media practically victimized Devore and made me out to be the villain in this whole mess. I ought to sue those nosy reporters who played up Tobin's loss and termination for … for defamation of character."

"Actually, I think they portrayed you quite accurately. For once everything they printed was the truth. Wasn't it?"

His eyes widened at her boldness. So desperate to please him, she'd so often stifled her opinions to be in his favor. But in light of everything that happened, and his ever-present egocentrism that still held firm despite it all, she knew she could never earn her way into his good graces.

She steeled her breath, bolstered her courage, and let go of her composure. *Please, let him hear me.* "Listen, Dad … I know losing Mom changed everything."

"Joselyn, this is not the time—"

"You never have time." She said with a fierce sort of calm. "And I'm not waiting any longer to tell you that you've failed. The great Declan Whyte failed. Big time."

Something chilled in his eyes, but this time the ice couldn't reach her.

"Your wife died that day. But your daughter didn't. I'm still here. But you're too self-absorbed with your success and your campaign to see me. You missed everything. My whole life."

The pent-up emotional purge unlocked something so guarded that the freedom of the words unleashed twenty years of heartache and loneliness. The tears were still warm when they coursed down to her neck. The words kept spilling through the breaking sobs.

"I needed you. And you abandoned me."

The line of his jaw was tight, his eyes downcast as if biding his time until her rant would end.

"Look at me!" she screamed.

He rested his eyes shut and lifted his chin, and then dragged them open again. She didn't know what it was she saw in them, but there didn't seem to be anything resembling regret.

"Do you even see me?" Not bothering to wipe away the mess on her face, she locked into his eyes, holding his stare with her iron will—the only thing she seemed to have inherited from him. "Don't you see that I am still that same little girl who wanted her daddy to wipe away her tears and tell her it would be all right?"

Breaking eye contact, he cleared his throat, but the gruffness still laced his words. "I did what I had to do to survive. I don't expect you to understand or forgive me, but I simply couldn't live with the constant reminder of all that I'd lost."

And there it was. The truth was a bitter pill—the effects,

she feared, were both fast-acting and extended-release.

After several long moments, Joselyn found the courage to speak again. "Well, then, you're a coward. You lost a lot more than you should have that day. And the sad thing is, you chose to."

With a final flash of his empty eyes, he turned to leave. The clicking of his expensive shoes across the hardwood floor felt like time counting down to the end of their relationship.

"Hey, Dad?" Heart in her throat, Joselyn held her breath. *Give me strength.*

Her father stopped, hesitating before looking over his shoulder.

"I forgive you." The utterance seemed to loose a boulder from her chest, and she drew in an easy breath.

He swiveled to face her. She couldn't read him. The twenty feet between them yawned like a chasm of a million miles.

"You don't deserve it. But true forgiveness can't be earned. And though I wish desperately that things could be mended between us, I don't need you anymore." She spoke tenderly, without a hint of the malice that used to consume her. "I've found a love that doesn't quit when times get hard. Comforts me when I'm frightened, dusts me off when I fall, listens and cares about the hurts in my heart. Unconditional, like a father's love should be."

He didn't move or speak. His face a placid mask of mystery.

"You may not need me, or anyone else in this world. But you need that love too. You're bankrupt without it."

It felt like good-bye. This thing they'd danced around for years had finally come to a head. The thought was both freeing and heartbreaking. If only he could understand all he was missing.

Turning to make his exit, he resumed his long stride without a word.

"I won't be here when you return." That stopped him one

last time, though he didn't turn. "I don't know when I'll see you again. And while I don't need you anymore, I will *never* give up on you, Dad. That's a promise."

Chapter 47

Finn Carson

Today was D-day.

Finn's nerves wrapped around his heart so tight he'd have sworn they would strangle the life out of the bleeding thing. But it was still beating. His emotions on a high of love and hope he could hardly contain.

Waiting at the altar between Archer and Sal, Finn curled his fingers into his slick palms. His right hand issued a complaint from the repercussions of his hot-tempered actions from yesterday.

Without closing his eyes, Finn could recall every trace of guilt on Cody's face before he'd rammed his fist into his nose. The fact that Cody had toppled head over heels over his desk from the force of the blow was so satisfying that even now a smirk played across Finn's lips. And when his old friend couldn't manage to get to a standing position, croaking out to his secretary for assistance, it felt like Christmas all over again. In farewell, Finn had flicked his lucky chip at the heap on the floor. Finn didn't need luck anymore. He had grace. Grace he extended to Cody out of consideration for Joselyn's privacy, but with a warning that if he ever hurt someone trying to get lucky again, no amount of money would save him from just how unlucky his punishment would be.

Was it Finn's classiest moment?

No. But it was better than being incarcerated for doing what he felt the prick deserved.

On his way out he hadn't neglected to tell an unusually

chipper Clarisse—the secretary who either hadn't heard or had purposefully ignored the pleas for help—to make sure Cody lived after receiving his beating. Mercy. Another step in the right direction.

Finn's conscience was clear.

Unfortunately, his hand was a key player in his plans for today. And his swollen knuckles and stiff joints weren't granting any hint of appeasement to his overwrought nerves.

The ushers were about finished seating the forty-some guests, and any moment the bridesmaids would start down the aisle. The anticipation was agonizing, but everything else about the ambiance was perfect and serene.

The understated elegance of the little stone chapel on a hillside was pure magic. A fresh blanket of snow hugged the endless horizon of hills and glinted a Polaroid-perfect amber glow of the setting sun through the wall of windows at his back. Ivory candles and rose petals littered the altar, and a slow, melodious serenade of the piano all tinted the air with warmth that could be seen and heard as much as felt.

The music changed, the pianist effortlessly tickling the keys of the baby grand. The old, jazzy tune, one of Sadie's favorites, filled the room to the tops of the stoned arches and hung in the air, thick with meaning.

Finn glanced at his soon to be brother-in-law. The look on Archer's face could soften the hardest, most cynical heart to its core. The man was in love, and it shone from every facet of his being.

Was that what Finn looked like? Could love really show on your face like a sign that read, *I'm hopeless. Done for. Stick a fork in me, baby!*

And would Joselyn be able to see it. See that he wasn't pretending and that the past didn't matter. That he loved her, and he'd do whatever it takes to prove that to her every day for the rest of their lives.

The first bridesmaid started down the aisle, and Sal started to choke on something. Probably his own saliva based on the appreciation that shone from his gaze. Hacking and wheezing, Sal leaned forward on his crutches and made a spectacle of himself until Finn had to give his back a solid thump.

Leave it to Sal to liven things up.

Candice, the medical examiner who worked with Archer, had become quite close with Finn's little sister. Sadie was like that. Always reaching out to new people.

Having been a strange mix between a tomboy and a princess, Sadie didn't quite fit the stereotype people cast her. Her life, while it had its detours, was closing in on happily ever after. And Finn couldn't be happier, or prouder, of the brave choices she'd made to find her way through the struggles to the beautiful future that lay ahead of her.

But the thought only made him restless. Was there such a future for Finn?

Could Joselyn truly forgive him? Or had his window for a future with her passed too many times?

Rounding the corner of the back pew, an usher pushed Joselyn down the aisle in her temporary wheel chair. Draped in a dreamy, blush-colored dress that looked soft and sweet, and yet caressed her subtle curves in a way that was temptation on heels—and wheels—she was the picture of elegance and composure. Her minky locks, affixed on one side with an antique diamond clip, fell in thick, tumbling waves over her shoulder. And though the whole package was stunning to say the least, her eyes were what captivated him.

They were luminous, the flash of the photographer's camera reflecting their rare and glittering beauty. He couldn't look away.

And when those unfathomable, violet-blue eyes landed on him, he prayed he would be able to see her love shining back to him. That maybe they would give her away, the way Archer's eyes communicated his love for Sadie. But before he could dive into them, and the mystery they held, she looked away, hiding away whatever was in her heart.

Once in her place at the altar, the guests rose from their seats and Sadie came into view. Archer's breath staggered in with a sharp sound. His eyes filled with tears, and his smile ignited brighter and more intense than any fire Finn had ever witnessed. The song swelled, the sound vibrant and pulling on every brewing emotion until the beauty of it was a palpable thing. It was a moment dreams were made of.

Finn couldn't help but realize that his own dreams hinged on this night. On one very important question.

He slipped his eyes from the tearful and radiant bride on his father's arm and stole another glance at the woman of his dreams. Longing welled up so strong it took every bit of his willpower to keep his feet planted in place instead of crossing the altar, taking her in his arms, and whispering the words of love caged in his throat against her lips.

But it wouldn't look very good if the best man interrupted the ceremony to profess his love for the maid of honor. This was Sadie's day. And she was already gracious enough to share it with him.

For the sake of appearances, he tore his gaze away from Joselyn and watched his sister join her life with the man who'd mended her broken heart.

The anticipation strung him along tediously, but then again, hope was better than defeat.

Finn knew he was going all in tonight and that the cards might not turn in his favor. He'd always been a keen poker player. Observing, calculating the odds, the risks. Reading his opponents with ease. But nothing that mattered was ever on the line. It had always been a distraction. A game. But right now, knowing he was about to show his hand made him realize something.

Never before had he gambled with his heart.

Chapter 48

Joselyn Whyte

Finn had disappeared.

Okay, so maybe she'd been keeping tabs on him a little bit throughout the night. It was only natural. She was the maid of honor, and he the best man. They were supposed to have the wedding party dance soon, and he was nowhere to be found.

Looking down at her seat on wheels she was tuned to a conclusion she hadn't thought about until this moment—she wouldn't be doing any dancing tonight.

Would he dance with someone else?

The thought stung more than she wanted to admit. There hadn't been an appropriate time to talk during the ceremony or during the pictures that followed. And most of the photo ops were staged with bridesmaids on one side and groomsmen on the other separated by, of course, the bride and groom.

But there had been a moment. More than a moment— though time didn't seem to exist for the shots she and Finn had taken side-by-side—when that fresh woodsy scent, enticing and masculine, like leather and cedar with a hint of sugar and spice, so unmistakably Finn, had invaded her senses, alerting her to his presence a mere moment before his husky voice warmed her ear.

"Hi, Joss."

Heat shimmied down her spine even now, over an hour— a dinner roll, a garden salad, a half of a stuffed chicken breast, a few nibbles of green bean almondine, and two pieces of raspberry-filled French vanilla cake slathered in butter cream icing—later.

Her stomach protested. Maybe she shouldn't have had that second piece of cake. But so far—other than the delirious happiness of her best friend—the day was not doing her any favors.

For one, she felt ridiculous being carted around like some Egyptian princess lounging on a litter. At least she'd shed the sling and bandages and was only contending with a small brace on her right wrist and decreasingly tender feet.

Two, her dress was uncomfortably clingy and somewhat skin toned. Permanently parked in the chair, she struggled to make adjustments to the stupid, but pretty, thing that made her feel like that naked thinking statue. She'd noticed a few guys in the band staring and felt exposed. Helpless and transparent.

And three, last but certainly not least, was Finn. He'd avoided her all night.

She hadn't known what to expect, but after hearing about his *Say Anything* inspired protest on her father's front lawn, she figured he'd have something to say to her. Maybe an apology?

But no. Other than the moment down the aisle when they'd locked gazes, and then of course their pairing for the pictures, she'd seen neither hide nor hair of the little coward.

The music continued, sauntering and sweet, while Archer held his bride on the dance floor. The joy on Sadie's face was as pure and ethereal as the soft flutter of organza and lace that billowed out from her tiny frame while Archer spun her out and dipped her as if she weighed no more than a feather.

When he brought her back up, his strong arms surrounded her, melding her as close as two people could be in public and remain decent. And then he partook of her lips so tenderly Joselyn had to look away. Because if she continued to watch her best friend be overcome with love, losing herself in the tender moment despite the prying eyes of the small crowd, Joselyn would only be consumed with longing for a love of her own.

There was only one person that came to mind. And he wasn't here. Nor did he seem to care that he'd shattered her heart into a million pieces. Again.

Leaning back into her chair, she closed her eyes, remembering—hearing nothing but the soft clicking of the shutter—but feeling … everything.

The faint stirring of his breath in her hair when he'd said her name. The tingling awareness of his arm slipping around her waist as they posed for pictures. Pressing her so gently to his side one would think she was made of the most delicate china. The smooth caress of his shaved, satiny cheek when he touched their faces together for the close-up. And the deliberate turn of his head, brushing his skin against hers for one heart-stopping moment when the world seemed to right itself.

But without a word, he was gone. And then the reception kicked off in the area below the chapel.

It was perfect. Joselyn took it all in with pride. The venue itself was breathtaking. A long wall of windows traversed the length of the elegant room and opened to a terrace overlooking the snow-snuggled Missouri River.

Despite the subzero temperature, the water tarried without a care down the spotless white riverbanks. And though the view was almost too pretty to be real, the reception hall proved as unique and dazzling. Creamy candlelight flickered from the hearts of countless glass hurricanes, and festive twinkling light and red berry-wrapped garlands enchanted the cozy space warmed by a rustic stone fireplace. And right now, a deep, mahogany-stained dance floor held the happiest girl in the world.

She'd promised herself she wouldn't cry. She would do nothing to distract from Sadie's perfect day. But as she sat imprisoned in her lonely wheelchair, all the love and happiness in the room became too much to take. Her nose tingled, and the first warm tear escaped the corner of her eye.

Joselyn unlatched the brake on her chair and started to

wheel toward the restroom, needing a moment to drown her sorrows in private. Too bad there was no chocolate in sight. A tragic oversight. Though another piece of cake might do the trick.

The crowd began issuing applause for the end of the first dance. Grateful for the distraction, Joselyn set all her attention to the task of wheeling her chair in short, awkward strokes.

She was almost there, tears brimming over the edge of her eyelids when a familiar riff from an acoustic guitar struck out through the sudden silence, stopping her in her tracks.

A voice followed. Full and rich ... and a bit shaky, but perfectly stunning as it wove though the crowd and reached into her heart.

"Baby why you wanna cry?
You really oughta know that I
Just have to walk away sometimes
We're gonna do what lovers do
We're gonna have a fight or two
But I ain't ever changing my mind ... "

It couldn't be. But it was.

Joselyn's breath caught. Her heart rent from her chest, coming alive with hope she'd not dared to even dream of. It was her favorite song, the one she'd sang in the car with Finn. Before she'd even turned to look she knew who was singing.

With trembling hands she eased the chair around and froze. Tears threatened anew. Even from a distance, those eyes grabbed on and wouldn't let go. Because there, on the stage, in front of a room full of people, was the admittedly stage-frightened Finn Carson ... singing a country song. For her.

"Crazy girl, don't you know that I love you?
I wouldn't dream of going nowhere
Silly woman come here let me hold you
Have I told you lately I love you like crazy, girl?"

And though she was frozen in the wonder of the

moment—enrapt by the man who, it would seem, was publically professing his love for her and paying up on their safe room bet—she was somehow moving toward the stage. Someone was pushing her, but she couldn't bring herself to look away to confirm it.

The lazy melody floated with newfound ease and silky smoothness off the lips of the man she loved. *Loved.* She could feel the weight of it crashing through her doubts. And the healing power of it piecing her together again. Different, but no less whole.

"I wouldn't last a single day
I'd probably just fade away
Without you I'd lose my mind
Before you ever came along
I was living life all wrong
The smartest thing I ever did was make you all mine ..."

Still singing, Finn had unhooked his shoulder strap, shed his guitar, and stepped away from the microphone. With each step in her direction the sound of his voice became a beacon of hope, drawing them together.

At the edge of the dance floor he stopped in front of Joselyn's chair. The words of the chorus declared his crazy love from an arm's-length away. And like the view and the euphoric atmosphere of love, it felt too perfect to be real.

But then Finn knelt in front of her, his strong hand clasping hers in her lap, bringing her back down to earth. She forced a hard blink to be sure he was really there, shaking loose a few more tears in the process.

His other hand, rugged and yet so tender, whisked the moisture from her eyes with the softest touch, his fingers lingering to skim over her cheek. The last note rang out, perfect and buttery, and she leaned into his hand, relishing the simple touch that was melting all her defenses.

He lowered his voice, deep and achingly vulnerable, for her ears only—though she suspected everyone in the room could hear. "Joselyn, there is so much I need to say. The most important of which is how I'm completely, hopelessly, out-of-my-mind in love with you. I always have been, ever since that first moment in the hallway in high school. I would say it was love at first sight, but it was more than that. More than simply being drawn to your beauty. When I looked into your eyes, I caught my first glimpse of your heart. And it was the most beautiful thing I had ever seen. So guarded and hurt, but so kind and hopeful. Full of this spark for life I'd never seen in anyone. I knew I loved you right then."

His eyes held hers, almost unblinking and so earnest she could see his heart too. And what she saw was all she wanted. Blemished but beautiful. Despite the past and the wounds she knew he tried to hide, his heart was a perfect match.

"Next, I need to explain about the money from your father. Joss, I'm so sorry I didn't tell you—"

"Finn, stop," she whispered.

His hand dropped away from her face, and his countenance fell as if she'd slapped him.

Lifting her hand, she brushed the hair away from his cheek and then let her fingers curl around his neck, threading through the soft strands of his sexy, surfer hair. "I've learned something very important. Something that affects you."

She could see his heart pounding in his throat, the questions and the hope in his eyes. "And what's that?"

"That love always hopes, trusts, believes. And it endures whatever comes."

A spark ignited in his eyes, spreading down to upturned and gorgeous come-kiss-me lips. "So … you're saying you love me?"

Unleashing her smile to match his, she leaned in to share her secret and nodded her answer before adding, "No matter what."

He released a short, comical sigh of relief. "That's very good news because I have something else I need to ask you."

She leaned in a little more, drawing reverent circles on the marred skin of his neck, tempting him to give in to her wanting lips. "Can it wait until after you kiss me?"

"Actually, it can't." Easing away a few inches, Finn brought his hand up between them, his eyes sparkling like the sunlight over an emerald ocean. She was sunk. "Joselyn Whyte, will you marry me?"

It was the moment she'd been waiting for her whole life. For someone to claim her. To chase away the loneliness. This man, the man she'd always loved, wanted to be her family.

She nodded her head and let herself cry without a hint of shame. "Yes. Yes, Finn Carson, I would love nothing more than to marry you."

She'd forgotten about their audience, but they burst to their feet in applause a mere moment before Finn slipped the ring on her finger, lifted her up out of her chair, cradling her to his chest, and sealed the whole thing with one heck of a crowd-pleasing, toe-tingling kiss.

Two weeks later...

Chapter 49
Finn & Joselyn

"Finn, how could you!" The shrill reprimand echoing through the earpiece forced a few extra inches of grace between his ear and his phone.

Joselyn fought back a giggle, having heard all of Sadie's meltdown from across the room and enjoyed discretely witnessing the comical sibling interaction.

Before Finn could articulate a response that was appropriate for his sister's ears, Sadie started back in. "Well, I guess I should have seen this coming after you two couldn't keep your hands off each other and practically made out for the remainder of my reception. Thanks for that, by the way."

Finn's face lit up, a devious grin tilting his lips. "No problem. And at least we excused ourselves to the coatroom. But, hey I gotta go. Time to make it official." Wagging his eyebrows, he sent a silent signal of his innuendo.

One Sadie obviously didn't need to see to pick up on. "Eww. Yes, go. And let's not talk for a while, huh? I'm glad you're happy, but I also want to be able to sleep at night— you know, without the nightmares. It's taken me two weeks to wash the image of you two on the dance floor out of my mind. The last thing I want to think about is those poor traumatized coats, let alone the evening you have planned tonight."

Finn laughed, deep and musical like the melody of any number of love songs he'd taken to crooning in her ear at every opportunity. "Okay, but tell Mom and Dad the news. Oh, and let them know they're gonna be grandparents again soon."

"Finn, seriously, I might throw up."

"Settle down, it's not what you think. We're adopting Kendi. It's not official yet, but Joselyn pulled some strings and it's looking good for us. Be happy, Aunt Sadie." After a marked influx of squealing, Finn haggled for a few more moments to end the call with his sister.

Joss watched him drop his phone on the end table, shed his suit coat, and tug to loosen his tie.

All those years dreaming about him, loving and hating him, had culminated to bring her to this moment. Tried by fire. Then and now. Each time their winter had burned to the ground, leaving them broken but not defeated. Because deep beneath the wreckage, the ashes still smoldered, kindling a new flame that couldn't be extinguished. Not even by her almost too-hot-to-handle firefighter. A man who rescued strangers. Who rescued dogs. And orphans. And the one who helped rescue her frozen heart and set it on fire.

A true hero. Down to the marrow.

He had even gotten to explain that the "payment" was a term her father enforced to maintain the upper hand in their arrangement. After persistent refusal, Finn had relented with a counteroffer—that a generous donation be made, and determined, by Declan Whyte to the struggling group home where Kendi lived.

Her father had accepted. Only last week were they informed of how generous her father had been. A million dollars would go a long way in helping countless young kids find security at Trisha Bollivar's home. If all went as planned, Kendi wouldn't need to be one of them. She'd have a family of her own.

And maybe, just maybe, the generosity meant the tides were turning in Joselyn's father's heart too.

Nothing was impossible.

Joselyn stepped forward from the doorway of the bedroom suite. As if feeling her eyes on him, tuned to the sizzling frequency of her gaze, Finn turned at her soundless pursuit, her barely tender feet glided over the plush carpet as if walking out a dream.

His lips curled in a slow spreading grin, the appreciative gleam in his eyes mimicking the longing bubbling beneath her skin.

Crossing the space that separated them, he drawled teasingly, "I have a feeling you are going to make me an extremely happy man." He already was. Happier than he ever knew was possible.

"Care for a preview?" She threw his flirty words back at him, remembering that moment in his bedroom when they'd first been tempted to play with the fire of their attraction. Only now, they could play all they wanted. And though she'd never willingly given herself to a man, for the first time in her life she felt whole. Like what had once been stolen had been restored.

Like she had something special to give.

Matching his sexy grin, she slipped the tie from her robe and braved ahead the last few feet as it fell to the floor.

Revealing miniscule sheer white lace pieces that artfully covered nothing.

His mouth dropped open, the heat in his eyes a hundred times hotter than the five-alarm blaze that brought them together. Like the scrape of a match down her spine, every nerve ignited from his spark.

"No, Mrs. Carson." Tipping up her chin, he smoothed the back of his knuckles down her neck, luxuriating in the feel of her silken skin. "Not just a preview. I've waited my whole life for you. I want it all. And more."

Then, sweeping his bride up in his arms, his lips found their way to hers, hungry and cherishing, with the passion of star-crossed enemies who had just eloped after ten years of wrestling with love and hate.

His heart raced, strong and thrilling, against her chest. His arms held her tight in his grip, like he would never let her go.

His legs led the way to the intimate gift that awaited them. Over the threshold to the enormously decadent bed of the honeymoon suite. And then those lips again took their time … laying claim to it all. And more, just like he'd promised. A promise she echoed with her own. Cherishing every taste, every discovery of the man who was hers. Who proved the almost unbearable anticipation made every long-awaited touch irresistibly electrifying.

When they finally joined together, the miracle of it, of how they got here, crashed over her with emotions she'd never known. Love, devotion, passion, and tenderness pieced together in a stunning array of intimacy, held together by a covenant promise of belonging. Family. It stole her breath, pressed tears of joy behind her eyes, and poured bliss through her veins.

Fevered, but with heart-melting sweetness, they crested that glittery summit to heaven and back with sensational ease.

There was no fear. No panic. The cold darkness that had preyed upon her loneliness, the lies from the poisonous black serpent that had teased the fringes of her fears for so long, had been slain by love.

And she knew she'd been healed. Gloriously remade. A truth they cemented over and over and over, making up for lost time and enjoying every second of pure wedded bliss.

And when they could no longer summon the energy to move, holding each other until the sun dawned on their first day as man and wife, Finn tugged her closer. Splaying his large hand down her belly, nibbling gently on her smooth shoulder, he whispered, "I'm on fire for you."

Smiling to herself, she arched back into him enticingly before flipping over and pinning her firefighter husband beneath her. "I can help you with that."

The End

Dear Reader,

First, I want to say that there are hordes of books out there, so I am completely humbled and honored you took the time to read mine! From the moment I plopped Joselyn and Finn together on the page in *When Fall Fades* I knew something good was cooking. Their temperaments were as polar opposite as, well, fire and ice, but I loved exploring that fine line between love and hate where passion and perception cross wires. The barbs and the banter between these two! Such fun! I seriously had a blast constantly throwing them together and watching them fight a losing battle.

As a mother, I talk a lot to my wee ones about consequences. Luckily at this phase in my life those consequences are things like time outs, no candy, and losing privileges. I may compose stories about imaginary people, but fictional heiresses or ordinary stay-at-home-mamas, we're all flawed. Mistakes are part of the package. And I'd even venture to say that they can become the most beautiful product of that refining fire. But we all know some mistakes are harder to live with than others. It was heartbreaking to portray such devastating consequences for Finn and Joss. Despite their seemingly charmed lives and physical beauty, they each wore their most debilitating scars on their hearts, and yet still found the courage to reach for something more. Second chances are a beautiful thing.

But while this book is meant to be exciting and romantic, I chose not to shy away from several rather sensitive topics. Not because I wanted to add drama or darkness to the overall mood, but because life and love are messy. Pain is real, and it's something we all live with. Every single smiling, Facebook-perfect person hides a certain hurt or shame or insecurity that holds far too much power over the hope and the beauty available to every soul, no disqualifiers. I touch on things like depression, suicide, and abuse. Things we like to bury or ignore until we feel it's too late to escape. The Truth that can be so hard to see is, you were meant for *more*. So much more. No matter where you are at, or how alone you feel, no one is too lost to find their way home. If you've ever been there, you are not weak for struggling, but you don't have to go it alone, and YOU have the power to find the *more* you were called to be.

If you or someone you know struggles with depression or suicidal thoughts, talk. Fight. There are hotlines and ministries, local support groups and churches with compassionate people who truly can help.

And if you have a spare minute, I would be ever so grateful if you'd consider leaving a review. They really are an author's bread and butter, and they make all the difference. Besides, one way conversations are boring. Talk to me. ☺

Dream big!

Amy

**Keep reading for a sneak peek of Sal and Candice's story!

Acknowledgements

This is quite possibly my favorite chapter of this book! Arguably the most important! This book exists because of the champions who've made it possible for my stories to leave the nest and find their way into your hands. You're a HUGE part of my dream, and I couldn't do this without you.

To my husband, my muse, my very best friend, for perpetuating my love of happily ever afters by giving me one to live in every day. "I love … I love … I love you." And to the most awesome and adorable kidlets in the world—Kael, Rafe, and Eisley—who fill my days with more love and adventure than I could cram into a thousand stories as long as mine. I can't wait to watch you write your own dreams!

To my mom and dad, who taught me all things are possible. And whose prayers moved every mountain in my way. How blessed I am to have you.

To my family members who continually give their unwavering support. Jeremy Stehlick, Elsie Fitzgerald, Pete Simpson, Colleen Phillips, Karen Denson, Big Rick Simpson, and Britt and Patty Buersmeyer. You're the best!

To Eric Williams, for adding such beauty and artistry to the "fire and ice" artwork gracing these pages. It's all in the details, cuz, and yours are pretty remarkable!

To Pepper Basham, my crit partner and brainstorming buddy, faithful friend and sister of my heart. You inspire me to greatness. When I grow up, I want to be like you.

To the incredibly talented (writer and graphic designer) Angie Dicken, who gives her time to make me look good!

To Captain Russel Elzinga, who volleyed a few technical questions. I didn't want to be a pest, so any and all mistakes are mine. Creative liscence and all that.

To the most awesome early reader author pals, Jill Lynn

Buteyn, Amber Lynn Perry, and Nicole Deese. You know how wordy I am, but honestly, there aren't enough of them to thank you for the encouragement, support, and friendship. You're the reason I look forward to opening my messages every day!

To my blogging sisters and dearest writer friends the Alley Cats, as well as the Spicettes. It's so much more fun doing this together.

To amazing authors I am so blessed to know like Beth K. Vogt, Lynette Eason, Jennifer K. Hale, Irene Hannon, and Rachel Hauck—who gave me immeasurably helpful feedback from this book's very tentative beginnings several years ago.

To Serena Chase and Jeane Wynn, for having my back and being some of the sweetest women I know!

My super sharp editor Andrea Ferak, for making my words shine.

To Taryn Henry and Laura Hunt, for so patiently letting me go on and on about book stuff when I'm in the thick of the madness. (And never telling me to zip it already!)

To our heroes who fight a viciously unpredictable beast called fire. Who run into burning buildings when everyone else is running out. Courage doesn't begin to cover it. Thank you.

To my amazing readers, it is a privilege to connect with you through stories I love to tell. For every kind word, review, and copy, you make all the fears, frustrations, plot kinks, and sleepless nights worth it. Thank YOU for spending time with my imaginary friends and for reading every painstakingly vetted word of my labor of love. My heart is overflowing with gratitude!

And most importantly, to the Author of *my* story. Who wrapped me up in grace from my first breath, miraculously preserved my life against all odds, still relentlessly pursues my stubborn heart, and loves me and my crazy imagination like no one else. Again, this, and every other word I write, is for You. Always.

The third book in The Girl Next Door series …
Coming Spring 2018!

Chapter 2

Dorian Salivas

"Dorian?" Only Candice Stevens could deliver his name like an insult.

Her eyes shone bright with embarrassment, like a splash of sunrise through splintered glass. They were wide set, exotic, and as usual, completely disarming.

Of course, her being on top of him might add something to that effect.

"Listen, if you don't like the taste of it, you could always go with *Sal* like everyone else." By the time he'd finished the thought he was grinning again. She did that to him.

"Sal makes you sound like some tough, cranky mob boss. It just doesn't fit." Her smile was so patronizing she might as well have pinched his cheeks and called him "Buddy."

"Whatever makes you happy, Candi."

Her infuriating big sister look was instantly replaced by lines of tension tightening down her neck and flaring though the body still wonderfully atop his.

"How about we cool it with the nicknames. We're coworkers. Sort of. I'll be Dr. Stevens, or Candice since we have a shared group of friends. And you can just be Dorian."

Just be Dorian. He answered the exhausting woman with a sigh.

"What?" She shrugged, her hands resting on his chest, her body once again soft and perfectly mind-numbing. Lush tendrils of hair stirred on the wind, torturing him with the wild, sweet scent of her. "It *is* your name."

Oh, he hated how this woman looked at him like a five-year-old. Two could play that game. "You're a brat."

"Takes one to know one." The gleam in her gaze turned a little bit naughty, though he was sure she didn't mean it that way.

Candice wasn't the easiest person to read, but his abridged version said she wielded humor in an effort to stay detached. She was also completely ignorant of her appeal on the opposite sex, and incredibly sharp and driven, but under heavy guard from some sort of phantom pain hidden behind her smile.

Unfortunately for Sal, the heavy guard was more like a full suit of armor equipped with a bulletproof vest, chastity belt, and an iron will.

It was as if she denied herself any emotions or advances that might remind her she was a woman. Restaurant closed. Female on lockdown, reinforced with barbed wire and an electric current.

A current that was, at this very moment, live and zapping him with conductive skitters of testosterone.

Candice didn't seem to realize she was still lying on top of him. On the sidewalk. On Clark Avenue.

Loosing his hands from her arms he let them slip around to the small of her back. "Does this mean you might actually take me up on my offer to dinner?" He lifted an eyebrow in challenge.

"Oh, for—!" She squirmed. His body reacted and she froze. He saw the second she reacquainted with reality—and their horizontal status on the sidewalk. "Oh, geeze. Sorry." Shoving to her knees, she brushed off her hands as if contact with his coat had left her gritty.

He watched her as she stood. Twinges of pink blotted onto her café au lait-colored skin. Her breathing had quickened, her pupils dilating before her eyes averted.

Despite her brusque demeanor—and the way she'd just less than delicately tackled him—she held a certain grace about her when caught off guard. Her neck long and controlled, her shoulders pressed, the drift of her spine and her arms fluid like wind stroking sheer curtains.

She didn't offer her hand. And it would seem he did a poor job hiding his wince when he braced against his good knee and straightened because she gasped.

Her petite hand touched her lips before she stretched it out to touch his chest in consolation. "Did I hurt you? I'd forgotten about your surgery. Knee replacement, right?"

Even with the straggling pains darting through his nervous system he chuckled. "Is that a no for dinner then?"

She retracted her hand as if scalded. Some small realization blooming another spray of roses on her cheeks before she snapped back into character. *This* Candice smirked, crossed her arms, and jutted her hip like his asking, again, had been a complete waste of air.

"I feel so used." He smoothed a hand down his chest, making light of the ache this woman kept pounding into him with her persistent refusal.

This was only a hat-trick effort. It's not like he'd been pelting her windows with stones or spouting sonnets below her balcony at midnight. Though if she'd give him a date he'd agree to just about anything.

Something about her drove him a little bit crazy. Perhaps that's why he was so enthralled by her. She was part fascination, part mystery. And very seldom did Sal encounter a puzzle he couldn't crack.

Her secrets ran deeper than Sal's radar could reach. But his cold read said right now Candice had him quarantined, refusing to really see him lest he throw some color on her tidy, stark white life.

Lucky for him he could sense things she couldn't hide nor control. It'd only been a couple months. He'd get to her. Eventually.

With one blink, her sassy attitude dissolved faster than he could say "*adios.*" Her eyes sprang wide, her pulse pounded double-time at her neck. And then she did something odd. With a frantic jerk of her arm she stuffed her hand down her shirt.

"Digging for gold?"

She ignored him and continued to re-arrange herself, which he had to admit, he'd never seen a woman do with quite so much gusto.

"Aww, lighten up, that was funny."

She didn't laugh, and any element of grace she'd had was lost in the panic. When she finished frisking herself, she whipped her head around, scanning the sidewalk. Her silk-spun chestnut hair flipped and writhed with each agitated turn.

Before he'd inquired further, she'd dropped to the pavement, feeling around like a blind squirrel on a nut hunt.

Twisting to assist her search for whatever she'd lost, he saw nothing but city stained concrete until a strand of sunlight glinted from beyond the curb. Glass or plastic, and it looked like a—

"Move!" She barreled past, shoving him aside to fling herself into oncoming traffic.

She bent over her prize, unfazed by the SUV speeding toward her. With a driver who didn't seem to notice the excessively short woman crouching down in his lane.

"Candice." He warned. "Candice, look out!" Pain ripped through him as he lunged into the street, hooked an arm around her waist and dove back to the curb. They met the sidewalk hard and fast. The vibration of the tire brushed the sole of his shoe. He tucked his legs up and around Candice. A rush of air surrounded them, warning how close they'd come to being road-kill.

He kept his arms around her, not wanting to let go until he was sure she was safe. And maybe not even then.

The adrenaline started to recede, and the strain in his lungs shot fragments of painful awareness to his collection of injuries still in the process of healing.

Candice's back was against his chest, their breaths heaving in sync. The shock of the moment leaving them once again lying on the sidewalk. Only this time they were spooning.

He shifted her in his arms, turning her back to the ground so he could assess her for injury. Once he'd confirmed she was just as fine and perfect as ever, he pressed his forehead to her temple, closed his eyes, and willed his heart and lungs to reboot. "We have to stop meeting like this."

He didn't need to see her lips to know she was smiling. And for a solitary moment in time, she wilted, completely at rest in his arms. His touch, or perhaps just shock, short-circuiting her defenses.

"Yes, we do." Pulling up to a seated position, she lifted his arm that had tucked her against him and shrugged it off like a shackle of rope. Again she stood, this time offering her hand.

Sal took it and managed to get his feet beneath him. His knee throbbed. His left lung was stiff and aching. His head a bit swimmy. He was definitely gonna pay for all this later.

"So what's in the evidence jar?" He nodded toward her hand, her fist wrapped around the small vial she'd risked her life to protect.

Her eyes shifted, cheeks pulling taut like she'd clenched her teeth together. "Nothing."

"Liar, liar, pants on fire." He took a step closer. "You're not stealing evidence, are you, Doc?"

There was a moment's pause, the faintest gulp. Barely a hitch of hesitation, but it told him all he needed to know.

She shook her head, her eyes repelling from his. "No, I—"

"Save it." It was from last night's Vivaldi victim. He held out his hand, watching the guilt scan across her features like his own personal wire-tap into her psyche. "If you hand it over right now, I'll get it back before anyone notices it's gone. And I won't have the bureau press charges."

Sliding the contraband into her front coat pocket, her smile faltered. "I told you it's nothing."

More convincing, but still miles from the truth.

"Besides, you're not even active with the FBI right now. What makes you thing you have the authority to confiscate my personal property?"

Burn. She had him there.

She wanted to play dirty? Fine. She had no idea who she was messing with.

Her hand resurfaced empty, and she patted her pocket. Her confidence was back in full swing as the chilled wind tossed that smooth, silky hair over her shoulder. "I've gotta run."

He wasn't sure she realized what she was doing. Maybe she thought she was using her wiles to distract him for a clean escape—which was a very good plan—but he managed to remain on task when she leaned in and placed her cool palm against his shirt between the open front of his coat.

He tried not to let the press of her hand and the implied intimacy of her body language affect him. Did a pretty good job too because if ever a touch could be patronizing, Candice had it down to a science.

"Thanks for catching me, Dorian."

She'd set herself up perfectly. It was almost too easy. Using his index and middle finger he lifted the vial from her coat pocket, leaving behind the quarter from his, and casually shoving his hands back into his pockets.

As she walked past him he caught the faint tip of her lips, confirming she remained unaware of the shift of power.

"Hey, Brat." He waited until she glanced back and then he winked. "You can land on me anytime."